SEDUCED

"Celia, you don't know what you're doing," he began to say, but she interrupted.

"I know enough." She tilted back her head to look up at him, a movement he felt more than saw. "But I shall leave if you don't want me to stay."

"Celia," he rasped, clinging to his sanity and honor with great difficulty, "I must tell you—"

"I know who you are," she whispered. "I've known for some time, Anthony."

His name fell like an absolution on his ears. She knew. There were still reasons why he shouldn't do this—many, many reasons—but they fell aside under the weight of those words and the others she had said: *I want you.*

Slowly, reverently, he bent his head and brushed his lips against hers, once, twice. She stood quietly, her face raised to his, her hand still on his chest. He trailed one hand down the back of her neck, a feathery touch that made her lips part in a silent gasp against his. He deepened the kiss just a little, wanting to savor every moment, every bit of her. . . .

Books by Caroline Linden

WHAT A WOMAN NEEDS*

WHAT A GENTLEMAN WANTS*

WHAT A ROGUE DESIRES*

A RAKE'S GUIDE TO SEDUCTION*

A VIEW TO A KISS

FOR YOUR ARMS ONLY

YOU ONLY LOVE ONCE

ONE NIGHT IN LONDON

BLAME IT ON BATH

THE WAY TO A DUKE'S HEART

LOVE AND OTHER SCANDALS

IT TAKES A SCANDAL

LOVE IN THE TIME OF SCANDAL

SIX DEGREES OF SCANDAL

*Published by Kensington Publishing Corporation

A Rake's Guide To Seduction

CAROLINE LINDEN

ZEBRA BOOKS
KENSINGTON PUBLISHING CORP.
http://www.kensingtonbooks.com

ZEBRA BOOKS are published by

Kensington Publishing Corp.
119 West 40th Street
New York, NY 10018

All Kensington titles, imprints, and distributed lines are available at special quantity discounts for bulk purchases for sales promotion, premiums, fund-raising, educational, or institutional use.

Special book excerpts or customized printings can also be created to fit specific needs. For details, write or phone the office of the Kensington Sales Manager: Attn.: Sales Department. Kensington Publishing Corp., 119 West 40th Street, New York, NY 10018. Phone: 1-800-221-2647.

First Zebra Books Mass-Market Paperback Printing: June 2008
ISBN-13: 978-1-4201-4406-2
ISBN-10: 1-4201-4406-5

10 9 8 7 6 5 4 3 2

Printed in the United States of America

For Ruth and Lucas:
I miss you both.

Chapter One

Anthony Hamilton was born scandalous, and his reputation did not improve as he grew.

He was the only son of the earl of Lynley, but it was almost a proven fact that he was not Lynley's own child. Lady Lynley, a much younger woman than her husband, had not borne a child in the first ten years of her marriage and then, out of the blue, gave birth to a strapping, handsome lad who didn't look a thing like Lord Lynley, nor any of the Hamiltons for that matter. Lynley had not repudiated his wife or the child, but the fact that Lady Lynley and her son spent most of their time away from Lynley Court seemed proof of . . . something.

Mr. Hamilton had been a thoroughly wild boy as well. He was asked to leave no fewer than three schools— mostly for fighting, but once for cheating a professor at cards. He had finished his education at Oxford in record time, then set himself up in London to begin a life that could only be called, in hushed tones, depraved and immoral. That was when he had stopped using his courtesy title as well; he no longer allowed people to call him Viscount Langford, as befitted the Lynley heir, but insisted on being plain Mr. Hamilton. That, combined with his regular appearances at high-stakes gaming tables and the steady stream of wealthy widows and matrons he kept company with, painted him blacker than black, utterly irredeemable, and absolutely, deliciously fascinating to the *ton*.

There was the time he wagered everything he owned, including the clothing he was wearing at the time, at the hazard table and somehow walked away with a small fortune. There was his infamous but vague wager with Lady Nicols—no one quite seemed to know the precise details—that ended with Lady Nicols handing him her priceless rubies in the midst of a ball at Carleton House. There was the time Sir Henry Milton accused him of siring the child Lady Milton carried at the time; Mr. Hamilton simply smiled, murmured a few words in Sir Henry's ear, and within an hour the two men were sharing a bottle of wine, looking for all the world as if they were bosom friends. He was rumored to be on the verge of being taken to the Fleet one night, and as rich as Croesus the next. He was a complete contradiction, and he only inflamed the gossips' interest by being utterly discreet. For such a wicked man, he was remarkably guarded.

Celia Reece had heard all the stories about him. Despite her mother's admonitions, Celia had developed a fondness for gossip in her first Season in London, and all the best bits seemed to involve him in one way or another. Although Anthony Hamilton might not be—quite—the most scandalous person in London, he was the most scandalous person she knew, and as such she found his exploits hugely entertaining.

He had been friends with her brother David for as long as Celia could remember and had often come to

Ainsley Park, the Reece family estate, for school holidays. As he had grown more and more disreputable, he had stopped visiting—Celia suspected her mother had banned him from coming—but she still remembered him fondly, almost as an extra brother. He had tied her fishing lines and helped launch her kites, and it gave her no end of amusement that he was now so wicked, young ladies were afraid to walk past him alone.

Naturally, his reputation meant that she was never to speak to him again. Celia's mother, Rosalind, had drummed it into her daughter's head that proper young ladies did not associate with wicked gentlemen. Celia had restrained herself from pointing out that her own brother was every bit as wild as Mr. Hamilton, but she had obeyed her mother for the most part. She was having a grand time in her first Season and didn't want to do anything to spoil it, particularly not anything that would get her sent back to Ainsley Park in disgrace for associating with wicked gentlemen.

Fortunately, there were so many other gentlemen to choose from. As the daughter and now sister of the duke of Exeter, Celia was a very eligible young lady. The earl of Carrick sent her lilies every week. Sir Henry Avenall sent her roses. The duke of Ware asked her to dance more than once, Viscount Graves took her driving in the Park, and Lord Andrew Bertram wrote sonnets to her. It was nothing less than exhilarating, being courted by so many gentlemen.

Tonight, for instance, Lord Euston was being very attentive. The handsome young earl was a prime catch, with an estate in Derbyshire and a respectable fortune. He was also a wonderful dancer, and Celia loved to dance. When he approached her for the third time, she smiled at him.

"Lady Celia, I should like to have this dance." He bowed very smartly. He had handsome manners, too.

Celia blushed. He must know she couldn't possibly dance with him again. "Indeed, sir, I think I must refuse."

He didn't look surprised or disappointed. "I think you must as well. Would you consent to take a turn on the terrace with me instead?"

A turn on the terrace—alone with a gentleman! She darted a glance at her mother, several feet away. Rosalind was watching and gave a tiny nod of permission, with an approving look at Lord Euston. Her stomach jumped. She had never taken a private stroll with a gentleman. She excused herself from her friends, all of whom watched enviously, and put her hand on Lord Euston's arm.

"I am honored you would walk with me," he said as they skirted the edge of the ballroom.

"It is my pleasure, sir." She smiled at him, but he merely nodded and didn't speak again. They stepped through the open doors, into the wonderfully fresh and cool night air. Instead of remaining near the doors, though, Lord Euston kept walking, leading her toward the far end of the terrace where it was darker and less crowded. Far less crowded; almost deserted, really. Celia's heart skipped a beat. What did he intend? None of her other admirers had kissed her. Lord Euston wasn't quite her favorite among them, but it would be immensely flattering if he tried to kiss her. And shouldn't she have some practice at kissing?

Celia's curiosity flared to life, and she stole a glance at her companion. He was a little handsomer in the moonlight, she thought, trying to imagine what his lips would feel like. Would it be pleasant, or awkward? Should she be modest and retiring, or more forward? Should she even allow him the liberty at all? Should—?

"There is something I must say to you." Celia wet her lips, preparing herself, still trying to decide if she would allow it. But he made no move toward her. "Lady Celia," he began, laying one hand on his heart, "I must tell you how passionately I adore you."

She hadn't quite expected that. "Oh. Er . . . Oh, indeed?"

"Since the moment I first saw you, I have thought of nothing but you," he went on with growing fervor. "My will is overruled by fate. To deliberate would demean my love, which blossomed at first sight." He took her hand, looking at her expectantly.

"I—I am flattered, sir," she said after a pregnant pause.

"And do you adore me?" he prompted. Celia's eyes widened in confusion.

"I—Well, that is . . . I . . ." She cleared her throat. "What?"

"Do you adore me?" he repeated with unnerving intensity.

No. Of course she didn't. He was handsome and a wonderful dancer, and she probably would have let him steal a chaste kiss on the cheek, but adore him? No. She wished she hadn't let him lead her all the way out here. What on earth was she to do now? "Lord Euston, I don't think this is a proper thing to discuss."

He resisted her gentle attempts to pull free of his grasp. "If it is maidenly reserve that prevents you saying it, I understand. If it is fear of your family's disapproval, I understand. You have but to say one word, and I will wait a thousand years for you."

"Oh, please don't." She pulled a little harder, and he squeezed her hand a little tighter.

"Or you might say another word, and we could go to His Grace tonight. We could be married before the end of the Season, my dearest Lady Celia."

"Ah, but—but my brother's away from town," she said, edging backward. Euston followed, pulling her toward him, now gripping her one hand in his two.

"I shall call on him the moment he returns."

"I wish you wouldn't," Celia whispered.

"Your modesty enthralls me." He crowded nearer, his eyes feverish.

"Oh dear . . ."

"Sweet Celia, make me immortal with a kiss!" Celia grimaced and turned her face away from his. She was never going to dance with Lord Euston again. What a wretched first kiss this would be.

"Good evening," said an affable new voice just then.

Lord Euston released her at once, recoiling a step as he spun around toward the intruder. Celia put her freed hands behind her, suddenly horrified at what she had done. Goodness—she was alone, in the dark, with an unmarried gentleman—if they were discovered here, she could be ruined.

"Lovely evening, isn't it?" said Anthony Hamilton as he strolled up, a glass of champagne in each hand.

"Yes," said Euston stiffly. Celia closed her eyes, relief flooding her as she recognized her savior. Surely he, of all people, would understand and not cause trouble for her.

"Lady Celia. A pleasure to see you again." He gave her a secretive smile, as if he knew very well what he had interrupted and found it highly amusing.

"Mr. Hamilton," she murmured, bobbing a curtsy. For a moment everyone stood in awkward silence.

"We should return to the ball." Lord Euston extended his hand to her, pointedly not looking at the other man.

"No!" Celia exclaimed without thinking. Euston froze, startled. She flushed. "I shall return in a moment, sir," she said more politely, grasping for any excuse not to go with him. "The air is so fresh and cool."

"Yes," said Euston grimly. He didn't look nearly so handsome anymore. "Yes. I see. Good evening, Lady Celia."

Celia murmured a reply, willing him to leave. "Good evening, Euston," added Mr. Hamilton.

Lord Euston jerked, darting a suspicious glance at Mr. Hamilton. "Good evening, sir." He hesitated, gave Celia a deeply disappointed look, then walked away.

Celia swung around, bracing her hands on the balustrade that encircled the terrace. Good heavens. That had not turned out at all the way she had expected. Why had her mother approved of him?

"That," said Mr. Hamilton, leaning against the balustrade beside her, "may be the worst marriage proposal I have ever heard."

She closed her eyes and took a deep breath. It didn't work. The giggles bubbled up inside her and finally burst free. She pressed one hand to her mouth. "I suppose you heard everything he said?"

"I suppose," he agreed. "Including the part he stole from Marlowe."

"No! Really?" Celia gasped. He just smiled, and she groaned. "You mustn't repeat it to anyone."

"Of course not," he said in mild affront. "I should be ashamed to say such things aloud. It would quite ruin my reputation." Celia laughed again, and he smiled. "Would you care for some champagne?"

"Thank you." She took the glass he offered, and sipped gratefully.

He set the other glass on the balustrade and leaned on his elbows, surveying the dark gardens in front of them. "So you weren't trying to bring Euston up to scratch?"

"Don't be ridiculous." She snorted, then remembered she wasn't supposed to do that. "I would never have walked out with him if I'd thought he meant to propose."

"Why did you, then?" He glanced at her, his expression open and relaxed, inviting confidence. Celia sighed, sipping more champagne.

"He's a wonderful dancer," she said.

"And a dreadful bore," he said in the same regretful tone. Celia looked at him in shock, then burst out laughing.

"That's dreadful of you to say, but—but—well, perhaps he is."

"Perhaps," he murmured.

"And now he is probably telling my mother." She sighed. Walking out with Lord Euston, with her mother's permission, was one thing; lingering in the darkness with a man—let alone a notorious rake her mother strenuously disapproved of—was another. "I really should return."

"Did you want him to kiss you, then?"

She stopped in the act of turning to go. He was still facing the gardens, away from her, but after a moment had passed and she said nothing, he glanced at her. "Did you?" he asked again, his voice a shade deeper.

Celia drew closer. He turned, now leaning on one elbow, his full attention fixed on her. She didn't know another gentleman who could appear so approachable. She had forgotten how easy he was to talk to.

"You mustn't laugh at me, Anthony," she warned, unconsciously using his Christian name as she had done for years. "I—I've never been kissed before, and it seemed like the perfect night for it, and . . . well, until he started demanding to know if I adored him, it was quite romantic. It *was*," she protested as his mouth curved. "We can't all be disreputable, with all sorts of scandalous adventures."

His smile stiffened. "Nor should you be."

"But you should?" She grinned, glad to be teasing him instead of the other way around. "Every gossip in London adores you, you know."

He sighed, shaking his head. "I'm neither so daring nor so foolish as they like to think. Perhaps you, as a pillar of propriety, can tell me how to escape their pernicious notice."

"Why, that is easy," she said with a wave of one hand. "Find a girl, fall desperately in love with her, and settle down to have six children and raise dogs. No one will say a word about you, then."

Anthony chuckled. "Ah, there's the rub. What you suggest is more easily said than done, miss."

"Have you ever tried?"

He shrugged. "No."

"Then how can you say it's so difficult?" she exclaimed. "There are dozens of young ladies looking for a husband. You must simply ask one—"

He gave a soft *tsk*. "I couldn't possibly."

"You could."

"I couldn't."

Celia's eyes lit. "That sounds almost like a challenge."

He glanced at her from the corner of his eye, then grinned. "It's not. Don't try your matchmaking on me. I'm a hopeless case."

"Of course you're not," she said stoutly. "Why, any lady in London—"

"Would not suit me, nor I her."

"Miss Weatherby," said Celia.

"Too thin."

"Lady Jane Cranston."

"Too tall."

"Miss Alcomb."

"Too . . ." He paused, his gaze sharpening on her as he thought, and Celia opened her mouth, ready to exclaim in delight that he could find no fault with Lucinda Alcomb, who was a very nice girl. "Too merry," he said at last.

"Who would please you, then?" she burst out, laughing at his pleasant obstinacy.

He shifted, his eyes skipping across the garden again. "No one, perhaps."

"You aren't even trying to be fair. I know so many nice young ladies—"

Anthony gave a sharp huff. "This is quite a dull topic of conversation. We've had very fine weather this spring, don't you think?"

"Anyone who took the trouble to know you would accept you," Celia insisted, ignoring his efforts to turn the subject.

"You've gone and ruled out every woman in England." He leaned over the railing, squinting into the darkness.

"Except myself," Celia declared, and then she stopped. Good heavens, what had she just said?

Anthony seemed shocked as well. His head whipped around, and he stared at her with raised eyebrows. "I beg your pardon?"

Heat rushed to her face. "I—I meant that I know

you, and know you're not half so bad as you pretend to be."

His gaze was riveted on her, so dark and intense Celia scarcely recognized him for a moment. Goodness, it was just Anthony, but for a moment, he was looking at her almost like . . .

"Not half so bad," he murmured speculatively. "A rare compliment, if I do say so myself."

She burst out laughing again, relieved that he was merely teasing her. That expression on his face—rather like a wolf's before he sprang—unsettled her; it had made her think, for one mad moment, that he might in fact spring on her. And even worse, Celia realized that a small, naughty part of her was somewhat curious. No, rampantly curious. She might have let Lord Euston kiss her, but only for the satisfaction of being able to say she had been kissed. She had never expected to be swept away with passion by Lord Euston, who was, as Anthony had said, a dreadful bore. But a kiss from one of the most talked-about rakes in London . . . now, *that* would be something else altogether.

"You know what I meant," she said, shaking off that curiosity as shocking and obviously forbidden. "I know you've quite a soft heart, although you hide it very well. As proof, I must point out that you've stood out here with me for some time now, trying to make me feel better after receiving the most appalling marriage proposal of all time. David would have laughed until he couldn't stand upright, and then retold the tale to everyone he met."

"Ah, but I am not your brother," he replied, smiling easily although his gaze lingered on her face.

She was glad he couldn't see her blush. "No, indeed! But because you are not"—she took the last sip of champagne from her glass before setting it on the balustrade—"I must return to the ballroom. I suppose you'll continue to skulk in the shadows out here, and be appropriately wicked?"

"You know me too well."

Celia laughed once more. "Good night, Anthony. And thank you." She flashed him a parting smile and hurried away. Perhaps if she could make her mother see the humor, and idiocy, in Lord Euston's proposal, Mama wouldn't ask too many questions about where she'd been ever since.

Anthony listened to her rapid footsteps die away, counting every one. Seventeen steps, and then she was gone. He folded his arms on the balustrade once again, taking a deep breath. The faint scent of lemons lingered in the air. He wondered why she smelled of lemons and not rosewater or something other ladies wore.

"You gave away my champagne, I see," said a voice behind him.

Anthony smiled and held out the untouched glass sitting next to his elbow. "No. I gave away mine."

Fanny, Lady Drummond, took it with a coy look. "Indeed." She turned, looking back at the house. "A bit young for your taste."

"An old friend," he said evenly. "The younger sister of a friend. Euston was giving her a spot of trouble."

"Better and better," exclaimed Fanny. "You are a knight in shining armor."

Anthony shrugged. "Hardly."

"Now, darling, I wouldn't blame you." She ran her fingers down his arm. "She's the catch of the Season.

Rumor holds her marriage portion is fifty thousand pounds."

"How *do* the gossips ferret out such information?"

"Persistent spying, I believe. Fouché's agents would have been put to shame by the matrons of London." Fanny rested the tip of her fan next to her mouth, studying him. "For a moment, I thought you had spotted your chance."

Anthony tightened his lips and said nothing. The less said on this topic, the better. The scent of lemons was gone, banished by Fanny's heavier perfume.

"Have you?" pressed Fanny as the silence lengthened. She moved closer, her face lighting up with interest. "Good Lord. The greatest lover in London, pining for a girl?"

He turned to her. "She's just a girl," he said. "I've known her since she was practically a babe, and yes, I am fond of her. Fanny, you would understand if you'd heard what Euston was saying to her. I spoke as much to close his mouth as anything else."

"And yet, there *was* something else," she replied archly. He sighed in exasperation. She laughed, laying her hand on his. "Admit it, you've thought of it. She would solve all your problems, wouldn't she? Money, connection, respectability . . ."

He pulled his hand free. "Yes, all I would have to do is persuade the duke of Exeter to give his consent, overcome the dowager duchess's extreme dislike of me, and then ask the lady herself to choose me above all her respectable, eligible suitors. I don't take odds that long, Fanny."

She smirked. "She was a girl a moment ago. Now she's a lady." Anthony looked at her in undisguised irritation. Fanny moved closer, so close her breath warmed his ear. "I wouldn't fault you for trying, darling," she murmured. "It needn't alter our relationship in any way . . . in fact, why don't you call on me tonight . . . later . . . and we can continue that relationship."

"You'll want to hear the news from Cornwall, I expect."

Fanny pouted at his deliberate change of subject, but she let it go. "I don't believe I would have let you seduce me if I'd known you simply wanted me to invest in some mining venture." He cocked a brow at her. "All right." She gave in with a knowing smile. "I would have still let you seduce me, but I would have asked for better terms."

"I like to think we shall always be on the best of terms with each other." He brought her hand to his mouth and pressed his lips to the inside of her wrist. Fanny's expression softened even more.

"I suppose we shall. Business terms . . . and other terms."

Anthony smiled, ruthlessly forcing his moment of gallantry from his mind, along with everything else related to Celia Reece. Fanny might make light of it, but he needed every farthing she would invest, and Anthony knew how to work to protect that.

He related the report from the mine manager, knowing Fanny, unlike many women, truly wanted to know how her money was faring. She had a sharp mind for business, and they shared a profitable relationship. Their other relationship was almost as valuable to him—Fanny lived in the present and didn't dwell on the past, especially not *his* past. That mattered a great deal to Anthony.

But when Fanny had gone back to the ball, Anthony found his mind wandering. Although Fanny was nearly fifteen years older than he, she was still a very handsome woman, with a tart wit and a marvelous sense of humor. She had a sophistication no young lady just making her debut could claim, and Anthony genuinely liked her. He liked the way her money made his financial schemes successful. He liked her acceptance of their intermittent affair with no recriminations or demands. But she didn't smell of lemons.

He pushed away from the balustrade, restless and tired at the same time. His plans for the evening had included some time in the card room, where he hoped to win a few months' rent, but he suspected he couldn't concentrate on his cards now. Damn lemons.

With a deep sigh, Anthony turned back toward the house. He repeated in his mind what he had told Fanny: Celia was just a girl; he spoke to her out of mere kindness. He tried not to hear the echo of Celia's words, that she was the only woman in England who thought him . . . how had she put it . . . "not half so bad as he pretended."

He slipped into the overheated ballroom, lingering near the door. Without meaning to, he saw her. She was dancing with another young buck like Euston. Her pink gown swirled around her as her partner turned her, her golden curls gleaming in the candlelight. Anthony's gaze lingered on her back, where her partner's hand was spread in a wide, proprietary grip. The young man was delighted to be dancing with her—and why shouldn't he be? She beamed up at him, smiling at whatever he'd said to her, and Anthony realized, with a small shock of alarm, that she was breathtaking. No longer a child or a young girl, but a beautiful young woman who would walk out with a gentleman in hopes of a kiss and end up fending off a marriage proposal.

He turned away from the dancers, continuing on his way without another glance back. He wound his way through the crowd, out through the hall, pausing only to collect his things, then down the steps into the night. He kept going, past the lines of waiting carriages, strolling along at an unhurried pace through the streets of London. The early spring air was fresh and crisp; it was a lovely night to walk, but Anthony didn't walk to enjoy the weather.

At last he reached his lodging, a rented flat in a house just clinging to the edge of respectability. Up the stairs he climbed to his plain, simply furnished rooms. Since sinking most of his funds into the tin mines, he had had to cut his expenses to the bone. There was little of luxury or comfort in his rooms, certainly nothing to tempt a duke's daughter. His lip curled derisively at his own thoughts as he shrugged off his jacket and unwound his cravat. There was little of anything in his life to tempt any lady.

And yet . . .

Except me, rang Celia's words in his mind. No lady in London would accept him . . . *except me,* whispered her voice. He unbuttoned his waistcoat and tossed it on a nearby chair. Everyone saw him as a wastrel and a hedonist . . . *except me.* Anthony pulled open his collar and yanked the shirt over his head. His skin felt hot and prickly. "She's your friend's younger sister," he told himself out loud. "Practically your own sister." But it did no good.

He could still close his eyes and see Celia as a redcheeked little girl, handing him the last scone from tea, wrapped in a handkerchief. He could still hear her angry tears when her brother had insisted she stay behind while they went fishing. And he could still see the glimpse of ankle as she danced, the curve of bosom as she curtsied to her partner, and the gleam of moonlight on her blond curls.

Anthony had liked Celia Reece very much as a girl, but he had never allowed himself to think of her as a woman. Ladies like Celia were not for him. And so long as she remained fixed in his mind as just a girl, everything had been fine. Tonight, though, he found with alarm that he could think of her as nothing but a woman—a young woman, to be certain, but a woman all the same. She had wanted to be kissed tonight, and Anthony knew just how easily he could have been the man to do it. *Except me,* echoed her voice again, and he remembered how her face changed when he looked at her then. She hadn't meant it that way when she said it, but he had seen the flush of awareness on her cheeks and the spark of interest in her eyes. And that awareness, to say nothing of the interest, just might have sealed his fate, forever ending any brotherly feelings he had for her.

He splashed cold water from the ewer on his face, letting it run down his neck and chest. Even if Celia would accept him, her family would never allow it. Surely not . . . except that the duke of Exeter had made a rather odd marriage himself last year, to a penniless widow from a country village. And Celia's other brother had married even lower. Lady David, Anthony knew, had been a common pickpocket at one time.

If the Reeces could overlook the lack of fortune, family, standing, and even respectability, perhaps . . . just perhaps . . . they could accept him as well.

Anthony Hamilton, widely regarded as the most scandalous rogue in London, lay down on his narrow bed alone and contemplated having six children and raising dogs.

Chapter Two

Much to Celia's relief, she was not scolded for her misadventure with Lord Euston. She managed to tell her mother about it in such a way that made them both laugh, and that had quite ended the matter as far as Rosalind was concerned.

Her friends, however, were not so easily put off. "Did he go down on one knee?" Jane Melvill wanted to know the next night.

Celia grimaced. "No."

"Did he kiss you first?" Louisa Witherspoon asked.

"Thank heavens, no."

"But you wanted him to," said Mary Greene.

Celia pondered. "When I agreed to walk out with him, I thought he might try to steal a kiss," she admitted. "And I suppose . . . I might have let him."

"Might?" squeaked Louisa in disbelief. "Euston's so wonderfully handsome!"

"And a wonderful dancer," said Jane, while Mary nodded.

"But he's a dreadful bore," Celia replied. "He began by saying he adored me."

"A fine beginning," someone murmured. Celia nodded.

"True. Fine enough. But then"—she glanced around to make certain no one nearby would overhear—"he asked if I adored him."

Jane looked at Mary, who looked at Louisa. Louisa shrugged. Celia suspected she admired Lord Euston more than the rest of them. "And I couldn't say yes, because of course I don't, even if he is handsome and a wonderful dancer."

Even Louisa had to admit one could not lie about that to a gentleman, no matter how well he looked or danced.

"Then he wanted to speak to my brother." Celia almost rolled her eyes but caught herself in time. "Of course Exeter would have told him no, but . . . well, I didn't want the poor man to go to the trouble when I don't want to marry him."

"Not at all?" asked Louisa, as if she could hardly believe it possible.

"No," said Celia helplessly. "Not at all."

"Did he appear distraught? Did he beg you to reconsider?" Jane's nose was almost twitching with interest.

Celia grimaced again. "*Then* he tried to kiss me. Make me immortal with a kiss, he said."

"Oh, that's Shakespeare," exclaimed Louisa. "How romantic!"

"It is not Shakespeare, it's Milton," Jane told her.

"Milton?" Mary's nose wrinkled. "Didn't he write that horrid poem about Lucifer? Was he comparing Celia to a devil? Or to an angel?"

"It's Marlowe," said Celia, saying a silent thanks to Anthony. She hadn't been quite certain herself, but if anyone would know a love poem, it would be Anthony

Hamilton. "And I didn't find it very romantic. He seized me by the hand and wouldn't let me go."

"How did you escape?" All three girls turned to look at her again, poetry forgotten. Celia opened her mouth, then closed it. She liked her friends very much, but she also knew they liked to gossip even more than she did. She didn't dare link her name to Anthony's, not after he had been so kind to her and there was nothing at all improper about his actions or hers.

"Someone came by then, and Lord Euston let me go," she said. "He returned to the ballroom, as did I a moment later."

Her friends all looked suitably impressed. "At least he didn't ask you in front of everyone," Mary said. "Sir George Lacey offered for Martha Winters in a theater box full of people. Imagine how hard it would be to refuse a gentleman then."

Celia nodded. "I never thought Lord Euston would propose marriage, not last night. I would never have walked out with him if I had."

"It does every girl good to get one offer of marriage she must refuse," said Jane with authority. "My mother says so."

"Oh dear. Here he comes," whispered Mary.

"Who?" Jane craned her neck in the direction Mary was facing, then jerked back to answer her own question. "Lord Euston!"

Celia recalled the strength of his grip and shuddered. She also recalled that he had not been pleased to leave her alone with Anthony Hamilton, even if only for a few minutes. She dared a peek over Louisa's shoulder. He didn't look like he was coming to apologize for his actions; he looked petulant and a little bit angry. Celia took the coward's way out. "I feel the need to visit the ladies' retiring room," she whispered.

"Shall I go with you?" Mary asked. Celia shook her head.

"Don't fear, Celia, we'll keep him from following," Jane said. "We'll try to get him to dance with Louisa."

Celia slipped away through the crowd as Louisa exclaimed in indignation. Keeping her head down, she made her way to the room set aside for the ladies to rest and repair themselves.

Anthony saw her slip out of the ballroom just as he was about to enter the card room. A quick glance along her wake showed Euston talking to the young ladies who had been Celia's companions only a few moments ago. Anthony's steps slowed, then turned. "Excuse me," he murmured to his companions as he walked away from them and headed out the same door she had taken.

He didn't know what he meant to do. The sight of her golden hair had caught his eye, and the furtive way she left had pricked his interest. She was avoiding Euston—small wonder there, he thought as he climbed the stairs, following her blue-gowned figure. She might not be pleased that he was following her, either, but Anthony continued up the stairs.

At the top of the stairs she turned into the ladies' powder room. Anthony stopped short. Of course; he should have guessed she was taking refuge where Euston unequivocally couldn't follow. Nor could he. And lingering outside the powder room to talk to her would only cause the sort of scene she was doubtless hoping to avoid. Tamping down the flicker of disappointment in his chest, he turned to go back to the card room.

"Hamilton," growled a voice behind him. "I'd like a word with you, sir."

Anthony turned, his features falling automatically into a disinterested expression. "Yes?"

The man stepped closer, until their toes almost touched. Sir George Howard, a baronet with a modest fortune and an ambitious wife. Not among Anthony's usual associates. He put his face up close to Anthony's. "What business do you have talking to my wife?"

"I suppose you've asked her already," he said in neutral tones. Lady Howard was difficult to avoid; Anthony would have sworn she was lying in wait for him, so often had he seen her of late.

Howard reached out and caught the front of his jacket, twisting it tight. Anthony let himself be yanked forward and shaken, only pulling back his head with an expression of distaste. Sir George looked as though he were just waiting for any excuse to call him out. "That's not what I asked," Sir George snapped. "I want to hear it from you."

Anthony sighed as if the whole thing bored him, even though the man was putting a severe strain on his clothing. Sir George was a few inches shorter than Anthony, but he was squat and broad and built like a bull; he had the fists of a pugilist. There was nothing at all to gain by provoking him, especially not when the only witnesses were a few of the baronet's friends. "Nothing but polite conversation," he said.

Howard gave him another shake, his eyes glittering. He was half-drunk, unless Anthony was very much mistaken. "Rubbish. Polite conversation doesn't take place with so many little smiles and end with three thousand pounds missing from my accounts."

Anthony raised one eyebrow. Three thousand pounds? Lady Howard had given him only two thousand, and that was after vowing her husband would never notice. "Are you accusing me of theft?"

"Not directly." Howard glowered at him. "Stay away from my wife."

Anthony inclined his head. "As you wish." The corridor was relatively empty, but the people who were about were watching as Howard continued to hold him by the jacket. Didn't the fool realize this would attract even more scandal to his name than any contact Anthony had with Lady Howard?

The vein in Howard's temple began to pulse. "I mean it," he said, his voice rising. He thrust his fist into Anthony's face and shook it. "Stay away from my wife!"

Now people were openly staring at them. Ladies going into the powder room and ladies leaving the powder room were standing, agog with interest. Anthony lowered his voice. "Let me go, Howard. I've never touched your wife."

"I don't believe you." One of Sir George's companions stepped forward, murmuring into his ear. Sir George shook like a wet dog. "Damned seducer," he snarled at Anthony. "Thief. I know what you do. Cozen some poor woman into thinking she's in love with you, then persuade her to give you money. You've gambled my three thousand pounds away already, haven't you? I see you every night at the tables. Never care whether you win or lose, do you?" The companion, glancing around nervously, whispered to Sir George again, and again the baronet shook him off. "Don't care, because it's not your money!"

From the corner of his eye Anthony caught a flash of blue, the same color as Celia's gown. Oh, Lord. He ought never to have followed her. He'd much prefer she didn't witness this. "Release me," he ordered in a low, even voice. "You are causing a scene, sir."

Glowering, Sir George wrenched Anthony's jacket, releasing him with a shove that made him fall back a step. "Stay away from my wife," Sir George said once more, pointing a thick finger at him.

"With pleasure," muttered Anthony, twitching his jacket back into place and moving to step around the man. He would return Lady Howard's funds tomorrow and avoid her like the deadly plague from now on. No investment was worth this.

But the baronet heard, and with a strangled roar he pulled free of his friend's restraining hold and lunged. His fist slammed into the side of Anthony's face, connecting with his nose and cheekbone and sending white-hot pain through his entire head.

For a moment he couldn't breathe. The force of the blow, coupled with the surprise of it, made him light-headed. Blindly Anthony groped behind him for support, only dimly aware that Sir George's friends had seized him and dragged him back. Damned fool, Anthony thought to himself, not to see that one coming.

He found the wall and leaned against it, his head ringing. He raised one hand to his face and it came away crimson. The lunatic had probably broken his nose, and now blood was dripping all over his waistcoat. Suddenly exhausted, he turned his back to the onlookers, resting his shoulder against the wall and feeling in his pockets for a handkerchief.

"Mr. Hamilton?" He stiffened at the cautious inquiry behind him. "Are you hurt?"

"No," he said, but his voice came out thick and muffled. He finally located a handkerchief and pressed it to his nose, hoping she would go away.

But she stepped around in front of him and gasped.

"No! Oh, you most certainly are hurt! How could you say no?"

"It's nothing," he said, trying not to wince at the way his own voice caused his head to vibrate with greater agony.

"Nothing! There's blood all over you. Oh, Anthony." Her eyes filled with dismay, Celia put her hand on his arm. "Stay right there. I'll be back."

He ought to walk away, to take himself home where he could bleed in private. This was not at all how he had hoped to approach Celia, and he most especially didn't want her to hear that Sir George had punched him because he suspected Anthony of having an affair with his wife. He should leave before she returned.

But she was back before he could gather his will to go. "Here, let me help you." With gentle hands she took the blood-soaked handkerchief away and replaced it with a clean linen, dabbing at the blood on his face. "What happened?"

"A gentlemen's dispute." For a moment he just stood slumped against the wall, savoring the feel of her hands on his face in spite of the pain.

Celia snorted. "A gentlemen's dispute! An obvious lie if ever I heard one. Someone in the retiring room said Sir George Howard called you a thief before he hit you."

"He might have done." As much as he was enjoying her ministrations, she was being too tender; blood was still pouring down his chin. "Here, let me. You have to hold it firmly." He covered her hand with his, taking the cloth. For a moment their fingers tangled together before she extricated hers. "You should go back to the ball," he said with a gruesome smile as he applied the cloth to his nose again, dropping his chin and squeezing firmly.

"And leave you here like this? Of course not." Celia looked around. "Come, there's a settee over here. Sit down."

He waved one hand in refusal, but she took his arm and tugged him toward it. When he sat, she sat beside him. "I'm quite all right," he tried to tell her one last time. "You needn't waste your evening tending me."

She laughed in disbelief. "Anthony, you can hardly speak! Your nose is going to be swollen, and your clothes are covered with blood. You are not quite all right."

He cast an awkward glance down at himself. "Oh dear. I do look a fright." His cravat was pulled askew and wrinkled, and it looked like a pair of buttons had gone missing from his waistcoat. Everything was flecked and splotched with blood.

"Your valet will be terribly upset," she said, looking at his clothes.

"Ah . . . yes. No doubt." Anthony shifted the cloth at his nose.

"You must make certain he brings you cool compresses for your nose," Celia told him. "David broke his nose once and Mama sent for ice. It helps the pain."

"I shall trust no one's advice but yours."

She beamed at him. "I could ask Mama for more information, if you like. Or is your man used to dealing with things like this?"

"Not so much," Anthony murmured wryly. She frowned, and he continued quickly, "He's a proud fellow. Nursing is quite beneath him, I've been given to understand. I dare not put him out too much."

She looked at him as if she couldn't quite believe it. "I can hardly see you being browbeaten by your servants."

Anthony sighed. "He'll scold me properly for getting

blood on this waistcoat, and tell me I deserve every ache and pain in my head for bringing home so many stains on my person."

"How terrible! You mustn't let him abuse you so. I'm sure it wasn't your fault at all." Her eyes flashed. "Sir George has an awful temper, and everyone knows it. Even David says he's a hothead."

"No doubt it was the wine." He removed the cloth and waited, but the bleeding continued. He turned the cloth over and pressed it back to his nose.

"That doesn't make it acceptable for him to go about punching people," Celia went on. "Whatever was he thinking?"

Anthony knew the answer to that, just as well as he knew how quickly everyone in London would seize on the story. No doubt within a week everyone would believe he was having a torrid affair with Lady Howard and her husband had been defending her honor. Oh yes, and that he had embezzled three thousand pounds from Sir George as well. Mustn't forget that bit. He slumped back in his seat.

"Are you feeling faint?" She scooted closer, her face anxious. "Should I send for someone? Fetch another cloth? Would you like a drink, or—?"

"No, no." He made himself smile. "Really, I am perfectly well. See, the bleeding has stopped." He took the cloth from his face. She inspected his injured nose closely, and Anthony almost held his breath as she leaned even closer toward him. Good Lord, her eyes were so blue. And her lips were so pink. . . .

"Celia."

Anthony glanced up from under his eyebrows to see Rosalind, the dowager duchess of Exeter, standing over them. From her polite but chilly smile, he guessed she was not pleased to find her daughter here with him.

"Mama, Sir George Howard punched Mr. Hamilton in the face," Celia said.

"Celia, let's not gossip," her mother said in a firm voice.

"It's not gossip, Mama, I saw it as I left the powder room. And look—he may have broken Mr. Hamilton's nose!"

The dowager duchess did not appear swayed by this. Her lips pinched together and she glanced at Anthony as he made to rise. She put up her hand. "Please don't, Mr. Hamilton. There is no need."

He ignored her, getting to his feet and giving a small bow. "Lady Celia has been most kind in assisting me."

The duchess smiled a tight little smile. "I am delighted to hear it. Perhaps someone should send for Lord Carfax's valet, Mr. Hamilton, to see to your injury."

"Should we send for some ice, Mama?" Celia asked. "As you did when David broke his nose."

"Mr. Hamilton is well able to send for anything he requires."

Unless what he required was her daughter's company. He gave another brief bow, this time in Celia's direction. "Yes, indeed. Thank you most sincerely, Lady Celia, for your kindness."

"Of course." She curtsied. "Do take care of yourself, sir."

He nodded once. "I shall."

The dowager duchess shepherded her daughter away, and Anthony contemplated the bloody cloth in his hand. He should take the duchess's demeanor as a warning, he thought. No doubt she viewed him just as suspiciously as the rest of society did, always ready and willing to be outraged by his actions, real or rumored.

Lord Carfax, the host, approached then. He apologized for Sir George's behavior and summoned a servant to help Anthony repair his appearance. Anthony went with the man into a guest room and cleaned his face and hands. His nose was already swelling and his head ached. His clothes were in a sad state; he gave them an obligatory straightening. Hopefully his landlady would be able to scrub out the blood.

His fingers lingered on his re-tied cravat as he stared at his reflection in the mirror. He didn't know what had possessed him to tell Celia those lies about his valet, a person who didn't even exist. Perhaps because she just assumed he had one, and he didn't want her to know he didn't. Perhaps because he had preferred to make her laugh at him instead of tending him. Her touch had been so gentle as she wiped the blood from his face.

Was he a fool? Most likely. With a sigh he turned from the mirror. The wise thing to do would be to return to the card room, win a tidy pile of money, and forget how she had fussed over him with such tender concern.

And Anthony always tried to do the wise thing.

Chapter Three

Celia didn't see Anthony Hamilton again for almost a fortnight. Her mother gave her a stern lecture about associating with scandalous people like him and then kept a closer eye on her when they were out. Although she didn't want to disobey her mother, Celia did want to know if he had recovered. It was easy to hear tales of his public behavior; she heard he returned to the card room after being punched by Sir George Howard and played piquet until dawn, still speckled with his own blood. But that told her nothing of his health, and finally she was forced to turn to her brother.

"Hamilton? He's fine," said David carelessly. His eyes were following his wife, Vivian, around the room as she danced with Lord Milbury. David made no effort to hide his devotion to his new wife, nor how protective he was of her. Vivian had been raised in the rookeries and made her way as a pickpocket before she met David, in a vaguely shocking way no one had seen fit to explain to Celia. David was always ready to step in if he perceived any slight to her. Celia thought it quite lovely of him, actually, even if it made him aggravatingly distracted at times.

"No, truly, David." Celia poked his arm. "He was hurt."

"What? Oh, yes. But he's fine."

"Are you certain?"

David finally tore his eyes away from Vivian for a moment. "Yes, Celia, I'm certain. It was a glancing blow."

"It might have broken his nose!"

Her brother waved one hand, making a face. "It was one punch. Hamilton's suffered a lot worse in his time. Don't worry."

"But I haven't seen him since then."

That got his attention. "Have you been looking for him?"

She flushed. "No. I just wanted to know he was well."

"He is." Her brother's eyes narrowed. "Your mother would have an apoplexy if—"

"Then don't tell her," Celia snapped. "He did nothing, I did nothing. I just wanted to know, and now that you've told me, I am satisfied."

David continued to look suspicious, but he didn't press her. "Excellent."

Celia shook her head and walked away from her infuriating brother, back across the room toward her friends. Why was she not allowed to ask after the health of an acquaintance, she fumed. Surely not even Anthony was so wicked that it was wrong to wish him well.

"Good evening, Lady Celia." The voice made her start. Celia whirled around to see the man himself, bowing in front of her.

"Good evening, Mr. Hamilton," she said with surprised pleasure. "I am *so* glad to see you again!" His eyebrows shot up. Celia gave an embarrassed little laugh, realizing how odd that must sound. "That is, I am so glad to see you are well."

"I am very well, thank you." He looked at her with a strange expression. "I hope you are well."

"Oh, yes, but when last I saw you, you were covered in blood."

"Ah, yes, that. A night's discomfort." His mouth quirked. "Surely you weren't worried?"

"Of course I was! You might have had a broken nose. I didn't see you anywhere after that, and David only said you were fine." She huffed. "Do gentlemen go about beating each other regularly? David was sure it was a common enough occurrence that you barely noticed."

His half-grin had faded. "I am flattered you would inquire after my health."

There was something in his voice that caught her attention, but when she looked, his face was inscrutable. Celia sighed and shook her head. "And I had no idea what 'fine' meant. David might be on death's doorstep and still he would insist he was fine."

"No, I am well. Quite well, in fact." He sounded somehow distracted, as he stared at her. "I wished to thank you for your kindness that night."

"It was the least I could do," she exclaimed. "I fear I was no real help to you at all. I'm afraid I haven't much experience at nursing."

"I could not imagine a better nurse." He gave a slight smile. "Although I should hate to appear to such a disadvantage in your eyes again. It was not the best way to renew our acquaintance."

She laughed ruefully. "No. But you were so gallant the previous night, when Lord Euston . . . Well, we have neither of us been at our best, perhaps."

"And yet I can see no fault in you."

"That is because you haven't seen me for several years," she scoffed. "A few more meetings, and you shall find me as tiresome as when I was a child."

"I never found you tiresome." He said it simply, calmly. Celia paused, contrite.

"No, you were always so kind to me. Kinder than David, especially! And I shall never forget it." She caught sight of her mother advancing on them with fire in her eyes. "But I must go. Good evening, Mr. Hamilton." She bobbed a quick curtsy.

"Good evening, Lady Celia." He bowed, and she hurried to intercept her mother and explain before Mama worked herself into a state.

Anthony didn't watch her go. There was nothing to be gained by antagonizing the dowager duchess. But his heart still pounded, and his hand trembled as he took a glass from a nearby servant and downed half the wine in one gulp.

She had been pleased to see him. And she had worried about him. Anthony took a deep breath, held it a moment as he contemplated that thought with unbounded and unwarranted pleasure, and swallowed the rest of his wine.

Anthony was a seasoned gambler. He held a bad hand now, and he knew it. There was no way he could bluff his way out of it; the scandal sheets had made his every misdeed public, and even given him credit for some misdeeds not his own. In fact, the best thing to do with a hand this bad was to bow out at once. Perhaps he could wait a year. A year was a long time, and he could mend his ways and get his life in order before attempting it. . . .

But she was dancing with another man. Lord Andrew Bertram, son and heir to the earl of Lansborough.

Another handsome, respectable gentleman like Euston. Anthony's eyes narrowed as he watched them, Bertram's fair head next to Celia's golden one. A year was too long, he decided abruptly. It seemed unlikely Bertram was looking to marry yet—he was a year younger than Anthony, and known for his merry, carefree ways—but there were sure to be others. If Anthony wanted any chance of winning her, he couldn't wait.

He caught sight of her again, beaming up at Bertram, and his heart seemed to stop in his chest. There was a glow to her face, a vivacity to her manner, that made him smile just to look at her. The only thing worse than holding a hand this bad was wanting to win this badly with it. He couldn't bow out, no matter how foolish it was not to. Some gambles were worth any odds.

For a fortnight he considered the problem. Events seemed to conspire against him—Lady Howard tried to refuse her money back, even when he told her he would tell her husband everything. She grew quite hysterical, throwing herself at him and tearing open her bodice. Anthony suspected she had expected a far larger return on her money than he had offered her, so she could return the full three thousand to her husband's funds with no one the wiser. When he refused her bared breasts, she took to following him about town, always approaching him in public and threatening a scene at any moment. He stayed away from society for four straight nights to avoid her, even though it cost him the opportunity to see Celia again, too.

Could Celia come to care for him? The likely answer was no, of course. He acknowledged that as he sat in dark, smoky card rooms and tried to keep his mind on his cards. He gambled with people from the whole width of society, yet knew he was perceived as somehow worse than the rest. Anthony even curtailed his gaming for a while, trying out his new, morally upright life, but then the bill from his tailor arrived and he had to return to the tables. Even in his tight financial circumstances, the one thing he could not scrimp on was his clothing. If he began to dress like a man in dire straits, people would stop giving him their money, and then he would be truly sunk.

But he still thought about her. Six children and a pack of dogs. The image was growing on him.

Finally he decided the key would be winning the duke of Exeter's consent. He had never asked permission to court a young lady before, and now—just his luck—he would have to ask the strict and grim duke of Exeter. But as Celia's oldest brother and guardian, his approval was vital, and once gained, it would surely go a long way toward winning the dowager duchess's approval, if not her blessing. To persuade the duke, Anthony planned to surrender at once: confess his sins, admit his failings, and swear a solemn oath to mend his ways. A lot of humility, he hoped, would go a long way.

He managed to get an invitation to the annual Roxbury ball, knowing that Exeter and Lord Roxbury were allies in Parliament and even friends, as much as Exeter could be said to have friends at all. He dressed with great care—more than any woman had ever done, he thought to himself in dark amusement—and set off.

After an hour, though, he had not caught even a glimpse of Exeter, his duchess, the dowager duchess, or Celia herself. Finally he located Celia's brother, his old friend David Reece, near the card room. "Is

Exeter about this evening?" Anthony straightened his shoulders, tense with apprehension.

"I believe so." David Reece peered into the depths of his empty glass. "He won't be in there, though."

"Right." Anthony glanced into the card room, automatically sizing up players. He turned resolutely away and walked back into the ballroom. Exeter was known to disapprove of gambling, and Anthony knew his reputation would hurt him in that regard. He hoped the duke would accept his explanation.

Reece followed him. "Do you have a particular question for Exeter?"

"What?" Distracted, Anthony scanned the ballroom for the duke.

"Why do you want to find him?" Reece repeated.

Anthony turned to look at his friend. "A question about an investment," he said vaguely. "Someone recommended his opinion."

Reece gave him an odd look. "Investments."

"Er—yes," Anthony said. "Of a rather delicate nature."

His friend did not look convinced. "Right. Here, I'll ask Vivian." His wife was winding her way through the crowd toward them. Anthony went still as he realized Celia was with her.

"There you are, love." David drew his wife close to his side, unabashedly affectionate. "Have you seen Exeter? Hamilton wants him."

"I'm to tell you they've gone home," she answered, a faint Irish lilt to her voice. "Her Grace felt unwell. They're nearly home by now, I expect."

"Ah. Bad luck, then," David said to Anthony.

He made himself smile and nod as if he didn't mind. "Another time."

"Was it an urgent matter, Mr. Hamilton?" Celia gazed up at him with wide blue eyes. She wore a very fashionable gown of pale blue, perfectly suitable for a young lady making her debut. Its very modesty made him burn to see her without it. Just her slim figure, clothed only by a cloud of golden, lemony hair . . .

"No, it can wait." But not long. He couldn't see her many more times without giving himself away. Wouldn't that give society a delicious spectacle: the notorious rake starry-eyed over a girl. "I hope Her Grace recovers."

Her smile was so warm. "I shall tell her you wish her well."

He nodded, and after a moment two young ladies came up to steal Celia away. The three girls departed, leaving Anthony alone with David Reece and his wife.

"I trust the delay won't affect your investments," said Reece.

Anthony started, tearing his eyes away from Celia's departing back. "No. I shall call on him."

The next morning he presented himself at Exeter House as early as was polite. The butler showed him into the duke's study, where Exeter did not look overly surprised to see him. Perhaps Reece had said something.

"Hamilton." The duke nodded in greeting. Anthony bowed. Exeter waved one hand. "Won't you be seated?"

Anthony sat, feeling rather like he was sitting down in a high-stakes situation with his every farthing in the center of the table. Outwardly he was calm, but inwardly his nerves were coiled tight. "I have come to ask permission to court your sister, Lady Celia."

The duke's eyebrows went up. He looked shocked. Anthony took a deep breath and plowed on. "I am aware that my reputation will make you hesitant. This is not a lark to me, nor a passing impulse. I have known Lady Celia since she was a child and have always felt the greatest affection for her."

"Er—yes," said the duke, still apparently caught off guard.

"I am well aware that there is gossip attached to my name. Not all of it is true—in fact, a fair amount of it is completely wrong," Anthony went on with his practiced speech. "You may be concerned that I will break her heart. I will not, to the very best of my ability. Whatever people say about me, I am a man of my word, and I give my solemn vow that I shall do everything in my power to make her happy and to avoid that which will make her unhappy. Your sister will never be disgraced by my actions."

"Indeed," murmured the duke. "Mr. Hamilton—"

"I will make amends with my father. We shall never be on the best of terms, but I am his only heir. I shall do whatever is necessary to ensure Lady Celia is received as a future countess."

"Mr. Hamilton . . ."

"And my finances . . ." Here he paused before going on, more slowly. "I am not a gambler by whim, Your Grace. It is my income. The earl has not made me an allowance in several years, since our estrangement. I had to have means to live. I have investments, though still modest, and can support a wife. With her dowry as capital, I shall be able to give up cards entirely." He realized he was gripping the arm of the chair, and uncurled his fingers as he waited for the duke's answer.

"Mr. Hamilton." Exeter leaned forward, fixing him with an unreadable gaze. "That is all very admirable, but I must tell you that I have recently given my permission to another man for Celia's hand in marriage."

It was so far from the answer he was expecting, Anthony couldn't comprehend it for a moment. "I see," he said after a pause. He had expected to have to plead his cause; he had even expected to be refused. He had not expected *that* answer, that he was too late entirely. "And she has . . . ?" He couldn't even say it. He'd put every farthing on the table and lost it.

The duke nodded. "She has."

"Right." For a moment he just sat there, trying to absorb it. Anthony had always known she might not want him and had braced himself for rejection. On a mad impulse he almost asked if he could still approach her, just to know if she might have accepted this other fellow only because he, Anthony, hadn't asked her—and if she might change her mind.

But no. Celia was too honest to do that. If she had accepted someone, it must only be because she wanted to marry him. She had surely never had a thought of Anthony Hamilton, debauched rake and notorious gambler. He was not only too late, he had never had a chance in the first place. "Of course," he murmured at last. "I wish her very happy."

Exeter inclined his head. "I am sorry."

"No," said Anthony. "There is no need to be." He forced a gruesome smile. "I hope you won't tell her of . . . this. She is kindhearted enough, she might feel sorry as well." He paused. "I do not want her pity."

"I shall keep your confidence," said the duke with a slightly more sympathetic expression.

"Thank you." Belatedly Anthony realized he had no more reason to stay, and got stiffly to his feet. His muscles, which had been so tense and tight when he walked into the room, hadn't yet relaxed. He cleared his throat, but there was nothing more to say. He bowed and murmured a farewell, and left.

Exeter House had come to life in the short time he'd been in the duke's study. Anthony followed the corridor toward the soaring main hall, passed by servants bustling back and forth with baskets of flowers. He heard his name and turned to see David Reece striding down the hall toward him.

"I say, Hamilton, finally tracked Exeter down, eh?"

"Yes." He had to say something else before David started asking again what he'd had to discuss with the duke. "I didn't realize the house was being turned upside down."

David grimaced. "A ball. The ladies are making wreaths or bouquets, I'm not certain which." He gestured toward an open door some way down the passage. Slowly, Anthony walked forward, just until he could see the interior.

She was sitting on a sofa with a small mountain of roses in front of her. The morning sunlight streaming in the windows behind her made her curls shine like gold, and pink and yellow petals littered her pale green skirts as she tied the blooms into small bunches. She looked like a Botticelli goddess, and just as attainable.

Behind him, David was still talking. ". . . after the wedding, of course. Rosalind is already determined it shall be the event of the Season."

"What?" asked Anthony, tearing his eyes off Celia. "What did you say?"

"Celia's to wed young Bertram," repeated David. "Young scamp. A bit dodgy, in my opinion, but my stepmother has declared Celia shall marry whom she chooses, and for some reason she's chosen him. Not even Exeter can deny her."

"Indeed," murmured Anthony. His gaze strayed back to Celia, still laughing merrily with the other ladies in the room. She looked blissfully happy—in love, he thought with a quiet sigh.

"Did you conclude your business with Exeter?" David interrupted his thoughts.

"Er—yes." Anthony roused himself. He heartily hoped the duke wouldn't tell a soul what they had discussed.

"And did he have the answer to your question?" David probed.

"Yes," Anthony murmured. There was another burst of female laughter and Celia blushed, from obvious pleasure. His throat felt dry. "It was a trivial matter. Nothing of significance."

"Ah. I see." David eyed him for a moment. "Well, I've some fine colts this year. Perhaps you'd care to see them, perhaps take one." David had become rather domesticated of late, since he married. He was setting up a stable with offspring from some of the finest horseflesh in England. If Anthony could have afforded a horse, he would have been severely tempted.

"Perhaps," he said instead. Very few people knew of his financial circumstances, and David Reece did not need to be one of them. For all that Reece was a capital fellow and an old friend, Anthony had too much pride to tell him. He had only revealed it to Exeter out of necessity, and look what it had gotten him: nothing.

He bade David farewell and left. The afternoon air hit him in the face, suffocatingly warm. For a moment he lingered on the steps of Exeter House. He hadn't realized until this moment, as he walked out of her home for possibly the last time, how much he had hoped . . .

But perhaps this was best. Who was he, after all, to aspire to her? There was a reason he had never before let himself think of her in that way, and the soundness of that reason had just been driven home. He was not the man she loved, or ever would love. He was just a friend of her brother's, and she had never thought of him as anything else. He would survive it. He had survived many other disappointments in his life.

Anthony drew a deep, resolute breath and walked down the steps without a backward glance.

The Journal of
Lady Celia Reece
Given with Love and
Affection on the
Occasion of her Marriage
by her loving Mother

June 1819

Tomorrow is my wedding day—at last! It seems a year at least since my dear betrothed husband-to-be went down on his knee and asked me to be his wife, although it has really been less than one month. I feel I am the luckiest girl in London, to be the bride of a gentleman of such manners, such charm, such dash! Many young ladies hoped for nothing more than a smile from him. And yet he chose me! So romantically, too. I feel I ought to record every detail of his courtship, to tell our children some day. That is in fact why Mama has given me this journal. She says a girl should have a place to save such happy memories, and I do long to. But oh—there is no time tonight! Suffice to say—for now—that no gentleman was ever more devoted than my beloved has been. He has quite spoiled me with his affection and regard, with poetry and flowers and such attentions as have made me the envy of every unmarried lady in London, and no doubt some of the married ladies as well! I cannot wait for everyone to see my gown. It is surely the most beautiful gown ever made, of blue French silk with seed pearls on the bodice and a great quantity of lace. I shall wear Mama's lace mantua over my hair, and the loveliest satin slippers—they are cunningly embellished with glass beads in the design of the lilies I shall carry. I am certain my entire ensemble shall be copied all over England.

I must to bed—in a mere ten hours, I shall be Lady Andrew Bertram!

June 1819

It is so lovely to be married. We have journeyed to the Lake District for our wedding trip. Although Bertie is not much interested in the scenery for himself, he has squired me about so devotedly. When I got a blister on my foot, he swept me into his arms and carried me back to the inn! We have had lovely picnics and romantic strolls, and he has read poetry to me. It seems impossible, but I am more in love than ever.

July 1819

Our first night in our new home, Kenlington Abbey. It is nothing like Ainsley Park. It is much older and used to be a monastery. At first glance it's a bit imposing and even intimidating, with none of the cheery comforts Mama has installed at Ainsley. Perhaps that is to be expected, though, as Bertie's mother died when he was a child and there has been no mistress at Kenlington since. I confess, I am cowed at the thought of having charge of such a place, but I shall do my best.

Bertie told me some of the history as we traveled, although he admitted he was not a great scholar of family history, as his father is. Every Lansborough heir for three hundred years has been born at Kenlington. I shiver to think I shall be part of that history. And perhaps soon—dear Bertie has been so attentive, and we are only a month married!

August 1819

A dinner party this night, with all the local families of standing invited. Lord L. is very conscious of standing; he never introduced me but as "the duke of Exeter's sister." I suppose that is to show how advantageous the match is for Bertie, but I do wish he would stop. I long to meet new friends and wouldn't want people to think me too proud.

(later)

An odd night. Of all the guests, only the Misses Blacke seemed particularly friendly. They are two spinster sisters who live near Keswick and are of great good humor and spirits. Squire and Lady Melton were also very kind, as were the other guests, but they were mostly of an age with Lord L. There were two single gentlemen as well, particular friends of Bertie's. Bertie was in high spirits all evening and is still below with Sir

Owen Henry and Mr. William Cane. I had hoped to meet more young ladies, or really any ladies, but I suppose there will be many more opportunities. Jane Melvill has written twice already, and I miss her.

September 1819

A quiet evening at home. Bertie walked out this morning with Sir Owen and Mr. Cane to hunt. Lord L. discouraged me from going with them because he fears for my health, that as I am not accustomed to the northern weather, I may take cold. It is no secret Lord L. wishes for an heir as soon as Bertie and I can manage one. Bertie is his only child, and the last of the Lansborough line at the moment. On our wedding day, he kissed my forehead and asked only that I present him with a grandson before he dies. I am certainly trying my best, but I would still like to walk out from time to time, even if the weather is not as fine as in Kent.

September 1819

A wretched day. Bertie and I argued. I wished to walk into town today, as much for the exercise and fresh air as to explore Keswick. Bertie refused to accompany me, as he had already made plans to fish with Mr. Cane. Lord L. encouraged him to walk with me, as it is quite a long way and Lord L. was afraid I might become lost or not be up to the walk. He is still very solicitous of my health, but Kenlington is too dull for words. No one comes to call, and there are few assemblies. Even a country dance would lift my spirits.

But Bertie would not accompany me. He said it would be rude to tell Mr. Cane he could not fish after all. Perhaps I ought to have been more considerate when he had already made an engagement, but I have no friends in the country to call on, and Bertie is perfectly aware that I spend most of my days at home. It did not seem such a terrible thing to ask of him. I am certain Marcus does not neglect Hannah so, nor David, Vivian.

Late September 1819

Bertie took me into town today to make up for not taking me the other day. We have rarely been alone together, and it was such a long walk into town, one might have thought we had never spoken to each other in our lives! He confided to me that he does not much care for Cumberland, and that is why he has been so out of sorts. Cumberland, for all that it is beautiful in its own way, is a harsher land than Kent, and perhaps this explains Bertie's restlessness of late. Still, we had a lovely walk and he even composed some poetry on the way, although very poor verse—so poor we laughed until our stomachs hurt.

In town we met a number of people. We stopped for tea with another newly married couple, a Mr. and Mrs. Winslow. Mr. Winslow, who has just been ordained, grew up in Keswick, and he and Bertie knew each other well. Mrs. Winslow was quite engaging as well, and I should like to know her better, but they are moving house to Mr. Winslow's new parish in Derbyshire soon.

November 1819

A letter from Mama and one from Jane. I am becoming quite a correspondent of late! Mama has invited us to Ainsley Park for the New Year, but Lord L. does not wish us to go. He still hopes for an heir soon and has quite a dislike of travel. He said I may invite Mama to Kenlington next year, if I wish, and I suppose that must do.

Jane asks when we plan to journey to London again. Bertie is as pleased as I am about returning to London in the spring. It will be so splendid to attend balls and the theater together!

January 1820

I am very dismal today. We are not to spend the Season in London after all. Lord L. has developed a rheumatism and is confined to a chair. The doctor says he must not travel for several months. Lord L. said that he cannot do without us, and he does not want us to go to London. I was quite upset, not just from the loss of London's entertainments but because I shall miss seeing Marcus and Hannah as well. Mama writes that Hannah will have a child before the year is out—I did not tell Bertie or Lord L. this, though. We still have no prospect of a child, despite diligent efforts.

I asked Bertie to ask his father again about the Season, but

*he will not. I know he is unhappy, though, for he has gone to
the pub in Keswick with Sir Owen and likely won't be back
before dawn.*

February 1820

*Oh, horror. After dinner, Lord L. asked me to read to him.
His eyes are growing weaker, and he takes great pleasure in
my voice, he tells me. I dutifully read for an hour, and then—
I don't know what came over me—I asked if we might go to
London for the Season.*

*"No, my dear. I explained it to Bertie," he told me. "Your life,
and his, will be here. You must learn your roles as master and
mistress. You are both needed here, and it will be good for
Bertie to settle down a bit."*

*"But Bertie had been in the habit of attending the Season,"
I dared to say. "And what of Parliament?"*

*"Bertie needed to find a wife—and a fine job he did, too.
When he is Lansborough, he will be in London for Parliament
and you may travel to London every spring. With my poor
health, I am unable to do as much as before, and Bertie must
begin to take over Kenlington, which he cannot do from
London. I hope it is not too distressing to you, my dear. Next
year you will take the* ton *by storm, I am certain."*

*He cannot go because he is in poor health, and he does not
want Bertie and me to go, either. I do not think life at Kenlington is so very complicated that we must spend every day of the
year studying it. Bertie shows no interest in the estate and
spends as little time as possible here, despite Lord L.'s admon-
ishments. If only Bertie would stay in at nights more! He is out
until dawn nearly every day now. I think he is as bored as I,
but he prefers to spend his time elsewhere. I believe we might
amuse ourselves well enough together, but apart it is terribly
quiet and lonely.*

May 1820

*A dreadful disappointment. We were to dine tonight at the
Meltons', but a fearsome rainstorm sprang up. Bertie declared he would go after all and not spend the night at home,*

even though his father begged him not to venture out. He persisted and went, but Lord L. and I stayed home, as it was quite fierce out.

I wonder that Bertie was so anxious to be out; he has not spent above ten days together here in the last month. His father's health has begun to decline of late, and he worries about Bertie worse than ever. I do wish Bertie would make more of an effort to handle more of Kenlington business, and spare Lord L. so he might recover.

May 1820

Bertie has not returned from the Meltons' these four days. He sent word that a party of guests from Oxfordshire was also detained, and as they were excellent company he found it gratifying to stay.

It is rather disappointing that my *company is not so desirable to him.*

June 1820

Bertie came home in high spirits. He is never so happy as in the company of good friends. His father, however, has taken very ill, and there was quite a row.

I have always tried to be as comforting and loyal after Bertie argues with his father, but in this, I confess, his father has a good point. Bertie ought to spend more time at Kenlington, not less. Bertie thought I was disloyal for saying so. Is it not my place to speak my mind? I had thought we could speak freely to each other, but Bertie seemed to resent it.

August 1820

A letter from Mama today. She writes of Marcus's newborn son, who will be christened Thomas. Lord L. expressed joy and bade me send his felicitations, but afterward he appeared tired and sad, and retired early. Bertie said I ought not to have told his father. When I said I should like to make a visit to see the child and the rest of the family, Bertie said it would only stir up trouble with his father, and perhaps he is right. I do not wish to bring any more despair upon Lord L., who longs so

*desperately for a grandson. Bertie said I may write Hannah
and Marcus, and send a gift.*

I do hope we shall attend the Season in London next year.

December 1820

*A quiet Christmastide at Kenlington. Mama was to come,
but a bad cold kept her home until the roads were too dangerous to travel.*

*She hints in her letter at my condition. No doubt she won-
ders why a year and a half of marriage has produced no child.
I cannot tell her the answer, that Bertie would rather spend his
evenings drinking at the Black Bull in Keswick than doing
anything with me. I fear his father's constant prodding and
prompting about an heir has given Bertie a disgust of the
whole business. So long as his father tries to push him into my
bed, Bertie runs the other way—leaving me to tell his father
every month that I am not expecting. Until we have a child,
Lord L. will keep at Bertie, and Bertie will seek other society
so long as his father hounds him. What a dreadful muddle.*

*Bertie does not shun me altogether; it is a bit worrisome
that we have not been blessed. Perhaps a child would revive
Bertie's devotion, as well as give me something to fill the hours
of the day.*

February 1821

*Mama sent me a packet of all the latest fashions. She won-
ders why we aren't to be in London this year again. I have
replied to her that Lord L. is in poor health and needs my care.
That is not completely untrue, but not completely true, either.
The truth is that Bertie will not even ask his father's permission, and without it, we have no funds for a Season.*

*I am not certain I would enjoy the Season in any event. I fear
I've grown unfashionably quiet and dull, although I have improved my needlework and read a large number of books.*

March 1821

*After luncheon today, Lord L. summoned me to his cham-
bers. He gave me a magnificent set of jewels, almost fit to rival*

the Exeter pearls. They were Bertie's mother's, he explained, and should be mine now.

I thanked him and left. I believe Lord L. begins to feel his mortality, and meant well, but I came back to my room in a dismal mood. I have no place to wear such jewels, here in the wilds of Cumberland.

April 1821

Mama asks if she might make a visit. I have cowardly told her no. She will bring news of Marcus's son, and that can only grieve Lord L. and annoy Bertie. It seems most things I propose annoy Bertie now, or are not interesting to him.

Before we married, Bertie swore he loved me above all others and that he would adore me forever. Either we disagree on what adoration means, or forever is far shorter than I expected.

May 1821

Jane Melvill is engaged to be married—to David's old friend Mr. Percy! At first her letter did not name him but only said we would nearly be sisters, her husband was such good friends with my brother. For a moment I thought she meant Mr. Hamilton, for all that she and every other young lady in London was in awe of him. The thought did not please me, I confess with shame. Jane is perfectly lovely, but she would never truly understand Mr. Hamilton.

Her news has made me think of him for the first time in months. Bertie would not be pleased, but I do miss the way Mr. Hamilton was so easy about my teasing. I never laughed so much as with him.

July 1821

Lord L. continues unwell. His poor health unsettles Bertie, who is almost never at home now. We have hardly traded two words this fortnight. I don't know what to say to my husband anymore. At home he is quiet and moody. In company he is charming and merry. I cannot fathom how I never noticed that before.

August 1821

Bertie leaves tomorrow for York. It is a shooting party for the gentlemen, at Mr. Cane's hunting lodge. Lord L. is not pleased. I overheard them shouting at each other for almost an hour last evening. Lord L. wants Bertie to undertake the management of Kenlington, but Bertie does not wish to. When I asked him why he didn't have more interest in his future estate, he said he would have years to deal with those worries when his father was dead, and why should he sacrifice his youth as well? He is seven-and-twenty; when my father died and left Exeter to Marcus, my brother was only twenty-three. I don't recall ever hearing him complain about "those worries."

For my impertinent question, Bertie called me a scold and said I should work more embroidery. I wanted to throw the hoop at his head.

August 1821

A letter from Bertie today, asking for funds. I am to ask Lord L. to send the money at once. At first I feared Bertie was in danger or injured, but surely his friends would come to his aid in that event. I wonder what the trouble can be?

August 1821

Lord L. does not wish to send the money, and I hope he does not! After dinner I overheard two maids gossiping. One said she had learned from the messenger who brought Bertie's message that the money is to hush up a scandal over a girl in York. Bertie trifled with her, it seems! It would make me very happy if he were forced to stay in York and suffer the consequences of his actions.

But I suppose that would leave the poor girl with nothing, and that wouldn't be fair. No doubt she, like others, was blinded by Bertie's charm and manner.

September 1821

Bertie returned from York today. He was in good spirits and greeted me and his father with great affection. I did not believe it for a moment. As soon as we were alone I asked if it were true, about the girl in York, and he upbraided me for not being more civil. He said not one word of denial.

I feel as though the scales have fallen from my eyes. This is how Bertie has always been: charming and dashing when there is an audience to impress, and selfish and arrogant otherwise. I have made a terrible mistake and do not know how to repair it.

September 1821

Bertie and I have not spoken in a week. He feels I am overreacting by scolding him for his behavior in York. I am at a loss as to how I could have been so blind to Bertie's true character. Not only has he not denied or rebutted the accusation of impropriety, he declares I am a shrew for speaking of it. As if it is wrong for me to want my husband to come home to me!

October 1821

Two letters from Mama this month. I don't know how to reply. I cannot bear for her to know how things stand between Bertie and me. She was so pleased to see me marry for love, and how it has turned out now. It would break her heart if she knew. I don't know how much longer I can deceive her, though. If she should visit, she would know at once everything is wrong.

February 1822

Lord L. has recovered some of his health. The weather has been very mild of late, and I persuaded him to walk with me in the garden every day. He vows it has done him a world of good. He is so improved, he declared we might attend the Season this year. I believe it was meant as a gift to me, after the way Bertie behaved last fall.

I waited up to tell Bertie the news, but he returned from the Black Bull very late, soaking wet and in a foul temper, and so drunk he didn't know what I said. He has begun drinking more than is healthy of late, but I dare not tell him this. All my suggestions are met with indignation or scorn. I hold out faint hope that time in greater society will improve things between us, but I do not know if we shall ever feel affection for each other as we once did.

February 1822

Bertie is ill. I sat by him last night, but he was so cross I snapped at him. Then he growled at me to go away, and so I did. It is not fair to make the maids stay with him, though, so I shall try again tonight. It is no doubt a wife's duty to sit by him, but I must say it is not the most pleasant duty.

Lord L. is not pleased. He said he had hoped marriage and responsibility at Kenlington would make Bertie more sober and dependable, but it has not happened. I'm not certain if he blames me or not. I have certainly become more sober.

Perhaps I am a disloyal wife for such thoughts, but it is hard to pity a man of nearly thirty years who cares for no one's comfort and amusement but his own.

March 1822

Bertie died this morning.
Acute pneumonia, the physician said.
Lord L. is devastated.

March 1822

Bertie was laid to rest in the Lansborough crypt this day. Lord L. wept in silent grief all day. He is the last of the Bertrams, now Bertie's gone without an heir. Lord L. looks a dozen years older than a fortnight ago.

Everyone has left me in peace, supposing me to be grief-stricken. Perhaps I am. I don't know. I feel no pain, no agony, no loss. I sit and stare at nothing, wondering why I feel so hollow.

I do not think I shall keep this journal any longer. I fear my thoughts are not worthy of recording.

Chapter Four

Spring 1823

Celia, Lady Bertram rested her cheek against the side of the carriage and watched through the window. It had been so long since she left London, she had forgotten how busy it was. The carriage passed through streets filled with other carriages, gentlemen on horseback, people on foot, and street vendors. It was loud and noxious after the secluded quiet of Kenlington Abbey, and so foreign she could hardly believe she had once lived here.

Her mother, who had dozed off some time ago, woke up as the wheels clattered loudly over the city streets. "Goodness, we must be nearly home!" She smothered a yawn behind her handkerchief. "Are you feeling ill, Celia?"

Celia sat upright again. "No, Mama."

Her mother beamed. "It is so good to have you back, dearest. I missed you so, these four years. You shall be shocked at how things at Exeter House have changed. Two young boys have a way of upending a household! And of course David and Vivian will be in town this fortnight as well. Oh, my dear, we have all missed you so . . ." She talked on, detailing everything that had happened since Celia left the city four years ago. Celia quit listening. She had been listening to her mother since they left Kenlington Abbey, over a week ago. Celia didn't realize how accustomed she had become to quiet until she had to listen to her mother talk for eight days.

When the carriage rolled to a stop in front of Exeter House, the footman let down the steps and Mama stepped down first. Celia climbed down herself, looking up at the house and waiting for the familiar surge of delight. Exeter House had always meant excitement to her. Coming to town had been like setting off on a grand adventure. She let her head fall back, taking in the full effect of the mansion's grandeur, and felt . . . nothing. No thrill of anticipation, no sense of coming home; it was like someplace she had visited a long time ago, just for a while. Perhaps she should have suggested to Mama that they visit Ainsley Park instead of London. Perhaps at Ainsley she would truly feel at home again, and not like an outsider who was trying to go where she no longer fit.

She followed her mother inside, past the curtsying servants. The hall looked the same, and yet different. The walls that had been white were now a soft yellow. There were lilies on the table near the door. Celia pulled loose the ribbons on her bonnet, feeling oddly like an intruder.

"Oh, you've arrived!" Hannah, the duchess of Exeter, emerged from the back of the hall and hurried forward. She embraced Celia quickly, then drew back to study her. "It is so good to see you again," she said warmly. "I hope the journey was not too difficult."

"No, no, we had good weather all the way," said

Rosalind. She had already removed her traveling cloak and bonnet and now came over to greet Hannah. "How was all in our absence?"

Hannah laughed. "Impatient! All we heard was, 'Have they come yet? When shall Grandmama and Aunt Celia return? Will it be today?'" She shook her head. "They are incorrigible, all three of them."

"All three?" Celia let the footman take away her cloak. An instant later she was sorry, realizing how grim she looked in her dusty, wrinkled black dress.

"Yes, Molly has told Thomas and Edward all about you," said Hannah with a smile. "They are wild to meet you." Her sharp blue eyes roved over Celia's face, but her expression didn't alter. Celia supposed she must look different to Hannah, just as Hannah looked different to her—her sister-in-law's dark hair was smoother than Celia remembered, no longer loose black curls, and there were fine lines around her eyes that Celia didn't remember. But Hannah had been in London with Marcus; she had had two children. Things had happened to her in the past four years.

Celia mustered a smile. "And I long to meet them. Mama has written quite a lot about them."

Hannah cast her eyes upward and laughed ruefully. "There is quite a lot to tell! You never saw two such scamps."

"I can hardly wait," said Celia softly.

"But first you must settle in after your journey." Hannah turned, beckoning the butler forward. "Harper, arrange for tea in an hour, please." He bowed and hurried off. "I've had your rooms prepared. No doubt you're tired and would like to rest."

Celia nodded, not so much because she was truly tired but because she found she needed a bit of time alone. The irony was sharp; how desperately had she longed for friends and family all those months at Kenlington, and now she felt a desire just as desperate to get away from them the moment she arrived in London. She needed some time to readjust to this house, to London, like a sailor back on land after months at sea. She followed Hannah and her mother up the stairs in silence, not knowing anyone or anything they were talking about.

Down the hallway they walked to the room that had been Celia's since she was a child. Hannah stopped at the door. "I shan't intrude on you right now. The children will be wild to know you've arrived, and I did promise to tell Molly the instant you were here. Oh, Celia, I'm so happy to see you again." And Hannah hugged her again.

Celia found a small smile on her face at the mention of Molly. "And I cannot wait to see Molly again. Shall she join us for tea?"

"I will invite her now," said Hannah with a laugh.

"Do you need anything, my dear?" asked her mother fondly. Celia shook her head.

"No, Mama. A little rest will do."

Rosalind squeezed her hand. "Then we shall leave you to it."

They went off down the hall together. Celia watched them a moment, then let herself into her room.

It was like stepping back in time. Everything was just as she remembered it. Hannah must have closed the room and never opened it. Celia walked into the center of the room, looking around in mild astonishment. The last time she had been in this room, she had been a new bride. Memories stirred at the edges of her mind. Her wedding dress had been hung there on a dressmaker's form so it would not wrinkle. For some reason Celia remembered her maid saying it had taken three hours to press it, and they didn't dare lay it flat even for a night. That had been the evening before her wedding. She hadn't gone to sleep until very late, so excited she could hardly stay in bed.

She walked over to the window and looked out. The gardens lay below, lush and colorful. Far more colorful than the Kenlington gardens; practicality had reigned there, for many plants couldn't survive the harsher northern winter.

Celia turned away from the window and sat at her dressing table. The plants weren't the only thing that had not survived well in Cumberland. Her reflection caught her eye. She leaned closer and studied herself.

She looked older, for certain. She had seen herself many times in this mirror, and for an instant, she almost expected to see the same pink-cheeked, smiling girl of old. Instead she saw a pale, thin face, blond hair scraped back into a subdued knot. Her blue eyes were somber, and there was no pink in her cheeks. The black of her mourning gown only made her look paler, more devoid of color. Her eyelids fluttered closed and for a moment memory intruded again; Bertie's handsome face smiling over her shoulder into this very mirror. His arms around her. His breath on her neck as he whispered words of love. Those words seem to echo mockingly inside the hollowness within her. She opened her eyes.

Bertie was not there behind her in the mirror. The charming boy she had married was gone, every bit as dead as the indifferent, distant husband he had become. Only she was left, and she wondered just how much of her he had taken to the grave with him.

Sluggishly she got to her feet. She supposed she was tired, and hungry, and all those things one ought to be after a long journey. But lying down held no appeal, and being alone had not brought her any peace, not even in the room that had once been her haven. She opened the door and left.

In the corridor she met Hannah again. "Oh," said her sister-in-law in surprise. "You're not tired?"

Celia gave a wan smile. "Not much. I've been away too long to want to sleep the day away."

"Of course." Hannah smiled, not asking anything further. Celia wondered what her mother had told Hannah. "I was just going up to see the children. Would you like to come with me?"

"Yes, thank you." She had never seen Hannah and Marcus's two young sons. "I hear the boys are quite a handful."

Hannah sighed and shook her head. "That they are. The baby of course is just a baby, but Thomas . . . oh my, Thomas. He keeps us all running from morning 'til night." She led the way upstairs to the nursery, which was now open and bright.

A little boy with wavy dark hair sat at a small table, arranging tin soldiers. At their entrance, he looked up, blue eyes brightening. "Mama!" he cried, leaping from his chair and running into Hannah's arms.

"Thomas," she cried back, scooping him up. "I have brought someone to meet you." She turned toward Celia. "Your aunt, Lady Bertram, has arrived."

The little boy pressed his cheek to Hannah's shoulder, studying Celia from the shelter of his mother's arms. He was sturdy and round, with bright, curious eyes. Celia stepped forward and made a slight curtsy. "I am delighted to make your acquaintance, sir," she said to him. "But you must call me Aunt Celia, instead of Lady Bertram."

"Ceelee," he whispered, then hid his face in Hannah's arm. Hannah laughed, and Celia smiled. She supposed she properly ought to call him Tavistock, as

Marcus's heir, but it seemed absurd to call a three-year-old child by his courtesy title.

"Might I meet your brother?" she asked him. Without looking up, Thomas nodded, and Hannah led her into the next room. In a cradle near the window, a baby with a round face and wispy curls slept, his tiny fingers wrapped around a wooden duck.

"He adores the duck," whispered Hannah, juggling her older son into a different position. "He cannot go to sleep without it."

Celia's mouth curved; she remembered choosing that duck for her new nephew before he was even born, from a man who lived in Keswick and carved startlingly realistic animals. That had been a week before Bertie took ill. Her smile faded, and she sighed silently. "He's a handsome child," she said in a low voice. A handsome child like she had never had.

"Thank you," Hannah replied, her voice filled with affectionate pride. "But we should go see Molly." She returned Thomas to his table, soothed his protests at being left behind, and they left him with his nursemaid, who had been waiting quietly in the corner.

Molly was in the schoolroom, where Celia vaguely recalled learning her own sums and letters. Celia remembered Molly very well, a darling child who loved to dig in the dirt and catch bugs and fish. She was brought up short by the girl who looked up when they entered the schoolroom.

"Aunt Celia!" The girl got to her feet and bobbed a brief curtsy. "How lovely to see you again!"

"And you, Molly," said Celia warmly. "Although I can scarce recognize you. You've grown so tall."

Molly grinned. She was tall, or seemed so to Celia, and her hair was no longer a tangle of long blond curls but a darker honey color, and neatly combed.

Her face had lengthened and taken on sharper contours, making her look more like her mother. Her hands were just as dirty as Celia remembered, though.

Molly must have realized it as well, for she blushed and put them behind her. "I'm sorry," she said. "I was working on my drawing."

"May I see?"

Molly nodded, and Celia moved forward to look. A tulip, sliced neatly in half, lay on the table. A half-finished drawing of the plant was next to it; Molly had carefully sketched the insides of the plant and labeled them. "It's quite good," she said.

"Thank you." Molly crossed the room and brought back a portfolio. "Here are the rest of them. Mr. Griggs has undertaken to teach me about all the plants in the gardens."

Celia's eyebrows went up as she turned page after page of drawings. "They're lovely," she said, amazed more at the dedication and effort than at the technical skill. She would not have had such patience, or interest, when she was only nine years old.

The girl beamed. "Thank you, ma'am."

Celia put down the book. "Please call me Aunt Celia, like you used to do."

Molly's face grew even brighter. "Gladly, Aunt Celia."

"It's time for Miss Preston's riding lesson, Your Grace," said a young woman then, who must have been the governess.

Hannah looked at Molly. "You may join us for tea after your lesson, if you wish."

"Yes, thank you." Molly grinned once more at Celia. "I shall see you then."

"Yes." Celia smiled and followed Hannah from the room as Molly went to change into her riding clothes. "She's grown so tall," she said again.

Hannah looked amused. "Hasn't she? She has also become an expert on everything. No question arises but that Molly has the answer—and she is quick to tell us so. Your mother says she has picked up a great deal of Marcus's manner, which I doubt is a good thing in a girl of her age."

"Where is Marcus? Will he be here?" For some reason Celia was hesitant to see her brother; she had a vague sense of foreboding. Marcus, after all, had been persuaded against his better judgment to give Bertie permission to marry her. She knew he wouldn't speak of it, but she knew he would remember.

"He should return soon. I've sent around to Vivian, inviting her and David to dine here this evening, if that won't be too tiring for you."

"No," Celia assured her. Perhaps being surrounded by her family again would revive her spirits and make her feel at ease again.

It did not.

David greeted her with a hug that pulled her off her feet. Vivian, whom Celia remembered as wary and reserved, had clearly fit into the family more, although she was still formal with Rosalind. Waists had dropped, and Vivian's gown displayed her rounding belly, proof that she would have a child in a few months. Marcus returned and greeted her almost as warmly as David had, but Celia feared his sharper eyes saw what David overlooked. As expected, though, he said nothing of it.

"To Celia," proclaimed David at dinner, raising his wine glass. "It's dashed good to have you in London again." Everyone raised their glasses and echoed his toast. Celia smiled uncomfortably.

"It is good to see you all again as well."

As if sensing she didn't wish to talk much, Hannah turned the conversation to other topics. Celia was free to sit and listen in peace as they discussed people and events she knew little about. She felt their eyes on her at various times, but as she had nothing to add, she ignored it. At long last, though, something did occur to her.

"David, is your friend Mr. Percy in town this Season?"

"Percy? He's about, I expect."

"He married my friend Jane Melvill," said Celia. "I should like to see her again."

"Oh. Er—right." David cleared his throat. "Yes, I expect you'll see them."

Celia smiled and nodded but had nothing else to say. After a moment's pause, David brought up a new topic of conversation. Celia kept her eyes on her plate for the rest of dinner, feeling more and more lost.

If she had felt quiet and ignorant at dinner, though, Celia felt even worse in the drawing room. David sat next to his wife on the small sofa and openly put his arm around her. The children were allowed to come in to say good night, and then Marcus and Hannah walked them back upstairs, baby Edward waving happily from his mother's arms as Thomas bounced atop his father's shoulders. Molly trailed after them, and Celia saw her return the little wooden duck to Edward's grasp as they left the room.

She alone had chosen badly. Both her brothers, whatever scandal and gossip had attended their marriages initially, were happy. Only she, who had had the wedding of the Season to a very eligible, respectable gentleman, was not. For a moment Celia wondered how she had done so poorly; if she had run away with an actor, or eloped to Scotland, or done anything else out of the ordinary, would things have turned out differently? Better?

"So." Her smiling mother settled into the seat next to hers, shaking Celia out of her thoughts. "I've given some thought to your wardrobe, and Madame Lescaut will be here tomorrow."

Celia stared at her in alarm. "Mama, I—I don't feel much like going out yet."

"Of course," her mother said at once. "But, dearest, it is surely time to leave off the blacks. And fashions have changed a great deal since you left London."

Celia sighed. Perhaps it was. Perhaps if she dressed less like a widow, she would feel less dead. "I suppose they have."

Rosalind beamed at her. "How I've missed you, Celia! A mother needs her daughter about."

Celia didn't know what to say. Did a daughter need her mother about? For some reason, she had felt nothing but dismay so far with her family. Instead of feeling like she had come home, Celia had the awful sense that she had no home anymore, no place where she would feel at ease. Exeter House was Marcus and Hannah's home, not hers. David and Vivian were happy without her, too. And Rosalind seemed determined to make Celia happy again just so they could shop and talk and carry on as they had before.

Celia looked around the large, bright room. *I don't belong here*, she thought.

Her mother would have talked more, but Celia couldn't bear it. She pleaded exhaustion and excused herself.

Chapter Five

After such an early evening, and since she was still accustomed to keeping country hours, Celia was awake early. When her maid came, she told Agnes she would eat downstairs. Partly she was determined to join her family, hoping to feel more at home again. Partly she wanted to get away from her room with its memories. She dressed and went down the stairs.

The breakfast room door was open. She heard her mother's voice, and Celia summoned a smile. She would be more pleasant this morning, she promised herself.

Then a snippet of the conversation in the breakfast room caught her attention, and she paused just outside the door.

"But is Celia happy?" Hannah was asking gently.

There was a pause. Celia remained silent and still, waiting for her mother's answer, as much to learn for herself as to know her mother's opinion. Was she happy? She didn't know. It had been so long since she felt anything. She didn't feel truly unhappy, but surely that was not the same thing as being happy.

"I am afraid for her," came Rosalind's reply at last.

It was so soft Celia had to lean closer to the door to hear. "She is so quiet."

"She has lost her husband," said Hannah. "It takes time for the grief—"

"No," interrupted Rosalind. "I don't think that is the trouble."

"Then what?"

"I fear . . ." Her mother's voice dropped even more. "I fear she has not been happy for some time."

"But her letters," Hannah protested after a moment. "She never said a word."

"No." Rosalind sighed. "I was a fool not to have noticed sooner. She never said anything bad—not about the miserable Cumberland weather, not about Kenlington Abbey, a drafty old place that's not been improved since Queen Elizabeth's day, not about waiting on persnickety old Lansborough. I loved my husband, Hannah, but he vexed me from time to time. I ought to have noticed that Bertram never seemed to vex Celia."

"It could have meant they were so well-matched." But there was doubt in Hannah's voice. Celia closed her eyes; she had lied to her family. She had written happy letters to make them think she was happy, and to hide how disastrous her marriage was.

"Not in this instance." Her mother's voice rose. "I should have known. I am her mother! Even if she could not bring herself to tell me, I should have sensed things were not as they should be."

"You are too harsh on yourself, Rosalind. We all ought to have made a greater effort to bring her back to London; surely Lansborough wouldn't have refused if Marcus had insisted. We ought to have visited. We are all to blame."

Celia clasped her hands together to stop their shaking. Who was to blame, she wondered wildly.

Bertie? She herself? Lord Lansborough, for keeping them in Cumberland when it was clear Bertie would never be happy there? Not her family. She had discouraged them from coming to visit and had done everything she could to make them think all was well. For that, she alone was to blame.

Her appetite gone, she backed away from the breakfast room door. She slipped out of the house, into the garden. Perhaps she ought to go back to Cumberland, she thought glumly as she walked amid the roses, just blooming. All she seemed to be doing in London was avoiding her family. She didn't see any way they could help her. Even sadder, she didn't know how she could help herself. She sank down on a bench.

In the long months since Bertie's death, Celia had tried to evaluate her life. She was only two-and-twenty; she couldn't spend the rest of her life in black and alone. What was she to do now? When her mother had arrived and announced she was taking Celia back to town, Lord Lansborough had protested. He was an old man, and if she left he would be utterly alone. Celia had felt sorry for him, and part of her had clung to the familiarity of Kenlington Abbey. She had lived there for four years, after all, and had grown accustomed to its quiet.

London had lost its appeal. She feared her memories of town would be dominated by her first and only Season, when Bertie had swept into her life with daily bouquets of flowers and sonnets to her eyes. He had courted her so ardently, so devotedly, so romantically. Almost before she knew it, he had been going down on his knee and begging her to marry him.

It took her two years to realize that her love for Bertie had never been as strong as on that day, when she accepted him. Celia had always believed in true love at first sight. It hadn't bothered her that she had known Bertie only two months before they were married. It had never occurred to her that while it might be enough time to fall in love, it was not quite enough time to really *know* someone. Foolishly, she had assumed they could spend the rest of their life together getting to know each other. Instead, it seemed that she and Bertie never really knew each other at all.

Only on looking back did Celia realize that Bertie's merry laugh rang out more often in crowds. He didn't like solitary pursuits, and while one person's company could be sufficient to entertain him, that person had better be an extraordinarily interesting person. Celia, it turned out, had not been interesting enough. If Bertie had to choose between a quiet evening home alone with his wife and a night of drinking with strangers at the local pub, he would choose the pub every time. Celia had still tried to be a good wife to him. She just didn't like him as much as she had thought.

But that was her fault. No one had forced her to choose Bertie, and she had tried to make the best of things. The best just hadn't been very good.

His father's demand that they live in the country in anticipation of a child, a son and heir, had only worsened the situation. Perhaps in town, Celia thought, there would have been enough happening around them to carry both of them through. If they had been in the midst of entertaining society, they might not have noticed, or perhaps not cared, that they were unsuited to each other. She found Bertie tiresome, and she suspected he found her dull. Soon enough there was little reason to anticipate a child of any gender, but Lord Lansborough insisted they remain. He controlled the funds, so they had remained.

She wondered if Lord Lansborough had known Bertie's true nature. Perhaps he thought that forcing Bertie to stay at Kenlington would eventually overcome his son's desire for society and entertainment. He had been so displeased with Bertie's lack of interest in running the estate, and yet Celia couldn't help noticing that Lord Lansborough had been very particular about matters. The few times Bertie had done something, Lord Lansborough had always taken him to task over it. In fairness to Bertie, he must have thought he could never please his father.

And that had left her stuck in the middle. She knew Lord Lansborough had hounded Bertie mercilessly about producing an heir. Celia truly hoped that, and not her own person, was behind Bertie's lack of interest in making love to her. She had quite liked that part of marriage, but her interest in lovemaking had dwindled with her affection for Bertie. Certainly after the affair in York, Bertie had never again come to her bed.

She was still sitting there, thinking, when her mother found her. "There you are," cried Rosalind. She swept Celia into an embrace, pressing her cheek to Celia's. "You weren't at breakfast, and Agnes said she didn't bring a tray. Are you feeling ill?"

"No, Mama." *Just a little heartsick.* She forced a smile. "I am out of sorts from the journey still."

Her mother's blue eyes scrutinized her face. "You must eat, dearest. You're much too thin as it is. Shall I have Cook prepare some currant buns?"

"No, Mama."

"Some scones? Crumpets? Some lovely fresh strawberries with cream, perhaps?"

"No, Mama," Celia repeated.

Her mother's forehead creased, but she abandoned the topic. "What would you like to do today? I sent for Madame Lescaut, but perhaps you would rather go walking or visit Bond Street. And you must be quite anxious to see your friends again."

Celia sighed. None of it sounded very appealing. "I don't know, Mama. I was just enjoying the garden this morning." Rosalind bit her lip, a gesture that betrayed her anxiety. Celia felt awful for causing her mother such distress. "Perhaps a drive, later today?" she suggested.

Rosalind beamed. "Yes, of course!" She clasped Celia's hand. "I shall order the carriage this afternoon." She hesitated. "Shall I send Madame Lescaut away as well?"

Celia sighed. She didn't feel like being fitted, but she did need new clothing. She had done too little lately, perhaps. "No."

Her mother's relief was almost palpable. "I shall tell her to be brief," she promised with another dazzling smile. "We mustn't overtire you."

She managed a wry smile at that. How could someone who did almost nothing feel tired? Even Celia didn't understand why she had so little interest in everything around her. She must force herself to do more and hope that the actions would help raise her interest.

"Will you come back to the house with me? There is still plenty of breakfast to be had. A cup of tea, perhaps?" Rosalind looked at her hopefully.

Celia took a deep breath. She really wasn't hungry. "Not yet. I think I shall sit here awhile. The garden at Kenlington wasn't half so lovely. I have missed this garden."

It was clear Rosalind was disappointed, but she only

nodded. With one more fond touch on Celia's cheek, she left, walking back to the house.

Celia turned her face to the sky and closed her eyes, letting the sun warm her skin. It was nice to be in London, she thought to herself; the sun wasn't warm this early in the day in Cumberland. And she did love the Exeter garden. She remembered playing hide and seek around the fountain with her father, long, long ago. He was only a dim figure in her memory, having died when she was only eight, and he hadn't been much inclined to play with children. It had been a rare day that he chased her around the fountain. She remembered him mostly as a presence, a force that sent the servants running and seemed to make the air hum with energy. Rather like Marcus, although she could never picture her father carrying a child on his shoulders as Marcus had done last night.

The crunch of footsteps interrupted her reverie. She opened her eyes and saw Molly, just turning to creep away. "Molly," she said with a genuine spark of pleasure. "Don't go."

Molly faced her again. "I didn't mean to interrupt," she said, sounding so grown up Celia could hardly believe it. "You looked so peaceful."

Celia smiled. "I was just enjoying the sun. It seems warmer in the south."

The girl came up beside her. "Does it? What is it like in Cumberland?"

She made a face and shook her head. "Darker. Colder. But beautiful in its own way." She patted the bench beside her. "Come sit with me."

Molly sat. She held a drawing case in her arms, which she put on the ground at her feet. "I am supposed to be finding new specimens to sketch," she explained. "Mr. Griggs knows everything about every plant in the world, I think."

"Your work is lovely."

Molly sighed. "Thank you. But I would rather not work on it today."

"No?"

The girl shook her head. "I would rather ride. Mr. Beecham comes twice a week to give me riding lessons. He's such a marvelous rider. He can do all sorts of things, like a performer at Astley's. I asked Mama to have him come three times a week, but she said no. I must study French, and soon dancing."

Celia had to smile at Molly's grimace. "You might like dancing."

"Perhaps," Molly grudgingly allowed. "But I shall never like French."

It made her want to laugh out loud. "I remember you used to like catching tadpoles in the pond," she said on impulse. "Your interests change."

A guilty look came over Molly's face. "I'm not supposed to catch frogs anymore," she whispered. "Mama told me. Young ladies don't go in the pond." She sighed darkly. "I expect she'll allow the boys to go in the pond, though."

"Ah. And how do you like having brothers?"

Molly made another face. "They're an awful bother. Edward is very sweet, but Thomas is a terror. He's forever getting away from his nurse and running after me. He grabs at everything. Once he spilled a bottle of ink on my drawings!"

Celia smiled, a little sadly. "I always wished to have a sister, you know. It was lonely with only my mother for company. When your mother married my brother, I was so pleased. It was almost like I got two sisters: your mother and you."

Molly looked up shyly. "Really? I wasn't a bother?"

Celia shook her head. "Not in the least."

Molly's smile grew. "I am so glad to hear that." She put her head to one side and thought a moment. "Boys must be different, I believe. At times I overhear Her Grace telling Mama tales of Uncle Reece, and he was even worse than Thomas, it seems."

"Well, my mother did not know David until he was almost ten years old," Celia told her. "So yes, I am certain he was a great deal more trouble than Thomas could possibly be yet."

"He'll get worse?" Molly heaved a tragic sigh, and Celia did laugh this time. Just a chuckle, but more than she had laughed in months. She ought to spend more time with Molly, she told herself. Celia had had a deep affection for Molly as a small child, and now the girl was apparently the only person in the house who wasn't watching Celia's every move with worry and despair.

"Shall we walk to the pond?" she asked on impulse.

Molly's face brightened. "Oh, yes!"

"Perhaps we shall catch a frog or two," Celia added, although she hadn't the slightest idea how one would catch a frog.

Molly looked at her warily. "For . . . Thomas?"

"Precisely. Someone must teach him these things so he can torment his tutors some day." She smiled, and Molly giggled.

"Yes, let's!" She pushed the drawing case under the bench and they went off together.

"Lovely legs."

"And a beautiful mouth; nice and soft."

"Hmm. How is she to ride?"

For an answer, David Reece beckoned, and the female in question obligingly trotted over. Her rider swung down. "Mr. Hamilton will take a ride, Simon," he said.

The young man nodded, handing the reins of the tall chestnut mare to Anthony. "She's as smooth as can be," he said.

Anthony mounted. The horse stood calmly as he adjusted things and took his bearings. She was an exceptionally handsome horse, good blood and better training. David's stable produced fine horses, but the young head groom, Mr. Beecham, turned them into excellent ones.

Normally Anthony wouldn't purchase a mare to ride himself, but David had sworn this was the best horse he'd ever bred, gentle but spirited, beautifully elegant in every line but sturdy, and virtually unspookable. He wheeled the horse around and circled the small space in the mews. A fine gait, and very smooth indeed. At a nod from David, he took the horse out into the street, watching her closely but finding no fault. When they reached the park, Anthony gave the mare her head, and her trot flowed easily into a canter, then a gallop. She turned at the slightest touch and obeyed his every command almost the instant he gave it.

He rode back to his house and dismounted. "Mr. Beecham, that is one well-trained animal."

The young man's eyes brightened with pride. "Thank you, sir."

"Reece, you've finally won me over. She's all you said, and I have no choice but to buy her."

David grinned triumphantly. He had been after Anthony for more than three years to buy a horse from him. "Excellent. I knew I had you with this one.

Simon, take her home, will you? Mr. Hamilton and I shall make the arrangements."

"Yes, sir." Mr. Beecham took the reins once more, stroking the horse's muzzle. As he swung into the saddle and rode off, Anthony led his old friend into his house.

"A fine head groom you've got," he said.

David grinned again. "Yes, haven't I? Bloody brilliant stroke of luck. Vivian wanted the boy to be a butcher, can you imagine?"

Anthony raised one eyebrow as they went inside. "A butcher?"

"Something like it. Something honest, she insisted."

"He would have been wasted as a butcher. Perhaps I shall steal him away from you, too."

David snorted. "You couldn't. He's only got one sister, and I've already married her. He's my family, and he's my head groom. Sorry, old chap."

Anthony chuckled. He led the way through the hall and into his library. He preferred to work in here instead of set up another room as his study. The library was a large, bright room with tall windows in between the shelves. The library was the reason he had bought the house two years ago, in fact. "Coffee?" he asked his guest. It was still early morning, much too early for anything stronger.

"Thank you."

Anthony rang for coffee, and they had settled on a price for the mare by the time the servant brought it. "A pleasure doing business with you at last," David told him as he accepted his cup.

He waved one hand. "The pleasure is mine."

"Simon will bring her over tomorrow." Anthony nodded, sipping. "It's a good time to move her,"

David went on. "We're all off to the country shortly, and I should hate to leave her here."

"Back to Blessing Hill?" Anthony asked, naming the country farm where David bred and raised his horses.

His friend shook his head. "Ainsley Park."

"Ah." The family estate. "It's a fine time to go to the country. I was to go see Pease's new railway undertaking in Durham, but he's put me off."

"Then come to Kent instead."

Anthony leaned back in his chair. "Whatever for?"

"My stepmother is having a house party."

"I doubt she would welcome me." Anthony smiled wryly. "But thank you for the suggestion."

"But the party is in Celia's honor," said David. "Or rather, for her benefit. She's back in town, you know, and we hardly knew her when she arrived." Anthony's cup paused in midair. "Bertram turned out to be a sad excuse for a husband—not that I'm happy to say it, but neither am I surprised."

"It was the match of the Season," murmured Anthony, staring into his coffee. "A love match. She seemed quite happy."

"I don't think it lasted long. The blighter got bored in Cumberland, no doubt. I can hardly blame him for that, but I've never seen my sister so quiet. It's unnatural." David got to his feet. "She's bloody miserable, and Rosalind's gone and invited several of her friends to Ainsley for a month. She's so determined to see Celia cheerful again."

"And you fear a party of her friends will fail to restore her?"

"She always liked you," said David. "I'm certain she would rather see you than a dozen gossiping, prying women. The poor girl's going to be pursued through the halls by people wanting to know every wretched detail of Bertram's incompetence as a husband, and I can't think that will help her much."

"I don't want to intrude on Lady Bertram's grief," Anthony demurred. The last thing he wanted to see was Celia, sad and mourning. Celia, vulnerable and brokenhearted over her late husband.

"Someone needs to," said David bluntly. "She's been marooned in it for over a year. If she's not shaken out of it soon, she may suffocate under it."

Anthony hesitated. "I've not received an invitation." His coffee had grown cold. Anthony carefully reached out and replaced it on the desk.

"The devil you haven't," David declared. "I issued one just a moment ago. In fact, consider it a plea. I shall surely go mad without a friendly face about." Anthony gave him an aggrieved look. David laughed. "You'll have it by tomorrow. But after I go to the trouble of getting Hannah to send one, you'd best swear to attend."

"I shall consider it," Anthony said, avoiding a real answer.

"Consider it imperative, for an old friend." David let himself out without waiting for a reply. Anthony inhaled and let the breath out slowly. He really ought not to go. He had other business to attend to, and there was nothing to gain by going to Kent for a day, let alone for a month. Lady Bertram couldn't possibly wish to see him, not if her spirits were as low as her brother said. David Reece had always been somewhat cavalier with the truth, inclined to exaggerate when it suited him. Any recent widow might be considered quiet and subdued. And the dowager duchess would rather see an American savage at her house party than Anthony Hamilton, bastard heir of the earl of Lynley. No, he certainly would not go.

But an invitation arrived that afternoon, delivered by an Exeter footman in immaculate livery. Anthony stared at the neat lines of the duchess's script. He really ought not to go.

Unfortunately, David's words rang in his mind. A sad excuse for a husband, he had called Bertram. Celia had been marooned in grief for a year. Had it really been a year? He remembered hearing news of Bertram's death. The name, of course, had caught his attention. He had listened carefully for any word of Bertram's widow; was she well? Had she caught whatever illness killed Bertram? No one ever hinted at such, but he still wondered. The chance to answer all his wondering lay before him on the desk, in elegant lines. A month in Kent, for the express purpose of cheering Celia out of her mourning.

He shoved himself away from his desk and paced to the windows. There was no good reason for him even to consider this. It had been a strange infatuation of his, a flight of fancy, that made him consider courting Celia Reece in the first place. Once he had gotten past the disappointment, he had seen it was clearly best that he had *not* courted her, let alone married her. His financial affairs had worsened that year, and only through some frantic bargaining and a few loans had he stayed afloat at all. The next year the Cornish tin mines had boomed, and he'd spent most of the year in Cornwall, living above the yawning pits in a mining town. It had made him fairly wealthy, and even more important, it had demanded every minute of his waking attention. He never could have done that with a wife, especially not if that wife had been Celia.

Of course . . . if he'd had a wife, a wife like Celia, he wouldn't have been almost bankrupted by his money troubles, and he could have hired someone to safe-guard his interests in Cornwall. His hand curled unconsciously into a fist, braced against the windowsill, as he thought what it would have been like if he had married Celia four years ago.

Anthony let out his breath in a long sigh. He was a fool, and a maudlin one at that, to stand here and pine for a woman he hadn't seen in four years, who might not even remember him. And it hadn't even been love he felt. It had been affection, with a strong touch of lust. That was slim basis to renew the acquaintance.

No, he certainly would not go to Kent.

Chapter Six

The next two weeks passed in a blur for Celia. Her mother announced, quite out of the blue, that she was having a house party at Ainsley Park. Hannah seconded this plan so promptly Celia suspected they had planned it together for her benefit, and then Marcus gave it his approval as well, confirming that suspicion. She knew they meant well, so she said nothing and let herself be swept up in the preparations. Although she had just arrived in London, there was still a great deal to be done before leaving again.

Despite her promise not to overtire Celia, Rosalind couldn't seem to help herself from ordering a complete new wardrobe for her. She must have paid Madame Lescaut a fortune, because every day, twice a day, large boxes arrived from the dressmaker. The bright colors looked odd and out of place to Celia, who had become accustomed to unvaried black in her wardrobe. With some trepidation she put away her mourning clothes. They had become a comfortable shield of sorts. Stepping out of them made her feel bare, but it was time for her to put the blacks away.

She discovered her mother's guest list for the house

party as people began writing to her. Old friends, people she barely remembered, people she hadn't heard from in years sent her notes, welcoming her back to town and expressing sympathy on Bertie's death. Only Jane Percy's genuinely lifted her spirits. Despite her vow to do more with her family, Celia still didn't feel at ease, and often she caught her mother watching her with worried eyes. Only Molly looked at her as just a normal person, without watching her every move with anxiety. Celia spent as much time as she possibly could with Molly, as much to escape her mother's frenetic planning as to simply be herself.

They arrived at Ainsley Park to find it scrubbed and polished to a shine, prepared for the guests who began arriving the day after the family arrived. Louisa Witherspoon, now Lady Elton, and her husband arrived, followed closely by Jane and Mr. Percy. Lady Throckmorton, Celia's godmother, arrived with her two eldest daughters, Kitty and Daphne, then Lord Snowden, whose property bordered the Exeter lands. Every time she turned around, it seemed more guests were arriving.

Finally she could take it no longer. Telling herself her mother and Hannah would see to the guests, she slipped out of the house. As nice as it was to see some of her friends again, she felt a bit suffocated. There were only so many times one could answer the question, "How have you been, Celia darling?" How was she supposed to answer, she wondered: truthfully? Politely? Neither option really made her feel better.

Far across the lawns, another carriage was approaching, rolling along the long gravel drive. Celia stopped. Oh, dear. More guests.

On impulse she turned and hurried around the house. It was rude of her, but she wasn't in the mood to greet people. Head down, she followed the well-worn path that led past the stables to the wood beyond. It had been her favorite escape as a child, and her heart lifted at the prospect of visiting it again.

Lost in her thoughts, she almost ran into the man before she saw him. "Oh," she exclaimed, stopping abruptly as the tall figure loomed in front of her.

He stopped, too. "Lady Celia," he said, then corrected himself as he bowed. "Lady Bertram."

For a moment she simply stared at him. Mr. Hamilton, whom she'd not seen in years, looked much the same, but she would have known him just from his voice. The way he said "Lady Celia" at first, in a half-startled, half-pleased way, just as she remembered him calling her for years. But then he said "Lady Bertram," in the low, condoling tone she had also come to know too well, the tone that reminded her she was Bertie's widow. "Mr. Hamilton," she murmured at last, dipping a brief curtsy. It seemed strange to stand on ceremony with him, but she'd not seen him in four years. They were strangers now, really.

Anthony had no chance to prepare himself. She simply appeared right in front of him, and he responded on instinct, calling her what he had always called her. But then she blinked, and he jolted back to himself. She was no longer Lady Celia, of course, and he was no longer even a slight acquaintance of hers.

He knew he should look away from her, but he couldn't. She had always been fair, but now she was as pale as a shadow. The blue eyes that once sparkled and danced were now somber. Even her shining golden curls had been tamed into a subdued, almost spinsterly knot. He had told himself there was nothing to mourn, that he couldn't miss what he'd never had. But as she stood there on the path in front of him, her lips parted in surprise, he couldn't move. He had thought he was prepared to see her and was caught off guard by how wrong he was.

"I was just seeing to my horse," he said when he realized the silence had gone on too long. "I've just bought her from your brother."

"Oh! Oh, of course." Faint color rose into her cheeks and for a moment she looked flustered. "I was just"—*avoiding any arriving guests,* he thought—"going for a walk." She seemed to know it was a poor answer, for she bit her lip. But instead of the sheepish smile he instinctively expected, she merely looked dismayed.

"My valet will be arriving with the baggage," he went on, trying to fill in the awkward moment and lift that shadow from her expression. "I sent him in the carriage. He told me it simply would not do to arrive with just a horse, so I must send a carriage. And if a carriage were to be sent, he would agree to ride in it, and possibly continue to serve as my valet, provided it was a well-sprung carriage and he was not jostled overmuch on the trip."

The corners of her mouth softened, but not enough to be called a smile. "Are you still being taken advantage of by your servants?"

He heaved a sigh. "It would appear so. There must be a sign above my door: Herein dwells an easy mark."

The faint curve of her lips grew. "I find that difficult to believe. Impossible, even. I don't think anyone could fool you, Mr. Hamilton."

"I am a much bigger fool than you've ever imagined," he told her with absolute sincerity.

The nascent smile faded. "I'm sure not." She hesitated. "It is good to see you again."

"I am glad to see you again as well." Best to get it over with at once. "I was very sorry to hear of your loss."

If anything, her face grew sadder. "Thank you," she murmured.

For a moment they just stood there in silence, looking at each other. Anthony finally felt obliged to say something, even though he would rather just look at her some more. "Your brother—" he began, just as she said, "I don't want—"

They both stopped at the same time, and Anthony held up his hands. "My apologies. You were saying?"

"I don't want to keep you," she said. "You must wish to change, or rest."

"Yes, of course." He didn't, much, but he could see she wanted an escape. "A pleasure, my lady."

That seemed to lift her mood some. "And mine." She bobbed a slight curtsy. "Until dinner, Mr. Hamilton."

"Until dinner," he murmured, bowing. She continued along the path, and Anthony turned to watch her go. When she vanished around the corner of the stable, he went on his way.

His valet, Franklin, had arrived with his baggage. Anthony met him in the house as the Exeter butler was directing the footmen where to take the trunk. Franklin bowed when he saw Anthony.

"Welcome to Ainsley Park, sir." The very proper Exeter butler bowed as well. "His Grace bids you welcome and invites you to retire to your room or explore the estate. He is detained at the moment, but should you require anything, ring for it at once."

"Thank you." Anthony inclined his head; it never paid to be short with the servants. "I shall." The butler bowed again and led him upstairs, showing him into a spacious, well-appointed bedchamber where his trunk already resided.

Anthony walked around the room after the butler

had silently bowed out the door. "No troubles on the journey?"

"No, sir." Franklin went to the trunk and opened it to unpack. Anthony glanced out the windows. His room overlooked the stables. He looked, but there was no sign of Celia along the path. Had she gone into the woods?

"Shall I draw a bath, sir?" Franklin interrupted his thoughts.

"No," he murmured, peering into the woods. "I shall take a walk before dinner, I believe. Prepare a bath when I return."

"Very good, sir."

He washed the dust from his face and changed out of his riding clothes, then made his way back outside. He cast a lingering glance toward the stables, but there was no one on the path. It would be too obvious to pay another visit to his horse; Celia—Lady Bertram— would be at dinner. Resolutely he turned toward the lake. He was not going to hound her.

He was more than halfway to the water when he heard his name. "Hamilton, by God, wait." David Reece strode up beside him, out of breath and a bit disheveled. "You came," he said, shaking Anthony's hand heartily.

Anthony smiled. "So I did."

"You're among the last to arrive." David fell in step beside him. "The house is full to the rafters." Anthony didn't say anything, especially not that he had been torn, up until the last moment, on whether he would actually attend. Even now he couldn't say what had decided him to come. "Rosalind is in her element," David went on. "I'm glad to see you, for I thought you would not come."

"You told me to come." Anthony clasped his hands

behind him, looking out across the water. "Commanded, really. Even threatened me if I did not."

David laughed. "And you've never been frightened of anything I said, even when you should have been."

"Ah, yes, I remember promises of drowning that went unfulfilled."

"My father would have had my head on a platter if I'd drowned someone in the lake outside his own home." His friend glanced at him. "Not that you didn't deserve drowning at times." Anthony just smirked as they reached a large flat rock projecting over the water, where they used to swim as boys. "You won everything at cards," David grumbled. "It really wasn't right. Did no one ever teach you proper respect for your elders?"

"You certainly didn't," Anthony replied. "And I hardly think seven extra years makes you much my elder."

David snorted. "I ought to throw you in right now, and no one would ever know you were here."

"Ah, but Lady Bertram met me on the path, and she would call your bluff." Anthony spoke lightly, trying to adjust to speaking of her again. He had never called her Lady Bertram in his mind but that's who she was, of course.

David sobered at once. "You met her? Good. In the crush of arrivals, she looked positively miserable."

That was not what he had intended to discuss. "She seemed quiet," he settled for saying.

Celia's brother shook his head. "And was she ever quiet? Do you see now what I meant? Hopefully my stepmother is right, and this will restore her spirits." He clapped Anthony's shoulder. "Shall we go back?"

Anthony took a deep breath, gazing across the lake. "No, I shall walk around."

"What, all the way?" Anthony nodded. "As you wish.

I'll see you at dinner." David turned around, and Anthony resumed his walk.

Celia didn't return to the house until it was time to dress for dinner. Her maid was frantic when she finally reached her room.

"La, madame, we shall have to rush!" Clucking in despair, Agnes hurried around the room, setting things out. "We shan't have time for ringlets tonight, although your hair—madame, you've got twigs in it!"

Celia smiled, trying to hold off the creeping tension in her shoulders. All the peace from her walk vanished in an instant as she contemplated the evening ahead. Just the thought of all those guests, looking at her, wondering about her health, her marriage, her state of mind . . . "Just brush it out, Agnes. I don't care for ringlets tonight."

"Well, very well, madame, if you say so." Shaking her head, Agnes did as she said, brushing out Celia's hair and pinning it up in a simple arrangement. "And the blue tonight?"

She looked at the dresses Agnes had laid out. A rich blue with white satin trim, a golden brown one, and a pale green. The darker the better, she thought. "Yes."

By the time she went downstairs to the drawing room, most of the other guests were already there. Her mother swooped down on her as she lingered in the doorway. "There you are!" Rosalind pressed her cheek to Celia's, then gave her a quick look. "You look lovely, dearest," she said fondly. "Blue suits you much better than black." Without waiting for a reply, she tucked Celia's arm through hers and led her across the room. "I don't think you've met everyone. Lord Warfield, may I present my daughter, Lady Bertram?"

They stopped in front of a tall, rather rough-featured man. He bowed as Rosalind completed the introduction. "A great pleasure to make your acquaintance, Lady Bertram," he said in a deep voice with a hint of Scot.

"And his cousin," Rosalind went on, "Mr. Edward Childress."

Mr. Childress bowed. He was a very handsome man, with fine features and dark hair. "How do you do, Lady Bertram?"

Celia murmured a reply. Oh, dear. How silly of her not to have realized earlier why Mr. Childress was here. He was not a friend of hers, nor even a friend of anyone in the family. She vaguely remembered her mother telling her he was quite the society darling, but Celia hadn't paid much attention. Now she had no choice. Mr. Childress could not have been more obviously meant for her escort if he'd worn a sign around his neck. She would have to speak to her mother about this.

But it only grew worse. There were more unmarried gentlemen, five in total, six if she included Lord Warfield, for all that he was surely twenty years older than she. Even the presence of their neighbor, Lord Snowden, began to look suspicious. All the gentlemen seemed perfectly polite and charming, but Celia was not looking for another husband. The people she genuinely wished to see, Jane and Louisa, were kept waiting as Rosalind led her around like a prize sow to meet every unmarried man in the room.

"Lady Bertram!" cried Jane's voice beside her as her mother talked with the last man, Lord Marbury. "It is so good to see you again." She threw her arms around Celia and embraced her. "Do come sit with me so we can reacquaint ourselves. May I steal her away, Your

Grace?" She smiled very sweetly at Rosalind, who had no choice but to smile back and nod.

"Thank you," Celia breathed as they walked away.

"You looked like you were going to the gallows," Jane returned. "I can't think that would appeal to any man."

"I don't mean to appeal to a man." Celia sighed as they seated themselves on a small sofa. "My mother means well."

"But she's a mother. She can't help herself." Jane smiled sympathetically. "And I can't help but thank her for inviting us all. I declare, Ainsley Park is the finest estate I've ever seen. I should be very happy to spend a month here, no matter what the reason, but it shall be so much nicer that you are here." She flipped open her fan and leaned close. "There is so much gossip to tell you, I don't know where to begin!"

"Tell me about you," Celia said instead. "Where is Mr. Percy?" He wasn't in the room.

Jane made a face. "In the stables, no doubt. Percy thinks of nothing but horse racing at the moment. I'm sure he only came to Ainsley Park because Lord David is here."

"Oh," Celia murmured. Mention of the stables made her think of Mr. Hamilton. He had arrived several hours ago, but he was not in the drawing room. Was he coming to dinner?

As if on cue, a murmur went around the room, and Celia looked up to see him in the doorway, along with David and Mr. Percy. Celia was struck again by how different he appeared. As a younger man he had had an air about him that positively drew people to him; more charming than anyone that wicked ought to be, as one gossip had put it. Celia herself remembered how open he was, how he managed to make her feel as though she could say anything to him and he wouldn't mock her or think her a simple child. Even as he had become more scandalous, people still seemed unable to ignore him.

Now he appeared more mysterious, more remote, as if he were holding himself apart from the rest. He was just as handsome as ever, but there was something indefinably different—and distant—about him now. He might have been alone in the room, instead of the focus of so many eyes and so much attention. He wore a faint, cynical smile she didn't remember as he strolled across the room. He looked colder, she thought; just like she felt.

"Good heavens, he looks as wicked as his reputation," said Jane behind her fan. Celia tore her eyes off Anthony, who had joined Lord Warfield and some other gentlemen.

Jane, though, did not appear to notice. She was watching him with a naked interest that surprised Celia. She glanced again at Mr. Hamilton. Jane had been terrified of him four years ago, and now she looked as though she would eat him.

"Jane, you're staring," she said under her breath.

"Every woman in the room is," replied Jane, still staring. "I can hardly believe he's here, in truth."

Celia frowned a little. "David invited him, I believe." She had overheard bits of conversation between her mother and Hannah. Her mother was not overly pleased Mr. Hamilton was here.

"Well." Jane gave her a sly glance. "My thanks to Lord David."

For some reason that didn't sit well with Celia. She was still frowning, just a little, when they went in to dinner. Her mother had paired her with the earl of Marbury, a nice enough man but rather quiet. In fact, that could be said for nearly everyone at Celia's end of the table. Celia was next to Lord Marbury, with Mr. Picton-Lewis on her other side. Lady Hillenby, the former Miss Mary Greene, was across from her, along with Mr. Childress, Lord Snowden, and Lady Throckmorton. Everyone was nice and very polite, but even with Hannah's valiant efforts, the conversation lagged. In contrast, the other end of the table, where Jane and Louisa sat, was quite boisterous at times, with much laughing and talking. David and Mr. Percy seemed to be the chief bon vivants, Celia thought, stealing a glance down the table from time to time. She felt so odd, wanting to know what was so interesting and entertaining at the other end of the table, and yet terribly certain it wouldn't seem half so interesting and entertaining to her if she were in the midst of it.

But she could see Mr. Hamilton. He was seated near the middle of the table. His dinner partner was David's wife, Vivian, and they seemed to be having a perfectly lovely time, conversing mostly with each other. Mr. Hamilton even smiled at Vivian, a true smile this time. There was the old Anthony she remembered in that smile, his eyes dark amber and his handsome face relaxed in amusement. No doubt Vivian was enjoying dinner much more than Celia was, from her expression. Celia gave a silent sigh as Mr. Picton-Lewis asked her about another type of bird in Cumberland, and tried to turn her mind back to him. She supposed if she found ornithology half as interesting as Mr. Picton-Lewis did, they could also have an engrossing conversation, but as it was, Celia could hardly wait for dinner to end.

After dinner the ladies left the men to their port and returned to the drawing room. This time Celia deliberately dodged her mother and sat with Jane and

Louisa and Mary in a quiet corner. This was what she had truly looked forward to, the chance to talk with her friends again after so many years away. This was what she had missed, those years in Cumberland: her friendships. It would be a delight to talk to other young women her age again, after being all but alone with her elderly father-in-law for a year.

Their conversation, though, was not what she had anticipated.

Chapter Seven

"I can hardly believe he's here," Mary said with barely repressed excitement.

"Lord David," Jane said knowingly. "He and Percy were always friends with him."

"Indeed." Mary and Louisa shared a glance.

"You don't mean Mr. Hamilton, do you?" asked Celia in cautious disbelief.

"Who else?" Louisa lifted one hand. "Celia, darling, it's an absolute shock to see him here. He rarely goes about in society—"

"Not in good society, at any rate," Jane interjected.

"But the tales of his doings . . . I do believe he singlehandedly keeps the gossip rags in business."

"People have talked about him for years," Celia said. "And I never thought half of it was true."

"Even if only half is true, he's about as wicked as one can get and still be received." Mary seemed pleased by the thought.

"He's received because old Lynley might kick off at any moment," said Louisa.

"He's received because he made a fortune in Welsh

tin or some such thing," Jane replied. "And an earldom, combined with that fortune and that face—"

"And that form," said Louisa on a sigh.

"—he'd be received even if someone could prove he *did* kill that man in Bath." Mary gave a decisive nod.

"What?" Celia gasped. "He killed a man? No!"

Jane lifted one shoulder. "Well, no one could prove it. Percy says he wasn't even in Bath then, but other people say he was."

"He would never do such a thing," Celia protested. Anthony, kill a man? It was impossible to reconcile that with her memories of him.

"He may have been provoked," Mary conceded. "They say the other man drew his pistol first."

"Because he caught Mr. Hamilton cheating at cards," said Louisa. "They say he only plays at the most notorious gaming hells now because no one else will sit down with him."

"I can't believe he cheated, or that he would kill a man." Celia cast about desperately for another topic of conversation.

"There's plenty else he's done," Louisa told her. "Mrs. Ridgely threw a fish at Lady Pierce because he tossed her over for Lady Pierce."

"Oh, I remember that!" Mary exclaimed. She made a chagrined face. "At the Nethercote ball. I was so sorry to miss it; Hillenby refused to go after Lord Nethercote voted in favor of some Irish bill Hillenby despises."

"We weren't there, either," Jane told her. "Percy won't go to Nethercote House because Sir William only allows penny stakes in his card room."

"I was there." Louisa's eyes gleamed with excitement. "And saw the entire affair."

"A fish?" Celia felt a creeping discomfort at the way

Louisa savored the story, and at Mary's disappointment in missing the spectacle.

"A whole poached salmon in cream sauce. She snatched up the tray from the table, and flung it at Lady Pierce just as everyone was going in to supper. It quite ruined Lady Pierce's gown, a lovely blue silk with gold cord trim and blond lace. It was so fashionable, and now no one can copy it because of the scandal attached to it." Louisa sighed, as if mourning the loss of a beautiful gown.

"But you can hardly blame Mr. Hamilton for what others did," Celia murmured.

Mary leaned forward, flicking one hand dismissively. "Oh, but we all know he's behind it. Really, can you imagine what sort of lover he must be, to make Catherine Ridgely destroy her own reputation over him? Mr. Ridgely dragged her off into the country the next day, and she hasn't been seen since."

"She must have been driven completely out of her mind to fly into such a passion," Louisa agreed with a shiver of delight. "It does make one wonder . . ."

There was a moment of silence as they shared another knowing look, and Celia fought back the urge to jump up and leave. She had always enjoyed a bit of gossip, but this was almost cruel. Not only were they gossiping, but Louisa and Mary were actually pleased that someone they knew personally had humiliated herself so badly. Celia didn't know Mrs. Ridgely, or why she had thrown a fish at anyone, but she felt very sorry for her all the same.

"How is Lord Elton?" she asked Louisa instead.

Her friend made a face. "Healthy."

"I never met him before yesterday," Celia said. "Is he amiable?"

Louisa looked surprised. "Amiable enough, I suppose. We aren't in each other's company often."

"He's a dry old stick." Jane laughed. "At least one can't call Percy dull."

"*He's* merely a drunkard." Jane rolled her eyes at Louisa's comment but didn't refute it.

"He'll be a baronet one day, and he's a handsome fellow. I do wish his father wouldn't dangle him on such a short string, though. I have to pinch the housekeeping just to pay the milliner."

"It's no better when your husband controls his own funds," Louisa replied. "He barely gives me enough housekeeping to pay the servants, and then complains if I don't serve beef every night."

"At least you control the housekeeping," grumbled Mary. "Hillenby only gives me a small amount of pin money and nothing else."

The gentlemen came into the room then. Celia caught sight of her mother heading her way, a gleam in her eyes. Rosalind had had her head together with Lady Throckmorton all evening, and Celia dreaded whatever exhibition they had planned. Her conversation with her friends had dampened her spirits even more, and her head ached. She couldn't bear any more, not when she suddenly felt like the latest object of interest: the tragic widow. Were the others talking about her sad life with as much relish as Louisa discussed Mr. Hamilton's allegedly wicked life? No doubt they were. They just weren't bold enough to do it in front of her—yet.

Celia got to her feet. "You must excuse me."

"Of course!" Jane pressed Celia's hand in hers. "Are you ill?"

She managed a halfhearted smile. "No, I just require a bit of air."

"Shall I come with you?"

She wanted to be alone. "I shall be fine," she said with a better smile. "Please stay and enjoy yourself."

Jane, who clearly was disposed to stay and enjoy herself, nodded and released her, and Mary and Louisa wished her well. Celia slipped out of the room. For a moment she stood in the hall outside the drawing room, listening to the murmur of conversation punctuated by moments of laughter. Everyone was having a fine time . . . except her.

She began to walk, wandering the corridors she had known since she was born. Ainsley Park, though one of the finest estates in England, was not an enormously large house. It had been built over many centuries by many different people, and as such included a variety of quirks like secret cupboards and hidden doors, but Rosalind had made it as modern as a house could be. Celia had explored every inch of it as a child, always delighted when some new feature was installed or some secret uncovered. Unlike the austere formality of Kenlington House, Ainsley was bright and lived-in. Every step she took held memories that made her smile.

She left the house through the side entrance. It was a beautiful night, with only a crescent of moon to compete with the stars. Celia stopped and took a deep breath, closing her eyes and raising her face to the cool air as she stood on the wide stone steps. Perhaps she did feel a bit more at home here—at least when she was alone.

Celia opened her eyes and gasped. A man stood in the shadows a short distance away from her, watching her. Her heart thudded against her ribs for a moment, and she pressed one hand to her chest. "I beg your pardon, sir," she said breathlessly. "You startled me."

Mr. Hamilton didn't move. "Then I must beg your pardon. I did not mean to."

Celia smiled. "We had best forgive each other at once, then."

"Done," he said with a chuckle. "Is the party moving out of doors?"

"What? Oh, no. I came for a breath of fresh air." She remembered what Mary and Louisa had said about him, that he was unbearably wicked and might have killed a man and caused women to have public brawls over him. Did he know? He must suspect. Perhaps that was why he was out here, too. She hadn't noticed he wasn't with the other gentlemen when they arrived in the drawing room.

"I did the same." Her eyes had adjusted to the darkness now; she could see the wry twist to his mouth. He knew, she realized. He knew very well what they were saying about him.

"Shall we take a turn about the garden?" Celia didn't mean to ask the question, it just came out. But she couldn't be so cold to him that she just walked away, not when he was escaping the same thing she was.

His hesitation was slight. "I would be delighted."

For a while they walked in silence. Anthony had come outside to be alone and to avoid any unpleasantness in the drawing room. No one could have missed the looks he got at dinner. Even Reece and Percy had merely nodded in understanding when he turned away from the gentlemen at the drawing room door and headed for the outdoors instead. He ought to be annoyed with Reece, Anthony thought, for pushing him to come to this house party knowing full well the talk it would cause. Lord Elton had watched him as though he expected Anthony to steal his purse, and Lord William Norwood seemed to have a desire to duel on the morrow, so provoking was he. Anthony was accustomed to people talking about him, even in front of his face, but he must be getting old and perverse; part of him had considered standing up and announcing that he was taking bets on which lady at the party he could seduce first, just to see Hillenby's face turn completely purple.

So he came outside. It was quiet outside, and a beautiful night as well. Ainsley Park was a fine estate, and it had been some time since Anthony had seen it. A solitary walk seemed just the thing before going to bed.

But then *she* came out, turning her face up to the moon with an expression of near-rapture. In the moonlight the changes in her face weren't as striking. Instead she was just as beautiful as he remembered— even more so, perhaps. She no longer had the rosy exuberance of youth, but sorrow hadn't destroyed her beauty. It had pared away the rounder, more innocent softness and left her with a mysterious quality that made her even more alluring to him.

She appeared too caught up in her own thoughts to be horrified by his presence as they walked. He found it hard to believe she hadn't already gotten an earful from Lady Elton, if not from her mother. When she had gasped at the sight of him, Anthony had braced himself for a cool retreat. Instead she invited him to take a stroll. Anthony remembered what her brother had said that afternoon, and saw it was true: Celia *was* far quieter than she had ever been as a girl. She was just walking beside him, absorbed in her own thoughts and unconcerned with his wicked reputation. Anthony found it remarkably peaceful and walked a little easier.

"Mr. Hamilton," she said abruptly. "You have never paid much mind to gossip. How have you managed?"

Years of practice, he thought. That, and years of getting pummeled for reacting to it. Indifference had been literally beaten into him. "There are far more interesting things to mind. It's not difficult at all."

"But when—I mean, if," she hastily corrected herself. "If you suspected people were talking of you, how could you bear it? Is it better to hear what they say, or to avoid it entirely?"

"It's often difficult to avoid it entirely. Some of it may be so absurdly wrong, it's amusing." He tried to answer lightly but still honestly. He didn't want to make her feel worse by admitting that some gossip, the parts that bit more closely to the truth, could maim a person's soul.

"I suppose," she murmured doubtfully.

Another silence ensued. They passed through the arbor into the more formal garden, silvery and shadowy in the moonlight. Anthony stole a glance at his companion; her expression was pensive and almost troubled, quiet and still, nothing like the ever-changing open countenance he remembered. He recalled how she had looked the day he learned of her engagement, covered in rose petals and laughing merrily, vibrant and pink with joy. Again he wondered what had gone wrong, how abominable a husband Bertram had been to transform her thus.

Perhaps that was wrong, though. He knew only what Reece had told him about her marriage. Perhaps her melancholy sprang more from grief, or guilt, or something unrelated. He must remember that he didn't really know her now. The Celia he remembered would have stopped in starstruck delight at the sight of a shooting star, but this Celia didn't even notice the streak of celestial light above her. Her eyes were only on the path in front of her, not on the skies or the gardens or him.

"Did you see that?" he asked softly. "In the sky. A shooting star."

"Oh?" She tilted her face upward, but there was still no joy in it. She was looking only because he had said something. "I missed it."

"Your question about gossip," he said. "My answer was too hasty." She looked at him, but Anthony kept his eyes on the sky, searching for any more shooting stars—wishing stars, his mother had called them. "It takes time to be able to ignore it. At first, one cannot help but want to know, to hear everything. It's impossible not to be appalled, humiliated, indignant, even angry. Often it's difficult to restrain yourself from retaliation of some sort. Unfortunately, that only leads people to talk more, and now you've given them grist for their mill. It becomes harder to ignore, as the tattletales try to provoke a reaction from you, giving them yet more to talk about. It's a cruel cycle, really.

"But eventually, if you very diligently ignore it and persuade everyone you don't care, they begin to leave you alone—somewhat. Often your best hope is that someone else commits a more scandalous act and diverts attention from you."

"That sounds awful," she said with a sigh.

"The cure, I was once told, is to be as dull as possible, and thus escape interest in the first place." He said it lightly, wondering if she would remember her own words to him. For a moment she didn't react, and he glanced at her from the corner of his eye. She didn't remember, he realized, and was about to speak again when recognition dawned on her face.

"That is not quite what I said—you did mean to

remind me of that? I believe I said settling down to a quiet life would quiet rumors about wickedness."

"You recommended having six children and a pack of dogs." She looked at him in astonishment, and he tapped his temple with a rueful grin. "I remember."

"Oh. Oh, yes, I do, too," she said slowly, a smile forming on her lips. "The night you saved me from Lord Euston."

Anthony pretended to shudder. "And the most appalling abuse of poetry I've ever heard, before or since."

"Surely not. Lord Farnsworth once recited his own poetry, 'An Ode on a Decanter of Brandy.'"

"A love poem, no doubt."

Celia gave a little gasp of laughter. "I do believe it was!" She shook her head. "Particularly as he was holding the decanter aloft during his recitation. It quite enlivened the evening." Her smile faded. The moonlight turned her hair dark silver as she bowed her head. "I feel such a hypocrite," she said. "I don't want people to talk about me and my troubles, yet I find it amusing when someone else stands on a table and declares his undying affection for the bottle."

"You're not a hypocrite at all," he told her. "A tipsy fellow climbing on a table and composing odes to cheap brandy makes himself a public spectacle and simply cries out to be a figure of fun to others. Farnsworth himself found it amusing, once his head stopped aching. A person's private troubles, on the other hand, are rarely amusing, and ought never to be proclaimed to all."

"Some seem to find them so," came her soft reply.

Anthony shook his head. "Not amusing. Titillating. They delight in knowing someone else's private concerns, whatever those concerns may be. It's not about the scandal or the force or the shock; it's simply about knowing something they have neither right nor reason to know."

Celia was quiet for a while. "I do believe you're right," she said at last. "I never thought of it that way, but . . . yes. That is very logical. How sensible you are."

"Ah, now I can retire with my mind at peace," he said with a smile. "I have said something sensible today."

"I am sure it is not the first sensible thing you've said today." They had reached the far end of the garden. Celia tipped her head back, looking at the starry sky above. "No more wishing stars," she murmured. "Just my luck, to have missed the only one tonight."

"You may have my wish, if you like."

She just shook her head. "I should go back. Mama will wonder where I've gone."

Without a word Anthony turned back toward the house. The garden was still and peaceful, with only the breeze rustling the trees. She walked with him all the way in silence, then bade him a quiet good night at the door. Anthony watched her go back inside the house; he wasn't ready to go in himself yet, and it made for an easier parting.

So others were talking about her, and she knew it. He tried to repress the swell of anger at those other guests, who had so little breeding that they would come to whisper about their hostess's sorrows. It was one thing in London, where razor-tongued old biddies would carve their neighbor's lives into bits for sport, but these were supposed to be Celia's friends. David had said so. And if this was how her friends would treat her . . .

"Lady Bertram?" Anthony started at the voice,

coming from the other side of the garden. "Lady Bertram?" it called again. Anthony shook off his thoughts and turned toward the man whose footsteps were already crunching toward him.

"Ah, Hamilton," said Ned Childress in surprise. Ned was nearly a sort of cousin to him. His father had been cousin to Lord Warfield, Anthony's uncle, and he and Ned had spent many summers at Warfield's Scottish estate as boys. Ned was one of Anthony's few friends. "I was in search of Lady Bertram. Don't suppose you've seen her?"

"Yes, for a few moments. She has returned to the house."

"Ah." There was a hint of disappointment in Ned's voice. "Her Grace asked me to see that she was all right."

"She appeared perfectly well when I saw her." Physically, at any rate.

"Right." Ned hesitated. "What are you doing out here?"

Anthony took a deep breath. "Taking the air, of course. Fine, fresh country air. Nothing like it."

Ned laughed, understanding at once. "And nothing at all like the air of a drawing room filled with gossiping women." Anthony smiled faintly and said nothing. "I never understand why they find you so interesting. You're one of the dullest blokes I know."

"Spoken like a true friend."

Ned laughed again. "Of course!" He glanced over his shoulder. "I should go back, if Lady Bertram is not lying ill in the garden. Join me?"

Anthony took another deep breath and let it out. Might as well, he thought, and get it done with. He could hardly spend the entire house party lurking in the shadows. And after seeing Celia and talking to her, of course it was clear he wasn't the only one chafing at the gossips—even if he were the one better equipped to deal with them. If all he did was divert the busybodies' attention from her onto himself, at least he would have accomplished something useful. "Of course."

Chapter Eight

The first few days of the party were unpredictable. That was the best way Celia could describe them. On one hand, it was lovely to see some friends again, to be in the country again, to be outside in the sunshine and wearing colors. At times she almost began to feel at home and happy again.

But on the other hand, there were times she wanted to flee the entire party. The more time she spent with Jane, Mary, and Louisa, the more she realized her marriage had not been the only one made on short acquaintance and uncertain affection. Louisa liked being a viscountess, but otherwise had little fondness for Lord Elton. Mary's marriage had been arranged by her parents, and she made no secret of resenting being treated like a child by her elderly husband. Jane was fond enough of Percy, but in a careless sort of way. She thought nothing of sharing his foibles and laughing at him with others. Celia remembered their days as unmarried young ladies having their first Season together, dreaming of romantic love matches with handsome young men, and wondered how they had all become such jaded women in only four years.

And the gossip. Celia had once liked to gossip. Her mother had constantly warned her not to engage in it, but she hadn't seen the harm in whispering with her friends. It always seemed the best bits had been kept secret from them in any event, as young ladies. Now that the restrictions had been lifted by their married status, though, Celia began to wish she had listened more closely to her mother's advice.

"Mary told me she intends to seduce Mr. Hamilton," said Louisa one morning as they sat outside watching the other guests bowl. Earlier the ladies had taken a turn at the green, but now the gentlemen were playing.

"Indeed?" Jane didn't seem at all as shocked as Celia was by this casual announcement.

"Hillenby wants an heir but doesn't appear capable of siring one himself, at least not to Mary's satisfaction." Louisa leaned forward to scan the trays of refreshments set on the table. "Are there any more of those sweet buns?"

"Mr. Hamilton certainly appears far more capable than Hillenby," said Jane. "I do wonder if she'll succeed?"

Louisa pushed away a dish of tarts and smirked. "I doubt it." She lowered her voice. "Does Mary seem like the kind of woman to attract a man like that?"

"Rumor holds he doesn't turn away any woman. Percy says Mr. Hamilton's always been able to get any woman he wants, just with a wink of his eye." Jane rolled her eyes. "I think he was quite jealous."

Celia turned to look at the man in question. She wondered if his ears were burning, as the old saying went; did he suspect people were talking of him, barely fifty feet away? He was with some other gentlemen at the green, no doubt talking strategy and shots.

From the expressions on some of the gentlemen's faces, Celia suspected there was money riding on some throws.

Mr. Hamilton was not obviously a rake. He dressed with perfect taste, but not at all in a way that drew attention. He was handsome, although not extraordinarily. Tall and well-built, he wore his rich brown hair cut shorter than was stylish, although it did seem to suit him. His most exceptional feature was his eyes, warm brown eyes that could be as warm as liquid gold, and the way they would fasten on a person and never once leave her, as if he simply couldn't bear to look away. Until one had the full force of his attention—and those eyes—turned upon her, one might hardly notice him in a crowd.

He caught her looking at him then and tilted his head slightly toward her. His eyes softened even though the smile didn't reach his mouth. Celia felt the warmth of his regard all the way across the lawn. His attention was so intent on her, unwavering, unflinching, but not bold or even unsettling. It was rather like stepping close to the fire on a cold day. Celia dropped her eyes for a moment, rather surprised at that feeling, and when she glanced back he had turned away, with no sign he had been looking at her, not even when Mr. Childress turned her way and doffed his hat slightly. With a start, Celia looked away from the gentlemen.

"But that's the point," Louisa was saying. "If he wanted Mary he could get her—why, I'll wager he finds her naked in his bed before the party ends. You know Mary never was shy or modest. But if he doesn't want her . . ." She smiled, a very superior look. "It's the chase that matters to rogues like him. If he can get a woman for a wink of his eye, why would he want her? A woman must be unobtainable—a challenge—to attract his attention."

"Isn't it odd what makes a woman appealing to a man?" Jane shaded her eyes as she looked toward the green. Her husband was lining up his shot, his face creased with concentration. "When a man is young, it's all in a woman's face and form. When a man wants to marry, it's all her fortune and family. And when he is already married . . ." She sighed. "Perhaps if she inherited a prize-winning colt he would be as entranced."

A shout went up from the green. Percy leaped into the air exultantly. "Did you see that shot?" he cried up at them.

Jane smiled. "Good show, Percy!" He turned back to the other men, laughing and talking some more, and Celia saw a few bits of money change hands. She wondered if her mother knew the guests were wagering on bowls. Mama did not approve of gambling.

"What do you think, Celia?" Louisa had located a platter of Cook's tender little muffins and put two on her plate. "You're so quiet, I do hope we're not droning on and putting you to sleep."

She forced a small smile. "No. I am just quiet lately."

"Of course." Jane nodded sympathetically. "Louisa, those muffins are dreadful for one's figure. I'm certain my corset is tighter after only two days of eating them."

Louisa made a face at her but put aside the muffins.

"I think you do Mr. Hamilton an injustice," Celia said. "Whatever affairs he has, I am sure he is very discreet. He doesn't like to talk about himself at all."

Louisa blinked at her in surprise. "I keep forgetting you know him. What was he like as a boy?"

"He was always very kind to me. I never saw any wickedness in him." Honesty then compelled Celia to add, "I did not know him well and haven't spoken to him in years. He is my brother's friend."

"Oh." Louisa appeared disappointed. "How interesting it would be to know someone so wicked, and to know what he had been like before."

"He's not wicked," Celia said quietly. "I cannot believe that."

Louisa looked doubtful. "Perhaps."

"It is possible," said Jane. "Everyone said Percy was almost as dissipated."

"Well, isn't he?" Louisa plucked another muffin from the tray.

"No," declared Jane in outrage. "At least, not that I have seen. He gambles a bit and spends far too much time at the races, and I suppose he drinks more than he ought, but I've never heard a word of him with a mistress or another woman."

"Aren't you fortunate," said Louisa. "I vow Elton must have a very expensive mistress, the way he scrimps and saves. He's not spending his income on me."

"I just wish Percy would show as much animation at home as he does when there's a game of bowls to be wagered upon." Jane reached for the tray of muffins, obligingly handed over by Louisa. "I am quite sure Mr. Hamilton doesn't talk of horses and cards in bed. He wouldn't have half so many lovers if he did."

"Perhaps he speaks of them with more spirit," suggested Louisa with a mischievous grin.

Jane frowned at her, then broke out laughing. "Perhaps. How spirited, I wonder? How might one make horse racing seductive?"

"If any man could, I'd lay money it would be Mr. Hamilton."

Celia turned her eyes on her hands in her lap. She hated to hear them talk about Mr. Hamilton that way, as if he were a hard-hearted rake who thought only of seducing as many women as possible. She knew there was more to him than that. But this was the sort of gossip she had once gloried in, Celia admitted to herself. She had been happily scandalized and had repeated the shocking tidbits with glee. Who was she to frown on it now, when she had been just as guilty herself?

She couldn't look at the gentlemen again.

"That's five pounds on a draw. Do I have that right?" A pause. "Hamilton?"

Anthony pulled his gaze away from the ladies on the terrace. "Certainly."

Ned grinned. Percy glared at him for wagering on the draw shot. Anthony lifted one shoulder in indifferent apology. Percy was a terrible bowler, and he was the one who had started the wagering in the first place.

Percy took his bowl and toed the line, his face grim. Anthony stole another glance toward the terrace. Lady Hillenby had drifted down near the green to join the Misses Throckmorton, two giggly young girls who applauded vigorously whenever Lord William Norwood stepped to the line. He could almost feel Lady Hillenby's eyes prying at his clothing. She had managed to sidle up against him after dinner last night and murmur a fairly blatant proposition. Even had he been attracted to her, Anthony would never for a moment consider anything so indiscreet at a house party—let alone at this of all house parties. He wondered what Celia had been thinking as she looked at him so thoughtfully just now.

"She's circling," Ned murmured. "Watch your back, Hamilton."

"Don't be ridiculous," said Anthony under the

shouts of the other gentlemen as Percy, shockingly, made his shot.

"If not your back, then your bed." Ned laughed at his repressive glance. "Rumor is Hillenby wants an heir."

"He should get one himself, then." Anthony grinned and tipped his hat as Percy turned to give him a victorious salute. "He'll not get one from me."

"I doubt he could tell the difference."

"You never know," said Anthony under his breath.

"If only ladies would throw themselves at me the way they do at you. I at least would appreciate the effort."

"This doesn't strike me as the proper setting," Anthony replied. "There are an awful lot of husbands present."

"A good point," Ned agreed. "Although, not all the ladies are married."

Anthony froze for a moment, then jerked around to follow Ned's gaze. Ned was looking right at Celia, still sitting on the terrace with Mrs. Percy and Lady Elton. "Lady Bertram is out of mourning now," Ned went on, lowering his voice but speaking warmly. "A very lovely lady. I vow, she's almost as beautiful as Percy's wife."

Anthony knew most men would consider Mrs. Percy the more beautiful woman, with her dark curls and plump little bow of a mouth, but for him Celia outshone her. Celia was certainly beautiful—he defied any man with blood in his veins to deny it—but her true beauty lay within. Somehow he didn't expect Ned to know that.

"I wonder . . ."

"Yes?" asked Anthony curtly when Ned let his wondering linger too long unspoken.

"I wonder if she's decided to re-enter society," his

friend said slowly, still watching her. "Perhaps marry again. What a fetching bride she would be. And she can't be above five-and-twenty."

She was just two-and-twenty, eight years younger than he. Far too young not to marry again. Anthony turned back to the bowlers, regrouping for another match. "I believe she is still recovering from the loss of her husband."

"But if that were so, would there be so many unmarried gentlemen in attendance?" Ned caught sight of his frown. "I was only speculating. You can't deny she's a handsome woman, and with money and position as well. I think I shall make my interest known to her—discreetly, of course—in case she has put off mourning entirely. It's time for me to marry anyway, and a wealthy widow is an ideal bride for a man in my position. What do you think? You know her family."

Anthony forced his mouth into a tight smile. "Not well enough to help your cause."

Ned laughed. "I hardly need help courting ladies. They might not fancy me as much as they do you, but I have my own charm."

"So you persist in telling me."

Ned waved it away, his mood unaffected. "Have pity, Ham. What of her family? Lady Bertram's a bit above me, widow of the Lansborough heir and sister of a duke. Have I got a chance, a mere gentleman?"

Anthony longed to say no. He risked another glance toward Celia. She had put her head down and turned away from the other ladies. In her straw bonnet and pale dress, she was blanched by the sun almost as pale as an alabaster statue, so still and remote. Who was he to say what would please her? He knew she didn't have any sort of immodest pride or ambition that would cause her to reject Ned just for his lack of title. He also didn't think

Ned would be the man to touch her heart . . . but who was he to say that, either? He really must stop thinking he knew anything about her. "As good a chance as any, if her heart is engaged," he said quietly. "She's a most gracious lady."

"Excellent." Ned's face cleared. "Most excellent."

Anthony didn't look at the ladies again.

That evening Celia made the mistake of sitting near the Throckmorton girls after dinner. She had thought to escape Mary and Louisa's chatter about scandal and lovers but soon found she had not improved her situation. Daphne and Kitty were only a few years younger than she, but they seemed decades younger as they giggled and chattered to each other. Celia had known them both for years, as their mother was her mother's dearest friend. It gave her quite a shock to realize Daphne and Kitty were the same age she had been when she married Bertie, and yet were still as silly as they had been at ages eight and nine.

"What a lovely party, don't you think, Lady Bertram?" said Kitty with a giggle.

"The finest party we've ever been to," put in Daphne before Celia could even open her mouth. "Mama was so delighted to tell us we were both to attend, because, of course, next year is to be our Season in London—"

"Although I still do not think it fair I should have to share my Season with you," Kitty complained. "I am older and should have my own Season."

"You are not even a year older, and why should I have to wait a year when I am prettier? I am quite sure I shall land a husband very soon and then you can enjoy your Season alone."

Kitty's eyes snapped. "Perhaps I shall have a husband even before next Season!"

"Well, if you mean Lord William I hope you don't hold your breath expecting him to propose," Daphne retorted. "Everyone can see he favors me. Lady Bertram, don't you agree? Surely you've noticed."

"Er . . ." Celia had been thinking of ways to change seats without seeming rude. "No, I haven't."

"Of course he does." Daphne ignored Kitty's delighted smirk. "Not that I would accept him, of course, not yet. I shall be the most eligible lady in town next spring—"

"After me," said Kitty through gritted teeth.

"I should like Lord William to propose then, after I've had my come-out ball and ordered a new wardrobe. Mama said this party would be a fine introduction to town manners and good society, but she steadfastly refused to order new wardrobes. I think that's dreadfully unfair, don't you, Lady Bertram? How can we appear to best advantage in these old gowns?" She waved one hand at her frock.

"There is more to appearing at your best than a new gown." Good heavens; had she been this silly as a girl? It was a wonder her family had put up with her. Celia finally abandoned subtlety and gave an excuse Kitty and Daphne would understand. "You must excuse me, I must speak to my mother."

"There you are." Rosalind beamed at her approach and made room for her on the sofa, giving her hand a squeeze. "I've not seen you all day."

Celia tried to appear cheerful. "How are you, Mama?"

Rosalind smiled. "Perfectly well. But how are you, darling? Are you enjoying the gathering?"

Celia looked around the room. Louisa was off flirting with Lord William while her husband dozed by the fireplace. Mary was watching Mr. Hamilton with hungry eyes; Lord Hillenby had already retired for the night, as he had every night after dinner. The Throckmorton girls were glowering at Louisa and whispering fiercely to each other, and their mother had made a table of whist with Lord Snowden, Mr. Picton-Lewis, and Mr. Percy, who appeared ready to play at anything where he might wager a farthing. Mr. Hamilton . . . he sat serene and solitary, reading a book. He alone among the guests appeared to be content with his lot.

Was this what she had missed, all those years in Cumberland? Whispered discussions of who was having an affair with whom, and how one might go about seducing a different lover? Celia wondered just how much of her own life had gone through the gossip mill. It seemed naive to think she had escaped entirely. Had Jane and Louisa been just as willing to discuss her and her marriage as they were to discuss everyone else's? She had always thought of them as her friends, but now she wondered if she could truly count anyone as her friend. She wondered if anyone in the world really knew her at all anymore, or if she really knew anyone.

Celia sighed. "Yes, Mama."

"Is there anything you would like to do tomorrow? Any diversion you would care to see? I considered hiring a troupe of players one night; what do you think?"

Celia closed her eyes as her mother talked, too brightly, of plans for the party. "Yes, Mama."

"Which part?" Rosalind peered closely at her face. "Celia, you're so pale. Are you feeling ill?"

Only in spirit. She gave a hopeless smile and shook her head. "Just a little tired."

Her mother was worried, Celia could see, but Rosalind tried to hide it. "Then go to bed, dear. You'll feel better in the morning."

If only that were so. Celia simply nodded, making her way upstairs alone, wishing she had not left Cumberland at all.

Chapter Nine

The next morning Celia decided not even to attempt to fit in. She hadn't seen Molly since the guests arrived, no doubt because Hannah was keeping her children well away from the guests. Celia suspected Molly was chafing under the confinement as much as she had as a child, when her mother had kept her confined when her brothers had guests. She went directly to the children's rooms after breakfast.

"Mama, make him stop!" Molly's cry reached her while she was still in the corridor. Celia quickened her steps as a child's wailing began, with a patter of running footsteps.

In the schoolroom, chaos seemed to reign. The table was covered with Molly's drawing materials, but it looked as though a vase of flowers had also been dumped out atop her papers and pens. Water dripped off the edges of the table, making colorful little puddles on the floor, and a number of wilted tulips lay scattered about. Hannah, looking harried, stood in the corner with baby Edward fussing in her arms as Thomas yanked at her skirts and wailed even louder.

Molly was on the other side of the table clutching her book of drawings to her chest, her cheeks red.

"Molly, he's just a child," said Hannah, handing the baby to the nurse and scooping up Thomas, who flung his arms around her neck and hid his face in her shoulder. "I'm sorry—"

"But he's spoiled my drawing—again!" Molly looked near tears. "Why must I draw in here? Why can't I go to the garden?"

"Molly, you know why." Hannah had to raise her voice over Thomas's crying. "Please understand."

"I understand that Thomas causes trouble and I always have to be understanding!" Two fat tears rolled down her cheeks. "It isn't fair!"

"No," her mother agreed with a sigh. "I'm sorry, Molly, but while the guests are here, you can't run wild about the grounds as usual."

Molly pressed her lips together, her face growing redder. Celia stepped into the breach. "I was about to go walking. I came to see if Molly might be excused from her lessons to walk with me this morning."

Desperate hope leaped into the girl's face, and she turned anxiously to her mother. "Of course she may," said Hannah, giving Celia a grateful look. "Put away your things, Molly, and fetch your bonnet." Molly whirled and ran from the room almost before her mother finished speaking. Celia came into the room, surveying the mess. "She feels so constrained," Hannah explained quietly. "Usually she is allowed the run of the estate, but I don't want her to interfere with our guests."

Celia smiled. "I remember that feeling well. With two older brothers, I spent many a day restricted to the nursery while they carried on something my mother didn't want me to see."

Hannah smiled again. Thomas had stopped crying

and was now just snuggling in her arms. She put him down, then knelt before him. "Master Thomas," she said firmly, "you are not to touch your sister's belongings."

His lower lip came out. "But Mama, Molly likes pretty flowers! I brought her more!"

"Yes, but then you spilled them on her work." Hannah put her hands on his little shoulders. "She is very upset. It was rude of you to pester her while she worked, even if you meant well."

"Molly sad?"

"Yes." Now the little boy looked a little sad himself. "If you don't learn to respect her, she won't want you about. You like doing things with Molly, don't you?" After a moment, he nodded. "Then you must apologize."

Molly came back into the room, and Thomas looked at her with round, sad eyes. "I 'pologize, Molly."

Her expression softened a little. "Thank you, Thomas." Celia saw Hannah's shoulders sag slightly with a breath of relief. "I'm ready, Aunt Celia," Molly added eagerly.

"We're off, then."

Molly fairly skipped along beside her as they walked down the stairs and out of the house. "Thank you for inviting me, Aunt Celia. I was almost wild to get out of the house!"

She smiled. "I could see that."

"Thomas won't leave me alone." She huffed. "Mama says he'll play with Edward once Edward grows bigger, and want nothing to do with me, but that seems an aw-fully long time away."

"At least they are younger," Celia told her. "My older brothers not only wanted little to do with me, they were allowed to do all sorts of things I wasn't. You at least will be ahead of them. I hear you are already a splendid rider."

Molly's face lit up. "It is all thanks to Mr. Beecham. Oh, I am so glad he came into Kent with us this time, for now I shall still have my lessons with him. He's the most marvelous teacher, Aunt Celia. I expect there's nothing he can't get a horse to do." She glanced over her shoulder, then lowered her voice. "May we stop by the stables on our walk? I should like to show you my pony."

"Of course." They turned down the path that wound past the stables. Celia remembered that Molly would wander off as a smaller child and was often to be found in the stables petting the cats or watching the horses being groomed. Now she led Celia to a stall where a gray and white dappled pony munched on hay.

"Her name is Lucinda." Molly gazed at the pony with pride. "I would ride her all the time if Mama permitted it." The pony swung her head around at Molly's voice and trotted over, pushing her nose into Molly's hand.

"She's a beautiful pony."

"Yes." Molly cooed and murmured to Lucinda, "Mr. Beecham says she's the finest pony he's ever seen." She looked over her shoulder. "There he is. I do wish I could have a lesson today. . . ."

Mr. Beecham, Vivian's younger brother, was a lean whipcord of a man. Celia knew he was about her own age. She had never really gotten to know him, since Vivian had married David only a few months before she herself got married and left for Cumberland, but she remembered Simon Beecham as a thin, quiet fellow with wary eyes. Now he appeared much more at ease as he brushed out the coat of a tall chestnut mare, whistling softly.

"What a beautiful horse," said Molly, walking up to him. The horse turned its head to look at her but otherwise didn't move.

"Aye," Simon said. He glanced at Celia and nodded. "Good day, Lady Bertram."

"Good day, Mr. Beecham."

"Is this one of Uncle Reece's horses?" Molly tilted her head back to study the animal with confident expertise.

"No, curious miss, this is Mr. Hamilton's horse. The finest horse your uncle ever bred, and before you ask, no, you may not feed her an apple. You'll not be undoing my hard work by spoiling her now." He flicked his sandy brown hair out of his eyes and winked at Molly. "If you stand there much longer, I'll set you to work combing out the tail."

Celia looked at the horse with renewed interest. Mr. Hamilton's. A mare. Bertie had never ridden any but the most spirited stallions, even when he could barely control them. Bertie had liked the danger of it. Mr. Hamilton obviously valued something else, for his horse seemed the most well-trained creature Celia had ever seen. Even with Molly flitting back and forth around her, the horse didn't stir.

After a while Molly tore herself away from the stables and they continued their walk. They took a very long walk, down all the wooded trails Celia had explored as a child and that Molly now haunted, and by the end of it Celia was fully informed on Molly's life, all the joys and tribulations a nine-year-old girl had. It brought a smile to her face, remembering her own self at that age, and all the things she had rebelled against and longed for and delighted in. In some ways she wasn't so different now—but in others she was completely changed.

As they reached the terrace, the butler came out. "A letter for you, my lady." He held out the letter on his tray. Celia took it, her raised spirits promptly dropping again as she read the direction. It was from her father-in-law, Lord Lansborough.

She looked at her companion. "Thank you for a lovely walk, Molly."

The girl beamed. "Thank you, Aunt Celia. I feel much better now."

Celia clasped her hand. "I'm so glad. Go tell your governess you've returned." Molly bobbed in reply and hurried off into the house.

Her smile fading, Celia took her letter into a quiet corner of the garden, around the eastern corner of the house. There was a secluded arbor there, a peaceful little spot one might hide away in. For a while she simply sat and held the letter. She had a feeling she would need to hide for a while after reading it.

Lord Lansborough had written to her nearly every week since she left Cumberland, and she had come to view his missives with dread. She had developed a great deal of affection for the old man during her marriage, but Bertie's death decimated him. Never exactly a jolly fellow, he had become tragically sad since his son's death, and he wrote of little but how much he mourned Bertie, how much he missed her, how something had reminded him of Bertie, how quiet Kenlington was now. He was old and lonely and had no one else. She didn't want to read his letter but couldn't do that to him. How could she abandon him now as well? With a sigh, she broke the seal and opened the letter.

Anthony was having a devil of a time concentrating on his work.

He had retreated to the library once it was clear the rest of the party would be outside for the day. He imagined this would leave everyone satisfied, and mostly it had. No one seemed to miss him and Anthony was perfectly content.

It was peaceful and quiet in the library; the room was at the back of the house and had obviously been improved in recent years, featuring tall French windows that afforded a sweeping view of the garden and lawns. It reminded him of his own bright, airy library in his house, and he had taken a table in a particularly sunny corner. He got on well enough for a while, working steadily through the letters from his solicitors, inquiries from inventors seeking investors, and so on, until a flash of blue caught his eye.

Through the window he could see a corner of the garden. The main party was out on the lawn playing at croquet or some other game, but Celia wasn't. If he moved his head just a little, he could see her, quietly sitting on a stone bench tucked under an arbor. He tried to ignore her, out there all alone in the midst of a party in her honor. Anthony leaned his head back, and saw the gentle curve of her cheek, the wisps of golden hair trailing from her bonnet. For a long moment he contemplated the slope of her shoulder and imagined running his finger down it until she arched her neck and let him press his lips . . .

He turned his head away. *Leave the lady in peace,* he told himself, forcibly concentrating on his letter. When it was done, he replaced the pen and sealed the letter, then again, from the corner of his eye, caught a glimpse of her. She hadn't moved.

Anthony realized he was drumming his fingers on the table, and folded his hands. He was not going to intrude on her. He ought to leave her alone. He had work to do, after all. Her shoulders rose and fell on a sigh, and he jerked his eyes away again. Since when had he done as he ought? With a sigh, he pushed back from the table, collected his papers and put them away, then strolled out into the garden.

She looked up at his approach, not quite hiding the bleakness in her eyes. "Good day, Mr. Hamilton."

"Good day, Lady Bertram." He paused, taken aback by that look. "It is very fine out."

"Yes, it is."

"And you have discovered the quietest corner in the gardens."

"Have I?" She sighed, folding the letter she had been reading. "I suppose so."

He hesitated a moment, then sat on the other end of the bench. For a moment both were silent, Celia with her head bent in somber contemplation of the letter in her hands, and Anthony in covert observation of her.

"It is from Lord Lansborough," she said. "My father-in-law. He is lonely, now I am gone from Kenlington."

"I am sure you were a great comfort to him," Anthony murmured.

"He is devastated by Bertie's death," she went on, as if he hadn't spoken. "Bertie was his only child. Lord Lansborough did so long for an heir, and I feel— I fear I disappointed him."

Anthony shifted on the bench. "Unless I have been seriously misinformed, creating an heir takes two people."

"But I am the only one left," she whispered.

"Does he reproach you?" Anthony asked after a pause, making an effort to keep his voice even. How dare old Lansborough heap guilt on her head, especially when there was nothing that could be done about it now?

She heaved a quiet sigh. "No. But perhaps—if I had

been more—" She broke off and looked away, blinking rapidly against the dazzling sunlight.

"Perhaps," he agreed. "And perhaps not. Not all things are meant to be, no matter how strongly one desires them."

She slanted him a curious look. "And is it so easy to put off the longing?"

A question he knew too well how to answer. "No, it's not," he said gently. "But—sometimes—it does help, knowing that it was unattainable from the beginning."

She frowned a little. "I don't see how that could be so."

"Well." He cleared his throat. "If you long for something impossible, it takes the sting out of failure. Too often, regrets spring from the things one could have done but didn't, and the chance that those actions might have led to success. It is the weight of personal fault that causes the pain, the feeling that but for being remiss in some way, you might have achieved your goal. If there is absolutely nothing else one could have done . . . it was simply not meant to be." He lifted one hand. "Have I managed to be sensible in any way?"

Celia sighed, but her expression had eased. "Yes. You always do. So what do you suggest?"

He tilted back his head to study the arbor above them. "When you want something, do everything in your power to achieve it. Leave no room for regret. And if you still fail in your objective, console yourself that it must surely not be your own fault, and you shall find a better opportunity."

"And when it is too late for that?"

For a moment he was silent. "Then one should go fishing," he said at last.

Her eyes widened, then she burst out laughing. She

stopped at once, looking around with an almost alarmed expression. "What good will fishing do?"

"Perhaps not much," he conceded with a rueful grin, "but it's more enjoyable than contemplating your woes."

Anthony could see she wanted to laugh again. She was biting the inside of her cheek to stop herself, but her mouth still curved. He felt ridiculously pleased with himself for getting her to laugh.

But after a moment the glow faded from her face, and she looked out across the garden to the other guests playing Pall Mall on the lawn. The occasional laugh or shout of triumph was barely audible from this distance.

"My mother thinks I am moping," she said suddenly. "She thinks I am still brokenhearted over Bertie and that it's time for me to leave off mourning him and re-enter society. All these entertainments and outings are meant to raise my spirits and take my mind off my grief."

"And are they succeeding?" he dared to ask after a moment.

Celia shook her head. "She's completely wrong. That's not the problem, and I don't think this house party is the solution." She heaved a sigh. "There may be no happy answer for me. I feel as though everything I believed in was wrong. I married not for advantage or wealth or connection, but for love—and I made a terrible choice. I always thought to marry for love meant one would be happy forever. It's such a lovely story, that a girl will meet a gentleman, they'll fall madly in love with each other, and live the rest of their days devoted to each other. But it doesn't always happen that way, does it?"

Anthony had no reply to that, so he said nothing. Celia's voice grew tighter. "And where does the fault lie in that story? If they are not happy together, does it mean they were never truly in love? Or were they truly in love, but love doesn't last? Or perhaps even that love doesn't exist?"

"Love exists," he said. "I've never seen a man more besotted than your own brother."

She gave a despairing little laugh. "Which one?"

"Both, actually."

"True enough." She sighed. "Yet neither of them was quick to recognize the fact. That's not much comfort, that your true love could be right before your eyes and you would still not know it."

Anthony didn't dare look at her. "They discovered it eventually."

"Hmm." She looked down at the letter in her hands. "I was too hasty."

"We all are, at times."

She nodded. "And sometimes not hasty enough. Oh, it is a wretched tangle, isn't it?"

Anthony smiled wryly. Yes, he had sometimes not been hasty enough. "Indeed."

Celia tucked the letter into her pocket. Go fishing, indeed. The thought almost made her smile again, and that alone made her feel a bit better. Anthony always seemed to have that effect on her. On impulse she grasped his hand. "Thank you. You have been so kind to listen to me. I do hope I'm not being too grim and ruining your visit."

His fingers tightened slightly around hers. His eyes seemed to gaze inside her, to the bottom of her soul. "Never suggest it."

For a moment she could only sit, caught in the spell of his attention. Again she felt the strange sense of warmth and comfort, just from sitting here talking to him. She had always felt at ease with him, but this time, something was different. . . .

"Shall we join the others?" His question startled her out of her thoughts. Celia nodded, her face growing warm. He helped her to her feet and offered his arm. Celia gave him her hand and walked with him down the lawn to join the other guests.

Anthony paced his room late that night. He couldn't sleep. The two halves of him were waging war inside him. One side, his cool, calculating side, favored doing nothing, or nothing more than he had been doing. Celia's happiness or unhappiness was none of his concern, not really. She was not his sister, his cousin, his lover, or anything other than an acquaintance he held in high regard. There were more arguments against his involvement in her life than he could count, and Anthony had learned to listen to such arguments.

But the other side of him, the reckless, impulsive side of him, burned with the need to do *something*. Being a constant friend wasn't enough to erase the shadows from her eyes, especially not after Lansborough's letter. What sort of gentleman would stand by and do nothing as someone he cared for struggled under great unhappiness? The trouble was, anything he did was bound to be viewed with suspicion, merely because *he* did it. The last thing he wanted to do was expose her to more gossip and even scandal by making his attentions, no matter how nobly motivated and innocently meant, obvious.

He gripped his hands behind him as he continued prowling the room in indecision. He could tell her brother about the letter . . . except it was not his place, and what could Reece do in any event? Perhaps one of her sisters-in-law, who both seemed very sensible ladies, would know how to comfort her against Lord Lansborough's words. But he didn't know either well enough to betray Celia's confidences. Those same reasons ruled out mentioning the letter to anyone else, someone he knew even less well. If Celia wanted her family to know, she would tell them. Anything Anthony did must be discreet, both for her sake and for his.

What could he do, though? He stopped pacing and flexed his hand, still feeling her fingers curling around his. She had thanked him—just for listening to her. He longed to pummel Lansborough for making her feel guilty, but that wouldn't help Celia. If anything, she'd be sorry for the old man, for whom she clearly had some affection and sympathy.

Unconsciously he began reviewing the items in his rake's bag of tricks. What would he normally do to please a woman? Something subtle, something personal, something . . . lovely. Most of the choices were unsuitable. The only one suitable, in fact . . . might be the best choice.

For a moment he paused, considering it. It needn't be too personal; in fact, it needn't reveal him at all. Anonymity might even be preferable. Yes, that might be just the thing. He could lift her spirits in a discreet way, without putting her into a difficult position because of his involvement. Before he could change his mind, Anthony unlocked his writing desk. Glancing around his empty room almost furtively, he drew out a sheet of paper and unstopped the bottle of ink.

He took his time dipping the pen. What to say? Something warm, flattering, admiring, not too ardent.

Something to appeal to a romantic heart, but leaving room for retreat if she took offense. Something she would never suspect came from him. He let out his breath; he was a fool for doing this, most likely. Then, casting aside his reservations, he began to write.

Chapter Ten

Celia was awake before dawn, but she made no effort to get out of bed even when her maid came. She had dreamed of Bertie's funeral during the night, of Lord Lansborough weeping brokenly, and had woken with tears on her face. She was tired of feeling sad and low all the time, but every time she began to feel more like her old self, something always seemed to come along and cut her legs out from under her. She knew Lord Lansborough didn't mean to make her sad by writing to her; that made it all the worse. She was here in Kent, surrounded by loving family and friends, while Lord Lansborough was alone in his manor, in failing health and with only his memories. It seemed dreadful to wish he wouldn't write to her, and Celia felt even more dreadful because she knew that and *still* wished he wouldn't write to her, at least not so sadly.

"Good morning, madame," whispered Agnes in surprise as she slipped into the room with a pitcher of warm water. "I hope you've not been waiting."

"No."

"Shall I go?"

"No," she said again. She could hardly stay in bed all day. "I'm ready to get up." Agnes bobbed and nodded, and slipped out of the room. She returned awhile later with a breakfast tray, and Celia made herself sit up. Her mother would worry if she stayed in bed all day. Celia wished, for a moment, she could go fishing, or out walking, or even just stay quietly in her room and read. Today did not feel like a day for merrymaking.

Agnes arranged the tray for her, and Celia surveyed the plates with disinterest. Not even Cook's tender little muffins with orange marmalade stirred any hunger. She picked up the cup of tea, trying to shake the horrible feeling that she was all but dying inside.

Tucked beside the saucer was a folded paper.

"Agnes," said Celia, drawing it out, "what's this?"

Her maid looked up from opening the drapes. "I don't know, m'lady. It was in the kitchen, with your name on it. Cook said I ought to bring it up."

Mildly curious, Celia broke the small, plain seal and opened the note. She read it, then read it again in growing surprise. "Agnes," she asked, "did Cook say who sent this?"

Agnes shook her head. "No, madame."

Celia read the note again. "Go ask."

"Pardon, madame?"

"Go ask Cook who sent it," Celia repeated.

Agnes dropped a quick curtsy. "Yes, ma'am." And she hurried out the door.

Celia laid the note aside. How odd, someone sending her a love note—unsigned, no less. The old Celia would have been wild with excitement. Now, of course, she was older and wiser and knew better than to believe such nonsense. No doubt it was just an attempt to make her feel better; she wouldn't be surprised if her mother had arranged it. She would have to put a stop to it at once.

But Agnes returned with no news. "Cook doesn't know, ma'am," she said, ducking her head. "It was left in the kitchen overnight, and no one knows who sent it."

"I see." Celia fingered the strange note. "I shall wear the blue striped dress this morning."

"Yes, madame." Agnes hurried to get the dress from the wardrobe, and Celia swung her feet to the floor. She plucked the note from the tray, crossing the room to the fireplace. The fire had not been stirred up, but there was warmth in the embers still. She stirred them with the poker until there was enough heat to ignite a corner of the note. Celia turned away as the paper burned. She certainly wouldn't be taken in by such empty-headed romantic nonsense again.

Still, all that day she wondered who had sent it. The handwriting had been unfamiliar, but that meant nothing. Who could it have been?

It could be a scheme of her mother's. Celia wasn't at all sure her mother wouldn't nudge one of the gentlemen into writing to her that way, and the sentiments could have been copied from any book of poetry. Mama was a terrible matchmaker. But with whom?

Lord Warfield was surely too old, and he hardly seemed to notice her in any event. He, at least, had not been invited for the purpose of catching her interest. Celia knew he and Marcus spent long hours in the study discussing some railway project, and Lord Warfield only infrequently joined the other guests. Lord Snowden was a neighbor and, she supposed, an eligible gentleman. She had simply never thought of him as such, and rather doubted he thought much of anything about her. Mr. Picton-Lewis was of a scientific nature and didn't appear to have much poetry—even bad poetry—in his soul. Lord William, though, certainly was capable of writing the note, as were Mr. Childress and probably even Lord Marbury. Mr. Childress especially was very attentive. To be perfectly honest, some of the married gentlemen weren't out of the question. Celia had noticed some of them giving her looks from time to time, as though wondering which sort of widow she was.

Oh, and Mr. Hamilton. Celia smiled wryly to herself at the thought of Anthony Hamilton, cool, polished rake who could have any woman he wanted at a snap of his fingers, writing such a letter—to her, of all people.

But that night there was another note on her pillow, and in the morning another on her tray. Undeniably curious now, Celia took the letters to her desk when Agnes had left. They were both banal, trite things, with little wit in them. She was as much annoyed by them as she was flattered.

Dear Sir, she wrote. *I have received your notes with great surprise. It is no wonder to me you have not signed your name, for why bother, when you have put so little effort into composing the message? Any volume of poetry supplies your sentiment. When I wish to read poetry, I shall visit the library. If you have nothing more original to say to me, anonymously or not, then please spare us both the trouble of corresponding. C. B.*

Anthony found the note on the wide trestle table when he slipped into the kitchen very late that night. TO THE CORRESPONDENT OF LADY B., it said on the outside. For a moment he froze, warily glancing around to see if anyone lurked in the shadows. The kitchen seemed empty, though, so he picked up the message. There was another letter in the pocket of his dressing gown, but he didn't put it on the table, as he had done before. Curiosity about her response ate at him; was it favorable? He had been watching her, covertly, for two days to see if there were any change in her manner. She seemed a bit more engaged, but it might have been due to anything. For all he knew, she hadn't gotten a one of his notes, even though he had dared to leave one right on the pillow of her bed.

He took her note back to his room, not wanting to linger a moment longer than necessary in the kitchen. He closed and locked his door, barely turning the key before tearing open the letter.

Its tart message brought a pleased grin to his face. Now, that was the Celia he remembered. The grin faded. What ought he to do now? Perhaps it was enough that he had gotten a rise out of her. Perhaps he had accomplished what he wanted to do. Perhaps he ought to let it go now.

And perhaps he could ignore the challenge in her words. He was already drawing out a clean sheet of paper to reply. After some thought he sat at his desk and took up his pen.

> *Dear Madame—*
> *Forgive my lack of original wit. The same hesitancy that leads me to withhold my name also led me to take refuge in the words of others, words I dare not speak myself. Know that my feelings, if not the words used to express them, are all my own. Wear a yellow ribbon in your hair on the morrow, and I shall understand that my sentiments as well as my words are unwanted.*
> *Your devoted servant*

* * *

"The peach dress today, Agnes." Celia tapped the latest note from her mystery correspondent against the edge of her desk. She hadn't entirely expected another note at all, but here one was. He was in full retreat. *Good riddance, then,* she thought, crossing to her dressing table and rummaging through a drawer in search of a yellow ribbon.

That morning she walked into town with Jane, the Throckmorton girls, and a few of the gentlemen. It was another sunny day, although with a brisk, cool breeze. For a while she walked with Jane but eventually fell back. Mr. Childress ended up walking beside her, then. He was very charming and witty, but Celia couldn't shake a vague discomfort. Only when she had returned to her room to change for dinner did she realize what had unsettled her. Mr. Childress reminded her of Bertie.

She supposed she was doing the poor man a disservice. He might be nothing like Bertie in other ways. But he paid her too much attention. He hung on her every word too obviously. His charm and wit were too cultured, not unforced and easy. He was clearly flattering her and doing his best to charm her, and she didn't like it. It was exactly how Bertie had won her heart years ago.

People would think her a lunatic, she thought with a wry smile as she washed, being disgusted with a gentleman paying her his attentions. Most women would no doubt delight in having a handsome society favorite like Mr. Childress devoted to them. Celia wondered if he had written those silly letters; they certainly fit his personality, although she would have thought he'd sign them, so as not to leave even a shadow of doubt about his intentions.

Thinking of the letters, she reached up to her hair,

meaning to remove the yellow ribbon she'd tied in it that morning. Perhaps Mr. Childress's attentions had been an effort to overcome the sight of the ribbon. But it wasn't there. She turned her head from side to side, frowning at the mirror, but there was no ribbon. It must have come undone on the walk. The breeze had been quite brisk on the way home.

Well, no matter. She dressed for dinner and went to join the others, feeling rather confident and self-possessed. Odd, really, when all she had done was reject someone, but it seemed important to her. Instead of falling into a fluttery swoon over trite flattery and silly gestures, she had recognized it for what it was and refused to be swayed by it. She enjoyed dinner more than usual that night, especially since her mother had paired her with Lord Snowden instead of Mr. Childress. At least she believed Lord Snowden's conversation to be honest, if a bit dull.

She was very much surprised to see yet another folded little note on her breakfast tray. "I shall start taking breakfast downstairs," she muttered to herself as she ripped it open, ready to throw it back in Mr. Childress's face and directly tell him she was not . . .

Dearest Lady—
Words cannot express my relief that you wore no ribbon today. After such a poor beginning, it would have been my just due to receive a dozen yellow ribbons from you. All night I lay in suspense, fearing to see even a bit of ivory. In the light of day I searched anxiously for it, hardly daring to hope. I can only hope—pray—that by its absence you allot me a second chance, another chance for my pen to whisper these words that know no tongue, no voice. Your censure for my timidity has unlocked the vault of my heart, and those thoughts, once imprisoned,

begin to riot so fiercely, I cannot restrain them any longer.
If you know what it is to have such longing and such
feeling bottled inside you, you must understand a
hundredth of the joy I feel, to let them escape and fly to
you, small and shy though they may be. They shall be
fluttering in the air about you, no more than a faint
whisper of admiration; of devotion; of hope.
    Ever your devoted servant

She had gone completely still by the end. Well. That
was not the tired ode to her eyes the first notes had
been. She put it, not in the grate as she had the
others, but on her desk. Celia eyed the paper thoughtfully as she dressed. What accounted for the change?

Perhaps she should write back again. It would only
be fair to let the fellow know she had indeed worn a
yellow ribbon in her hair and had no desire to continue to receive his letters. Yes, she decided, she would
do that.

But it slipped her mind that night. Her mother had
hired a troupe of players to perform a pantomime of
one of Shakespeare's comedies, and she found it rather
amusing, even though Mr. Childress contrived to sit next
to her and kept trying to make conversation. She
nodded and smiled, not listening to half of what he said.
Before she knew it, the evening had flown by. By the time
she fell into bed she had completely forgotten about the
letters, and didn't remember she had meant to write
back and end the correspondence until the morning,
when yet another folded paper was on her tray.

"Agnes," she said, holding it up. "Where do these
come from?"

Her maid looked worried. "I don't know, madame.
They're just on the table in the kitchen in the morning with your name on. Shall I not bring them up?"

Celia pursed her lips and opened the note. It was better; very nice, in fact. *Hope illuminates my world*, it read in part. *My soul begins to lift as I declare my affections. Some have said that love unrequited is the most painful agony, as if the outpouring of love saps one of will and life. It is not so; the more I lay bare my heart's desires, the more there is to bare, as if I have unstopped a never-ending tide of feeling that flows ever toward you.*

Who sent these notes? she wondered. "No, Agnes, keep bringing them," she said. But for some reason she didn't tell the maid to try to find out who sent them.

Chapter Eleven

Lady Hillenby finally caught Anthony unawares after luncheon one day in the corridor outside his chamber. He had successfully avoided her for a week since her invitation to visit her bed, but now here she was, pressing up against him as he tried to excuse himself. Where was a man safe if he couldn't retire to his room for a few minutes unmolested?

Of course, he had slipped away to write a reply to Celia's latest note. He could barely keep his mind on conversations now that she had started writing back to his messages; he was constantly composing replies, more replies than he could ever send. And now his inattention had led to this awkward confrontation.

"We could slip away this very moment," she was saying, her high, girlish voice making his head hurt. She seemed much too young to be doing this.

"I have a prior engagement."

"Pshaw." Her fingers walked down his chest until he caught her wrist. "It won't take long. It never does."

"Ah, but if something is worth doing, it's worth doing right," he said gently. "I suggest you ask your husband to show you."

"I want you to show me." She pouted, trying to pull free of his grip. "I'd not be the first one you've shown, would I?"

"Lady Hillenby—"

"Mr. Hamilton." The voice stopped Lady Hillenby cold. For a moment fear flashed across her face, then disappeared under recognition. Anthony looked over her shoulder to see Celia standing there, watching him try to keep Lady Hillenby's hands off him.

"My brother is looking for you," Celia said. "He would like to have Mr. Beecham show your horse."

"I was on my way to the stables just now," he replied. "Thank you for passing on his message."

"I beg your pardon. I hope I did not interrupt." Celia gazed right at Lady Hillenby, who assumed a small smirk.

"Oh! Not too much." Lady Hillenby gave Anthony a look from under her eyelashes. "I must be going, sir. Hillenby will want me."

Good, thought Anthony, *for I never shall.* He bowed his head and she strolled away, brushing past him a little too closely. When she had gone he looked at Celia. "Thank you," he said again.

A hint of a smile curved her mouth. "You are most welcome. I hesitated to interrupt, but then I sensed you would not mind."

Anthony glanced down the corridor again, to make certain Lady Hillenby was truly gone. "I shall be eternally grateful you interrupted." Her hint of a smile grew. She had definitely smiled more in the past few days, Anthony was positive of it. He had certainly been watching her closely enough to know. "I was indeed on my way to the stables. Is Reece there waiting on me?"

"Impatiently," she confirmed. "I believe Lord William has piqued his temper with claims about his horse, and

David wishes to prove him wrong by offering a comparison to a horse from his own stables." She paused, pink coloring her cheeks. "I believe there may be money riding on the outcome."

"Ah," said Anthony. "Then Percy is there as well." This time Celia laughed. He felt a ridiculous burst of satisfaction at the sound. Lord, he loved her laugh. "Will you be viewing the contest?"

"I am to be a judge, along with the other ladies," she said, and when he offered his arm, she laid one hand on it.

As they walked she explained what had occurred. Lord William and some other gentlemen had gone for a ride and upon their return had met some of the ladies out walking. Lord William had begun to demonstrate his horse's fine points, and his actions only grew more extreme as the two Throckmorton girls exclaimed in awe and applauded his every move. But he had unsettled the other horses by doing it, and when Percy's horse reared and almost threw him, David had called Lord William a buffoon and told him he ought to get a horse he could control—perhaps a pony. Lord William had retorted that he knew as much about breeding horses as David did. Before long, money had been wagered on who kept better horses, and now most of the party was assembled near the stable yard to see. David wished to have Mr. Beecham show off Anthony's recently purchased mare, Hestia, as a testament to his stables. The gentlemen being involved in the wagering, it was decided the ladies would judge whose horse was superior.

"Because ladies," Celia finished dryly, "surely cannot be swayed by affectation and favor."

"Are you implying the Throckmorton ladies are not impartial?" he asked with a chuckle.

"They have already assured Lord William he shall prevail." Celia sighed and shook her head. "Such silly girls. They are sweet enough, but their heads are so easily turned."

"They are young."

"They are old enough to make a terrible mistake," she murmured. "Being young and naive would be small comfort then."

Anthony thought there was a world of meaning in that statement. He wondered yet again how unhappy she had been in her marriage, and how deep her regrets might be. But Celia's brow was clear. The shadows that had clouded her eyes were almost gone. She was still quieter than she had been as a girl, but she no longer seemed sad. Anthony realized they had reached the stable yard, and it was not his place to inquire anyway. David Reece strode up to them.

"Hamilton, there you are." He flashed a grin at his sister. "Thank you for offering to fetch him, Celia."

"It was my pleasure," she said, taking her hand off Anthony's arm. He felt its absence even as he tucked David's words away in his mind. She had offered to fetch him? She walked over to join the other ladies, and David grew serious.

"I say, would you mind if Simon took your mare out for a turn? I'm determined to show up that ass, Norwood, and you've got my best foal to date."

"Of course," Anthony said. "I shall never hesitate to hand any horse of mine into Mr. Beecham's hands. I still nourish hope he'll leave your employ for mine."

David laughed. "Not a chance! I only hope you've not undone all my good work."

"I've only owned her a month."

"Precisely. A month in your company is enough to ruin any female."

Anthony gave him a black look, but David just laughed again and walked off, calling to his groom to fetch Mr. Hamilton's horse. Anthony knew David spoke in jest, but still . . . He risked a glance in Celia's direction. She was standing beside a young girl in a green riding habit; the duchess's daughter, he remembered. The other ladies were several feet away from them. The men were on the far side of the yard, engaged in fierce debate. He should follow form and join them, at least for a while. Without looking at Celia again, he headed for the gentlemen.

"But why must Uncle Reece do it now?" Molly kicked at the bottom slat of the fence, her face wrinkled up in a scowl. "I'm supposed to have my riding lesson now."

"It shouldn't take long, Molly," said Celia with a smile. "Half an hour, no more."

The girl rolled her eyes and let out a gusty sigh. "An eternity! If only this house party were almost over. I cannot wait for everything to go back to normal."

Celia shook her head, clasping Molly's hand. She glanced over her shoulder, then leaned down to whisper in Molly's ear. "I cannot either. But we must both bear up as best we can, hmm?"

"Aren't you enjoying it?" Molly's brown eyes opened wide. "Betty and Miss Parrish said the party was all for you."

Celia's smile grew strained. Betty the nursemaid and Miss Parrish the governess shouldn't gossip around such keen ears. But then, a small part of her had to admit, in all fairness, she was enjoying the party now. It just wasn't due to the guests—or rather, one particular guest was responsible for her increased enjoyment of the other guests' company. Just the sight of the little folded notes on her breakfast tray made Celia happy. Molly hardly needed to know that, however. "It is, in a way. My mother invited several of my friends to welcome me back from Cumberland."

Molly looked doubtfully across the yard at Lord William, who was turning his horse through tight figures as the Misses Throckmorton giggled and waved their handkerchiefs at him. "Oh. I didn't realize they were all your friends, Aunt Celia."

Celia looked at Lord William, too. She couldn't guess why her mother had invited him, except that he was handsome, heir to a marquis, and—most important— unmarried. She sincerely hoped her mother didn't think she would fall in love with the likes of Lord William. "Well, some of them are my dear friends," she said. "Not all."

Her companion thought for a moment, watching the prancing horse and preening rider. "I hope he's a very good dancer," she said at last. "He's certainly not a very good horseman."

Celia choked and had to clap one hand over her mouth to keep from bursting out laughing. Trust Molly to speak as she felt.

"Are you well, Lady Bertram?"

She jumped and lurched around, almost losing her balance and falling backward. Anthony caught her, his hands at her elbows, and for a moment Celia swayed in his grip. Out of nowhere it occurred to her that she had never realized how strong he was. "Yes," she said breathlessly, gazing up at him. "Quite."

"I see," he said slowly. For a moment he scrutinized her, and then his expression eased. He released her and his hands fell away. Celia took a step back and looked away, flustered more than she ought to have been.

"Are they nearly done?" asked Molly in a hopeless tone, still watching Lord William.

Anthony tore his eyes off Celia, and his mind off what might be making her choke on laughter, and turned to the little girl. "Not quite. I believe Norwood has nearly finished, though."

The child turned. "Is the other horse yours?" she asked with more interest. She was charmingly direct.

Anthony nodded. "Indeed it is."

She looked at the horse, which Mr. Beecham had just led out. "She's a beautiful horse. We saw her in the stable the other day."

"Thank you. I am proud to own her."

"Molly, have you met Mr. Hamilton?" Celia asked, finally composed again. "Mr. Hamilton, may I present to you Miss Molly Preston, my niece. Miss Preston, may I present Mr. Hamilton, a friend of mine."

Anthony bowed, and the little girl dropped a very proper curtsy. "It is an honor to make your acquaintance, Miss Preston."

"And I yours, Mr. Hamilton." She then ruined her serious demeanor by declaring, "And I hope your horse wins, because it is far better than his!"

Anthony laughed, and Celia smiled. Their eyes met, and for a moment Anthony forgot everything around him. There was a glow about her face that hadn't been there even a few days ago.

"Are you not watching with the other gentlemen?" Celia asked him.

"Er—no. I have been dismissed on grounds of bias." Percy had said he must go away and not win all their money. So here he was, far happier to be standing with Celia instead.

Across the yard, Lord William had finished his performance and leaped off his horse's back. With an elaborate flourish, he gave a deep bow in the direction of the ladies. As he did so, the tail of his riding whip slapped his horse on the nose. With a loud neighing, the already excited, high-strung stallion reared up. Lord William fell on his face in the dirt, scrambling away like a crab as his horse bucked a few times, then started racing about the yard.

As the ladies screamed in alarm and the gentlemen came running, Anthony looked to his own horse, vulnerable for being in the same enclosure. Mr. Beecham was ahead of him, though. He tossed Hestia's reins over the fence to Anthony, then took off after the snorting stallion. The young groom came to a stop in the center of the yard and whistled. The stallion slowed, turned toward him, then charged. Just as Celia gasped and clutched at Anthony's arm, Mr. Beecham stepped to the side a moment before he would have been trampled, grabbed the stallion's mane, and swung himself onto the horse's back. It took him two more circuits of the yard to calm the animal down to a trot, but by the time he did, the men were cheering, the ladies were applauding, and Lord William had crawled through the fence, red-faced and covered with dirt.

"Bravo, Mr. Beecham!" cried Molly, clapping her hands and stamping one foot. "Bravo!"

"Good show, Simon!" David shouted, leaping over the fence as two more grooms warily approached the stallion. Anthony looked down at Celia. She gave him a sparkling smile, her eyebrows raised.

"I believe you won, sir." Aside from flicking her ears and tossing her head once, Hestia hadn't stirred during the commotion, not even when the stallion flew by her.

"Yes, I expect I did." Her hands were still wrapped around his arm; prize enough, to Anthony's mind.

"And now I can have my riding lesson," said Molly happily. The two grooms were leading Lord William's sweating, snorting stallion away, and David was shaking Mr. Beecham's hand. "I should go see that Lucinda is saddled at once." Without a word of farewell, she ran past them toward the stable.

Celia released his arm as if she had just realized she was holding it. "Molly loves to ride," she said, a note of apology in her voice.

"And she clearly recognizes quality horseflesh." Anthony nodded. "I believe I like the young lady exceedingly."

Celia met his eyes again and burst out laughing. Anthony felt something shift inside him as he gazed into her face, cheeks pink and eyes bright with laughter. *Lord help me,* he thought, knowing it was useless; he was almost surely long past help.

The rest of the party converged on them then, in a frenzy of amazement at Mr. Beecham's bravery and skill. Celia gave him a wry glance and slipped away with the other ladies. Anthony tried not to watch her go, but it was hard. His eyes seemed drawn to her no matter where he was, no matter where they were. He would give himself away if he weren't more careful.

That evening was no different. Twice he caught himself looking at her across the room. It was a weakness, he knew, but one he was increasingly helpless to resist. Every time he heard her laugh, or even just her voice, he instinctively looked her way. Each night that he poured out his heart to her on paper, he lost a little more of his protective armor, his ever-present shield of indifference. As long as he didn't care—as long as he could tell himself it was solely in the name of lifting her spirits for her sake alone—he was invincible.

The trouble was, her answering letters made him *want* to care. They made him begin to think impossible things possible. And he didn't think the impossibility of his hopes would comfort him when they came to naught, no matter what he had once told Celia. There was a growing connection between them, for all that it passed unseen and unspoken, a connection that reached past his affection for her, through his jaded history, and into a heart he had long since ignored. It colored every thought he had of her and was beginning to affect his actions around her. He was dropping his guard far too often.

It was unnerving. Anthony was not accustomed to losing his head over a woman. Normally he was the one who looked away from her, and he certainly never gazed longingly across a room at a woman. And yet tonight he'd caught himself doing it twice.

"You look damned pleased with yourself." Ned had come up beside him and laughed at his startled expression. "Surely not just the triumph of owning a superior horse. What is it, I wonder? A tedious new invention to fund? A new way to double your funds on the Exchange?" Ned cast a glance at the ladies on the other side of the drawing room. "A new woman to warm your bed?"

He made himself smile negligently. His heart still knocked against his ribs at being caught without his mask in place. "Nothing half so interesting."

"That's a disappointment," said Ned in disapproval, taking out his watch to check the time. "I expected more of you."

"You've always assured me I'm a dull fellow. How

pleased you must be to find yourself in the right for once."

"So you are, so you are. Still, there's a number of handsome women about. And I believe . . ." Ned lowered his voice. "I believe I am making rather good progress with one lady."

Anthony glanced down. A ribbon the color of spring daffodils was tied around Ned's watch fob. "A token from the lady?"

Ned started, then looked down. He stuffed the ribbon into his pocket, although not before a fleeting expression of satisfaction crossed his face. "Perhaps."

He looked away, letting it go. His thoughts churned. It could be from any lady, of course. Ned might have had it for months. But from the way Ned was watching the ladies across the room—including Celia—Anthony suspected he had not. And it was yellow.

But did it follow that Celia had given him the ribbon? No, he thought, watching her. The words of her last note ran before his mind's eye: *I believe you have known heartbreak and loss as I have, for no one else could understand the despair one suffers from being so mistaken in love.* She had had her heart broken; she had been mistaken, and she had suffered for it. Celia would not go about handing out ribbons as tokens of affection to a gentleman who wasn't even certain of her regard. Even if she had meant that yellow ribbon as a sign for him, she had been answering his letters ever since.

He wondered if she thought Ned wrote the letters to her, as he sat at his desk later that night to write to her again. The idea was utterly laughable to Anthony, but Celia didn't know Ned as he did. Ned counted on his face and his manner to win a woman's affection. He had no fortune of his own, and no title. He also had no scandalous reputation to detract from his charm. He had no need to hide behind anonymous notes.

Anthony didn't care, though, as he dipped the pen and began to write. The words Celia wrote were for him and him alone, whether she knew it or not. He might never have more of her than a handful of letters, but it was more than he had had before, and it was enough, for now. If this were the only way he could bare his soul to her, he would do it.

Chapter Twelve

Rosalind had worried for a while that the house party had been a bad idea and had pushed Celia even further into her gloom. For the first week Celia had been quiet and withdrawn, when she hadn't just gone missing entirely from the party. It had given Rosalind several sleepless nights, fearing that she had done exactly the wrong thing by inviting everyone to Ainsley Park. Perhaps she had misjudged the composition of the guest list. Perhaps she had invited too many people. Perhaps she ought to have waited a year and allowed Celia to rusticate in peace.

So she was overjoyed when she noticed signs of Celia's melancholy lifting. At first the signs were slight. Instead of retiring early or slipping away from the party, Celia would stay. Then Rosalind realized her daughter was smiling more often and even laughing from time to time. She joined in the parlor games, and bowled and walked out with the others. She was still far more quiet and reserved than she had once been, but it was a vast improvement from the somber, silent young woman who had returned from Cumberland.

That Celia had terrified Rosalind, and her disappearance was cause for great joy to a worried mother.

The one dark spot on Rosalind's happiness was Anthony Hamilton. The man was an unrepentant rake. Rosalind was quite sure he was carrying on with Lady Hillenby, right under Lord Hillenby's nose; Lady Hillenby was a bold thing, for all that Celia called her a friend, and Rosalind was sorry to have invited the Hillenbys at all. And that would be bad enough of Mr. Hamilton, but she now suspected he was setting his sights on her own daughter. Twice she had caught him watching Celia across the dining table, and more than once she suspected the man had lain in wait for Celia somewhere, so he could escort her back to the other guests. An affair with Lady Hillenby was one thing; Rosalind expected little better of him, after all. But this was utterly intolerable.

One couldn't baldly warn him off, of course. Rosalind didn't know what designs he harbored on her daughter, but she was determined to prevent them all. With some subtle manipulation, she contrived to keep him away from Celia. She moved Mr. Hamilton to the other end of the table and sat Celia next to a different gentleman every night. She was never more thankful that she had invited the very well-liked Mr. Childress, who was surely capable of charming any woman alive and who could always be counted on to act as Celia's escort. She was more vigilant during the evenings, and devised entertainments that didn't permit quiet moments apart. She even took to playing at bowls with the guests during the day. At first she had stayed back and out of the way, until discovering that David's rapscallion friend Edward Percy had enticed all the gentlemen into wagering on the game. It was best that she keep a closer eye on things for many reasons.

And it worked. She still caught Mr. Hamilton watching Celia, but as Celia's spirits improved, so did her circle. And since she no longer withdrew from the party, there was no chance for Mr. Hamilton to catch her alone. All in all, Rosalind felt things were going fairly well now.

She was sitting at the writing desk in the morning room, writing out the menu for the next day and contemplating the success of her endeavors, when the door swung open behind her, then closed with a bang. "Madame, you are making a mistake!" said an angry voice.

Rosalind whirled around, her mouth dropping open. The earl of Warfield stood in front of her, his hands in fists at his sides, his face dark as a thundercloud. Tall and red-haired, the Scottish earl had not been on her guest list originally. Marcus had added him at the last moment because they were contemplating a canal project together, and so far the earl had been closeted with Marcus much of the time. This was fine with Rosalind. Lord Warfield was a good-natured sort, she supposed, but he was, to put it politely, rough around the edges. He had a booming laugh that rang out far too often. He had little delicacy in his address; Rosalind had distinctly overheard him refer to her as "a fetching lass." As if one called any dowager duchess, a woman with a grown daughter, a lass. And worst of all, Lord Warfield was Mr. Hamilton's uncle. Somehow that seemed an odd connection, the bluff, hearty earl and the cold-hearted rake, but Rosalind wasn't fond of either of them.

She recovered her voice. "How *dare* you!"

"How dare I?" He advanced on her. Rosalind rose, drawing herself up to her full height and assuming her frostiest expression. How dare this man, this uncouth

Scot, scold her as if she were a child? "How dare *you!* You are humiliating a decent man!"

She gasped. "What? Sir, you overstep your bounds!"

Warfield slashed one hand through the air. "Someone must, if you will persist in marking Hamilton as an outcast."

Rosalind raised an eyebrow. "Heavens. I never knew I had such power. Pray, how have I marked him—or any of my guests—as an outcast?"

"You know what I mean," he growled. "You have deliberately seated every unmarried gentleman next to your daughter at dinner—except Hamilton. You have asked every unmarried gentleman to read aloud at nights—except Hamilton. You have tried your best to get every unmarried gentleman to sing with Lady Bertram—except Hamilton. For God's sake, woman, do you think people are blind?"

"My daughter," said Rosalind with cool, composed fury, "is in a delicate state. I prefer to spare her any discomfort. She is recently out of mourning for her husband, and—"

"You've an odd way of showing such compassion," he interrupted. "Anyone with eyes can see the lass is quiet and withdrawn, but the one person—sometimes the *only* person—she speaks to is young Hamilton. I think you know it, you don't like it, and you're doing your damnedest to separate them. Why?"

Rosalind simply stared him down for a moment. Of course he was right; every word was true. But it was not his concern. "If I have been ungracious as a hostess, I apologize," she finally said in a glacial tone. "Please convey my regrets to Mr. Hamilton, since you appear to be his representative in these matters."

"Bollocks," said the man rudely. Rosalind gasped in shock. "That's not what I want you to do, even were it a true apology. I want to know why. If you intend to shun the man, why even invite him?"

"I did not invite him," she snapped. "David did. There. Are you satisfied now?"

Some of the anger drained from his face. A slight frown took its place, more bemused than anything else. "What have you got against him?"

She pressed her lips together. "Nothing more than any mother in England would have against a rake who likely sees my poor bereaved daughter as nothing more than a wealthy widow, ripe for sport."

"He's not nearly as bad as the gossips say," said Warfield, sounding more and more puzzled. "I thought you had more discernment than that. Has he ever done the slightest thing against Lady Bertram?"

"No," Rosalind was forced to admit.

"Has she said she wishes him to keep a distance?"

Rosalind lifted her chin. The answer to that question was the same as the previous answer, but she was not about to tell him. "I keep my daughter's confidence, sir."

"All right." He folded his arms across his chest and leaned closer, his sharp green eyes searching her face. "Then why don't you like him?"

"I hardly have to explain myself to you."

"Why not?" he asked, his voice growing softer. "If you've an honest opinion, there's no reason not to say it."

Rosalind met his gaze straight on. "His reputation is unpardonable. His mere presence casts a whiff of scandal, if not brimstone. I wonder why I bear the weight of your scorn when he clearly does not. Perhaps if you counseled him to mend his ways, women such as I would not recoil at the sight of him. You think I am a hypocrite and a scandalmonger, but you're wrong: I am a mother. I will do anything to protect my daughter from further misery, and if that includes offending the greatest rogue in Christendom by not asking him to read poetry aloud after dinner, I will do it without hesitation or regret. Have I finally explained myself clearly enough to you?"

Warfield's face sank into weary lines. "Yes," he said quietly. "You have explained yourself perfectly." Rosalind inclined her head in acknowledgment. "You're wrong about him, though."

"Perhaps." The word was dry with doubt.

He shook his head. "One day you'll see it. I hope I am around on that day." Warfield turned to go but paused at the door. "I'll be ready to accept your apology then."

"Good day, Lord Warfield," said Rosalind coldly, infuriated by the way the corner of his mouth turned up as he let himself out. If anyone were wrong about Mr. Hamilton, it was surely his too-forgiving uncle.

Besides, she knew her daughter far better than Lord Warfield did, and she was certain Celia wanted nothing to do with Mr. Hamilton, not really. Mr. Hamilton was the very last sort of person who could make Celia happy. A man like that would crush her daughter's fragile spirit, seducing her and then leaving her just as he left every other woman, broken and disgraced.

Her anger cooled into determination. Celia's spirits had improved a great deal. If there were a gentleman at the root of it, she should know. She was Celia's mother, after all; it was her duty to know these things. If there were a man, she ought to know who he was, to make certain he was acceptable. If there were no man, she should still know, so that she might encourage whatever had revived her daughter from her melancholy.

She located Celia in the garden. Her daughter wore a small smile as she strolled idly along, and Rosalind realized Celia looked truly happy again for the first time since returning from the north. Her maternal heart swelled with delight; she just knew it had been the right decision to bring Celia back from Cumberland. It had been like bringing her back from the grave.

With renewed purpose she headed toward Celia, thankful to have caught her alone. "There you are, dearest," she called.

Celia looked up at her mother's voice. "Yes, Mama?" She had hidden in the garden to read the latest note from her secret admirer. She re-read each message several times now.

Her mother took her chin in one hand and inspected her face. "It is so good to see your smile again." Her voice trembled very slightly.

Celia blushed a little. "It is good to smile again."

Rosalind smiled, releasing her. "It's good to be home, is it not?"

"It has been good to be back, but this is no longer my home," said Celia wryly. As much as she loved Ainsley Park, it really wasn't home anymore.

"Nonsense," cried her mother. "Even when you have another home, you shall always be welcome at Ainsley Park."

"I know," Celia assured her. "I only meant that it feels like a visit, not as though I am returning to stay."

"Indeed." Rosalind linked her arm through Celia's and they walked on together. "Do you have reason to believe you will be leaving soon?"

Celia ducked her head, pretending to study the roses. Her mother's question was too careful. "No, Mama. I simply know I shall, some day."

"Of course, of course," said her mother quickly.

"Naturally a young woman will wish to be mistress of her own home." Again Celia refused to answer the underlying question, and finally Rosalind continued, "You are much too young to spend your life alone."

The words of the note on her breakfast tray this morning ran through Celia's head, and she couldn't keep a small, pleased smile from her face. She didn't feel alone anymore. "No, Mama."

"Are you . . ." Rosalind paused, watching her closely. "Dearest, has one of the gentlemen . . . perhaps . . . touched your heart?" Celia glanced at her guardedly. "I ask only because I am so relieved to see you happy again. Oh, child, I was so worried when I arrived in Cumberland. You were so silent, so sad! However natural it might have been after losing your husband, it broke my heart, Celia. And to see you smile again, to hear you laugh and talk as you used to . . ." She trailed off, squeezing Celia's hand in hers. "I promise not to interfere, if it is a gentleman."

Celia stopped, turning to face her mother. "Please don't worry about me. I think I am done with being sad and silent. Mama, in Cumberland—"

"You don't have to tell me, dearest," Rosalind interrupted. "It is in the past, and I don't wish to dwell on it."

She shook her head. "I want to tell you. I—I did not choose well in Bertie. He and I were not nearly as suited as I thought. I never truly knew him before we married, and that is a mistake I shall never make again. Don't blame yourself," she said as her mother's face grew more and more dismayed. "You were everything a loving mother should be; you allowed me my choice. It is not your fault I was wrong.

"And don't blame Bertie. He thought we would get along. He married me with the right intentions. Lord Lansborough kept us in Cumberland, hoping Bertie would settle into managing the estate and being a husband. No one is to blame, really. We all acted as we thought best." She paused. "We were all wrong."

"Why didn't you tell me sooner?" whispered her mother.

Celia bit her lip. "I didn't want you to know."

"Oh, my dear child . . ."

"But I have learned from it. Yes, there is a gentleman who has engaged my interest, but I am determined to be more circumspect this time, and not to rush matters."

"I understand," her mother said at once. "I shan't interfere or press you. It is enough for me to see you happy again." She squeezed Celia's hands, giving her a tremulous smile. "I shall leave you in peace," she promised once more. She leaned in and kissed Celia's cheek. "I only want you to be happy."

Celia smiled. "I know, Mama. Thank you."

Still beaming, her mother left her. Celia turned and resumed her stroll through the garden. For all her mother's promises and best intentions, Celia knew she would be queried more and more about this mystery gentleman. Her mother's curiosity was like an unstoppable force; her desire to know was too strong to be denied, especially with regards to Celia. In the years between her father's death and her own marriage, Celia had been her mother's constant companion. She had been fortunate to have such a loving and devoted mother, but Celia also knew she had had few, if any, secrets from her mother. With no ill will, her mother had managed to know almost everything about her life.

But now Celia wanted to keep her secrets secret. She didn't want her mother to know about her mysterious correspondent. If it were just any man, she wouldn't want her mother to know, simply to prevent any attempts at matchmaking. In this case, though, Celia was certain her mother would cause even more trouble, because she was certain her mother wouldn't approve of the gentleman—whom Celia was quite sure was Anthony Hamilton.

She had no proof, but the feeling grew stronger with every note. She couldn't imagine those words coming from any other gentleman at the party. Every conversation they had made her realize she felt more at ease with him than with anyone else. He was the first person she had really told about her marriage—intimate details like the lack of children and her own guilt over that—and never once had she regretted opening her heart to him. And no one had been a better comfort to her when the guests had started to suffocate her, when she had felt so alone and isolated from them. Isolated from them all, except from him, she amended. Never once had she been sorry when he approached her, or wished he would go away and leave her alone. No one else could make her laugh like he did; no one else seemed to be able to read her mood as he did.

The anonymous notes had been something else. They had quickly gone from romantic drivel to heart-felt letters revealing an understanding and sensibility that she had never seen in another man. Only Anthony, she was quite sure, would have written such things to her and taken pains not to reveal himself. And Celia had not pressed the matter, content to enjoy the exchange on its own merits.

Now her mother was alerted, though. Celia foresaw an endless parade of gentlemen seated next to her, introduced to her, matched with her at cards, all while Rosalind watched with the keen eye of a general. Her mother wouldn't be able to resist. Celia hadn't enjoyed it thus far, and she didn't want to endure any more of it. She would have to find out, for absolute certain, who was writing her those notes, and she'd have to do it before her mother found out. Agnes was already sworn to secrecy, but Celia would speak to her again and make clear she wasn't to tell even the dowager duchess. Celia thought her mother wouldn't dare to question the guests' servants, but she should probably discover which of the Exeter servants knew.

Then she would just have to persuade her mystery man to meet her face to face. If she were wrong, and it was not Anthony, she would be in a terrible position. She didn't want it to be anyone other than Anthony, so her impulse was to tell him to stop . . . and yet, the notes themselves compelled her not to. Celia tucked that worry into the back of her mind. It would be Anthony. She was sure of it.

She just had to get him to admit it.

Chapter Thirteen

Franklin held out the small folded note as soon as he entered his room to dress for dinner that night. As the frequency of his correspondence with Celia increased, Anthony had instructed Franklin to watch for any messages for him in the kitchen. He still left his messages for Celia on the long trestle table, and hers appeared there for him. Anthony took the note, his mood buoyed as always, and tore it open at once.

The message inside, though, punctured his cheer. He read it twice before believing what it said. *If you are truly my friend, meet me tonight,* she wrote. *After dinner, in the library. I shall wait for you there.*

Bloody, bloody hell. Of course he couldn't go.

Anthony dropped the note on the writing desk and let Franklin help him out of his jacket. All he had to do was write and plead timidity. He was too shy to meet her, he could say, and what could she do then? He stripped off his waistcoat with too much force, and a button flew off and rolled across the floor. He tossed the coat at Franklin and strode to the window, hands on his hips.

Meet her. The last thing, and the only thing, he

wanted to do. Why did she want to meet him? Had his words touched her heart? Or did she merely want to know who was writing them? Had she tired of the exercise and wished to put an end to it, or did she have some other intent?

Of course he couldn't go.

This had gotten out of hand. He had only meant to send her a few flowery notes to pique her feminine pride and revive her joie de vivre. It surely would have worked on most women, without the need for anything else. Anthony didn't feel he was vain to think he knew what women liked. But somehow he had poured out his heart to her, the woman he couldn't have but had wanted for years, the girl who had no thought of him but as a brotherly friend. He had revealed himself, all right; the only mystery left was his name.

But if he went, she would know. If he claimed he had only written to make her feel happier, she would feel deceived, and rightly so. If he admitted he had meant every word . . . then she would know he had meant every word. The best choice was to stay away and avoid both possibilities.

He tucked her note into his writing desk with the others and went back to dressing for dinner.

Dinner that night seemed to last an age. Celia could hardly eat from the fluttering of her stomach. She sipped her wine and tried to pay attention to the conversation around her, all the while trying to steal glances at Anthony to see if he, too, suffered from the same anxious anticipation she did.

He didn't, as far as she could tell. That only made her stomach lurch more. Celia was sure, quite sure, he was the man, but if . . . just perchance . . . she was wrong, she ought to be prepared. If Mr. Picton-Lewis appeared, or Mr. Childress, or even Lord William, she would thank him politely, she decided, and tell him they must stop writing to each other. Anything he wished to say to her from now on must be said openly. Not that she wanted any of them to declare themselves openly, but at least she could refuse them just as openly.

But it would not be one of them, she assured herself. Anthony would come to the library. She knew it.

Finally dinner ended, and the ladies went to the drawing room. Mama proposed a musical evening and began soliciting the other ladies to sing and play. Celia tried not to fidget. It suited her very well for everyone to be engaged in the drawing room listening to an impromptu concert, but she had to leave before her nerves snapped. When her mother turned to her, looking hopeful, Celia shook her head.

"No, Mama."

"Very well. Would you sit with me, then?" Rosalind took her hand, still smiling fondly.

"No, Mama." Celia placed one hand against her stomach to hide its nervous trembling. "I feel a bit unwell. I was thinking to retire early."

Concern filled her mother's face. She took Celia's chin in her hand and scrutinized her. "Oh dear. You are a bit pale. And you didn't eat much at dinner."

"I am sure I shall be fine." Celia managed a weak smile. Her mother nodded and released her.

"Good night, then. I shall make your excuses."

On shaking legs Celia left the drawing room. The gentlemen were still at the table, sharing their port. Once assured the corridor was empty, Celia picked up her skirts and ran to the library.

It was empty, and very dark after the brightness of

the drawing room. Celia walked slowly into the room, waiting for her eyes to adjust. The tall French windows let in the weak moonlight; most of the drapes had been drawn, and even after several minutes, she could still hardly see anything. Perfect. She moved farther into the room, trying to calm her nerves. She had never seduced a man, nor had one seduced her. Was this a suitable place for a seduction, even? She swallowed a nervous laugh at her own wondering. Perhaps no one would be seduced tonight. Perhaps it would end up an awkward meeting. Perhaps he wouldn't come at all for some reason. She would feel a complete fool, sitting here waiting all night.

Behind her the door swung open, then closed with a gentle click. Celia held her breath, her heart suddenly hammering so hard she had to grip the chair to steady herself. *Please,* she begged Fate silently, *please . . .*

For a moment there was silence. Then a soft footstep, followed by another.

And she knew. Just from that step, and the change in the air around her, she knew. Her trembling vanished; her heart seemed to pause, and then begin beating with hard, slow pulses of excitement. She closed her eyes and thought, *Thank heaven.* And a small smile curled her lips.

When he first stepped into the library, Anthony couldn't see anything. The room was pitch dark, and for a moment he thought she had changed her mind and not come. It was almost a relief; he had worried all through dinner, covertly watching Celia pick at her meal in silence and wondering what she was thinking. Anthony was just as happy to go on as they were, unknown and unseen. From the solitude of his chamber he could say what he felt, bold in obscurity. He had finally come tonight after deciding, reluctantly, that

keeping his secret wasn't fair. She deserved to know—
and reject him, if she wished.

A whiff of lemons gave away her presence. He
walked slowly into the room and could see her now.
She took a step toward him, her blond curls and pale
gown just barely visible. The weak moonlight limned
her figure in silver, the slope of her bared shoulder,
the curves of her bosom, the sweep of her skirts as she
moved. A surge of pure, unalloyed desire rolled over
him, nearly obliterating his more honorable urges.
His breath felt sharp and hot in his chest; this had
been a mistake, just as he had told himself every step
of the way to the library. Now he was like a man picking his way through a burning forest blindfolded.
One wrong step and he would be consumed. But was
the wrong step forward, or backward?

"You came." She sounded pleased.

Or possibly surprised.

He swallowed. "I should not have." Instinctively he
made his voice lower and rougher, clinging to anonymity.

"I'm glad," she said at the same time. She took another step toward him, her skirts rustling.

He made an odd noise, trying to force a chuckle
through his dry throat. "Don't be."

"But I wanted you to come."

"You shouldn't." His voice was almost a croak. Stay
back, he wanted to tell her, but he couldn't, and she
kept walking, one slow, tantalizing step after another
around the wide map table, until finally she was right
before him, only an arm's length away.

"Why not?" she whispered. It took him a moment to
think what she meant.

"We should light the lamps," he said instead. "This
isn't . . . prudent . . ."

"What is prudence, but cowardice seeking to justify itself?" She closed the final distance between them and laid her hand on his chest.

He wanted only this, he thought numbly. He wanted only a touch—a single touch—to bring him to his knees. In all the years he had known her, he had never once touched her except very properly on the hand, on the elbow, and once on the back, when he had helped her into a carriage. His fingers cramped as he clenched his hand into a fist, trying to resist. She didn't know it was he, here alone in the dark with her. He shouldn't take advantage of her. He couldn't. He wouldn't.

"Don't you want me?" She inched even closer. "Don't you want me as I want you?"

"Celia, you don't know what you're doing," he began to say, but she interrupted.

"I know enough." She tilted back her head to look up at him, a movement he felt more than saw. His face must be as indistinct to her as hers was to him. Not that Anthony needed light to know every line of her face. "But I shall leave if you don't want me to stay."

Anthony closed his mouth; those words he couldn't say. He had spent too long trying to convince himself he didn't want her, and been too unsuccessful at it. At best, he could bury the feeling deep inside himself. He could control his actions far better than his feelings, and in the bright light of day he would never have allowed things to progress this far. He wasn't sure she knew it was he. If she were here with him now because she thought he was someone else—if he did as she was tempting him to do, and as his body was burning for him to do—he could destroy a friendship he had valued for years and consign himself to eternal misery.

"Celia," he rasped, clinging to his sanity and honor with great difficulty, "I must tell you—"

"I know who you are," she whispered. "I've known for some time, Anthony."

His name fell like an absolution on his ears. She knew. There were still reasons why he shouldn't do this—many, many reasons—but they fell aside under the weight of those words and the others she had said: *as I want you.*

Slowly, reverently, he lowered his head and brushed his lips against hers, once, twice. She stood quietly, her face raised to his, her hand still on his chest. He raised his hands and caressed her cheeks, then trailed one hand down the back of her neck, a feathery touch that made her lips part in a silent gasp against his. He deepened the kiss just a little, wanting to savor every moment, every bit of her.

Her hands slid up his chest, around his neck. She tugged, pulling him closer. Anthony let his fingers continue to drift, down the slope of her shoulder, still amazed to find himself here with her. But Celia made a soft, contented noise in her throat and pressed against him. After a moment's surprise, Anthony gathered her into his arms and held her snug against him. Oh, Lord, she felt so good. So right.

All Celia's thoughts and worries about who might seduce whom evaporated as he held her. There were no fears left, only a deep certainty that this was *right.* She felt alive again, finally, vitally, fully alive in Anthony's arms. Desire radiated off him, for all his touch was still gentle and slow. She ran her fingers over the nape of his neck, openly exploring. The muscles of his shoulders tensed as she combed her fingertips through his crisp chestnut hair. He broke off the kiss to whisper her name as he dropped faint little kisses across her forehead. "Yes," she said on a sigh. "Oh, yes. Kiss me again."

He didn't say anything, but his breathing deepened. She knew he had heard. His mouth returned to hers, hungrier, more demanding. The last traces of melancholy and hesitation burned away under the heat of Anthony's kiss. For a moment, it occurred to her to wonder just how long he had wanted her this way and why she had never known it before, but then the dam seemed to break. His arms tightened around her, molding her against him. Celia gave a little moan of delight. She wanted him. It was a hot, urgent need within her, to hold him, touch him, kiss him. It was Anthony, the man who made her laugh, who now made her burn. She had never felt it this urgently before but knew it at once for what it was: desire.

What began tentatively quickly grew more heated. It was almost as if he could read her thoughts; no sooner did Celia begin to wish he would touch her than he did. She pushed at his clothing as if it were a barrier between them. He pulled his arms free of his jacket, letting it fall. She unbuttoned his waistcoat and slid her hands beneath it, marveling at how warm and solid he was.

While she worked at his clothing, he was doing the same to hers, loosening her bodice until it gaped above her corset. With wordless murmurs, he bent her back over his arm to trace his fingertips over the exposed mounds of her breasts. Celia shivered, and he sucked in his breath before ducking his head and pressing his lips to her cleavage.

Celia threw back her head and clutched him to her. Her skin seemed to prickle and tingle all over as he trailed soft little kisses across her bosom. His hands pressed and gripped her lower back, rhythmically pulling her body higher and tighter against his until she was almost on her toes, breathless and dizzy and barely able to stand.

His hands slid down, over her waist and hips, and then lifted her, setting her on the edge of the table she had forgotten was behind her. There he paused, resting his cheek on her shoulder, his chest rising and falling rapidly and his hands still around her bottom. Celia wiggled toward the edge of the table, parting her legs and trying to hold him closer. She desperately wanted to feel his body pressed full-length against hers, and whimpered as he shifted.

He lifted his head. It was too dark to see his expression, but Celia could almost feel his emotion: he wanted her, but he was holding back. He wasn't sure. He was waiting for her to decide. Celia had no qualms or hesitation. She slid her hand to the back of his neck and pulled his lips back to hers.

Anthony felt strangely unbound as he kissed her again. He had tried to fight against his desire for her, and she refused to cooperate, only tempting him more by wiggling against him, sighing against his mouth, pulling at his clothing. Now he gave in to the desire. She wanted him to make love to her, and he could no longer remember why he shouldn't.

With a light touch he whisked up the skirts of her gown, gliding his palm over her silk-covered leg. She lifted her knees beside his waist, panting softly in encouragement. He untied her garter, slipping the stocking down. His hand was warm against her bare skin as he hiked her knee higher, until she could put her leg around his waist. He pulled her almost off the table, until her hips were just perched on the edge. Celia nearly lost her balance, tipping backward, and only keeping herself upright by clutching at his shoulders.

He kissed her again and bore her down, onto her back. Now she did curl her legs around his hips, aware of how wicked she was being. His hands cupped her face, then smoothed down her neck and shoulders easing her flat on the table. With tender but efficient care, he pulled her bodice down more, baring more of her breasts.

Celia sucked in her breath as he touched her nipple with his tongue. Oh, heavens. His hands, his mouth . . . oh, heavens. She was already warm and wet by the time his hand slipped between her legs, through the slit in her pantalets. He made love to her breasts with his mouth, and with his fingers he drove her to the point of delirium until she was shaking and gasping for air.

On trembling arms she pushed herself up and reached for him. He gave a harsh groan as she brushed one hand down the front of his trousers. "Celia, I can't make love to you on a table."

"On the sofa, then," she murmured, kissing his jaw and stroking him through the fabric.

His groan turned into a strained chuckle. "Temptress."

"Don't tease me," Celia whispered, still stroking. Her pulse seemed to beat strongest between her legs. Her entire body throbbed with hunger for him. Kicking off her slipper, she rubbed her foot along the back of his calf.

He just laughed under his breath, kissing her softly as he pushed up more of her skirt. Celia had to brace her toes on the floor for balance as he moved between her thighs and unfastened his trousers. He took her hand in his and drew it down between them, wrapping her fingers along his naked length. Celia whimpered as he exhaled sharply, and she guided him to where she wanted him so badly.

Anthony pressed inside her slowly. Celia went still, hardly breathing as his flesh filled hers. It had been so long since she had made love to a man, and her every muscle felt drawn so tight she thought she might snap. When he paused, deep within her, Celia let out her breath in a drawn-out, shuddering sigh of pure bliss.

He nudged up her chin, brushing his mouth against hers. His hands gripped her hips, holding her steady as he began to move. She rocked against him, meeting his thrusts as best she could, beginning to shake. He was so gentle yet so expert, as if he had studied her body for years and knew just what to do. She wrapped her arms around his chest and threw back her head as he moved in her again and again, his hands moving over her, his lips touching here, there, and everywhere, whispering endearments she barely heard, until the ecstasy finally consumed Celia and she sobbed out her joy.

Anthony held her until she quieted. Just to hold her was a pleasure; to hold himself inside her as she convulsed in climax was heaven. She rolled her head forward, laying it against his shoulder. He rested his cheek against her golden curls, a little disheveled now, and breathed deeply of the glorious scent of lemons.

Chapter Fourteen

Celia shifted her weight after a few moments and slipped. She fell against him, grabbing at his arms and gasping a little laugh. Anthony realized he had perched her on the edge of a high table where her feet could barely touch the floor. He should let her go. He even started to pull back, easing his arms away from her. Her grip tightened, and she turned up her face, murmuring a protest in a drowsy, seductive voice. Anthony couldn't resist her when she used that voice, so instead of helping her down and stepping away from her, he wrapped his arms back around her and lifted.

Celia gasped, then giggled, clinging to him with arms and legs. She kissed him on the mouth again as he carried her across the room and sat with a great thump on the sofa. There she relaxed again, astride his lap, draping herself over him and letting her skirts bunch up around her knees.

He didn't know how long they stayed there. Anthony just stroked her back, plucking up a loose curl from time to time and winding it around his finger. He knew they had to talk, but the feel of her on top of

him, in his arms, was just too distracting. He had kept
his control and not spent himself inside her, but
this . . . this contented, easy companionship stole away
his discipline. He didn't want to do anything but sit
here with her for the rest of the night—for the rest of
the foreseeable future, perhaps. He rested his head
against the sofa back and let his eyes fall closed, holding her against his heart. He would have to plant a
grove immediately, for he didn't know how he could
do without the scent of lemons from now on.

Dimly, Anthony became aware of sound—voices.
Not just any voice, but David Reece's voice. Laughter, and other voices. In the corridor, very nearby. He
opened his eyes. What were the odds, he thought with
a spark of black humor. He'd been an utter monk
until the last hour and had been left mostly alone,
even shunned at times. The voices grew louder, closer.
He said a swift, urgent prayer that they would continue down the corridor, past the library, away from
him and Celia and their highly compromising situation. He squeezed her tighter in his arms, as much
hoping they could escape by being silent and still as
to cling to her a few moments more, in case they
didn't. The steps were too close; Celia's dress was half-
undone, and his jacket and waistcoat were somewhere
on the floor. There wasn't time to compose themselves in any event.

The library door swung open, and light seeped into
the room. "You're a bloody fool, Norwood, to take
that bet," boomed David's voice into the quiet. "If Her
Grace says it's so, it must be so. But I'll be glad to take
your money, once we . . ." He stopped abruptly, and a
collective intake of air sounded behind him.

Anthony let his head fall back against the sofa
again. He should have known his luck wouldn't hold.

"Celia?" said David, as if he couldn't believe his eyes.

Slowly she sat up. Anthony let his arms fall away from her, and his hands landed on her thighs, bared beside his. As discreetly as he could he pulled her rucked-up skirt over her knees. He raised his eyes at the same moment she did. For a moment they shared a heated gaze, and then she looked away.

"I see," said David dazedly, then his voice filled with anger. He set down his lamp with a clank on a nearby table. "Out, the lot of you."

Anthony caught bits and pieces of the murmurs as David's companions filtered out of the room. "No shock, really . . . Hamilton's as wicked as they come . . . Not so grief-stricken any longer . . . Fine legs on that filly . . ."

"Celia, repair yourself," snapped David. "Hamilton . . ."

Silently Celia climbed to her feet. Anthony exhaled as her soft, warm weight lifted off him. She turned her back to her brother, straightening her clothing in silence. Anthony gave David a long look as he retrieved his waistcoat and put his own appearance to rights. His friend's mouth was a thin line, his eyes black with fury. His hands clenched and unclenched at his side. "Give me one reason," said David in a low, ominous voice. "One reason why I ought not to break your neck right now."

Anthony finished buttoning his waistcoat. "The presence of a lady."

David's expression didn't change. "Celia, go upstairs."

"No," she said, turning to face him. She sounded fairly composed, although Anthony noticed her fingers shook the tiniest bit as she smoothed her skirts into place.

"Go," he repeated.

"No, I won't." She glared at her brother. "Why should I be sent to my room like a child for doing something I know you've done many, many times, David?"

David's mouth flapped open and closed, like a landed fish's, and a look of horror flashed across his face. "You shouldn't—that's not the same—Celia!"

"I'm not twelve anymore, David," she flung back at him. "Did you think I was deaf to all those stories about you? You're a complete hypocrite if you upbraid me now." Her brother turned a shade of dull red. Anthony wasn't certain if it was fury or embarrassment, but he wasn't foolish enough to call attention to himself by asking, not when Celia was handling things rather well herself.

"And why is David upbraiding you?" asked a new voice. Anthony exhaled a silent sigh. The duke had arrived. He straightened his shoulders and thought about how best to defend himself, or if he should even attempt it.

Celia swung around to her other brother, just closing the door behind him. His face was set in grave lines, and Anthony was quite sure Exeter knew just what David and his friends had interrupted. "Marcus, this is none of your concern," she said.

His eyebrow quirked. "Indeed. Then perhaps you can tell me how I ought to react when half my houseguests are in the hall saying my sister spread her legs for a scoundrel?"

Celia clamped her lips together, looking wildly annoyed. "You should throw them out of the house."

"Ah. And then?"

For the first time her composure faltered. She glanced at David, then back to the duke. "And you should not tell Mama."

"I don't believe I shall have to; someone else will be glad to do it."

Even as he said it, the dowager duchess's voice could be heard in the hallway, raised and anxious. A moment later she burst through the door behind the duke. "Celia—where is Celia?" she asked breathlessly, pressing one hand to her bosom. Her eyes landed on her daughter before anyone could answer, and then skipped to Anthony in his shirtsleeves. Even in the dim light, everyone could see the flush on Rosalind's skin. "What have you done?" she cried.

"Mama, calm yourself," said Celia firmly.

"Calm myself?" Her voice rose. "When that—that scoundrel has defiled my daughter?"

"Rosalind," said the duke in clear warning as Celia gasped. The duchess whirled on him.

"Marcus, surely you won't allow this—this fortune hunter to seduce and ruin your sister!"

"Mama, no," Celia said.

Exeter's eyes moved past his stepmother to Anthony again. "Not everything is in my control."

"Surely this is!" She stormed across the room to seize her daughter's arm and pulled, sending Celia stumbling. "Stay away from my daughter!"

"Mama! Stop!" cried Celia.

"Rosalind," said the duke again.

"I didn't—" Anthony began, appalled that anyone would think he was after Celia's fortune. Of that, at least, he was innocent. Only that, perhaps.

"Didn't?" David exclaimed. "You're a liar now, too?" Before Anthony realized what he intended, David's fist crashed into his jaw.

Undefended, it was a stunning blow. His head snapped around, his teeth rattled together, and he lost his balance, stumbling to the floor.

"David, stop it!" Celia shrieked, trying to wrest free of her mother.

"Get up," David growled at him. "Take your whipping like a man, Hamilton."

"Quiet!" Exeter's voice cracked like a whip. "Rosalind, compose yourself. David, enough." The dowager duchess pressed one hand to her mouth. She released Celia, who wormed between her brothers to lean over Anthony anxiously. Over her shoulder, he could see David Reece still glaring at him, but his fists lowered to his sides. Cautiously Anthony climbed to his feet, touching his jaw gingerly.

"It's all right," he said to her, very quietly. Celia's expression eased and she gave a small nod. The duke lowered his upraised hand as the room settled into quiet.

"Lest we all rush into misapprehension and make things worse than they need be, let us strive for some semblance of sensibility. David, clear the hallway. Rosalind, I am certain you will wish to reassure our guests there is no scandal brewing." Rosalind's tear-filled eyes darted past him to where Celia still stood with Anthony, but she nodded, drawing herself stiffly erect and walking out of the room with David, who had also plastered a grimly congenial expression on his face.

Exeter turned back to them. Anthony almost preferred David's white-hot fury to the duke's cool, implacable command. At least he knew what to expect from David. The duke looked at him a long moment, and Anthony didn't know if he should start apologizing, explaining, or writing his will. "Whatever you may have planned as a result of this evening, it would appear reconsideration is in order." He waved his hand. "Sit."

Anthony took the seat indicated. Celia sat on the

sofa. The duke folded his arms and looked from one to the other. "Normally I would not intrude on what is surely a private matter, but privacy seems to have been tossed out the window this evening. What do you propose to do now?"

For a moment neither said anything. Anthony glanced at Celia from the corner of his eye. What was she thinking? he wondered, as she sat with her head down and her hands tightly clasped in her lap. The neckline of her gown was slightly askew; he could see the shadowed valley between her breasts, and he wanted her again so badly he felt like a complete cad at once. If only he had a clue to her feelings . . .

"Well?" asked Exeter. "Celia?" She bit her lip and said nothing. "Hamilton?"

"I could leave," he said, leaning back in his chair even though his stomach felt twisted into a rock-hard knot. Might as well get it over with, since Celia didn't appear to have any solution to offer. "Within the hour."

She turned toward him with large, startled eyes, and he wondered if she were relieved he had suggested it so easily. She would suffer, no doubt, but more as an object of pity, for being seduced and ruined by the infamous Mr. Hamilton. People would whisper that he took advantage of her, that she was still vulnerable in her grief. But she would be free, and not tied to a man she didn't want.

"No," said Exeter. Anthony jerked his eyes back to him, instantly wary. Why not? he wanted to ask. Surely they all wanted him gone, especially after that scene . . .

"That will destroy Celia's reputation," continued Exeter in the same level tone. "I can't allow it."

"Marcus, I am not a child," Celia burst out.

"I am not treating you like one."

"Then you cannot make him stay and marry me!"

"I never said he must marry you, or that you must marry him," pointed out the duke. "I merely said he won't leave in the middle of the night like a thief afraid of being caught." He walked across the room to stand in front of his sister. "But you must know this could cause a dreadful scandal."

"But only about me," she declared. "It wouldn't disgrace the whole family."

To Anthony's surprise, the duke of Exeter laughed. "You would hardly be the first to disgrace the whole family, Celia. David did more than you could ever hope to achieve, and even I did my share. But I suggest you consider your own name and future as well as Mr. Hamilton's. This is not merely your decision to make. Perhaps you need some time alone to discuss it." He smiled at her once more in sympathy, then went to the door.

"And—and you will respect my decision?" Celia asked uncertainly.

The duke raised an eyebrow. "Haven't I always?" Celia closed her mouth, looking nonplussed. Exeter gave Anthony a speaking glance and left.

The room was quiet for a long minute after he closed the door behind him.

"I am very sorry for that," Celia said in a stilted voice.

"Don't be." Anthony sighed, feeling a little sick. Just this afternoon they had been friends; this evening they had been lovers. Now they could barely look at each other and had nothing to say to each other. What a fool, he berated himself. Hadn't he told himself this would happen? "It was my fault—"

"Would everyone please stop trying to take all the

blame?" she snapped, surging to her feet. "I am not an innocent victim!"

"I heard voices in the hall," he said. "A moment before they came in. If I had acted—"

"Oh, who cares that they came in!" Celia pressed her hands to her temples and began pacing a very short path in front of the sofa. "It was my fault there was anything for them to see." Anthony made a quiet sound of disbelief in his throat, and she whirled around to face him. "Do you disagree? Would you have been here if I hadn't told you to meet me here? Would you have—" She stopped short. "But now what are we to do?"

That was the question. Anthony knew he had no right to answer it. If he didn't marry her, everyone would whisper that she was just another widow of loose morals, open to propositions from anyone. If he did marry her, it wouldn't be because she wanted him, but because they had been caught in an indiscretion. Either course would be like digging out a piece of his heart, day by day.

"My marriage wasn't awful," Celia said suddenly. "Bertie never struck me, or locked me up. He just—" Her voice broke. "He just didn't love me."

Anthony knew the words that would set her at ease—perhaps. Bertie had once said he loved her, too. But he couldn't say it. He didn't think she would believe it if he did. "That was his failing, not yours."

She threw up one hand to stop him. "Don't, Anthony. I don't want pity and consolation. It was my choice to marry him. I—" She paused. "I chose badly. I thought I was in love, the sort of love poets describe, the romantic, foolish feeling."

Anthony hesitated, uncertain what to do or say. She studied him a moment, a crease between her eyes. "I can't do it again," she said, almost to herself. "I can't marry you just because of what happened tonight. I can't marry you just because my brother will shoot you otherwise. There must be a *good* reason."

Anthony opened his mouth, mildly offended that her first reason against marriage was his lovemaking, and that her second reason was her brother, and then he stopped. He couldn't think of a good reason for any woman, let alone Celia, to marry him, either. He closed his mouth and wiped his face clean of expression, awaiting her verdict.

"Could—could we try it?" she asked, her voice shaking a little. "Go on for a bit and see if we suit each other before we decide?"

"I shall do whatever you want," he said.

She shook her head, a sharp jerky motion. "No! That is exactly what I do *not* want you to do. What do *you* want, Anthony?"

I want to take you away, he thought. *Away from prying eyes and suspicious family and painful memories. I want to have you to myself so I can make you smile and make you laugh and make love to you all day long.*

He gave a silent sigh. "I want to do what is best for you."

"What about for you?" Frustration edged her voice. "Don't you have a care for yourself?"

He thought a moment. Getting caught making love to a woman was one of the lesser sins he had committed in society's eyes. This would be a mere footnote to his other crimes. And whatever he suffered for it . . . ah, it still couldn't make him sorry. "No, not really." She looked at him skeptically. "I have long since learned people will say, and believe, what they want about me," he said gently. "Nothing I do or say appears to affect it. So no, I don't much care for satisfying appearances, not for myself. But for you, I do care. If you think a marriage will be best, I will do it. If you think I should disappear and never be seen near you again, I will do it."

"Why don't you care?" She sat on the edge of her chair, leaning toward him, her blue eyes searching his face. "Why do you always say that?"

"Because it's true." He made a careless gesture with one hand. "I don't care."

"Why?" she persisted.

Anthony just shook his head. "My answer to your question is yes. We shall carry on for as long as you like, until you decide."

He could see she wasn't entirely satisfied with his response, but her expression softened. "Thank you," she murmured.

"It is the least I can do." And really, it was. Spending more time with her, under any pretense, was the easiest punishment he could imagine.

She nodded. For a moment they sat in awkward silence. Celia got to her feet. "Well, thank you," she said again. She bit her lip. "Good night."

"Good night," he said quietly. She ducked her head and let herself out. Anthony unclenched his hands, hung his head, and sighed.

Chapter Fifteen

At first glance, the corridor was empty. Celia breathed a sigh of relief and turned toward her room. Her hands were shaking, and she gripped them tightly in front of her, walking quickly. Her emotions were a wretched tangle of longing, hope, fear, and panic. Caught making love in the library, by her own brother! Part of her didn't care—the part that had made her throw respectable caution to the wind when she realized it was indeed Anthony—and part of her was mortified. Not only scandalous, but foolish, too.

Celia knew there were two likely outcomes from tonight. She had managed to delay the decision, but it couldn't be put off forever. And whatever she and Anthony decided, she'd have to screw up her courage to carry it off. Mere contemplation of the word *marriage* had rendered her mute with anxiety. Bertie had wanted to marry her as much as she had wanted to marry him, and look how badly that had turned out. She couldn't bear to commit herself to another marriage without being more certain of herself. Anthony's notes—and then his lovemaking—made her want to say yes; but when Marcus pressed him, he had offered to leave right off. Surely marriage to someone who didn't even want it in the first place would be worse. The prospect of repeating the long, lonely years of her marriage to Bertie—only worse, for this time it would be Anthony turning from her in disinterest—kept her mouth closed.

She was frightened, there was no denying it.

Which was absolutely dreadful of her. By her silence, she had allowed the burden of the blame to slide onto Anthony, and he, manfully, had taken it on his shoulders and not said a word—except that he would do whatever she wanted him to do. How could she blame him for not wanting to marry her when she had been so spineless?

But the other option—not marrying him, or even, as he suggested, never seeing him again—was even worse.

"Celia!" She jumped as someone called her name. Louisa hurried over, having been lurking closer to her chamber. "Are you . . . ?"

"I am perfectly well," she said when the question trailed off. Her friend smiled encouragingly, then stepped closer.

"Well?" Louisa lowered her voice. "Was it . . . ?"

Celia frowned. "Was what?"

"With Hamilton." Louisa's eyes sparkled with interest. "Was it good?"

"Louisa," said Celia, aghast.

"But I'm dying to know, and you've actually had him! Mary's been trying to seduce him for a week with no success, and he's rumored to be the most skilled lover in London. So, was it good?"

"I refuse to answer that," said Celia, thin-lipped with anger. "It's coarse and demeaning."

Louisa blinked in astonishment. "I didn't—but

no—oh, dear. I didn't mean it that way. I say . . . Celia. I didn't even know you fancied him."

"I don't think it's any of your concern."

Louisa hurried after her as Celia turned and stalked off down the hall. "Forgive me! I didn't know! I just assumed . . . well, because we talked about him—"

Celia spun around. "*You* talked about him."

"Yes, I did," she relented at once. "But you never said a word!"

"What should I say? He's a man with a mind of his own, not a new bonnet you can just decide to have because you want it? You're a married woman, and your husband is right here in the house?"

Louisa gaped at her. Celia's anger faded a little.

"I'm sorry."

Louisa rushed after her again to take her hands. "Never be! Oh, I am a poor friend. I do so want to see you happy again. It's just such a surprise that he's your choice. And now—after that scene—oh, I do hope you aren't being forced into something you shall hate."

Celia drew in a long shuddering breath. "No." She had not been forced; in fact, she had done her best to lure Anthony into making love to her. And even then she had managed to avoid any painful consequences.

Louisa pressed her lips together as if to quell a torrent of further queries, then gave an awkward smile. "Good. I could not bear to see . . . Well. Good." She gave a quick nod. "Good night, then."

"Good night," Celia murmured. She was right outside her room. She opened the door and went in, closing the door and leaning against it. *Was it good?* Louisa wanted to know. Celia touched her abdomen lightly. She could still feel Anthony's hands on her skin, still feel his mouth on her, still feel him moving within her, still feel the shuddery quakes of pleasure as she came apart in his arms. Her knees went a little weak at the memory, her breath came a little faster. Oh yes, it had been very good.

If only she knew what to do next.

Warfield was waiting for him when he finally left the library. Anthony took one look at his stern expression and sighed. He nodded once and Warfield fell in step beside him, following him all the way to his chamber.

"I should be asking after your intentions, young man," said his uncle when he had closed the door behind him.

"Are you?" Anthony peeled off his jacket, waving Franklin away when his valet slipped into the room. Just as silently, Franklin slipped back out.

"No. I'm hoping you'll tell me yourself."

Anthony lifted one shoulder. There was still a whiff of lemons about his jacket.

"I'm telling myself, young Hamilton would never trifle with a lady for sport. I'm promising myself, I know the boy better than that. And I'm reminding myself that it's not my concern, and if he wanted me to know what he feels for the lass, he'd tell me."

Anthony tossed the jacket on the chaise. "Does it really matter what I say on those counts?" he asked in a low voice.

His uncle jerked his head once. "Aye, to me it does."

"Then you're absolutely right. It's none of your concern." He turned away and began unknotting his cravat.

"Damn it all, lad." Warfield ran his hands through

his hair, standing it on end. "Tell me you're having a care."

"Obviously not enough of one," Anthony muttered, "or I'd have locked the door."

"I don't mean the bloody door, I mean for the lady. Do you fancy her?"

He jerked the linen from his neck, another testy reply on the tip of his tongue. But Warfield was watching him with the cross concern that only sprang from affection. Anthony subdued his temper. "Yes," he murmured.

His uncle's face cleared at once. "Wonderful! I knew it. Then everything will end well."

Anthony gave a dry laugh. "Don't be so hasty. She doesn't want to marry me, and Exeter isn't making her."

Warfield waved it away. "Of course he shouldn't force her. A bad beginning if ever there were one for a marriage. No, you must persuade her—and as you fancy her already, it shouldn't be a trial. A man can't really appreciate something unless he works for it."

"She doesn't want to marry again," said Anthony. "Her first marriage did not give her a liking for it."

"But that wasn't with you," Warfield retorted. "Look, lad. I know you've got the knack of making ladies like you. Don't be modest, it's true, and anyone with eyes could see them taking your measure this past fortnight. And I know you've applied yourself to it in the past," he added, quirking one brow knowingly.

"That was different."

"Worse," corrected his uncle. "There was no affection."

To Anthony's mind, the presence of affection was not an obvious benefit. Without affection involved, it didn't matter if he failed to catch a woman's interest. There were other women, after all. It was true, he had applied himself to winning a woman before; but if he had failed before, it mattered only a little, and mostly to his pride. But with Celia . . . it wasn't just affection or pride. Anthony knew that he was painfully, hopelessly in love with her. He would rather not try at all than try and fail. "I fear—" he began. "I fear . . ."

His uncle's footsteps sounded behind him as he tried to put his fear into words. Warfield laid one hand on his shoulder. "We all fear," he said kindly. "Particularly when there's a woman involved."

"But this isn't just any woman." He bowed his head to ease the tension in his neck.

"Then you mustn't persuade her in the ordinary way." Warfield slapped him on the back, grinning again. "She's the one, aye?"

Anthony glared at him. "You are not helping matters."

"What? Haven't I seen for days that the lass fancies you? Didn't I tell her mother to stop her meddling between the pair of you? And now you've gone and . . . Well, now you've just got to persuade her to have you. As a husband, that is."

"You told her mother . . . ?" Anthony stared in shock as Warfield grinned triumphantly, rocking on his heels. "Good God, I'm done for. The duchess has hated me for years."

"Persuade the daughter and the mother will follow," said his uncle with a gleam in his eye. "Your happiness is right in front of you, if you're not too much a coward to seize it."

"Oh, is that all I have to do," said Anthony dryly. Warfield nodded. "I'll undertake the duchess."

"No," said Anthony at once. "Don't. I beg you."

His uncle flipped one hand. "Nonsense. She's a mother, and she's worried, but she's an intelligent woman. She'll see reason soon enough, once her daughter comes around. I'll just whisper a good word for you in her ear."

"Whisper anything you like in her ear, except my name." He collapsed into a nearby chair and scrubbed his hands over his face. "She despises me."

"Eh, she doesn't know you." Warfield dismissed it with another wave of his hand.

"Nor does she want to."

"Lad. Anthony. Listen to me." He looked up. Warfield almost never called him by his Christian name. His uncle was unusually somber as he spoke. "Don't be a fool. Since when are you put off by a frowning mother? And you said yourself this isn't just any woman. You admit she's worth more than other bits of skirt. You'll deserve your misery if you don't even attempt to persuade her."

He let his head fall back and closed his eyes. Warfield was right. And perhaps . . . A little tendril of hope sprang up in his chest as he remembered Celia's response to him in the dark library. Perhaps it wasn't hopeless. The dowager duchess hated him for certain, and David Reece would probably still like to thrash him, but Exeter hadn't reacted as strongly as he might have. And Celia had only asked for time; she wanted to see if they would suit. That meant she considered it possible that they would.

Perhaps all he needed was that possibility.

Chapter Sixteen

Whatever Marcus had done or said to the guests, Celia never knew. Rosalind had arranged a picnic for the day in a lovely spot near the ruins of an old chapel and she did not change her plan. From her mother's relentless good cheer, Celia suspected she was hoping that if she carried on as if the previous evening had never happened, it might in fact fade away into nothing. Celia of course couldn't forget a moment of it, not the reverent way Anthony touched her face when he first kissed her, not the way he played with her hair after they made love, and certainly not the way he made her feel in between.

No one said a word to her about the scene in the library, although it was impossible that they weren't thinking of it. It ought to have bothered Celia that people were talking about her, and for such a scandalous action, but somehow it didn't. Every time she caught sight of Anthony—always from a distance—she noticed that he, unlike her, was alone. No one seemed to be speaking to him, and he spoke to no one except Lord Warfield. That bothered Celia, that Anthony was bearing the brunt of the scandal while she was protected from it. But he never approached her and only once looked her way.

They drove out in four carriages, a party of uncertain temperament. Jane chattered determinedly with Louisa. Lord Elton dozed in a corner of the carriage beside her, snoring softly. Mr. Percy rode up from time to time from his place with some of the other mounted gentlemen to inquire after their comfort, obviously at David's prodding. Celia wished they would all go away so she could think.

"There," exclaimed Rosalind with satisfaction when everyone had disembarked from the carriages. Servants had come ahead with the picnic things, and luncheon could be served at a moment's notice. "Isn't this lovely?"

Celia managed a smile. "Yes, Mama."

Her mother beamed. "Do enjoy yourself, darling. Mrs. Percy is waiting for you."

She looked. Jane was waving at her, urging her to join her and Louisa on a stroll through the ruins. Celia could almost hear her mother's voice telling Jane to keep her far, far away from Anthony Hamilton. With a sigh, Celia went to them.

Anthony thought it best if he did not go on the duchess's picnic. It would be awkward for everyone, and he didn't want to put Celia in that position. But Warfield routed him from his chambers, refusing to be put off. He was part of the party and he was going on the picnic if Warfield had to drag him along behind his horse, the earl said, and so Anthony went.

As expected, it was a strained outing. A few of the ladies seemed to form a wall of chatter around Celia, and he saw her only from a distance. The ladies and some of the married gentlemen were to go in carriages, but the other gentlemen were riding. Aside from Warfield, only Percy spoke to him, and that was in apologetic whispers. Anthony nodded and waved him on. He knew well enough what had probably been said about him, and about Celia, last night. He was quite content not to talk to anyone at the moment, to be honest.

The picnic seemed to go on forever. He sat a discreet distance away from Celia but couldn't help stealing a glance at her from time to time. Once or twice her eyes met his, wistful and wondering, and it was all he could do not to go to her. It would only cause more disquiet, though, so he stayed where he was.

"You should just go talk to the lady," Warfield observed at one point. "You're naught but a smoldering cauldron of frustration here."

Anthony looked away from her to glare at his uncle. "How poetic you are today."

"Oh, aye?" Warfield laughed. "Might as well put it to use, then, oughtn't I?"

He got to his feet, giving Anthony a significant wink. Anthony's eyes narrowed as he watched Warfield stroll across the grass toward—oh, good Lord. Warfield was heading for the dowager duchess, sitting with Lady Throckmorton on the other side of the clearing.

"Hamilton." He looked up to see Ned standing over him. All morning Ned had been closemouthed and distant; he'd not said one word to Anthony so far, but then most of the party hadn't. Ned bent his head toward the brook. "Take a stroll to the water?"

Anthony stole another quick glance in Celia's direction. She was talking with Mrs. Percy. Warfield had stopped to speak to David Reece. Perhaps this was an opportune moment for him to make an escape. He got to his feet and followed Ned. His friend walked in silence until they reached the rushing brook.

Ned's face had settled into a frown. "Last night," he said abruptly. "I wanted to speak to you."

"Ah." Anthony suddenly realized what Ned was about to say. He had completely forgotten Ned's hopes regarding Celia.

"Lady Bertram." Ned seemed incapable of speaking in complete sentences. "I did not know your interest lay in that direction."

"I did not set out to seduce her, if that's what you are asking."

"No." A muscle flexed in Ned's jaw as he stared across the stream. "I just—I just wanted to know for certain."

"I have admired her for some time." An enormous understatement, but close enough. Ned's shoulders fell slightly.

"Good. Good." He nodded once, sharply. "She's a lovely lady. Very kind and . . . charming."

Anthony inclined his head. "Yes."

Ned shook his head with a strained chuckle. "You know, I never really thought I'd see . . . But of course, she's no ordinary woman, is she? Still in a delicate state and all, but sure to be highly sought after. I didn't figure her for your kind of woman, to be honest, Hamilton."

Anthony was very still. There was an edge to Ned's voice he'd never heard before, and didn't like. "How so?"

Ned laughed again, a little harsher this time. "Oh, she's a wealthy widow, all right. That attraction is clear. And beautiful. But you've been friends with Reece for ages, and I simply thought . . . well, it takes tact to carry off, doesn't it? An affair with a friend's sister."

"It is not an affair." He bit off each word. *Not for me.*

"Isn't it? Well. Bravo," Ned said. He seemed to make a visible effort to swallow his bitterness. "Fortunate chap."

Anthony said nothing, and after a moment Ned muttered something about getting a drink and went back to the picnic. So Ned felt cheated of Celia. It shouldn't be a surprise; Ned had no fortune of his own, although Warfield had made him an allowance for as long as Anthony could remember. But it left a very sour taste in his mouth to think of Celia in Ned's arms. Ned, Anthony knew, was a society favorite, a man of great wit and charm and highly regarded by many society hostesses—perhaps even by the dowager duchess, since she had invited him. No doubt Her Grace would much rather see Celia fall for someone like Ned than someone like Anthony. He wondered if she would encourage Celia more heartily to consider other men—like Ned. No matter what Celia felt, Anthony thought she didn't deserve to be badgered that way.

And of course his greatest fear was that if she took her mother's advice, she would easily find someone more suitable than he.

He wrenched a long, willowy reed from the riverbank. For several minutes he stripped it, making a switch. He felt like beating something, and the grass would have to do. Footsteps behind him made him look up warily. Who had come to needle him now?

"All right, Hamilton?" Percy gave him a crooked smile. "Didn't fall in the brook, did you?"

"No." He turned back to his reed.

"Good, good." Percy slapped his shoulder. "I'd hate to have to tell the ladies that news."

"Would they care so much?" Anthony turned the reed over, running his thumb along the stem. "Would Mrs. Percy?"

Percy jerked, sudden alarm coloring his face. "I say, Ham," he began.

Anthony waved one hand, scowling. "No. No! By God, why does everyone in the house think I'm after his wife?" He slashed violently at the tall grass with the switch.

"Oh," said Percy a moment later. "I ought not to have thought that. Of course you'd never . . . Well, not with a mate's wife, surely. Not Jane, at any rate, even though she is a decent wife."

"Then keep her happy." Anthony flung the switch into the brook, watching it bob on end before slowly twirling around and floating away in the current. "I never met a happy wife who wanted an affair on the side."

"Indeed?" Percy looked at him with interest. "Not many happy wives, then."

"No," said Anthony grimly, watching his switch vanish around the bend.

"Jewels, I suppose," said Percy. "That sort of thing. Jane's been after me about her pin money, too. She wants a carriage—"

"Percy," Anthony interrupted him, "if you want to make your wife happy, talk to her. Listen to her. Write to her when you're away from her. Take her to the theater or the opera now and then if she likes them. Make love to her until neither of you can walk. If you don't do those things, someone else will be glad to."

Percy looked shocked. "Write to her?" he exclaimed. "Whatever for?"

"Because when you write to her, you are thinking of her." The words he had poured out on the page to

Celia ran through his mind. Thinking of her to the exclusion of all else. Anthony shook his head. "Never mind."

"No, wait! I make love to my wife." Percy ran after him as Anthony turned and strode back toward the others. "Every week!"

"Good work, Percy. How punctual."

"But she likes it!" Percy was now quite flushed.

"Excellent," said Anthony over his shoulder.

"Hamilton!" He walked another few steps and then stopped, only swinging around to face his friend when Percy spoke again. "You're mad for her, aren't you." It wasn't a question, but a somewhat amazed statement.

Anthony didn't reply. He simply stood there in the middle of the field, the wind blowing harder every moment, and looked into Percy's face, a face rapidly filling with understanding. How odd, thought Anthony in detachment, that Percy should become perceptive for the first time in his life at this moment.

"But that's good, then, isn't it?" Percy cocked his head. "Half the battle, I'd say. Got an earldom in your pocket and a fortune in the funds. Most men would conclude the business within a week." Anthony sighed and looked away. "And if you're mad for her, and do all those things . . . writing letters and whatnot . . . she'll have you and be glad, won't she?"

He hoped. Anthony slowly shook his head as he raised his hands. "I haven't the faintest bloody idea, Percy."

Chapter Seventeen

Rosalind, dowager duchess of Exeter, was in terrible danger of losing her temper.

The lovely house party she had planned with such hope was entirely spoiled after the wretched debacle last night. Her own daughter, caught in a very compromising situation with a notorious rake! Even worse, a rake she had been forewarned against for over a decade. Rosalind had allowed David to invite the young man to Ainsley Park years ago because David had told her his friend had nowhere else to go on holidays. Although the young Langford—Rosalind simply could not think of him any other way, no matter how he styled himself now—had never behaved any worse than David's other friends, there had always been something about him that made her wary, a feeling that although he was with David and the other young men, he wasn't really one of them, that he was somehow a bit removed from them. A lone wolf, she had always thought of him, and she had eventually told David not to invite him again, all for the sake of protecting her growing lamb.

And now . . . It made her almost ill to see the way

Celia watched him. Her daughter was pale and quiet again, as when she had first returned from Cumberland. Not quite the same, Rosalind reluctantly admitted; she no longer looked sad. She looked thoughtful. And that was perhaps even worse, for if Celia set her heart on him . . .

"I really don't know why you invited him," said Harriet Throckmorton.

"You know I didn't," returned Rosalind, thin-lipped. "Hannah did. David prompted her."

"I don't mean to interfere, but really, Rosalind. He is too terrible. I would have interceded and asked that he not come, not when there were to be so many young ladies present." Harriet was watching her own two daughters, who sat giggling together and watching Mr. Beecham.

Rosalind sighed. "Fortunately for you, he does not seem interested in your girls. Only mine." On the other side of the clearing, Mr. Hamilton looked up, meeting Celia's eyes. Neither looked away until someone spoke to Celia, and even then she appeared reluctant to turn away. Rosalind's stomach knotted. Oh, dear. Even from across a field she could see the longing that burned between the two of them, and she had to fight back the urge to run across the field and stand protectively in front of Celia.

"I almost count Celia as one of my own," Harriet was saying. "If Throckmorton were here, I'd set him after that rogue with instructions not to let him out of sight for an instant."

"Believe me, if I'd any notion of what he would do, I would have insisted Marcus speak to him." She would have insisted he toss Mr. Hamilton out on his ear. As she watched, the man in question got up and strolled off toward the nearby brook with Mr. Childress, and Rosalind breathed a little easier—for the moment.

"You have more forbearance than I have," Harriet said. "Now the harm's done. She's smitten, I fear. It's understandable, perhaps, given what the poor dear's been through."

Rosalind didn't reply. Her thoughts were the same. Her daughter still hadn't recovered from her disastrous marriage, and Rosalind had vowed never to let Celia fall victim to such a mistake again. It was her duty not to. She had been at fault before, for she had been the one to insist that Celia be allowed to choose her husband. She had persuaded Marcus, against his inclination, to grant young Bertram permission to marry Celia. Marcus had thought the boy too young; he had thought Celia too idealistic about marriage. Rosalind had convinced him otherwise, and she had been wrong.

But this time there was even more evidence that this match would not work. Celia had had her heart broken once, so who knew what state it was in now? Rosalind had lost a husband herself, and she knew all too well the loneliness of widowhood, the craving for a man's touch, the need to be loved and held and desired. The longing not to be *alone*. Mr. Hamilton was certainly capable of meeting the physical cravings, but everything Rosalind had heard of him indicated he couldn't possibly meet the deeper needs of a woman's heart. He was not faithful; he was a dedicated gambler; his fortune seemed to rise and fall with the tides. The only family he had had cast him out years ago. There were rumors of every sort of debauchery and mischief, even whispers of murder. He was the last sort of man she would wish for her daughter.

"If only he were respectable," she said with a sigh.

"If he could be the proper man for Celia, I would be very happy for them both—even including the indiscretion of last night."

"That alone must persuade you he is not." Harriet moved closer, lowering her voice. "Any man who would tempt a woman into making love out in public view like that must be a thorough scoundrel."

"It was not in public view, it was in the library," said Rosalind testily. "Harriet, please."

"Well, yes, of course, he didn't seduce her on the drawing room hearth in front of us all, but anyone might walk into the library," Harriet replied. "I would call that a very public place, in a house full of guests who might want entertainment."

Rosalind closed her eyes and pressed her fingertips to her temples. Harriet was right—well, she was half right—and there wasn't a thing Rosalind could do about it.

"Oh, dear," murmured Harriet. "The earl is coming to us." Rosalind drew in a deep, calming breath and opened her eyes.

"What—? Oh." That earl. Not Marbury, but Warfield. Rosalind was not in the mood to speak to him at all today, but her quelling look didn't deter him. He walked right up to her and Harriet and bowed.

"A grand day for a picnic, Your Grace."

"Thank you, sir." She smiled coolly, hoping he would go away.

"I've a fancy for old ruins," the wretched man went on, oblivious as ever. "Would you do me the honor of a stroll through the chapel?"

Her teeth hurt behind her smile. She longed to say no—if he said one word about his abominable nephew, she knew it would be impossible to maintain her composure—but could think of no excuse. Harriet sat quietly at her side sipping lemonade, no help at all. And there was no one else nearby, since she and Harriet had deliberately sat off by themselves to talk. There was only one thing a polite hostess could say. "Certainly, sir."

He helped her to her feet, and she put her hand on his arm. Harriet gave her a sympathetic glance as he led her away, up the hill toward the ruins. Rosalind returned a pointed look; Harriet might have tried to engage him in conversation at least, and delay the matter until Rosalind could think of a reasonable excuse.

"I must tell you I am not an expert," she said. "If you wish to know more than a general history, you shall have to consult the library." She barely restrained a wince as the last word left her lips. Rosalind didn't want to think of that room again.

"No, no, general history's more than enough," he said easily. "I like to discover things myself and not be fed someone else's opinion." She glanced at him suspiciously, but he gave no sign of meaning anything deeper. She forced her thoughts away from that. Warfield was a guest. She must be polite. A quarter hour's conversation, a brisk walk, and she could excuse herself.

"Well." She collected herself. "The chapel is all that remains of the old abbey that used to stand here. The first Exeter, then an earl, was a patron and gave generously to build it, until the papists fell from power and the abbey was destroyed during Cromwell's reign. Subsequent generations dismantled and cleared the abbey, except for this chapel. The stained glass alone has somehow survived." She was out of breath by the time she finished, for Warfield had been dragging her up the hill at a quick pace.

"Ah, yes, I see." He didn't stop, but kept going, right across the grass and into the stone nave. Only parts of the walls still stood, providing some shelter from the stronger breeze here on top of the hill. Warfield stopped and looked down at the cracked, sunken slabs of the floor. "Who's buried here?"

"Mostly priests and prelates, as far as I know. The family crypts are some distance away."

"Hmm." He scuffed delicately at some of the stones with his boot, but the writing had been worn away by years of feet and then exposure to the elements. He walked away, into the crumbling shell of the transept where the altar would have been. Here the end wall rose straight and true above them, with a triptych of stained glass windows that miraculously remained almost intact. Warfield tilted back his head to examine the glass.

"Odd to find something so fine out here in the middle of a field," he said. Rosalind smiled politely. The breeze had picked up, especially here. She was more than ready to return to the rest of the guests. "What is the scene portrayed?"

"Er . . . St. George, I believe." Rosalind tucked her lightweight shawl more closely about her and glanced at the clouds beginning to gather on the horizon. "We should return, sir. It may rain."

"It might rain at any moment of any day," said Warfield absently, still studying the stained glass. "It's impossible to see from this side. Come around."

Rosalind closed her eyes and inhaled deeply. The earl was waiting for her. Curbing her impatience, she followed him, taking his hand and letting him help her skirt the rubble. On the other side of the wall, the wind was even stronger. It whipped her skirts around her legs and threatened to tear her bonnet from her head. "We should return," she said again, raising her voice to be heard above the wind.

"Look." He pulled her farther around the wall, pointing up at the window. From this angle, the sun shone through the ancient glass; the colors blazed with life, a jewel-toned portrait of St. George slaying the dragon as hosts of angels and saints watched.

"Ah, there I see it. It's brilliant, from this point of view," he said, looking down at her. "I couldn't even guess what it was from inside the kirk. It all depends on how the light strikes it."

"Yes," said Rosalind, distracted by holding onto her bonnet. "The wind, Lord Warfield—"

"It seems to me that most things depend on how the light strikes them," he went on, stubbornly refusing to move. "In one light, they're black as night. In another, brilliant and colorful. See how fierce the dragon is, how noble St. George—when you see them from the proper point of view."

Rosalind held back a sigh of exasperation. "No doubt. Shall we join the others now?"

"Aye," he finally relented, just as a stronger gust of wind lashed the hill, catching the edge of Rosalind's bonnet and sending it tumbling across the grass.

"Oh!" She took a few stumbling steps after it, clutching at her shawl to save it from a similar fate, but Warfield loped past her, scooping up the bonnet just before it would have gone over the crest of the hill and down toward the brook. "Thank you," she said as he returned with it. The wind whistled through the ruins behind them, drowning out her words.

"Here," he said over the wind. "It's windy out!"

She tried not to show her impatience. "Yes. Indeed it is." She reached for the bonnet.

He held it out of her reach. "Your hair . . ." He

brushed loose curls from her forehead with his other
hand.

Rosalind flushed. Her hair must be a dreadful sight,
thanks to the wind. The earl just stood over her, staring, and it was unsettling as well as impolite. "Thank
you," she said again, taking her bonnet from his hand
and trying to smooth back her hair so she could put
the bonnet back on and they could rejoin the other
guests before being blown into the brook.

But the gale did not cooperate. The ribbons slapped
across her face, her hair was becoming more unkempt
by the moment as she tried to stuff it back into the
bonnet, and the long ends of her delicate shawl were
filling like sails and flapping about her. "Oh!" she finally exclaimed in frustration as the wind snapped one
end of the shawl loose.

"Blast!" The flapping cloth seemed to startle
Warfield. He caught the loose end, then the whole
shawl as it came out of her arm. "Here," he said, taking
her hand and leading her across the grass to a quieter
point, sheltered from the wind between the chapel
wall and a cascade of slate that must have once been
part of the roof. Then he turned his back to the wind,
shielding her from the brunt of it as she repaired her
appearance, settling the bonnet as best she could. She
reached for the shawl, but he lifted it over her head
and draped it across her shoulders himself. For a
moment his arms were on either side of her as he
plucked it up around her shoulders, clumsily trying to
arrange it properly. It was a hopeless task, of course.

"Thank you," she said breathlessly, taking over. His
hands fell away. Rosalind looked up to find him
watching her with a curious expression in his sea-
green eyes. The earl was a tall man, and broad. He
loomed over her, sheltering her fairly well from the

wind, and for a moment Rosalind did feel protected, blocked in the corner by his body.

"Do you never think," he said, somewhat humbly, "that perhaps what's true of the glass is true of people? That it all depends on how you look at them, how they appear?"

Rosalind could not miss his point. "If you refer to your nephew, sir, I assure you I bear him no particular ill will," she said, her temper flaring again. "I simply find him completely wrong for my daughter."

"What?" He blinked, and his face fell. "Oh, yes. You've nothing to fear from Hamilton. He'll never harm a hair on your daughter's head."

"I never thought he would," said Rosalind after a moment. What had he meant, if not to defend Mr. Hamilton? Hadn't that been his purpose in dragging her up here? "I fear for her heart, as you know."

"He'll most likely guard it more carefully than his own." He appeared ready to say more but didn't; he simply stood there, blocking the wind and looking at her with a strange intensity.

An unfamiliar feeling unfurled in Rosalind's stomach. "I am glad to hear it. And now we really must return to the party. I cannot leave my guests when it looks like rain."

He sighed. "Aye. O' course not." He moved aside and let her pass. Rosalind hurried back around the ruin, clinging tightly to both shawl and bonnet. The wind died down as she descended the hill, but her heart still thumped. She was imagining things. She had been a widow for fourteen years; men had approached her before. She had turned down marriage proposals from a marquis, two earls, and a baron. It was utterly ridiculous that an uncouth, loudmouthed Scot would even attempt—especially *that* Scot. She must be imagining things, she told herself. Lord Warfield knew very well what she thought of him.

But he didn't follow her down the hill.

Harriet had already instructed the servants to pack the picnic things. Lady Hillenby and Lady Elton were urging people back into the carriages. Rosalind arrived out of breath and out of sorts.

"What did Lord Warfield do?" Harriet looked at her curiously. "You were gone an age."

"The wind." Rosalind patted her bonnet. "It carried off my bonnet."

"Ah." Her friend was staring at her oddly. "That must explain it. You look upset."

"Of course," she said. "It's about to rain on my lovely picnic. Thank you for seeing to everything. Celia, will you ride back with me?" she called to her daughter, only a short distance away.

"No, Mama," she replied. "I shall ride with Hannah."

Rosalind had no choice but to nod and smile. She had hoped to avoid Harriet's too-curious eyes on the way home. Imagination, she reminded herself.

"Oh, Mama, may we ride with Her Grace, too?" cried Daphne.

"Yes, please?" Kitty added her voice to her sister's. "Please, Mama?"

Rosalind started toward the carriages as Harriet spoke to her daughters and gave them permission to ride with the duchess. She suspected the girls were more interested in Mr. Beecham, who had driven Hannah's open carriage. Harriet should be more watchful of her daughters if she didn't want to find a scandal on her hands involving one of them. Like Rosalind. She walked a little faster. Damn Mr. Hamilton. Damn his uncle. She would be very happy never to see either of them again.

By the time Harriet joined her in the carriage, Rosalind's temper was at full boil. Only through decades of discipline was she keeping her composure.

"Warfield harangued you, didn't he," said Harriet sympathetically.

Rosalind pressed her lips together and said nothing.

"The man looks guilty," continued Harriet, peering back at the picnic area. "And not a little frightening. Goodness, I admire your fortitude in going off with him."

"Harriet, please," commanded Rosalind.

"Just like his nephew." Harriet clicked her tongue in disapproval. She was so intent on watching Lord Warfield, she was completely ignoring Rosalind and was therefore unaware of her fraying temper. "There's just something about the two of them. But they're not related by blood, are they? The younger is more the siren, luring women to him, while the earl is a hunter. Couldn't you just see him seizing a woman and carrying her off to do heaven knows what to her? Do you know, when he demanded you take him to the ruins, I half expected the man wanted to ravish you! It's that fierce Scot blood, no doubt—"

"Do be quiet!" Rosalind cried. "He did nothing!"

"Well!" Harriet was taken aback. "I'm sure I didn't deserve that."

Rosalind glared at her, and mercifully the Eltons joined them in the carriage soon, putting an end to that conversation, if not to Rosalind's highly vexing thoughts.

Chapter Eighteen

Celia began to regret her decision to ride with Hannah the moment Daphne and Kitty pleaded with their mother for permission to join them. She had hoped to have a quiet ride home but instead realized it would be nonstop nonsensical chatter. The Throckmorton girls had evidently decided Lord William was not as charming as he had been before he had to crawl out of the stable yard to avoid his own rampaging horse, and had transferred their admiration to Mr. Beecham instead. There could be no doubt that his position as Hannah's driver had spurred the girls' desire to ride with them. Celia cast a look at her sister-in-law, whose quirked brow eloquently expressed her silent agreement with all Celia's thoughts.

Simon brought the carriage up as the other carriages departed, and jumped down to help Hannah and Celia into it. Kitty pushed past her sister then, managing to be next, but Daphne was not to be outdone.

"Oh, oh, my parasol!" Daphne cried, clinging to his hand as he helped her up the step. "Mr. Beecham, I've forgotten my parasol!"

Simon gave her an odd look, but he obediently helped her back down.

"Do you know where you left it, Daphne?" called Kitty, hanging over the side of the open carriage.

Daphne looked around, then fixed wide, helpless eyes on Simon. "I don't know. Perhaps we should walk about."

"I'll come with you." Kitty climbed down from the carriage.

"No! There's no need," Daphne told her sharply. "We can find it without you."

"Nonsense. Three pairs of eyes are better than two, are they not, Mr. Beecham?" She batted her eyelashes at Simon.

He shot a nervous look at David, who had ridden back to see what was keeping them. David just raised his eyebrows, and Simon reluctantly agreed with Kitty. A girl on each arm, he started off, apparently the only one of the trio at all interested in Daphne's missing parasol.

"Poor Simon," said David mildly, watching them go.

"You did precious little to help him," said Hannah, grinning. David laughed.

"Oh, he's safe enough from them. Two silly girls without a sensible thought between them? The boy handles blooded stallions every day."

"An altogether different species than silly girls."

David waved one hand. "He'd best learn how to deal with them now. See, he has the matter in hand." Simon was charging briskly across the grass, towing the Throckmorton girls along behind him.

"You're wretched to abandon him to them," Celia told her brother. "They shall chatter until his ears fall off."

"Oh, and I should let them inflict that on me?"

"They wouldn't chatter so in your company," Celia pointed out, unable to think that if Anthony hadn't ridden on ahead with the other gentlemen, he would have saved Simon from Daphne and Kitty. His presence alone would have terrified them into near-silence, and Celia had seen him use that fact—the more she thought about it, in fact, the more she realized he often used his scandalous reputation to some advantage.

"Really?" David pulled a face. "I doubt anything could stop those two from chattering like magpies."

Far across the field, Simon had located the parasol. Daphne and Kitty seemed to be doing their best to slow him, each pulling at his arm and attempting to engage his attention. By the time they reached the carriage, all three of their faces were red, Daphne's and Kitty's from breathlessness, no doubt, and Simon's from impatience. But as David had said, even that was not keeping Kitty and Daphne from talking nonstop as they fought for Simon's attention.

"I believe I shall walk." Hannah pushed open the carriage door and climbed back down. Without pause, Celia followed.

"But it must be three miles!" cried one of the Throck-morton girls.

"Barely two, across the fields," Hannah assured her. "I haven't had a good walk in an age. You go on. Your mother will miss you."

"Oh, of course." Daphne looked happily at Simon, who said nothing as he helped her into the carriage.

A groom had ridden back from the main party, no doubt to see what the delay was. David must have had some pity for Simon, for he called to him. "Here, Ben-wick, take the reins and give Mr. Beecham your horse."

The exchange dampened Daphne and Kitty's joy.

Celia shot her brother a glance, and he grinned. "Can't have them drive the boy mad," he murmured to her, watching the carriage set off with Simon riding safely ahead. "I need him."

"I would have gone utterly mad if forced to listen to those two another moment," Hannah said.

David grinned. Celia choked on a laugh. "I wasn't the only one?"

"Goodness, no." Hannah shuddered. "I cannot think their mother knows how silly they are."

"Mothers rarely do," said Celia wistfully. She saw Hannah glance at her, but her understanding sister-in-law said nothing.

"Hannah, are you certain you wish to walk?" David asked. "Shall I ride on and send back another carriage for you?"

She laughed. "No, I really do wish to walk."

"As do I," Celia added.

"Shall I walk with you, then?"

"No, no," Hannah repeated. "We shall be fine. Go see that Mr. Beecham doesn't keep riding all the way to Essex."

He laughed and put up his hands. "As you wish. Marcus will call out the militia if you're not home in good time."

They just waved, and set off across the fields. For a long while they walked in companionable silence. Hannah at least didn't feel the need to inquire after her health every hour, or persuade her to buy something, eat something, go here and there. Celia wished her mother could be as sensitive.

"Is something wrong?" asked Hannah.

Celia started. "Why?"

"You sighed very heavily. Are we walking too quickly?"

"No." Celia sighed again. "I was enjoying the peaceful quiet."

"I can summon Daphne and Kitty if it grows too quiet for you." Hannah flashed a wicked grin. "Or are your ears sore enough?" They both laughed.

"Hannah," said Celia on impulse, "may I ask you . . . That is . . . Well, there is something very private I should like to know. About being a widow." Hannah had been married to Marcus for so long, Celia had almost forgotten that she had been married before. But she had been, for several years, to a country vicar. After he had died, David had met her and thrown her together with Marcus.

"Of course. You may ask me anything. We are sisters."

"I wondered," began Celia, as they climbed a gentle hill, "how long it takes before you stop comparing everything to your marriage."

"Hmm." The taller grass caught at their skirts and muffled their steps. The breeze was still brisk, but the storm clouds remained far off on the horizon. "It depends, I suppose, on what happens to you after the marriage."

"What if nothing happens to you?" Celia said softly.

Hannah smiled. "Something always happens, even if it doesn't seem like much at the time. I can only speak from my own experience, but it seems to be the most unexpected things which have the greatest impact."

"Unexpected" did not begin to describe her relationship with Anthony. He was possibly the last person she would have anticipated falling in love with. She recoiled at once from that word. Once she had dreamed of nothing but falling in love; now she was almost afraid to think of it. Would she make another dreadful decision if she lost her heart and her head over a man again? And yet, was it even something she could control? "Were you afraid to fall in love again?" Her face felt warm as she blurted it out.

Hannah's expression turned somber. "I wasn't even thinking of it. My circumstances were not ideal; I needed other things than love. Love was the last thing I expected from Marcus, in fact."

"But when you realized . . . Did you fear it? Having been in love and suffered a loss, was it frightening to contemplate it again?"

Hannah stopped and turned to her. "I knew Marcus would never deliberately break my heart," she said. "I knew he was too honorable for that before I loved him. But yes, it was a bit frightening. It was an awful risk—we were so unsuitable for each other—"

"No!" Celia exclaimed.

Her sister-in-law smiled wryly. "Oh, yes. A common country widow, with no name or fortune, marry a duke? It was absurd, and you know it. I expect it never would have happened without your mother's prodding and encouragement; without her I should never have even been able to act the part of a duchess, let alone become one. No one would have accepted me if not for her." She paused. "But despite the risk, it was worth taking. If I had been cowed by his station, I never would have told him I loved him, and then how much would I have missed? Not just you for my sister, but Vivian and David, your mother, and of course there would be no Thomas or Edward."

"And Marcus," said Celia, staring at her. "You wouldn't have Marcus."

Hannah's smile deepened. "No," she agreed in a low, warm voice. "I would have missed him most of all."

The expression on Hannah's face made all too clear what she meant. Celia thought again of the previous night, how Anthony had held her and touched her and kissed her, as if she were the most precious thing in the world to him.

"I don't know what to do," she whispered. "I don't know what I feel for Anthony. I've known him for years; there is certainly affection between us. I never feel ill at ease with him, and he always makes me laugh. I know he's not as wicked as gossips say. But everyone tells me he's not the sort of man who could be happy with one woman, that he'll use me and discard me. I don't know if I can survive that."

"What does your heart tell you?"

Celia didn't say anything. Her heart yearned for Anthony to be the constant, faithful man she wanted, not the hardhearted rake everyone named him. She thought he *was* that man. But she wanted to be sure.

"Before I married your brother—when we were only acting at being married—people said he must have married me only because he'd got me with child," said Hannah, finally breaking the silence. "They said he had no heart, and was cold and arrogant and incapable of love, especially not for a poor country girl. I am quite persuaded those people didn't know him in the slightest."

"No," Celia murmured. "I just—I just wish I knew . . ."

"There is only one way to discover the truth." Hannah put her hands on Celia's shoulders. "We all of us must take the risk, sooner or later. There is never any way to know for certain until you chance it."

"What do you think of Mr. Hamilton?" Celia gazed anxiously at her sister-in-law.

Hannah smiled and shook her head. "I've seen so little of him, I shouldn't even attempt to give an opinion. It might turn out to be just as wrong as you hope the others' are. But I know you, and I trust you'll see the truth yourself, whatever others tell you."

Celia sighed and they started walking again. Of course she knew it was up to her. It did seem no one else saw Anthony the way she did. But she didn't trust herself, not after she had been so horribly wrong about Bertie. As much as she didn't think it was possible for Anthony to be callous and selfish, there were so many stories and rumors that claimed the contrary. Her mother strongly disapproved of him. Celia had always been able to count on her mother's support and indulgence; perhaps she had been a bit spoiled in that, but now it was all the more daunting to have her mother not just unhappy with her actions but pleading with her to reconsider and to stay away from Anthony. Celia felt as though she was walking into a dark, vast unknown, with her faith in Anthony her only assurance that she would survive.

"Where are the ladies?" Anthony demanded when David Reece rode up at last. He had been lurking near the stables ever since hearing the last carriage had been delayed. The two young Throckmorton ladies had returned a short time ago, sulky and petulant but without the duchess or Celia.

"They chose to walk." David swung down from his horse and handed it off to a stable boy.

"What, all the way?" He spun around to peer at the sky. The storm clouds that had been threatening all day were moving closer but were still in the distance.

"It's not above two miles," said David. "And Celia knows every inch of the property. She grew up here, you know."

"Of course." But he kept looking for them anyway.

Behind him David cleared his throat. "Ah . . . Hamilton. Last night."

Anthony stiffened. He'd forgotten, for the moment, about that. Bracing himself, he turned warily. "Yes?"

His friend scowled. "I shouldn't have struck you. My apologies." Surprised, Anthony jerked his head in a nod of acknowledgment. "My sister is old enough to take care of herself," David went on. "It was not my place to . . . interfere."

"Thank you." They eyed each other, then Anthony put out his hand. David clasped it a moment later.

"Of course, if you break her heart, I shall break your neck."

"Understood."

David went into the house and Anthony took a stroll around the garden, keeping a keen eye out for Celia and the duchess. At last they came into sight, windblown and out of breath, but laughing. The duchess said something to Celia, who put her hand on her stomach and laughed. Anthony smiled in relief just to see her, her color high, her hair falling down, her skirt dirty, and laughing so hard she had to hold her stomach. She was safely back. He didn't want to intrude on her conversation with the duchess, so he took himself off to think.

Today he had stayed away from her. Even when their eyes met and he felt an almost visceral pull, he kept his distance. He knew his uncle had persuaded her mother to take a stroll—Anthony suspected Warfield meant to give him a chance to speak to Celia—and the duchess returned looking out of sorts. Whatever Warfield had said to her had not pleased her. Despite David's apology, Anthony knew he was still suspect in her family's eyes.

Today he had tried to carry on as if last night had been nothing more than a typical brief affair, a trifle that could be forgotten if no one spoke of it.

But tonight . . . he meant to start persuading her it wasn't.

Chapter Nineteen

Celia could barely keep her eyes open through dinner. Her long walk with Hannah had made her thoughtful and footsore. The bath she'd had upon returning to the house had made her sleepy. The other guests seemed quiet, too, and she wasn't the only one who excused herself early.

She dismissed her maid and brushed out her hair herself. She was glad to have a bit of quiet tonight. Her conversation with Hannah had run through her mind several times. Eventually she must risk her heart again; if she didn't, she would be certain to avoid another broken heart, but just as certainly she would avoid any chance at love and happiness. And Anthony . . . Anthony was worth the risk.

A tap at the door startled her out of her thoughts. To her surprise, it was the man who had avoided her all day but still plagued her thoughts.

"What are you doing here?"

"Shh." He slipped into the room and softly closed the door behind him. "I'm persuading you."

"Persuading me? To what?"

He just gave her a naughty smile. A rake's smile.

"Anthony," she tried to protest, but he pressed his finger to her lips.

"Salve my manly pride by allowing me to try for a bit, please." Celia rolled her eyes, and he grinned. "Besides, it took me some time to sneak here unobserved, and I doubt I could make it back with the same success at the moment. So I can leave, and be caught sneaking out of your room, or I can stay, and at least if I'm seen sneaking out later, you'll know whether it was worth it."

"You," she informed him, "are outrageous."

He laughed. "And I've not even begun yet."

"So, you're going to persuade me to do something." She sat on her dressing table chair and clasped her hands in her lap, gazing up at him expectantly. "Get on with it, then. It's been a tiring day."

He shrugged off his dressing gown and laid it on her dressing table. "Lie down on the bed." Celia's eyes widened. "You'll be more comfortable. Go on." He made a shooing gesture with one hand, reaching into the dressing gown folds with the other.

Still eyeing him curiously, Celia slowly went to the bed and sat on the edge. *Take the risk,* she reminded herself. "Lie down," he said again, crossing the room toward her. He looked dangerous and alluring at the same time, his dark trousers outlining his legs, his white shirt falling open at the neck. Swallowing a little flutter of excitement, Celia laid back on the mattress. She heard a soft scrape as he dragged a chair across the floor to sit near her feet, and licked her lips nervously. Good Lord; did he intend to ravish her? Here? Now? And most important, how? Her heart nearly broke her ribs from pounding so hard.

"Pull up your skirt," he said. Eyes fixed on the ceiling, she did, up and up and up and—"Not that far," he said with a smile in his voice. She froze, bewildered. Then he took hold of her foot in both his hands and began to rub, pressing his thumbs into her aching sole.

Celia gasped in pure pleasure, a pleasure all the greater for being completely unexpected. "You've a naughty mind, my lady," said Anthony, soft and low. "I admire that in a woman."

Celia tried to laugh, but he started rubbing the ball of her foot, right under her toes, and all that came out was another sound of ecstasy. "How did you know?" she said on a moan.

He chuckled. "A woman who walks two miles across a field in those ridiculous slippers must have sore feet."

"I love those slippers." She wiggled her toes, and he obligingly returned to them. He had some ointment on his hands, and his fingers slid easily over her foot. "They're the most beautiful shoes."

"They're made for dancing in a ballroom, and not outdoor walking."

"They make me taller," she said, which sounded like nonsense even to her, but he seemed to have reduced her to an idiot. Oh, goodness, how did he know what to do to her foot?

Anthony laughed again. "And I did appreciate the lovely turn of ankle they displayed. But you are quite tall enough."

"Mm-hmm." His fingers were kneading her ankle, running along the bones of her foot. For several minutes she just wallowed in the luxury. By the time he released that foot and moved on to the other, her toes were tingling and her whole foot felt warm and soft.

"Better?" inquired Anthony's low voice as he worked the same magic on her other foot.

Celia smiled without opening her eyes. "That's the worst that could be said. A hundred times better. Oh, that's lovely . . ."

He began rubbing each toe individually, his touch gentle but firm. "Only a hundred times? I shall have to do better."

"I should probably expire in bliss if you did any better."

"A notable challenge." She pushed open her eyes to see him watching her with a wicked, knowing smile.

"Mr. Hamilton, is this all a plot to take advantage of me?" He laughed, pressing his thumbs into the ball of her foot, and Celia let her eyes fall closed again. "If so, it's working splendidly. Oh, heavens. There—oh, there. Oh, Anthony . . ."

"I love to hear you say my name," he whispered. "Particularly in that voice." His fingers stroked up the back of her leg. "Perhaps I should buy you another pair of slippers with a raised heel, so you'll welcome me into your room every night."

"Make them blue," she murmured. "To match my new evening gown."

Anthony chuckled. "Ah, but then your knees would soon be sore." He slid one hand up her leg to her knee, his fingertips circling her kneecap. "And then your entire leg." Now his hand was on her thigh. Her eyes still closed, Celia lay motionless. Her feet felt wonderful, but as his hands continued to move up and down her legs, pushing her nightdress a little higher each time, the rest of her body began to warm in anticipation.

"I couldn't contribute to that," he murmured, and then he pressed his lips to the inside of her knee. The muscles of her calf quivered as his tongue flicked over her skin. "I shall have to tempt you with something other than slippers."

"With what?" she asked breathlessly. His hands had moved to her inner thighs, still stroking lightly. The air on her bared skin only heightened the sensation, although she wasn't cold at all.

His laugh was quiet and full of promised pleasures. "I shall have to think. Jewels are too hard, too cold." Her nightdress slipped up over her hips, pooling around her waist. Celia lay still, her breathing turning shallow. "Roses are too fleeting." His fingertips skimmed her belly, and she gasped. "You deserve more than that."

"What?" She had to wet her lips to speak at all. "What do I deserve?"

"You deserve to be worshipped." He took her foot in his hand again, cradling it and lifting it. He kissed it, right on top above her toes. "Every inch of you." His hands slid up her leg, holding it up for the succession of lingering kisses he pressed every few inches along the inside of her calf. As he moved, he raised and bent her knee before resting her foot on the bed, right below her hip. He moved to the other leg and repeated his slow, unhurried caresses and kisses, and Celia sucked in her breath as he propped that foot on the bed, too. How wicked she must look, with her knees raised wide, her most private place fully exposed and right in front of him.

"There is something about a woman's body," came Anthony's velvet voice. "Something exotic and enticing. I could spend my life exploring and worshipping yours."

Her breath came in little pants now. She kept her eyes closed but couldn't erase from her mind the thought that he was staring at her, between her legs, where she was already growing wet. Could he tell by looking at her there? He must know what he was doing to her. He ran his hands lightly down the tops of her thighs, easing her legs further apart. A tiny spasm rippled through her womb, and Celia gulped in a shuddering breath.

"These valleys and swells, so foreign, so mysterious," he whispered. Now his hands were stroking over her hips, her belly. "All shadow and temptation." He brushed the curls that covered her there, and Celia's neck arched, her hips unconsciously tilting toward him. "Here," he whispered, his voice growing even softer. "The last veil. A woman concealed, yet bare. A hidden oracle." His finger glided through the springy curls, parting them. "The map to a treasure man would give his life to find."

Celia made an inarticulate sound as his fingertip rolled over and around that spot, that spot, oh, that *spot*. Her hands fisted in the coverlet beneath her. "Let me adore you," Anthony murmured, nipping the flesh of her inner thigh until she moaned. "Let me worship . . . here." And he put his mouth where his fingers had been.

Celia's mouth fell open in a soundless cry as he kissed her, licked her, suckled her. There, on that *spot*. Oh, God, she never knew . . . Her hips rose off the mattress, straining closer to the pulsing pleasure in his mouth. Every sweep and thrust of his tongue jolted her to new awareness of how sensitive, how primitive, her body could be. She clutched at him, tangling her fingers in his hair. She wanted him to keep going, she wanted him driving inside her, she wanted him . . . wanted *only* him . . .

Anthony tore his mouth away, taking little kissing bites of her thigh again. He pushed one finger, then two inside her, and Celia gave a low, keening moan.

"Celia, darling," he said, his voice rough and ragged. "My God, how beautiful you are like this." He suckled on her some more as his fingers stroked hard and deep inside her. Celia was shaking, real tears running down her face. She could feel it, winding tighter inside her, that exquisite tension, that desperation for release.

"An—Anthony," she gasped. "Please . . . You . . . Not just your mouth . . ."

"Come for me first," he whispered, his breath hot against her sensitive, aching sex. Celia tossed her head from side to side, almost whimpering in ecstasy. Her breath caught and held; she trembled as he sucked at her with long, hard pulls. Her climax pooled in her belly like a knot of heat, then it cracked and split, reverberating through her entire body. Celia arched her back with a choked cry, quaking with each wave of pleasure.

Anthony lurched to his feet. A moment later it wasn't his fingers inside her, but his cock, thrusting slick and hard. Celia cried out again as her body clenched around him, as if to hold on to him and draw him deeper inside her. Anthony's hands on her knees flexed, taking a firmer grip, and then he began a hard, slow, steady rhythm. Every time he came into her it bowed her spine and made her breasts bounce. The soft silk of her nightdress felt like coarse wool against her skin, made exquisitely sensitive from his touch and his words.

"Touch yourself," he commanded, thrusting into her after each word. "You want to."

Celia blinked aside the traces of tears and stared at him as she pressed her hands to her breasts, rubbing her palms against her nipples. Anthony's face darkened, and the muscles in his neck tensed. He squeezed her knees, pushing them farther apart and back into her chest. She was bent and curled, completely open and helpless beneath his relentless, driving possession. And she had never felt more alive in her life.

"Touch here." He seized one of her hands and brought it to his mouth. He sucked on her finger, his tongue swirling around it as he had done to another part of her body, and Celia's breath hitched again. Without looking away from her face, he guided her hand from his mouth to that—oh *heavens*—to *that* spot between her legs. His fingers covered hers, guiding hers, showing her just what he wanted her to do. Celia felt him inside her, above her, all around her. As she felt another wave building inside her, insanity rolled over her. She dug her toes into the mattress and began meeting his thrusts harder, bucking her hips into him, thrilling when his eyes flared and he seized her waist, dragging her toward the end of the bed and tilting her hips as he changed the angle of his thrusts. Sharp and short, hard and fast; Celia spread her hands on her belly and felt him moving inside her.

With an astonishing snap, her climax came over her, so fast she wasn't prepared for it. Her body simply seized, her back arched and taut, her hands closing in fists around the folds of her nightdress. Dimly she heard Anthony's victorious growl, and then his head sank and his shoulders heaved, and he was still.

After a long moment Anthony raised his head. His eyes were soft and golden as he regarded her. He reached out and brushed his knuckles down her cheek with sweet tenderness. "Darling," he murmured. "Oh, Celia."

She couldn't speak. She wrapped her fingers around his hand and turned her head to press her lips against his palm. He had upended her world, scattered her thoughts, and left her not knowing what to think. For now she only wanted to lie here beneath him, luxuriating in the aftermath of his lovemaking.

After a moment he shifted, sliding out of her. Celia made a soft noise of regret, and he smiled. He turned away, doing something she couldn't see, and a moment later fastened his trousers, leaving his shirt hanging out.

He leaned over her again, pressing a kiss to her stomach before pulling her nightdress back down over her. Celia smiled lazily at him. "What's that?" she asked, reaching for his hand.

Anthony caught her hand and brought it to his lips as he sat beside her on the bed. Celia rolled onto her side, wanting to curl herself around him. She wanted him to stay. She wanted to know what it was like to sleep in his arms, to wake with him beside her. At this moment, being with him didn't feel like a risk; it felt like a necessity.

"It prevents conception," he said then, showing her what was in his other hand. Celia looked up, surprised out of her dreamy thoughts.

"Oh." It looked like a crumpled piece of wet silk. "Why—I mean . . . I might not even be able . . ."

His smile this time was bitter. "I swore never to have a bastard. It would ruin the mother, and the child . . ." He shrugged, still holding her hand next to his cheek. "It wouldn't be fair to the child, saddling it with a life-time of misery just for my night's pleasure."

"Oh. Then . . . Then you don't . . ."

He sighed, replacing her hand on her stomach. "No. Not one." He got up and crossed the room to pull on his dressing gown, then shoved the crumpled sheath into the pocket, as well as a small jar that must hold the ointment he had spread on her feet. Celia just watched him move around her room. He didn't look out of place at all, or ill at ease. He never did, she realized. No matter where he was or what he was doing, Anthony always managed to appear composed. Controlled.

He came back across the room to her side. "Good night, my lady," he said softly.

"Must you go?" She reached for him again.

"Yes, you know I must." He pulled the coverlet over her, smoothing it around her shoulders. His eyes crinkled again as he grinned at her. "Sleep well. Until tomorrow." He kissed her forehead and left.

Celia curled her arms around herself. He used a sheath to spare any children of his the pain of being bastards. And to spare her the shame of having a child out of marriage. He might be a hedonist, as people said, but he certainly wasn't reckless or selfish in his pleasures.

She snuggled into her coverlet. Her pulse seemed to echo between her legs, strong and steady and blissfully sated. It would be very easy to get used to being worshipped by Anthony.

Chapter Twenty

The next morning the Hillenbys left for London. Mary said goodbye in a subdued, almost fearful tone, often glancing at her husband. Celia decided *she* must be the reason Lord Hillenby wanted to return to town early, from the cold look he gave her as he said farewell. Mary walked out to the carriage behind him, her shoulders stiff despite the rain drumming down on her. She didn't look back as the carriage drove off, even though Celia watched them to the gates.

That could have been her life, Celia realized. Not because she would have been married to an old man like Hillenby, but because she and Bertie had already fallen into a similar life of silence and resentments. She just hadn't been afraid of him, as Mary clearly was of Hillenby.

She went back into the house and found Louisa in the drawing room. Elton, a round, soft pudding of a man, always slept late. Louisa was normally glad of this, but today she seemed out of sorts. It gave them little to talk about, as Celia was still preoccupied with thoughts of the previous night. And Jane came down late, which seemed to vex Louisa most of all.

"There you are," exclaimed Louisa when she finally appeared. Her eyes narrowed. "And don't you look pleased!"

Jane drifted into the room, a contented smile on her face. "Good morning," she said graciously, dropping into a chair next to Celia. "What a splendid day."

Two thin lines appeared between Louisa's brows as she glanced at the rain drizzling down the windows. "Why is that, Jane?"

Jane gave Celia another wide, almost silly grin. "It could only be a splendid day, after such a night."

"What about your night?" Louisa was in a peevish mood today, thought Celia. She felt much more in charity with Jane, whose expression mirrored her own mood.

"Mmm. Percy." A tinge of color rose in Jane's cheeks, and suddenly Celia knew exactly what Jane had done last night. She resisted the urge to feel her own cheeks as her blood warmed again.

"That's all you can say?" Louisa scowled at her. "What about Percy? Did he come and talk to you of horses?"

Jane laughed, the full, rich laugh of a well-satisfied woman. "Not one word of horses! Oh, good heavens, no. At first I was quite astonished to see him; he nearly followed me up to bed, which is out of the ordinary. And especially in such company! He's more likely to sit up late and play at cards or billiards than come to bed early. But last night . . ." She sighed, her eyes drifting closed. "He asked me if I were happy, and if he could make me happier—as his wife. I was so surprised I scarcely knew what to say at first."

Louisa's face had been growing stonier and stonier. "What did you tell him?"

Jane blushed again and lowered her voice. "I said I

wanted a child. We have been married almost two years, and although Percy feels no urgency for an heir, I—I would like a child."

This time Louisa just stared at her. Celia's lips parted in surprise, and Jane gave her a hesitant nod.

"And he agreed." Jane's voice warmed, and her smile returned. "Oh, how he agreed. And after, we talked until late at night. Did you know, I never knew Percy liked a well-played violin? I never thought he had musical opinions at all."

"And what brought this on?" Louisa recovered her voice to ask.

Jane glanced around, then leaned forward. "That was the most astonishing thing," she confided. "When I asked what made him so attentive, he apologized for not being so earlier—Percy, apologize!—and then he said he had had an enlightening conversation with Mr. Hamilton. Mr. Hamilton, of all people! I asked what he meant and he said it was Mr. Hamilton who put it in his head that he ought to pay attention to me!" Her eyes glowed, and Jane actually giggled. "Well, it was astonishing, but I must say, Percy ought to spend more time with Mr. Hamilton, if this is the result."

"It is incredible," said Louisa after a moment.

But Celia didn't think so. She wondered if Anthony had meant to send Mr. Percy into Jane's arms, or if he had just spoken sense to Mr. Percy, but she rather thought he would be quite pleased to see Jane's happy glow this morning.

"And this morning, Percy composed a verse to me as I was dressing." Jane giggled again, drawing her fingertips along her collarbone. "It was dreadful, of course, but so dreadful it was amusing. I couldn't help but laugh and laugh, and then it took ever so long to get dressed."

"What a dreadful pity Elton won't speak to the man," Louisa lamented, beginning to look peeved again. "How convenient it would be if my own husband could be persuaded to care for my happiness and satisfaction."

"Oh, yes," said Jane on a sigh. "Much more convenient than dancing around a lover, trying to be discreet, and of course the uproar if you can't manage it. My father-in-law is such a martinet, I would be pilloried for that sort of scandal. And I wouldn't mind in the least if Percy and I were to become one of those disgustingly devoted couples. After this visit, seeing His Grace and Her Grace together, and Lord David and his wife . . . well, it looks rather pleasant."

Yes, Celia thought warmly. It did. She remembered again Hannah's face yesterday: *I would have missed Marcus most of all. . . .*

"But who would have thought such a thing of Mr. Hamilton?" Louisa asked. "Certainly not I. Are you sure he didn't give Percy the idea that perhaps he meant to seduce you, and that spurred Percy?"

"No," said Celia before Jane could answer. "Of course not." Louisa looked at her in surprise. "He would never do that," Celia repeated.

Louisa cleared her throat delicately. "Er—no. Perhaps not."

"Oh, do stop," Jane told her, unperturbed. "Percy's not precisely the jealous sort. He did not specifically say, but I believe Mr. Hamilton's words were more in the nature of advice. And I for one should like to thank him for it. He can give Percy all the advice he likes in this vein."

It wasn't until after luncheon that Celia had an

opportunity to speak to Anthony. Someone proposed going boating once the morning rain had been driven away by sunshine, and so a small party walked to the lake. Celia contrived to end up alone in a boat with Anthony, even sending her brother David a fierce look when he seemed about to approach and join them. It wasn't quite private, but they could talk without fear of impropriety.

"You have made Mrs. Percy very happy," she told him as he rowed them out.

"Have I?" He cocked his head curiously, pulling on the oars.

Celia grinned. "She barely made it downstairs before luncheon."

His eyebrows went up. "I had no idea."

"Hmm." Celia twirled her parasol. "And yet you are to thank, according to her."

Anthony gave her another quizzical look as he removed his hat and jacket. The sun was bright and hot in the middle of the lake, despite the cool breeze. The other men had already removed their jackets. "I don't believe I've spoken to Mrs. Percy in several days."

"Oh, but you spoke to her husband, and that made all the difference."

Comprehension dawned in his face. "Ah," he murmured with a slight smile. "Then I am delighted to have been of some small service to her."

"What did you tell her husband, I wonder?"

He squinted across the water at the other boaters, rowing them farther out. "How to win at the races."

Celia dipped her fingers in the lake and flipped water at him. Anthony laughed, flicking the end of an oar and sending a light spray of water back at her. "What did you really tell him?" she demanded, laughing.

"How to please a woman." He gave her a speaking look, flexing his arms as he rowed.

Celia pretended to take affront and tried to ignore the healthy display of masculinity in front of her. "And I suppose just because everyone considers you such an expert—"

"Everyone? Really, I had no idea my fame was that widespread."

"—you think you know all there is to it—"

"I am always ready to learn more, madame."

"You're such a scoundrel!" she exclaimed. He just gave her a sinful smile in reply, until Celia blushed. "So what is the secret, then? What did you tell Mr. Percy?"

Anthony shrugged. "Oh, nothing much. Start by rubbing her feet—" He broke off, laughing, at Celia's horrified exclamation as she looked wildly around to see if any of the other boats were near enough for the occupants to overhear. "Of course not. I didn't know that would please you. You might have turned me out on my ear, scandalized at the very suggestion of someone fondling your naked ankles."

"You manage to make it sound even more wicked than it was." Satisfied no one could hear him, she settled back into her seat.

Anthony dug in the oars again, sending the boat across the lake with a lurch. "Ought it to have been more wicked? You must tell me these things."

"You aren't answering my question, so I shan't answer yours. What did you tell Mr. Percy?"

Anthony rowed in silence for a few minutes. At this rate, he would take them all the way across the lake. "I told him to pay attention to his wife," he said finally. "To talk to her. To listen to her. I told him that a happy wife is a faithful wife. What Percy did after we spoke, I cannot say. I did not mean to advise him on his marriage."

"How do you know so much about marriage and wives?" Celia leaned forward, studying him.

His mouth twisted. "I've seen a lot of bad marriages, and even more unhappy wives."

"Then what makes a marriage happy?"

Again he hesitated a long time. "I know an unhappy marriage is one where there is little affection or respect between the parties," he said. "A companionable warmth, even, will make each person care more for the other's happiness, and therefore do less to ruin that happiness. An unhappy wife will do things a woman who is even moderately contented would never do."

"And what makes a wife happy?"

He looked at her, then grinned. She realized she had been holding her breath for his answer. "I am still hoping to learn, when I have a wife of my own."

Celia licked her lips, feeling very daring. "And what would you do, if you had a wife?"

He leaned forward under pretense of rowing, bringing his face very near hers. "Right now, at this moment?"

She nodded.

"In this boat, on this lake . . . with my wife?" he asked.

Celia nodded. He leaned back on the oars, looking thoughtful, then leaned close again as he brought the oars forward for another stroke. "I think . . ." His golden gaze wandered over her face. A sensual smile curved his mouth. "Ah, what a question you pose, my dear."

"And you have no answer?"

"Oh, I have an answer," he replied softly. "Many

answers. I was merely savoring the prospect of my answers."

"Now you must tell me."

Anthony grinned again, leaning back on a stroke of the oars. "I should prefer it a bit darker." He rowed again. "As dark as night, in fact. Yes, that would be best. A night with no moon, but a warm breeze."

"Night?"

Anthony made a low noise of assent. "Late at night, when all others have long since retired to their beds. But we—my wife and I," he clarified with a gleaming look. "We would steal out of the house together and row out on the lake until it was just the two of us, alone. Just like this." He leaned toward her again and his voice dropped. "Then I'd put up the oars, and we would lie down in the bottom of the boat . . ."

"And?"

That wicked smile returned. "And count the stars." He pulled back on the oars. "What else would one do out on a moonless night in a boat?"

"Wretch," she said with a laugh. "You know I thought you were going to say make love!"

"Make love in a boat?" He made a scandalized face. "How obscene. How shocking. I can't believe you would suggest such a thing."

Celia blushed but laughed again. "Now you're making sport of me."

Anthony grinned. "Not at all. Never suggest such a thing. But perhaps you've been contemplating it," he said suddenly, his eyes lighting up. "Is this a fancy you've taken lately, my lady? Far be it from me to refuse—"

"No!" she cried, feeling the blush extend over every inch of her skin. "Of course not!"

"Hmm." He rowed again, watching her with a devilish smile. "How unfortunate."

"I shan't speak to you anymore," she announced, turning in her seat and presenting him with her profile. Anthony grinned again and rowed some more, leisurely. They were quite alone on the water now. The others had not kept pace. He pushed aside the thought that it was not entirely proper. He was alone with Celia, at her instigation, and he was savoring every moment of it.

"Anthony," Celia said after a while, "I have been thinking about something you said last night. I—I have been wondering what you meant."

"What is that?" Unconsciously he tensed, wondering what the hell he had said that made her hesitant.

"You said you had come to persuade me." She turned back toward him. "What did you mean?"

"Ah." His shoulders eased. "To persuade you that I'm a decent fellow."

She dismissed his light comment with a wave of her hand. "I've known that for years." He glanced at her sharply, but she was already speaking again. "What did you really mean?"

Anthony rowed again, turning the boat in a wide, lazy circle. "That is what I meant. To persuade you that I won't hurt you. That I don't want to disappoint you. That you wouldn't be throwing yourself away, if you were to decide . . ." Anthony let the sentence remain unfinished as she jerked her gaze away, her cheeks scarlet. *Oh, Lord,* he thought in sudden dismay.

"Why?" she asked, head bent. Her fingers were white around the handle of her parasol.

"Why?" he echoed stupidly.

"Why would you want to persuade me of that?" She lifted her eyes. "Why *me?*"

He was so surprised by the question, he couldn't reply. Why Celia? *Because it couldn't be anyone else,* whispered a voice in his head. Because he cared what she thought of him, when he didn't give a bloody damn what anyone else thought. "What do you mean?" he asked cautiously.

She twisted the parasol handle between her hands. "The other night . . . in the library. I said nothing when my mother and David accused you of . . . of seducing me and ruining me. But you wouldn't have been there if I hadn't told you to meet me there, and I don't think you would have . . ." Her whole face was scarlet now but she plowed onward. "I don't think you would have made love to me if I hadn't thrown myself at you. And yet when everyone blamed you, you didn't say a word."

Anthony raised his eyebrows. "Should I have said something?"

"I would not have faulted you," she said somberly. "And afterward, I wondered why on earth you would even agree to my request to pretend that we are considering marriage. I was a complete coward. I did nothing to help you or defend you. And when you said you wanted to persuade me . . . I had to wonder why on earth you would harbor any kind feelings for me at all." Anthony stared at her. Celia raised her hands helplessly. "I—I know you could have any woman you wanted. I just can't think of any reason why you would want me."

No, he thought. *There's not one reason, there are a thousand.* He put his back into another stroke of the oars, turning them back toward the shore where they had departed. David Reece would follow them and toss him in the lake if they lingered too long. "I can have any woman I want? What a relief it is to hear that."

She pressed her lips together in a reluctant, reproving smile. His own grin faded and he shook his head.

"If you were any other woman I would think you were trying to tease compliments from me. But I know you. I have always had a very high regard for you. I have always considered you my friend."

"A friend," she repeated slowly.

Anthony winced at his own carelessness. *What words of passion and devotion,* he told himself. *Is it a wonder she's not swooning at your feet already?* "A very dear, trusted friend," he tried to clarify. "But also a beautiful woman. And dear to me. And—" He stopped, wondering when he'd become such an imbecile.

"Oh," she said. "I see." But he knew she didn't.

"You think I am not sincere?" he asked, trying to shift the conversation to safer ground. He would much rather hear her thoughts and feelings than try to express his.

Her gaze was pensive, a bit troubled. "No. I don't know. I know you are sincere in your efforts to help avoid a scandal, and I thought—I hoped—your letters . . ." She looked away. "I have been thinking about our bargain," she said. "And I believe—"

A shout from another boat interrupted her. David, rowing his wife, and the Percys had caught up to them, drawing alongside and exchanging good-natured teasing about rowing abilities. Anthony tamped down his urge to row away again and ask Celia to go on with what she was saying, as she laughed and talked with Mrs. Percy and Lady David. Had she decided what she wanted to do? Anthony rather thought any scandal wouldn't be extreme. They were surrounded by Celia's family and friends, none of whom would likely wish to tarnish her name, particularly not by linking it with his. If she decided to refuse him,

Anthony thought she needn't suffer much—at least in society's eyes.

But that meant she must decide whether she wanted him for himself, and not to preserve her reputation. *Why me?* she had asked, as if anyone would need a reason to love her. She was beautiful, exquisitely desirable. She was generous and kind—the kindest person Anthony knew, most likely. She was charming and well-mannered, loyal and passionate, strong and loving. She was even wealthy and well-connected, which didn't matter much to Anthony but he knew that alone would draw men to her like flies to honey.

Which meant she was nearly everything a man could ask for in a wife, while he . . . he was nearly everything a woman would *not* want in a husband.

Percy challenged him and David to a race back to shore. David shook his head at once; his wife cradled one hand around her swelling stomach and grinned. But Anthony took up Percy's offer, relieved to banish his dark thoughts with exertion, even nodding when Percy leaned across the water to murmur something about ten pounds to the winner.

He concentrated on rowing then. Celia and Mrs. Percy cheered them on with much laughter and cries of delight. Celia put down her parasol and held tight to her bonnet as they flew across the water. "Oh, we're leading," she exclaimed, looking at him with glowing eyes. Anthony, never one to lose a wager willingly anyway, redoubled his effort, and they reached the shore almost a full boat length ahead of the Percys.

"Well done!" cried Celia, leaping out of the boat and splashing ashore with no regard for her slippers and skirt. Anthony jumped out after her, dragging the punt onto the grass as Percy staggered ashore pulling his own boat.

"Hamilton, you bloody scoundrel," he panted. His fair hair was plastered to his forehead with perspiration. "I might have had an apoplexy trying to keep up with you."

Anthony laughed even though it made his chest burn. "More sport, less brandy, Percy."

His friend groaned, then leaned over to cough violently. His wife hurried up to pat him on the back as David rowed his boat up, shouting with laughter at them. Celia turned to Anthony, tucking her hand through his arm very naturally. "Good show," she whispered with a sparkling glance.

He grinned at her, his own breathing still harsh. "I like to win."

She laughed, and they all started back toward the house. Mrs. Percy was clinging devotedly to her husband, and Percy seemed to be soaking up her attention with pleasure, letting her blot his flushed face with her handkerchief. David helped his pregnant wife along with great tenderness, sweeping her into his arms and carrying her across a patch of mud despite her shriek of protest. Celia's hand nestled in the crook of his arm as if it belonged there, and Anthony, surrounded by happy married couples, began to think it did.

Because this, he thought to himself as they walked leisurely back to the house, this was what it would be like to be married to Celia. Her hand on his arm. Her warm presence at his side. Her face turning toward him, bright with joy over something as silly as a boat race. He had never felt so content and peaceful in all his life. He never wanted this day to end.

When they reached the house, the Percys went

upstairs together, still arm in arm. Lady David tried to hide a yawn, but her husband saw and led her off. Anthony and Celia stopped in the wide, airy hall, a bit awkwardly. Of course he couldn't escort her up to her room, or to his, not in the bright light of day.

"I should change," she said ruefully, lifting her skirt a few inches to examine her soaked slippers and stockings. "I was so excited to win, I jumped right into the lake."

"It was a hard-fought battle," he said, admiring the trim, wet ankles she displayed. She laughed and bid him farewell, and he stood at the bottom of the stairs watching until she had disappeared up them, with one last tiny wave and a smile at the top. He lifted his hand and grinned back at her, but then she was gone, and he was alone again.

As usual. But perhaps . . . not for long.

Chapter Twenty-One

Celia tried without success to find another chance to talk to Anthony alone in the next week. A few days of rain kept the party housebound, and someone always seemed to be nearby when she got up her nerve to discuss that topic: why he would want to persuade her to marry him. Celia couldn't help but think she was a fairly ordinary woman, even before one considered how many more beautiful and sophisticated women Anthony must have known and could have pursued.

She didn't want him to pursue someone else, of course. She wanted to be the one he wanted above all others. But she was afraid of disappointing him, as she had clearly disappointed Bertie, and Celia thought she would rather have her heart crushed now than later. The fact that Anthony was so charmingly self-deprecating and evasive in their conversation in the boat, when she had tried to ask what he saw in her, only made her wonder more.

He still paid her attentions, although in more subtle ways. A tiny boat, folded of silver tissue paper, was on her breakfast tray one morning. Agnes cheerfully admitted he had given it to her in the hall, and Celia set it on her mantel, smiling every time she saw the little reminder of their triumph on the lake.

Another morning a box with her name on it was delivered from a fashionable London shop. Mystified, Celia opened it to find a pair of sky-blue satin slippers with a small raised heel and ribbons to tie around her ankles. Her mouth dropped open, and she took one slipper out to admire it. What lovely, lovely slippers, embroidered with flowing vines and adorned with tiny beaded flowers.

It was a shockingly personal gift, and one she should refuse. She and Anthony were not even engaged, of course, and it would be highly improper for her to wear them. But she spirited them up to her room anyway, delighted and a little surprised to find they were a perfect fit, and an exact match for her new evening dress. How had he known? she wondered as she studied the shoes in the mirror, holding up her skirts to see them as she turned her feet this way and that. And again, he hadn't taken credit for it, although no one else could have possibly thought to send her slippers like these. There was no card in the box. It seemed he listened to, and remembered, every word she said. Celia let her skirts fall as she stared at herself.

Was she worthy of such a man?

She began watching him more thoughtfully. No wonder he was an enigma to most of society, she thought, watching one night at dinner as he waded through a barbed conversation with aplomb. Lord William seemed to want to provoke him and was constantly making little comments that seemed innocent, except to Celia. Anthony deflected them all with a slight smile, as if nothing could dent his armor. He ignored comments that probably would have brought David or Mr. Percy to the brink of violence, and Celia realized that he valued control.

After dinner the mood was lazy. The gentlemen joined them early. Several people wandered into the garden to enjoy a warm, clear night after all the rain, and the ones left in the drawing room were enjoying quiet pursuits. Celia sat with Vivian, helping her untangle the embroidery threads she was using in a tiny frock for her baby. Vivian's pregnancy left her tired and ill much of the time, and she had not joined the guests for most of the party. This was the first time she had stayed after dinner, in fact.

"You needn't hide away in the corner with me," Vivian told her as Celia sat near her on the sofa.

"Oh, no! I long to have a quiet bit of conversation. And I've hardly seen you at all."

"For all that there's a bit much of me to see," grumbled Vivian, discreetly pressing one hand to the small of her back. "Worse than a broken leg."

Celia smiled. "David is so certain it will be a son."

Vivian grimaced. "He is, and the babe kicks a bit harder every time he says it. I can't decide if it's a son stretching his legs or a daughter protesting."

"David will be pleased, no matter which it is. He was always fond of Molly, and quite gentle with her."

Vivian sighed, poking at the twists of colored floss. "So long as it's easy to birth, I'll be pleased, too." Celia choked back a laugh, stealing another glance at Anthony, who sat nearby reading a book. "It's been quite a party, I hear," Vivian remarked. Celia barely heard her, caught by a sudden thought. What did Anthony think of children? He said he wanted to spare any child of his the cruelty of growing up without a father, but what sort of father would he be?

"You really needn't stay by me," Vivian said, and Celia jerked her eyes and her thoughts away from him. "You ought to go about with your guests."

"Oh, no, I am perfectly happy to sit with you." Celia picked up some tangled threads and began picking at them with great care. From the corner of her eye she saw Vivian glance Anthony's way, her mouth curved in a knowing little smile. Celia flushed. Vivian didn't say anything else, though, and bent her head over her work.

For a while it was comfortably quiet, a soft murmur of conversations around the room not distracting anyone from reading or winding thread. But then some gentlemen came back in from outside, and the evening began to disintegrate.

"We need a fourth," Lord William announced as he and Mr. Percy and Mr. Childress sat down with a deck of cards. "Hamilton, join us."

Anthony didn't look up from his book. "Thank you, no."

"I insist." Norwood laughed. "I should like a chance to sit at a table with you once." Anthony's eyes shifted up to look at him for a long, measured moment. Then his eyes went back to his book. He didn't say anything. Lord William's face flushed. "I say, Hamilton, that was rude."

"Let it go, Norwood," said Mr. Childress as he shuffled the cards. "Your manners."

"Manners be damned. The fellow looked right through me, as though I weren't fit to play with him."

"It's penny stakes, Norwood," Percy said, a bit downcast. "Not much worth a fuss. Billiards?"

"No, I want to play cards. I want to see if his reputation is all it's cracked up to be." Lord William drained the rest of his wine and got to his feet. Celia glanced up anxiously. Vivian gave a tiny shake of her head. Rosalind was still on the far side of the room in conversation with Lady Throckmorton. David and Marcus had disappeared somewhere and not yet joined them. The other guests either didn't notice or didn't care.

"Norwood, you're drunk," said Mr. Childress in a low, firm voice. "Sit down."

"But I can beat him!"

"No, you can't." Percy yawned and checked his watch. "No one can."

Celia wished Mr. Percy would keep his mouth closed. Lord William's face turned scarlet. "The hell you say," he growled.

There was a soft snap. Anthony rose, putting aside the book he had been reading. "Very well, Norwood." He strolled across the room to the table, seating himself across from Mr. Percy and leaning back very elegantly in his chair. With a sharp nod and an air of triumph, Lord William dropped back into his seat.

Celia breathed a sigh of guarded relief. It was very bad of Lord William to insist, and Anthony ought not to have been pressed into a game he didn't want to play. She realized he had done it to avoid a scene, of course. She made herself look away, not wanting to make it any more awkward than it already was.

The gentlemen played for a while. The occasional mild oath and the murmured calls were the only conversation. After a while the mood appeared to ease, and Mr. Percy especially grew quite jolly as a servant brought more wine. Celia stole a glance at the table from time to time, and Anthony seemed perfectly calm. She was feeling rather grateful that he had given in so gracefully and headed off an argument or worse, when Lord William erupted.

"Impossible!"

The room fell quiet. Even Rosalind and Lady Throckmorton looked up. Lord William was breathing hard, his handsome face flushed. He gripped the edges of the table and his eyes, feverishly bright, were fixed on the cards.

"Norwood, it doesn't matter," said Mr. Childress as he laid down his own cards. "It's just a hand of cards."

"It's penny stakes," said Mr. Percy again, as if that were the most important point.

"No!" Lord William lurched to his feet, sending his chair over backward. "It's impossible! It cannot be allowed!"

Mr. Childress rose as well. "Still up for a round of billiards, Percy?"

"Certainly!" Percy bounded out of his seat with an anxious look at the lone remaining player at the table.

Anthony was as calm and composed as ever. Unhurried, he started to rise. "Then I shall—"

"Stay!" Lord William pointed a shaking finger at him. "Stay where you are, sir, and explain yourself."

"He had good luck," said Mr. Childress.

"I told you no one beats him," said Mr. Percy.

This did not, as it was perhaps intended, console Lord William. With a snort, he lashed out, sweeping all the cards off the table in Anthony's direction. "Good luck, my arse," he snarled. "You cheated!"

Celia caught her breath. No one made a sound. Every eye was fastened on him. Anthony gazed at Lord William with unreadable eyes for a long moment, still half-risen from his seat. Then he straightened, gave a little bow, and walked out of the room. Perfect control, Celia thought, even when insulted to his face.

"Let him go," whispered Vivian, grabbing her hand as Celia made to follow him. Mr. Childress gave Lord William a deeply disgusted look, then turned and walked out. Mr. Percy stood rather aimlessly by the table for a moment, then quickly walked out after Mr. Childress. A murmur of interested conversation had already sprung up.

"How dare that man call him a cheat," Celia exclaimed to Vivian. "How dare no one else say anything! Let me go!"

"A man's got pride," Vivian said, clinging harder to her hand. "If you run after him, how will that look?"

"I don't care!"

"He might," said Vivian softly. "Gentlemen are particular about things like that."

She hesitated, then shook her head. "Perhaps. But I think this particular gentleman has endured it for too long. Someone needs to stand up for him." And this time Vivian let her go.

Chapter Twenty-Two

Anthony walked back to his room in an odd state of detachment. Norwood had called him a cheat in front of everyone, including Celia. At one time Anthony would have risen to the bait and gotten into a fistfight with Norwood or called him out, but not now. He was just tired. No matter what he did or said, or didn't say and didn't do, he was wrong.

He used his unnatural memory and talent with numbers, and he was labeled a cheat. He found ways to support himself when his father threw him out, and he was named a speculator. He invested money for women whose husbands gave them little, and he was called a seducer. He stopped it all, and he was a fortune hunter. Even with Celia, he had done everything wrong. She had looked just as shocked as the rest when Norwood uttered his slander. Her expression had been the last blow; he couldn't watch her, too, recoil from him in disgust. Not after he had begun to hope . . . to believe she was on the verge, perhaps, of accepting him. . . .

He had probably been wrong about that, too, though. Anthony was tired of pretending not to notice how the women watched him with fascinated speculation, how the men watched him with suspicion, and how the dowager duchess watched him with barely concealed hostility. Who was he to think Celia would choose him and his sordid reputation over—against— the advice and protests of her family and friends? He knew it had been a mistake to come. Before this party he had been content with what he had. Now he felt as though he had suffered some great loss, when in reality it had all been nothing more than a phantasm of his hopes and desires, teasing him with what he would never have.

Franklin was waiting for him. Word must have spread like wildfire through the servants' quarters. Anthony removed his coat and waistcoat, then stripped off his cravat. He told Franklin to pack first thing in the morning; they would return to London on the morrow. His valet bowed, and Anthony told him to go off to bed. He didn't want anyone about tonight.

Wrapping his dressing gown around him, he walked to the window. The drapes were still open, revealing the moonlit lawns and stables of Ainsley Park. Anthony leaned against the wall, looking out. He had looked forward to coming here as a young man. Whatever David Reece's faults, the man had been a good friend to him, an arrogant, proud, lonely lad with nowhere else to go once the earl had told him not to return to Lynley Court. Anthony supposed he ought to have been grateful Lynley paid the bills for his education, but he had vowed then never again to take anything from Lynley. The earl didn't want him or need him, and Anthony wouldn't need or want anything from the earl, ever again. And he hadn't, not even when he'd been in dire financial circumstances and reputed to be the most scandalous man in London.

At Ainsley Park he had been almost accepted, even after David had left school. But eventually he had not been welcome here, either. This time there was no doubt what was behind it. He had never done a single improper thing toward Celia, but he knew the duchess hadn't wanted him around her daughter, just on general principles. Anthony supposed he couldn't fault her for it. His reputation had already outgrown him.

Ah, well. He had long ago learned there was no point in agonizing about it. Norwood's outburst had perhaps been a blessing, for it gave him an excuse to leave. It would give Celia a kind way out as well. . . .

A sharp knock on the door broke into his thoughts. For a moment he didn't move, but the knock came again. It was probably Percy, or perhaps even Ned, wanting to assure him—away from public view, of course—that they didn't believe he was a cheat. His friends were like that.

He went to the door and opened it, mildly surprised to see Celia standing there. "I'm sorry," she burst out. "Lord William is a buffoon."

He flicked one hand, falling instinctively into an attitude of careless disregard. "Oh, it's no matter. He's a bit in his cups, no doubt."

"But he called you a cheat," she exclaimed, "with no basis, and no one knew what to say or do, and I am so sorry you were so rudely spoken to at my house party."

A reluctant smile crossed his face. "Thank you for your concern."

Instead of easing, her expression only grew more worried. "May I come in?"

He hesitated only a moment, then pushed the door wide. She slipped past him, and he closed the door.

"I don't understand," she said, her voice quivering.

"I don't understand why you never defend yourself when—"

"How should I defend myself?" He leaned against the door. "Demand he prove it? Protest my innocence? Did Norwood look inclined to take my word as a gentleman?"

She bit her lip, acknowledging the point. "But you said not a word."

Anthony sighed, pushing away from the door and crossing the room. He ought not to have let her in; a few soothing words and he could have sent her on her way. "I'm leaving in the morning. It didn't seem worth the fuss."

Celia grew more agitated. She paced the room, her skirts swinging around her. "I thought—I know—Of course it is your right not to say anything when someone insults you. Even when it alarms and distresses others. But I wish—I do wish you could trust me enough to explain why you don't seem to care when others malign you."

He closed his eyes and rubbed his forehead. "It's not a matter of trust. It simply doesn't matter."

"To me it does. I think it is the key to understanding you."

Anthony raised his head and stared at her. Celia stared back, her eyes pleading with him. He looked away.

She drew in a breath, then turned and walked toward him, and for a moment he braced himself. But instead she went to the desk and took a deck of cards, then went back across the room, right to the bed, where she climbed up and sat. She shuffled the cards and looked pointedly at him, then at the bed. Reluctantly he sat, sitting just on the edge opposite her.

"Play me for the reason," she said. "If I win, you tell me. If you win, I shall cease asking."

"No."

"Why not?" Celia tossed a card at him. He caught it and laid it on the coverlet between them. "Are you afraid I'll beat you?"

"Terrified," he replied.

"I'm not so bad at cards," she told him, riffling the deck. "David taught me several tricks."

"You'd probably better not use them. They're bound to be highly suspect, and of doubtful assistance."

"Pooh." She tossed more cards at him. "I thought you would have more backbone than that. You refuse to answer my questions and shun my challenge. I thought you liked a challenge. What are you afraid of?"

Anthony ignored the cards in front of him. "Celia, I don't want to play cards with you."

"Don't change the subject. What game do you favor?"

He sighed and looked away. "No."

Celia heard the underlying steel in his voice and put down the cards. "Why not? You play with Norwood and the others, even when you don't wish to."

"Yes, and none of them come away pleased." He didn't meet her eyes but flipped a fold of his dressing gown back and forth in his fingers.

"Because you win," she said.

"Because they think I cheat." He tilted his head back and looked at her from beneath lowered eyelids. "You know that."

Celia gathered up the scattered cards. "You can't cheat at this," she said, dealing. "It's pure chance."

"At the beginning," he murmured.

"What does that mean?" He shrugged, and she leaned forward. "You can trust me, you know," she said softly. He looked at her again, his golden eyes cynical. "I wouldn't tell a soul, even if you told me you were cheating. Not that I think you are."

For a long moment he just looked at her. Celia almost held her breath; this was a turning point, she realized.

She had heard the whispers, that he was a card-sharp and a cheat. She had never believed them, not really, but it did seem odd that he was so successful at the tables when other people—including David—seemed to lose as much as they won. What was Anthony's secret? Could he actually be cheating? Celia didn't believe it, but . . . Would he tell her? Did he trust her that much?

"I can count the cards," he finally said.

Celia frowned. "Count them? You know how many there are."

"I can count them by suits and numbers," he said. "As they are played."

It took her a moment to realize what he meant, and how that would help win. "Can you really? No, you are teasing me," she said. Anthony pushed himself up against the headboard and took the cards from her, then dealt a round of *vingt-et-un* for four. Under his long fingers, the cards seem to fly to their places like trained birds.

Then he began flipping cards, as if four players were playing, but all hands shown. At the beginning, he explained, he just watched and played on instinct; often he lost money, but he was careful to wager only small sums. But as the deck in his hand grew smaller, his wagers grew larger; he could remember which cards had been played, and—more importantly—which cards had not been played.

"For instance," he said, "I should not play on this"

—he waved at one hand of cards on the coverlet— "because I know there are still five face cards unplayed; they are still in the deck. My chances of drawing one, and ruining my hand, are much greater."

Celia frowned, looking at the piles of cards. After a moment's counting, she realized he was right. "And you know it, just like that?"

"Yes, more or less. See what happens." He laid out another circle of cards atop the previous one, and Celia's lips parted as a jack of hearts landed on the hand in front of Anthony. A queen also turned up. Two of the four cards turned over were face cards. She looked at him, her mouth still agape.

"That's amazing."

He pulled a face. "No, it's not."

"It is," she insisted.

He gave her a twisted smile. "That little skill got me thrown out of three schools as a boy. Everyone was certain I was cheating. I was too young and full of myself to let them win, and I suppose I gloated, too. A mathematics lecturer declared I couldn't beat him, but like a fool, I did. He was so annoyed he wrote to my father, and that was the end of that school. All school, in fact."

"But why didn't you tell your father?" Celia protested. "Wasn't he upset that you were falsely accused?"

Anthony slouched against the bolster and fixed his gaze on the card deck still in his hand, face down. "There's the answer to your question, my dear. He didn't care why or how I had beaten a lecturer at cards. He only cared that I was accused, and therefore disgraced him." He held up the remaining cards, and without looking at them, said, "Ace of spades, queen of hearts, jack of hearts, a nine, two sevens, an eight, and a two." With a flick of his wrist he tossed down the cards, face up. Each card he had named spilled across the counterpane. Celia let out her breath.

"Amazing," she whispered again.

Anthony gave a disgusted snort. "The hell it is. I didn't even try to win tonight; truthfully, I tried to throw the game to Percy. He's just such a clodpole at cards he never took advantage."

"I shall never play whist with anyone but you ever again."

"I don't like whist."

"You should," she said. "We could win everything David and Mr. Percy own."

"I don't play to beggar other people."

"But David deserves it," she muttered. "So you're going to leave in the morning because you can do something no one else can."

"I'm going to leave in the morning because I don't want to be called a cheat again. And because . . ." He hesitated. "Because I don't want to bring you down with me."

"You're abandoning me, too?" she exclaimed. His face darkened even more.

"I'm releasing you from an awkward position." His words were clipped. He swung his feet to the floor and put out his hand to help her down, too. "Come. You should go."

Celia stayed where she was. "Why did you write those letters to me?"

A muscle in his jaw tensed. "To lift your spirits."

"Is that all?"

Anthony sighed. "Celia, you shouldn't be here. I was wrong to allow you to come in."

"Is that the only reason?" she pressed. He wasn't looking at her, and the pulse in his throat beat rapidly. "Just tell me," she said quietly. "If that was the only

reason, then I should thank you; it did raise my spirits."
He turned his back to her and walked to the window
alcove, hands on his hips. Celia got off the bed and
followed him. "Was that the only reason?" He didn't
reply. She touched his arm. "Anthony . . ."

He turned. In an instant he caught her face in his
hands, his mouth descending on hers in a punishing
kiss. With two steps he bore her back into the wall
behind her. Celia melted into him, meeting his unspoken desire with her own.

She reached for him. He caught her wrists and
pinned them to the wall beside her head. His mouth
moved down her throat, sucking lightly at her skin.
Celia sagged backward, held up only by his hands at
her wrists and the weight of his body pressed into
hers. Yes, she thought in exultation, *yes* . . .

"Celia," he breathed, catching the lobe of her ear
between his teeth for a second. "Stop me."

She thrashed her head from side to side. "No."

He rested his forehead in the curve of her neck and
moaned. "You must." He moved against her, his knee
sliding between hers with a slow, delicious rhythm. His
lips brushed the hollow at the base of her throat.
Celia closed her thighs on his, pushing her hips into
him. She didn't need to hear the answer to her original question. His body was telling her what he wouldn't
say out loud.

With a strangled curse Anthony jerked away from
her. For a moment he stood there, hands in fists at his
side, chest heaving, eyes dark. They stared at each
other, then Celia threw herself at him. She clutched
handfuls of his shirt, resisting when he tried to set her
away. She pressed her lips to his throat, and he froze.
When she took his arms and pushed him back into

the opposite wall of the alcove, he let her. "Celia," he said helplessly. "Please."

"Shh." She put her fingers on his lips and gazed up at him steadily. "You don't have to say anything."

After a moment he closed his eyes, letting his head fall back in surrender. His arms, taut and flexed in her grip, relaxed. Cautiously Celia released him, but he didn't move. Anthony stood tamely in front of her, at her mercy. Her heart skipped a beat and a tingle rippled across her skin in anticipation.

She pushed the dressing gown off his shoulders, sending it to the floor. She reached for his shirt, pulling the soft linen folds free. His chest filled for a second as the last of the shirt came out of his trousers, but he said nothing. Celia gazed at his face as she worked at the buttons on his trousers. In the dim light his features were harshly shadowed, but with desperate longing. He looked so alone then, and she remembered what he had said to her so many times: *it doesn't matter.* But some things did matter, and she wasn't leaving until he understood her.

His erection sprang free. Celia took him in her hands, stroking the full length as his breathing changed, becoming deeper and slower as her fingers slid up and down. She wrapped her hands around him, caressing him; his breathing stopped altogether for a moment until he inhaled sharply, his arms twitching. Celia smiled softly and sank to her knees.

He was hard and warm under her lips. She flicked her tongue tentatively, and his hips jerked. The muscles of his legs were like stone, rigid and braced. She licked again, and his whole body seemed to spasm. Feeling utterly alive and wicked, Celia circled her tongue once more over the tip before taking him all the way into her mouth.

Ever since he made love to her with his mouth the other night, Celia had wondered, in a deep, secret way, what it would be like to do the same to him. The thought of driving him to the same ecstasy had made her so restless and hot, she'd had to press her hand between her legs. And now here she was, on her knees before him, making him tremble. His hand came up to tangle in her hair, his fingers tensing as he showed her the right rhythm. Celia just wanted to please him; she moved under his hand, reveling in her effect on him and growing wet herself remembering what he had done to her.

Abruptly he shoved her back on her heels, then yanked his shirt over his head and tossed it aside. Breathing hard, he fell to his knees before her. His eyes were almost black with desire and the tendons of his neck stood out. "You should have left when you had the chance."

Slowly she shook her head, her skin prickling under his intense, hot gaze. His jaw tightened, and he reached out and stroked her cheek. Celia turned her face into his hand, pressing an open-mouthed kiss to his palm, swirling her tongue over the base of his thumb. Flames seemed to leap in his eyes.

He thrust his hand into her hair and pulled, baring her neck. Anthony put his lips to the arch of her throat, hard, hot kisses that made her moan. She gripped his arms, digging her fingernails into his flesh. He growled deep in his throat. With sharp, short movements he unfastened her bodice, yanking it down. "Untie your chemise," he commanded in a rough voice. Celia pulled the ribbon loose, almost gasping with relief as he dipped his hand into her corset to raise her breast, then bent his head and took her nipple into his mouth. Celia arched her back, shamelessly offering herself to him, begging, demanding, as he laved one breast and then the other. The bodice was still tight around her arms, preventing her from doing more than clinging to his waist. Without lifting his head, he took her hand and brought it to his erection, wrapping her fingers around him. She stroked him firmly with both hands, imagining that it wasn't her hands he was sliding between.

He tore his lips from her aching nipples and pushed her backward, onto her heels and then onto her back. Her skirts bunched in a tangle around her legs between them. With ruthless efficiency, Anthony shoved the mass of fabric out of the way. Her delicate pantalets came off in the blink of an eye. He loomed over her, dark and sensual, staring between her legs as he pushed one of her knees up and to the side.

"How beautiful you are," he murmured. "So soft and wet." He stroked her there, and Celia arched off the floor, gasping. "So beautiful," he breathed. "Hold." When she moved too slowly, he swept his hand up behind her knee, pushing her thigh back onto her chest and completely exposing her. "Hold it there," he said again, and then he thrust inside her.

It was hard and dominant and fast. There was no seduction or tenderness, only raw want. Somehow her leg worked its way over his shoulder as he stroked into her, hard and fast. She cupped her breasts, rolling the nipples between her fingers, as aroused by the feeling of her own hands on herself as by the taut expression on Anthony's face as he moved above her, his arms rigidly braced beside her and his gaze locked on her hands.

"Vixen," he gasped, his thrusts growing even harder. "What you do to me . . ." She raked her fingernails down his chest, and he grunted, slipping his hand between them to tease her, stroke her there. He pushed her leg higher, farther apart from the other. Just when Celia thought she might split apart, pleasure ripped through her. She threw back her head and slammed her hands down on the floor. Her hips jerked off the floor, straining closer to Anthony as he thrust deep inside her once more and stayed there, pouring his own pleasure into her with a hoarse exclamation.

Anthony's head cleared slowly; he came back to himself when his knees started to hurt. The black haze that had overcome him dissipated, leaving him feeling naked and exposed. Celia was still on the floor beneath him, her chest heaving, her legs still around him. Her hair lay in a tangled golden veil over her face. He brushed it away, his fingers lingering on the satiny smooth skin of her jaw, and she quivered—but she didn't move away.

He closed his eyes. He had told Celia to leave as a last effort to preserve the option, for both of them, of walking away. Now he didn't see how he could let her go, not even after he'd all but thrown her to the floor and made brutal love to her without consideration or restraint or even a sheath. He'd lost control, the first time in many, many years he'd taken complete leave of his senses and been ruled entirely by his passions. No, he'd lost more than his control. He'd lost everything—his heart and his very soul—to her.

Percy had been right. He was mad for her, and always would be.

"Celia," he said, her name just a sigh. Slowly she turned her head to look at him, her eyes bright and unfocused. Anthony released her and got to his feet, tugging his trousers back into place for the moment.

"Come, darling," he told her, helping her to her feet before scooping her into his arms. "Come to bed."

"With you?" She smiled dreamily at him, looping her arms around his neck. "Always."

He laughed softly as he carried her to the bed. "Do you realize we've never been naked together?" She laughed, too, as he finished undoing the fastenings of her dress and lifted it over her head. He raised an eyebrow as he slipped off her shoes, the beautiful blue silk slippers he had sent her, and Celia laughed again. When he had stripped her, he discarded the rest of his own clothes and joined her in the bed, pulling her into his arms. "I'm sorry," he whispered.

"For what?" She twisted to look at him over her shoulder.

"For being . . . indelicate." He shook his head. "It was not what I intended to happen."

"No," she said softly. "But it's what you needed."

Anthony closed his eyes and rested his forehead against her shoulder. She understood—or thought she did, which he supposed was good enough. She cared for him, at least enough to want to understand. Could she possibly know what that meant to him? "May I try to do better?" he asked instead.

"Better?" she repeated with a startled little laugh. "If you didn't notice, I found it quite enjoyable."

"That's why I said better, impudent wench," he retorted, laughing with her. "An improvement on good—"

"Very good," she murmured.

"I accept your challenge," he said, flipping her onto her stomach and ignoring her delighted shriek as he rolled on top of her. It felt as natural as breathing to move between her thighs and slide back inside her.

She was still slick from before. "Trust me," he told her, kissing the back of her neck.

"You know I do," she replied with a little kick of her feet.

He made love to her tenderly this time, but no less thoroughly. For a while he simply held her, whispering endearments as he stroked and caressed her body. He was inside her, but mostly holding still; every few minutes he would withdraw almost entirely, then leisurely slide back home. It was entirely intimate without being demanding. And Celia found that that intimate connection, even without the pleasure associating with motion, was no less arousing and warming than their frantic, needy coupling on the floor had been.

After a time he rose onto his knees, pulling her to her hands and knees. Now he started making love to her, but still leisurely, his hands exploring without hurry. Once, twice he brought her to the brink of climax, only to retreat at the last moment. When she was almost begging incoherently, he brought her to completion, driving inside her as she heaved and sobbed her release until he reached his own, and both collapsed on the bed, exhausted.

And in the quiet moments after, while their bodies still twined tightly together and the blood surged hard and heavy through her veins, Celia realized what had brought her to Anthony's room tonight, what had made her stay when he told her to go: it was love. Not the giddy, effervescent infatuation she'd felt before, but real love, the deep, true feeling for another that didn't need poetry and flowers to thrive. It was not the hothouse plant her affection for Bertie had been, but a strong and vibrant thing. It hadn't withered and died at the first storm but had grown only stronger with each trial it endured, until the roots of it spread through her entire being. She could never rip it out without ripping out a piece of herself. And Celia knew, with the same certainty, that what Anthony felt for her was just as strong. She didn't need to hear him declare it when he had proved it to her so many times.

"Yes," she whispered, hardly hearing her own voice over the thump of her heart. "Yes."

He kissed the nape of her neck, his breath on her skin sending a shiver through her. "Yes, what, darling?"

"Yes," she said again. "I'll marry you."

Chapter Twenty-Three

Marcus accepted her news without blinking an eye. "I wish you very happy," he said, kissing her cheek.

She beamed at him. "Thank you."

"Would you like me to tell your mother?"

"No," she said, still smiling uncontrollably. "I know she'll be pleased." Marcus raised an eyebrow but said nothing more. Celia went to find her mother. Of course her mother would be reluctant, but surely once she saw how happy Celia was, Mama would relent. She always did.

Rosalind paced the room several times with her hands clasped before her as if in prayer, eyeing Celia worriedly, after hearing the happy news. "Dearest," she began very carefully, "are you certain?"

"Yes, Mama, I am."

Her mother sighed. "Then—But—It's not that I do not want to see you happy, but I worry . . ."

"I know. You must trust me."

Agony flickered across Rosalind's face. "I trust you. I do. But I do not trust *him.*"

"Now, Mama," said Celia in reproach.

Rosalind quickly sat in the chair opposite her. She

took Celia's hands in her own. "Before you accuse me
of being unfair and judgmental, listen to me," she
begged. "Celia, I am your mother. I saw you miserable
in marriage before, after being so certain Bertie was
the one man you loved, and I cannot bear to see it
again. Will you please, just for a moment, hear my
concern?"

Celia thought to herself that this circumstance was
nothing like when she had married Bertie, and she
couldn't stop a twinge of irritation that Mama had to
mention that now, but her mother's distress kept her
from saying it. She nodded.

Her mother gave a tight, bright smile. "Thank you.
I don't wish to cause you pain; on the contrary. But
you must know, dearest, that Mr. Hamilton is not a respectable gentleman."

"Haven't you always told me not to listen to gossip?"

Rosalind flushed pale pink. "Yes. I have. And mostly
I am right, but in this—Celia, you have been away
from town for four years. You can't expect to know
what he's done in that time."

"Do you?"

"Of course I would not condemn a man based only
on gossip," Rosalind went on, ignoring the question.
"But many of the stories I know to be true. He is not a
faithful man, dearest. I doubt he has told you of all
his lovers. I can name four women who shared his
bed, and mind you, they were not the sort of women
a man marries. There were rumors, quite supported
by facts, that he seduced wealthy women in order to
gain access to their funds, and then threw them over
once he had wagered their money away. His gambling
habits are beyond the pale. It is no secret that he fre-
quents the most notorious gaming dens and has done
for years, mostly because it is widely believed he is not

honorable at the tables. Your godmother, Lady Throckmorton, told me—in confidence, mind you— that Mr. Hamilton was in such dire financial straits only a few years ago, he was almost taken to the Fleet for debts. Lord Throckmorton saw the warrant himself. There is even evidence he killed a man in Bath last year over a dispute at the hazard table. Darling, is this such a man you wish to marry?"

Celia met her mother's anxious eyes evenly. "There is more to him than you know—and less. If there is proof he killed a man, why is he not in prison? If he gambles so intemperately, why did Lord William have to bait him into joining a simple hand of casino the other night? And I think, if society were to turn out every man who'd had debts in his life, there would be precious few dancing partners for the ladies."

Rosalind closed her eyes in despair. "I knew it," she said, her voice breaking. "I knew it! He's seduced you and cast some sort of spell over you to make you agree to this!"

"For what purpose, Mama? He's already made his fortune. He shall inherit an earldom." Celia paused. "And he has not tried to coerce me at all."

Her mother gazed sadly at her. "You would make him respectable," she whispered. "And that is something he cannot inherit or create himself." Celia bit her lip, and Rosalind reached out to cup her cheeks in both hands. "I cannot bear to see him break your heart."

"Send for David," Celia said, recognizing that her mother's fears were too great to be set aside by her own declaration. "If he, who knows Anthony so well, will condemn him, I shall delay. But if he vouches for Anthony, *you* must reconsider, Mama."

Rosalind didn't appear entirely pleased with this,

but she nodded and rang for a servant. "Tell Lord David I should like to speak to him at once," she told the maid who answered. "I am not certain David's opinion will be the most objective," she muttered.

"But neither is yours." Celia smiled sheepishly. "Nor mine."

When David appeared, Celia got to her feet. "David, we would like your opinion."

"Oh? On what?" he asked easily. Suddenly Celia recalled how ferociously her brother had attacked Anthony the night they were discovered in the library, and felt a prickle of apprehension.

"Of Mr. Hamilton," said Rosalind. Celia was grateful that she didn't say more.

David's eyes shifted from Celia to Rosalind, then back. "Why? What's he done?"

"Nothing," Celia said swiftly as her mother opened her mouth to reply. "You know him best. What sort of man is he?"

Her brother continued to watch her guardedly. "He's a decent fellow," he said at last.

"Is that all?" she burst out. "You've known him for fifteen years and that's all you can say for him?"

"No," said David. "But I think you have more to say about him as well, and if you don't care to say more, then neither do I."

Celia glared at him as her mother exhaled in obvious satisfaction. "He has proposed marriage to Celia."

"Ah." David nodded. "And I suppose Celia wants to accept him, while you want her to refuse him."

"We would like your opinion," said Rosalind very civilly. "Is he an honest man? A kind man? A respectable man?"

David glanced at Celia for a long moment. "Yes."

Celia took a deep breath of relief. Her mother took a deep breath of outrage. "What?"

"He is honest," David repeated. "Although not always to people who are not honest with him. If you ask him a direct question, he'll answer in kind. Oddly enough, he's a quiet chap. Keeps his own counsel most of the time, but I expect that'll be because his father tossed him out when he was fifteen. He's bloody brilliant with money. Once he got enough to do something, his fortune was made."

"What about the gambling?" Rosalind cried. "The debts?"

David looked abashed. "He was no worse than I, Rosalind. Had much better luck at it, too. I believe the debts sprang from investments that took some time to prosper. I'll tell you this: if ever I needed to turn one hundred pounds into five hundred, I'd give the whole sum into his hands without hesitation."

"He is not respectable." Rosalind drew herself up as if this were the last word. "You can't deny that."

David shrugged. "What is respectability? It's not his fault the gossips latched onto him at an early age."

"His actions—" began his stepmother.

"Rosalind, he's a decent fellow," David repeated. "I don't know why the gossips made such hay over him. I've never known him to lie, to cheat, or to abuse a confidence. Nor has he ever trifled with a lady; if he's offered for Celia, he must be mad for her."

A quiet glow of delight suffused Celia at her brother's words. She beamed at him, and he gave her a wry look in reply.

"Then why did you strike him the other night?" Rosalind looked anguished. David's grin disappeared and he cleared his throat.

"Ah—that. I was surprised and acted rashly."

Rosalind closed her eyes in defeat. Celia bit the inside of her lip to hide her delight.

"Dearest," said Rosalind one more time. "Are you truly certain? This is marriage. It is the rest of your life, Celia."

"I know, Mama. And I am certain."

Her mother stared at her for a long moment with worried eyes. Then she mustered a smile more tragic than joyful. "Then I shall make the arrangements."

Celia threw her arms around her mother. "Thank you, Mama."

Rosalind's arms about her tightened. She drew in a deep breath, compressing her lips into a tight line as if to bite back any more argument. "I only want you to be happy." Her voice wobbled.

Celia nodded. "I will be."

Walking a bit stiffly, Rosalind excused herself. Celia turned to her brother when she was gone. "Thank you, David."

He leaned back, crossing his arms. "If he puts so much as a toe out of line, I'm thrashing him senseless."

She bristled. "You just said he's a decent fellow!"

"He is," David said. "Most of the time. I know things about him you should never suspect."

"I expect he knows things about you that you'd prefer no one else knew, too." She smiled sweetly at his scowl. "And if you interfere in my marriage, I'll find out, and I'll tell Vivian."

"Vivian trusts me."

"And I trust Anthony. We should have no worries, then, either of us." David just looked at the ceiling. Celia lowered her voice and stepped closer. "After all, I know how he wins at cards all the time. I daresay you don't."

Interest sparked in her brother's face. "Oh? How?"

"It's not cheating, it's just a natural talent he has." She sighed dramatically as David's face darkened again. "One you must certainly lack."

"Well, it doesn't matter. I've mostly given up cards." David started toward the door, then swung around. "Is it something one can learn?"

"No. I don't think so."

"Hmph. I've wondered for years," he muttered. "It's unnatural."

Celia just grinned. "Thank you for reassuring Mama, David."

He sighed, finally pulling her into his arms. "It was the least I could do," he said, "since your betrothed is undergoing the Exeter inquisition as we speak. Not quite sporting to put the fellow through that and then let Rosalind scotch the works."

She gasped. "What? Marcus wouldn't—"

David laughed as she rushed for the door. "Oh, Marcus would!"

Anthony had never been so glad in all his life for an expansive memory as he was that morning, as the duke of Exeter asked question after question after question of him. He had gone to make certain the duke wouldn't prohibit him from marrying Celia. She was a widow, but she was also the duke's younger sister, and Exeter was known to be protective of his family. The last thing Anthony wanted to do was make a muck of things by being careless or foolish, and not paying proper respectful deference to the duke would be very foolish and extremely careless.

Exeter had been waiting for him. Celia had already told him the news. Anthony searched for any sign, any hint of what his response to her had been, but there was nothing. The man had a face like marble. Anthony unconsciously assumed his own mask, bracing himself.

The duke knew more about him than Anthony had suspected. His questions probed into areas of his life that Anthony had felt were very discreet. Still, this was the price he must pay to marry Celia, so he answered with unflinching candor. From time to time the duke would incline his head ever so slightly, but that was the only encouragement he received.

When he was beginning to think he had shared every detail of his life he could remember, there was a rapid knocking on the door, then it flew open. "What is going on?" demanded Celia, out of breath and flushed.

Exeter got to his feet, as did Anthony. "We are getting acquainted, since we are to be family."

She shot a questioning glance at Anthony, who gave her a small, hopeful nod. Her face lit up. "Then you didn't—you haven't—?"

The duke smiled, coming around his desk. "You're babbling, Celia." She blushed. "I wish you both much joy."

"Thank you, Marcus." She went up on her tiptoes to kiss his cheek. "David said you were giving him an inquisition."

Subdued amusement lit the duke's dark eyes. "Not at all. It was all quite cordial."

Anthony thought that he'd rather not discover the duke's unfriendly side, if that were a cordial conversation, but then Celia turned to him, her face glowing. "Then everything is settled?"

He couldn't help grinning like a fool. "Yes, I believe so." Exeter said nothing to contradict him, and

Anthony's grin grew a little wider. "It is," he repeated more definitely.

She beamed back at him. "I shall go tell Mama. Thank you, Marcus. You must know your approval will be a great comfort to Mama."

He just chuckled, and Celia hurried out the door ahead of them. Exeter put his head to one side, watching his sister go. "I've not seen her this happy in years. Perhaps never."

"I shall do everything in my power to protect her happiness," said Anthony gravely.

Exeter glanced at him. He gave a suddenly open grin. "Oh, no need for that. I shan't take your head off. You'll answer to Celia from now on, not to me."

"Ah . . . right." Anthony still remembered how quickly David, his supposed friend, had charged at him. "Of course."

The duke shook his head, still grinning. "David feels the same. Come. Luncheon awaits."

Chapter Twenty-Four

The duke announced their engagement at dinner that evening. David Reece was the first on his feet to propose a toast to the new couple, and Percy seconded it. Everyone raised their glasses quickly, as if they had been expecting such a thing for some time and were glad to have it out in the open. The announcement seemed, in a way, to release the tension in the party, as if the normal order of things had now been righted and the little scandal in the library had been put to rest. The conversation flowed more easily that night after the ladies left, and Anthony felt completely at ease for the first time as the other men congratulated him.

Except Ned, that is. He drank more port than anyone else but said the least. Anthony remembered their conversation by the stream and wondered just how strongly Ned had hoped to wed Celia himself. He had never seen the slightest preference for Ned in *her* behavior, but perhaps Ned had seen things differently. And of course, were their positions reversed, and Ned were receiving congratulations on his upcoming marriage to Celia . . . Well, one bottle of port probably wouldn't have been enough for Anthony in that event.

"Well done, lad, well done!" Warfield slapped him on the back as the men moved to join the ladies in the drawing room, and they had a moment to speak quietly. "And the lady looks as happy as a bride ought to look."

Anthony smiled. "I intend to keep her so."

His uncle laughed. "No doubt! And you never fail in what you set out to do; damned admirable, I say. May you and your wife enjoy a long and happy life together."

Anthony nodded in thanks and in doing so caught sight of Ned. Ned was watching them, his face set, and when Anthony met his gaze, he turned on his heel and left the room. Anthony's grin faded.

Warfield noticed and frowned after Ned. "A bit disappointed, that one."

"Yes."

"Well, he'll get over it. 'Tis clear her heart was never engaged there, and his disappointment is more for the match than for the lady."

"Of course," Anthony murmured.

"Shall we join the ladies?" Warfield asked with a gleam in his eye. "I like to see the way her eyes light up when you come into the room." Anthony shot him a quizzical look, and Warfield laughed heartily. "Oh, Lord, boy, to see your face! Aye, it's true, and you'd notice if you weren't so busy trying not to stare at her like a hungry dog after a meaty bone."

"A mutt and a bone," said Anthony wryly. "You flatter us both. I shall gladly leave you at the door for better company."

"That you shall, my lad." With another slap on the shoulder, they followed the rest of the gentlemen.

That night Anthony felt almost a part of the family. A spirited game of charades left the company in gales of laughter, especially after Mrs. Percy called her husband an elephant when he was attempting to be a Roman general and he in turn called her a whirlwind when she was portraying the Three Fates. Celia sat beside Anthony on the sofa, where he could touch her hand discreetly from time to time to make her cheeks turn pink. And at the end of the evening, they managed to walk more slowly than anyone else up the stairs, until they were quite alone in the corridor.

"Good night, my darling," he whispered, pulling her close outside her door.

"And to you." She raised her face to him, a dreamy smile on her lips. Anthony kissed her, lightly, then deeply, until she was clinging to him breathlessly and he had to brace one hand against the wall. "Come to me later," she whispered, her eyes glowing and her breathing rapid.

He touched her lower lip. "No." And kissed her again.

"Why not?" She moved against him, running her fingers through the hair at the nape of his neck. Anthony chuckled and trailed one hand down her back until she arched, pressing her breasts against him.

"We're going to wait," he murmured in her ear, still stroking her back. "Until our wedding night. And then I shall have my wicked way with you all night long, until you cannot breathe or speak properly. You'd best get your rest now, my lady."

"What shall you do?" Celia's voice was husky with desire. He laughed again, even more softly, and she shivered. They were standing in the corridor, where anyone might walk by and see them wrapped around each other, but Celia didn't care a bit.

"I plan to tie you to my bed," came his dark, seductive voice in her ear, his breath on her neck sending shivers down her spine.

"You won't need to," she told him. Her knees were already weak.

"But I want to." He brushed his lips across the rapid pulse below her jaw, and Celia's breath came out in a sigh of want. "I want to taste every inch of you, from every angle. I want to make you weep with need, and then I want to satisfy that need until you can't even beg for more."

Celia moaned. "Why wait?"

He nuzzled her neck once more and released her. "Because I made a vow, just last night, that I would never again make love to any woman other than my wife."

Celia's heart quivered. *How romantic,* whispered a little voice in her head, a voice momentarily at odds with the demands of her body. "But *I* am your wife," she argued softly, tugging at his jacket.

"Not yet." His smile was full of promise, and Celia swallowed. Mutely she nodded acquiescence and released him. He opened her door, watched her go through it, and then closed it.

In her room she leaned against the wall to catch her breath. How long until the wedding? A fortnight. She pressed one hand to her heated face. Goodness, that seemed a long time all of a sudden.

But his vow . . . Celia closed her eyes, another smile curving her lips. She liked that vow very much.

The next week passed in happy contentment. Although all the houseguests had been invited to extend their stay for the wedding, many had to leave.

Soon it was just the Percys, Warfield, and Ned. Anthony would really have preferred the last gentleman leave as well. Ned kept to his rooms and avoided Anthony, and was distant when in company. Anthony took the hint and ignored Ned in return.

With the house emptier and quieter, there were more opportunities to steal away with Celia for an hour or two. He loved surprising her. He loved seeing her eyes open wide when he whispered something shocking in her ear, and he loved the naughty smile that went with her blush even as she went along with his ideas. He loved that she allowed him liberties even when they shocked her. He loved everything about her.

Although he kept his vow not to visit Celia's bed again, he saw no need to deprive either of them of lesser pleasures, in stolen moments here and there. Still, it wasn't quite the same, and he took to early morning rides to take the edge off his hunger for her. Perhaps he had been too hasty in declaring he wouldn't make love to her again until they were wed. But no; anticipation was a potent aphrodisiac. He could wait another week. It felt like he had waited his entire life for her, and in a week's time she would be his, forever.

He rode so early, the rest of the household was usually not awake, but one morning that was not the case. He came downstairs dressed to ride as usual and Ned was there, in his traveling clothes, slapping his gloves into his palm. A trunk sat in the hall, and a footman was carrying out a valise. As Anthony came down the stairs, Ned looked up and his expression eased.

"Hamilton," he said, sounding relieved. "There you are. I was about to leave you a note."

"Oh?"

"Yes." Ned cleared his throat. "About . . . That is,

to wish you well." Anthony inclined his head. Ned hesitated. "On your marriage."

"Thank you."

"I have been . . ." Again Ned seemed to struggle for words. "I have not been gracious."

Again Anthony merely bowed his head. Ned had been far from gracious, barely speaking a word to him in the past week or more. "You are leaving?"

"Yes, I have some business that requires my attention." Ned gave a gruesome smile. "My immediate attention, unfortunately. I made my farewells to Warfield and our hosts last evening."

Anthony unbent a little. He knew that feeling all too well. Who was he to judge another man in tight straits? For all he knew, Ned had been under strain for reasons completely unrelated to Anthony's engagement to Celia. Ned had been a friend to him for years, and he was uncharitable to mistrust every word the man said now. "Safe journey back to town."

"Thank you." He grinned, finally looking like the same Ned of old. "Convey my felicitations to the bride, would you?"

Anthony smiled back, clasping Ned's offered hand. Ned donned his hat and they walked out to where his horse waited behind the small carriage carrying his baggage and his valet.

"I shall miss this place," Ned said, squinting against the sun as he tugged on his gloves. "The finest estate in Kent, they say."

"Yes, I've always thought so."

"Ah, yes. I forget you were often here as a boy."

Anthony glanced at him, but Ned was still surveying the grounds. "Not often."

Ned sighed. "Oftener than I. Fare thee well, Ham."

Anthony stood on the steps and raised one hand in

farewell as Ned mounted his horse and touched the brim of his hat in reply before riding off.

He walked to the stables and saddled Hestia himself, not bothering the grooms. He rode out around the lake, heading for the open fields and meadows. There was really nothing like riding early in the morning, Anthony thought, filling his lungs with crisp fresh air as Hestia stretched out her stride. He liked this part of the country. Perhaps he should surprise Celia with a property in Kent. He hadn't yet thought of another wedding gift for her.

He had reached the dirt road that led to the ruins where they had picnicked several days earlier when he heard a sharp crack somewhere to his left, in the woods. His horse laid her ears flat back on her head and snorted. Anthony pulled her up, glancing into the trees. That had sounded an awful lot like a pistol shot, but no one from the house was out shooting. Surely there wouldn't be poachers out this near the house.

The second shot took off his hat. Too startled even to curse, Anthony ducked low on Hestia's neck, instinctively grabbing for the hat. Who the bloody hell was shooting—and why? It was damned careless. "Hold your fire!" he shouted.

The third shot sounded closer than even the second. Hestia whinnied sharply and lunged forward, breaking into a gallop. It was all Anthony could do to keep his seat as she tore up the road. Another shot cracked, and Hestia swerved abruptly to the right, veering up the slope of the hill. The shift took Anthony off guard and he lost a stirrup, leaving him no choice but to cling to the horse's neck. He supposed Mr. Beecham hadn't trained the poor animal to remain calm whilst being shot at. Anthony found it rather alarming himself, particularly as he still had no idea who was doing the shooting, where they were hiding, or why they had taken such a dislike to him. Instead of trying to bring Hestia under control, he gave her her head and concentrated on staying in the saddle.

She must have run three miles or more before she finally slowed to a trot, her sides slick with sweat. Anthony guided her into the shelter of a stand of oaks before pulling her up and gingerly sliding to the ground.

The horse trembled as he examined her. She favored her left hind hoof, lifting it just off the ground, and Anthony finally realized what had made her bolt: a long, oozing gash across her flank. It wasn't clear if the pistol ball had gone into or merely scored her flesh; there was too much blood to tell. She snorted and stamped her hooves as Anthony probed the wound. "Shh," he crooned to quiet her, leaving it. There was nothing he could do to help her out here. He'd have to take her back to the stables.

Assuming he didn't get shot first, that is. All the while he tended the horse, Anthony kept one eye out for any sign of the marksman. The first shot had gone wide, the second struck his hat, the third his horse, and the fourth was also nearby. There was no conclusion to make except that he himself was the target.

Unfortunately, he wasn't quite sure where he was at the moment. In giving Hestia her head, he had let her outrun the boundaries of what he remembered of Ainsley Park. He set his hat, which he'd been unconsciously clutching all the while, back on his head and tried to think. They had headed south from the ruins for some time. His eyes constantly moving from side to side, Anthony adjusted the saddle and tack before swinging back onto the horse's back. He'd lead her if he could, but in case the fellow with the pistol had followed, he judged it better to be mounted.

"All right, let's go home," he murmured, wheeling her around and setting her into a walk. "The long, cautious way."

Chapter Twenty-Five

Although Celia had told her mother it was to be a small wedding, Rosalind insisted some things simply could not be omitted.

"Just because it is a small wedding it needn't be a plain wedding," she said as they walked in the garden. "Have you given any thought to what you shall wear?"

"No," said Celia, leaning down to sniff the just-opened rosebuds. It had been a week since they announced their engagement, and Celia had not spent much of it on the wedding. The Eltons and the Throckmortons had been called back to London, and Lord Snowden had also returned home to his nearby estate after the other guests left. The quieter house had meant more opportunities to sneak away with Anthony for an hour or two, and although he had stuck fast to his vow not to make love to her, they had found other, nearly as delightful, pleasures. Just yesterday he had pulled her into a linen cupboard and—

"I have sent to Madame Lescaut, although perhaps we shall just remake one of your newer gowns," Rosalind went on. "Hannah might lend you the lace mantua from her wedding, and of course you must wear some of the pearls."

"Mama, I don't care for pearls or lace." A rose had broken off, the bud hanging from the stem by a thread of green. She broke it off and held it up. "I shall just wear some roses in my hair. They smell so lovely."

Her mother sighed. "Of course, dearest, if that is what you wish."

Celia smiled, the same contented smile that she seemed to wear all the time now. "It is." She twirled the bud between her fingers, inhaling its soft fragrance. "There's no need to make over a gown. My blue silk will do. And we shall just have the guests who are still here."

Rosalind made a soft noise in the back of her throat. "What of the earl of Lynley?"

Celia paused. Anthony's father. They ought to invite him, but she suspected Anthony wouldn't want him. The little he had said about his father had not been warm. "I shall ask Anthony," she said at last. "But Mama, I think he may not wish to come in any event. He and his son do not get on well."

"Yes, I know. But Lynley is his father. We must invite him for propriety's sake."

Celia nibbled her lip, still fiddling with the rosebud. "I shall ask," she said again.

"Celia, I really think if you insisted—"

"Yes." She stopped and faced her mother. "Yes, Mama, if I insisted, Anthony would agree to invite him. But why must I insist? For propriety's sake? I don't care if Lord Lynley is here. I suspect Anthony would rather not see him, and why must I force the earl upon him on our wedding day?"

"Darling," began her mother in the calm but firm

voice that normally was not to be refused. "You shall
be a countess one day. Even if your husband does not
stand on these ceremonies, you must. It is the proper
thing to do, and it is your place to see to it."

"Mama, I want to be married quietly and happily.
Must we argue?"

Rosalind closed her eyes and took a breath, as if
praying for patience. "No," she said. "We must not."

"I *am* happy," Celia told her in a rush. "You do know
that, don't you? You have always done so much for
me, and for us all, and I don't want you to think I
don't appreciate your efforts, but in this I just want to
revel in being happy. I don't want to worry about appearances, not when the appearances might cause my
husband to be unhappy."

Rosalind sighed. "You are right. It is your wedding,
and I shall not overrule you. I—I am not accustomed
to seeing you as an independent woman, Celia. It is
hard for me to stop mothering you, especially after
you were gone so long and I've only just gotten you
back. I missed you so, dearest."

"Perhaps you don't need to stop mothering me,"
she replied with a grin. "Just treat me as you do Hannah
or Vivian."

Rosalind gave a tiny, embarrassed laugh. "As much
as I love my daughters-in-law, they are not you." She
reached out and laid one hand gently alongside
Celia's cheek. "You are my only child. For so many
years it was just we two, together, while your brothers
went off to school and had their own lives elsewhere.
I am not used to sharing you, nor being without you."

Celia suddenly realized what her mother was trying
to say. Rosalind had devoted her life to Celia. She had
been widowed before she was thirty, but she had never
remarried, instead staying quietly in the country to

raise Celia and to be as loving a mother as she could be to Marcus and David. Celia's happy childhood, her carefree life, even her impetuous first marriage, had all been due to Rosalind's care and attention.

And what would Celia have done, if she had had a child with Bertie? Would she have brought the child back to London after Bertie's death, or would she have stayed to raise the child in its father's home at Kenlington? It was a sobering thought. If she'd had the child she longed for, she would have stayed at Kenlington—and she wouldn't have fallen in love with Anthony. In that moment Celia was very selfishly happy she had not had a child after all, and at the same time she saw what her mother had given up for her. She threw her arms around her mother. "You must visit us often, Mama," she said, "for I cannot do without you, either."

Rosalind embraced her, then stepped back, her smile more firmly in place. "You must see that your husband finds a suitable estate, then. I can't have my daughter living in a cottage." They both laughed.

"Celia."

She looked around to see Marcus on the path. "Yes?"

"I must have a word with you."

A whisper of foreboding stole up her spine at her brother's words and manner. Something was wrong. "About what?"

Instead of answering he held out one hand. "Come with me."

"Marcus, what is it?" asked Rosalind in concern. He barely glanced at her.

"I am not certain. Perhaps only a misunderstanding. Celia?"

She shook herself. Perhaps it was only a misunderstanding. But she could see that Marcus didn't think it was. She squeezed her mother's hand and turned toward the house. "Yes, I'm coming."

Marcus wouldn't tell her anything as they walked. Each step along the gravel path seemed to twist the knot of anxiety in her stomach a little tighter. Before long the dread outweighed the curiosity, and when they reached Marcus's study and found David waiting outside the door, his face set, Celia had to fight off the urge to run away from whatever they had to tell her.

Her oldest brother ushered her into the study, and David closed the door behind them. Warily Celia sat down, glancing between the two of them. For once they looked completely alike, and identically grim. "What is it?" she asked again.

"Do you know where Mr. Hamilton is?" asked Marcus. "No one seems to have seen him in some time."

"No," she said slowly. "No, I haven't seen him since last night. Has he gone missing? Have you asked his valet?"

"The valet knows only that he rose early and went out dressed to ride," said David. "His horse is gone from the stables."

"We must go out looking for him!" Celia started to rise. "He may be hurt—"

"No one suspects that," said Marcus, putting out his hand to stay her. "We merely want to speak to him, but he is nowhere to be found. It seemed reasonable that you might have more knowledge of his whereabouts or plans than either of us."

She shook her head. "No." Her brothers exchanged a look, and Celia leapt to her feet. "Tell me!" she exclaimed. "What is wrong? Why are you looking for Anthony? Tell me this instant!"

Again they glanced at each other. "We're not certain," said Marcus.

"Celia, has he never mentioned anything about another attachment?" asked David. She stared at him in bewilderment. David cleared his throat. "About another woman," he clarified.

"No," she said.

"Did he never hint there might be difficulties regarding your marriage?" he pressed. "Any obstacle?"

"No."

"Did he ever tell you he had been married before?" asked Marcus softly.

She blinked, then gave a gasp of shocked laughter. "No. Not at all!"

David sighed and hung his head. Marcus closed his eyes. Celia threw up her hands.

"If you won't tell me what the matter is, I shall leave!" She turned toward the door.

"There is a woman," said Marcus behind her. "Here, in the small drawing room. She says she is Mrs. Hamilton. She says she is his wife."

For a moment Celia stood motionless with shock. She couldn't possibly have heard that correctly. Slowly she turned to face her brothers. "Impossible," she said numbly.

"She claims they have been married for some time. She heard news of your engagement to him and rushed here to prevent a scandal. She arrived this morning."

"Impossible," Celia whispered again.

"Celia, she has a child," said David gently.

She clutched her hands to her throat. Her chest seemed to be caving in on itself. Anthony, a liar and a bigamist? Could he have lied to her so much—and to this other woman as well? A black pit seemed to open in front of her, and for a moment she teetered on the brink of falling into it. Behind her the door opened quietly. A hand rested lightly on her shoulder. Celia started, jerking her head around to see her mother standing beside her, her face filled with compassion.

"It's impossible," she choked, wanting someone, anyone, to agree with her.

"Of course," said her mother at once. "Hannah told me the story. Marcus, you spoke to this woman?"

Without taking his eyes off Celia, he nodded. David crossed the room and held out a piece of paper. "She said this was his last message to her. Celia, do you know Hamilton's hand?"

She eyed the letter with alarm. Yes, she did know his hand. She knew every spike and slope of his writing, how he crossed his Ts with sharp slashes, how his words ended with a little curl to the last letter, a final flourish to the word. She couldn't bear to see that writing to someone else—to his wife.

She covered her mouth with one hand. Disloyal, treacherous thought—that meant she suspected he might be guilty. And she didn't, truly she didn't. Except . . . that letter . . .

As she stood in mute despair, her mother reached out and took the letter. She unfolded it and held it in front of them both, where Celia could see it without touching it. She tried to focus on the writing without taking in the words, but couldn't help it.

Dearest Fanny—
Received your note with great pleasure; it seems an age since I have seen you. I regret being unable to tell

you the latest good news in person but circumstances
require my presence here. No more than a month more,
I hope; I have missed you.

> *Yours ever,*
> *AH*

The silence in the room seemed to last forever. Finally Rosalind looked at David. "You must know his hand. Is this . . . ?"

David hesitated. "I am not certain."

Celia's stunned eyes moved back to the letter. It *was* very like his hand. She just couldn't believe it. "No," she said faintly.

"It's not?" David stepped closer to her, studying her intently. "You're certain it is not?"

"No." Carefully she shook her head. "I'm not certain. I just don't know." David exchanged another look with Marcus.

"We have to find him," he said.

"No," said Celia, her voice growing firmer and louder. "This letter makes no sense. He would never do such a thing, to me or to any woman. If he had a wife and child, he would never abandon them. He would never deceive me like this. What would he gain by it?"

"Celia, you are a very wealthy widow," said her brother. "Probably wealthier than he is."

"You don't know that." She turned to her mother. "Mama, you believe me, don't you?"

Rosalind blinked several times. "Celia, we should ask the man to explain," she began. Celia pulled away from her.

"Perhaps you require that, but I don't. I know he would never do this."

For a moment the room was silent again. Marcus

looked at David, who looked at Rosalind, who looked on the verge of tears as she wrung her hands and watched Celia.

"The stories about him, dearest," whispered her mother in anguish.

"Are mostly lies!" Celia burst out. "Where is Lord Warfield? He knows Anthony. Ask him!"

"And what are we to tell the woman?" Marcus leaned back against his desk, arms folded over his chest. "The one claiming to be his wife."

Celia pressed her hands to her temples. "I don't know—perhaps there is another gentleman with the same name. This woman might be confused, or mistaken. She might have never laid eyes on him before, and it will all turn out to be a terrible mistake."

David coughed. "Ahem."

"What?" He ignored her, instead looking at Marcus. Marcus's face had settled once more into forbidding lines. "What is it?" Celia demanded again. "Tell me, David!"

"She's laid eyes on him before," said her brother reluctantly. "I remember they were . . . companions. Years ago."

"And since?"

David was shaking his head even before Marcus's question. "I don't know. Hamilton and I aren't much in company anymore. He went off to Wales or someplace for a year or more, and we spoke only infrequently after he returned."

Marcus's eyes moved to Rosalind. She flushed. "I— I really don't know, Marcus. I have not been as much in London these past few years."

"Then we shall wait," said Marcus evenly.

"Wait?" Rosalind echoed.

"Until Hamilton returns," he said. "As Celia says,

there may be a terrible mistake. A man deserves a chance to explain. But if he's not back today, Celia . . ." His gaze softened on her. "It would look very bad."

"I don't know where he went!"

"I'll get Warfield and Simon," said David. "We'll ride out and have a look."

Marcus nodded. "Hannah will see to the woman and keep her quiet. I'll send into Maidstone and try to discover anything about this letter, and if it was sent from here."

"Celia, come with me," said her mother, laying her hands on Celia's shoulders. She shook them off and stood, tense and wretched, in the middle of the room.

"No," she said in a quavering voice.

Marcus came to stand in front of her. His face was etched with concern. "You must trust me in this."

"But you don't trust him," she whispered.

He sighed. "I want to know the truth."

"As do I."

"But you are in love with him," he answered gently. "I know what it is to love another so much that you would do anything for him, even sacrifice yourself. I need to know this man deserves you and your trust in him." She closed her eyes, and a tear leaked out to slide down her cheek. Marcus drew her into a firm embrace. "I love you, too," he whispered. "You are my only sister. I want you to be right about him."

Celia nodded, swiping at her eyes. "I know. Thank you, Marcus. I know he will prove honorable."

He smiled, touching her cheek. "Good girl. Now let David find him, and we'll sort this out."

She wiped away the rest of her tears. "I want to see her. The woman."

Rosalind gasped. Marcus's eyebrows went up. "Why?"

"I need to."

"Dearest, that's not wise," murmured her mother. Celia shook her head.

"I am not a fragile flower, Mama. Where is she?"

Marcus looked at Rosalind, then back at Celia. "In the small drawing room."

Celia walked through the house, feeling almost as if she were watching herself do it from some distant vantage point. She knew—she *knew*—Anthony hadn't betrayed her, not like this, but beyond that she couldn't say she knew anything. Who was this person? Why was she here? And what did she really want from Anthony—or was it something else altogether?

She slowed as she reached the drawing room door. She wanted to see the woman, not go in and converse with her. A maid approached with a tea tray, on Hannah's orders, no doubt. She bobbed a curtsy to Celia, then opened the door and went in with her tray. Celia inched forward and peered around the open door.

The woman was older than she'd expected, tall and handsome but with unmistakable traces of gray in her dark hair. Her clothing had probably been very fashionable a year or two ago but now showed signs of wear. As Celia watched, she selected a small cake from the tray and handed it to a child sitting beside her, a boy so small his feet dangled in mid-air off the edge of the sofa.

Celia gazed at the little boy. A handsome little boy about Thomas's age, with curly light brown hair and dark eyes. She remembered Anthony's face when he showed her the sheath, after he made love to her: *it prevents children,* he had said. *It spares a child from a lifetime of misery, not knowing who his father is.* Celia took in the serious little face, the chubby little hands that reached for the cake eagerly. Anthony would never abandon a child of his.

Silently she backed away from the open door, leaving the woman and boy to their tea. With slow, deliberate steps she walked away. Where was Anthony? He would explain all this away when he returned. Somehow.

Chapter Twenty-Six

Overflowing with fury, Rosalind stormed through the halls to her quarry's chambers. She knocked on the door and then threw it open. "Well?" she demanded. "What have you got to say for your nephew now?"

Lord Warfield looked astonished; the beaming smile that had spread across his face at her entrance faded. "Eh? What's that?"

"Your nephew. The liar, the seducer, the attempted bigamist. Imagine my surprise," she said in affected surprise, "when Exeter announced that Mr. Hamilton's *wife* had arrived. No, don't simply imagine *my* surprise; imagine my daughter's."

"Wife?" Warfield appeared thunderstruck. "Hamilton's not got a wife."

"And a child," she retorted viciously. "Here in the drawing room at this moment."

The earl put down his pen, got up from his desk, and slowly approached her. "It's a misunderstanding, no doubt. . . ."

"The only one who misunderstood," she replied coldly, "is I. I, who repressed my own doubts about him and didn't ask him to leave weeks ago. I, who said nothing as he seduced my daughter and persuaded her to marry him. I, who listened to assurances from you and David and Celia that he was honorable when I knew he was not!"

"Shh," he murmured. "You're overset, my dear."

"Don't call me that," she warned him. He stopped, looking abashed.

"What would you have me say, then? I tell you Hamilton's not married; you say he is. Your opinion is based on the word of some woman—I assume you don't know her?"

"I know of her." Rosalind lifted her chin. "The former Lady Drummond. Don't think I don't recall the gossip linking them, years ago. I simply never heard of their marriage."

"Drummond," Warfield muttered. "Certainly he never said a word about her to me. The lad's been nearly a recluse for the last few years, I promise you."

"He found time enough to father a son."

"Now, there's how I know it cannot be. Hamilton would never leave a child of his, not after the way his own father turned him out and let him believe himself a bastard all these years." Warfield's face creased. "And he wouldn't lie to your daughter. He's not that big a fool, no matter what else you think him. It makes no sense, aye? Bigamy's not easily hidden and swept under the rug. He'd lose everything."

Rosalind looked away from him. She didn't want to hear reason. She wanted confirmation and consolation. She wanted Anthony Hamilton publicly flogged and ripped limb from limb. She was so angry at him, for making her daughter so happy again and then bringing this upon her, she couldn't bear to hear anyone defend him on any grounds. "Celia will be devastated. I cannot bear to see that happen to her."

"But I say it can't be true." The sympathy and concern in the earl's face threatened to undercut her outrage and expose her despair. Rosalind clenched her jaw tight as he moved even closer. "If it is true, I'll take a whip to the lad myself," Warfield went on. "If it is true, I'll not say another word in his defense. You can abuse him to no end, toss him out, and cut him forever, and I'll not protest. But for your daughter's sake, you must wait until it's absolutely certain Hamilton's guilty."

She could only shake her head. "Celia," she said, her voice beginning to tremble. "She believes in him. . . ."

The earl took her hand. After a moment's resistance, she let him lead her to the sofa. Rosalind sank down, Warfield beside her. "Nothing has gone as I intended," she said in despair. "I hoped this house party would revive Celia's spirits—she was so downcast and quiet. As silent as a wraith, and almost as pale. I almost feared for her life, she was so melancholy. I never expected she would take up with anyone this month, certainly not in such a shocking way with such scandalous results. I missed my daughter, Lord Warfield. I just wanted her to be happy again."

"Of course you did." He took her hand and cupped it between his. "As any mother would want."

"And I could be happy for her if only I could be certain Mr. Hamilton would guard her heart and be worthy of her love. But I cannot shake my fear that he will leave her even more brokenhearted than before. What am I to do?"

"I don't know," he confessed. He was rubbing her hand very soothingly. Rosalind thought she ought to pull away, but it was too comforting. She was tired of worrying. It made her sick, not pleased, to have proof of Mr. Hamilton's duplicity. She had suspected him of seducing Celia, of taking advantage of Celia's grief and loneliness. She had never suspected him of this. The horror and betrayal on Celia's face was stamped on her mind. She closed her eyes, giving in to the comfort he was offering.

There was a knock on the door. Warfield released her hand, and Rosalind put it in her lap, unsettled by the feeling of loss. He had large, strong, warm hands, and it had been a long time since a man held her hand like that. She turned away from him, and he went to answer the door.

It was David. He explained in a few low words what had happened, inviting Warfield to go out looking for the missing Mr. Hamilton. The earl nodded once, looking rather grim. David caught sight of Rosalind then and paused, no doubt surprised to see her in Lord Warfield's rooms. She just nodded at her stepson, and he left without another word. Warfield closed the door and turned back to her.

"We're going out to find him."

She nodded again. She ought to go, but stayed where she was. Warfield approached her again and knelt in front of her. "He'll explain himself, and this mess, or he'll not darken the doors of this house again," he added, his voice hardening. "I give you my word."

And Rosalind felt a little of the tension ease. He would, she realized. It felt so good to feel reassured about something, she impulsively reached out and clasped his hand. "Thank you, sir."

He stared at her hands a moment with an odd expression. "Of course," he mumbled. Then, hesitantly, he lifted his hand, and hers with it. He brushed his lips across her knuckles and then rested his cheek against the spot for a second. It was unbearably tender. Rosalind's lips parted in astonishment, and he let go of her hand.

The earl avoided her gaze as he climbed to his feet. "I'll have to change," he said. "I'm to meet Reece in a half hour at the stable to ride out."

"Yes." She cleared her throat. "Thank you."

He nodded, staring at the carpet. Was that a flush on his neck? She crossed the room and left, hearing him shout to his valet as she closed the door.

In the hallway she paused again. A rough-mannered Scot. Unconsciously she rubbed her thumb over the spot where he had pressed her hand to his cheek. It was still out of the question, of course, but . . . Still clasping her hands together, she headed toward her chambers.

Anthony didn't know how long it took him to return to the house, but the sun was past overhead by the time he led Hestia into the Ainsley stable. The stable was emptier and quieter now that many of the guests had gone, so he took her into the stall himself, unsaddling her and examining her wound more carefully after sending a stable boy to look for Mr. Beecham.

The pistol ball had left a deep gash across his horse's flank, but Anthony eventually satisfied himself the ball itself wasn't embedded in her flesh. Mr. Beecham arrived, and Anthony explained what had happened. The young groom's eyes widened, and his mouth settled into a line, but he merely nodded and set about cleaning the injury.

"She'll be fine," Mr. Beecham told him when they had dressed the wound. "It'll leave a scar, no doubt, but better the horse than you, sir."

Anthony glanced at his horse, now standing quietly

in her stall, eyes half-closed in exhaustion from her ordeal. "Yes. Some comfort, but not much. Another foot lower and she'd have to be put down."

Mr. Beecham nodded. "Another foot higher and it might have put *you* down, sir." He squinted at Anthony's hat. "Always better the horse than you."

Anthony removed his hat, finally noticing what had attracted Mr. Beecham's attention. A hole, right above the brim, straight through. He stuck one finger through it; nice and clean on both sides. The shot had been fired from nearby. Unless there had been a pheasant perched unnoticed on his shoulder, this shot, and the others with it, had been meant for him. The skin on his neck prickled, and he fought the urge to turn in a circle and see if anyone watched him.

Someone had tried to kill him. But who? And why?

He left Mr. Beecham to watch after Hestia and walked quickly back to the house, tense and on edge. His eyes darted back and forth, alert for any sign of movement. He didn't exhale until he reached the safety of the mansion, but even then none of the tension in his shoulders eased. With no idea who was behind it, he hardly knew what to do. He must tell the duke, of course. The entire party should be careful until they had more knowledge of who was behind it and why. It could have been a poacher, who might have shot at anyone who happened to be there. Four shots could mean more than one shooter, or one man who reloaded. Neither possibility was reassuring.

David Reece met him just inside the hall. He was dressed to ride, and—Anthony couldn't help noticing—carried a pair of pistols. David stopped short at the sight of him. "Hamilton," he said, half-relieved, half-warily. "There you are."

"Yes." Anthony slowed to a halt himself. "Here I am. Was I wanted?"

David drew closer, watching him with unexpected scrutiny. "I should say so. Where were you?"

From long habit, Anthony withdrew into reticence when questioned. "Riding."

"Where?"

"About the estate."

"Long ride," David observed. Anthony merely nodded once. What the devil was going on? "Planned?"

"No," he said. "Not particularly." David's eyes narrowed. "Who wanted me, then? Celia?"

David took his time replying. "I suppose she might. Perhaps not. I should like to have a word with you myself."

"Ah. No offense, but I'd rather see her."

"I wouldn't be so sure of that, if I were you," muttered David. "You've had a caller this morning."

"Indeed?" Anthony wished David would just come out with whatever was making him tight-lipped and enigmatic.

"Indeed." David bent a piercing stare on him. "Your wife."

For a moment Anthony didn't understand. He frowned. Celia wasn't yet his wife—and David had already said she wanted to see him. Why would David say that?

"Not my sister," said David with cold clarity. "Your first wife. And her son."

Anthony felt a strange sense of unreality steal over him. "My wife," he repeated in a blank tone.

"And son," David added.

He didn't have a wife or a son. But if a woman and child had arrived and claimed to be such . . . and

David Reece believed them . . . "Where is Celia?" he asked again.

"In the library. Perhaps she'll see you, perhaps not." Anthony nodded mutely. David frowned. "Haven't you anything to say for yourself, Hamilton?"

"No," he murmured, his mind racing frantically. Who the devil could it be? Did Celia know? What must she believe? "Where . . . ?"

"The small drawing room. Come, man, explain yourself!" David said. "No one wants to believe it, but if you don't even deny it—"

"Excuse me." Absently Anthony handed David his ruined hat and turned toward the small drawing room, ignoring David's surprised exclamation behind him. Had he been shot at to keep him from returning to refute this woman? Was she behind the shooting? Or was he just having a spectacularly unlucky day?

Outside the drawing room he hesitated. Who would be on the other side of the door? Slowly Anthony let himself into the room. A woman was bent over a little boy, wiping his face with a serviette from the tea tray on the table, but she straightened at the sound of the door, turning to face him. For a moment they stared at each other in silence.

"Fanny," said Anthony, his voice sounding distant.

She curtsied. "Anthony."

He had not seen her in at least two years, not since he returned from Cornwall. They had corresponded for some time, but he hadn't heard from her since her marriage; she had removed to Yorkshire shortly thereafter. She looked much the same, but the years had left their mark. Her dark hair was now threaded with silver, and there were fine lines around her mouth and eyes. It gave him an odd feeling to see her again.

He waved one hand at a pair of chairs. She took

one, and he took the other. "What a surprise to see you again."

Color rose in her cheeks. She gave a forced laugh. "Is it?"

"A very great surprise. I thought you happily ensconced in Yorkshire."

She abandoned all pretense of a smile. "No. Or rather, I was, until recently."

The child followed her then, glancing at Anthony with curious but wary eyes. Fanny pulled him close to her side, smoothing one hand over his curls. "A handsome child," said Anthony.

She smiled fondly at her son. "Thank you." She glanced at him. "I'm sorry I may have allowed the duke to think him yours."

"Yes, people do seem to have that impression," replied Anthony dryly.

Fanny flushed. "And I am sorry. But Anthony—I had little choice. My circumstances are wretched."

"Are they?" He felt no sympathy, still thinking of what Celia must have thought when she heard Fanny's false tale. "And am I to blame?"

Her cheeks grew even redder. "No," she said shortly. "But I am desperate, and for my son I'm willing to sacrifice some honesty."

"And my name, apparently."

Fanny's mouth tightened. "I have nowhere else to turn. I hoped you would help me, out of affection and perhaps in thanks for my help to you when you were in similar circumstances."

He looked at the boy. A dark-eyed, curly-headed child, somberly watching and listening to every word. "I am not certain I understand you."

"You know very well what I mean!" She surged to her feet. "I gave you ten thousand pounds to start your tin mines. Without me, you'd have no fortune at all. You'd be just another gambler, just another rake in London. Now you're a gentleman with airs and servants and an heiress bride."

"That is true," he agreed. "Your money helped me make my fortune. But it also made yours. I paid you a healthy rate of return, turning you a very handsome profit. It was a business arrangement, Fanny, and one that served you very well."

"Well, it's gone now!" Her son whimpered, and she patted him on the back. "It's all gone. My husband was not good with funds. He ran through it and then had the gall to break his neck and leave me alone. I didn't know until he died that he'd lost it all. His creditors took everything within a month of his death. I have nothing, Anthony. Nothing."

"So you've come to blackmail me for more."

"I have nowhere else to turn!" she said again.

Anthony sighed and hung his head, massaging his brow. "Fanny, don't. Did you think I wouldn't have helped you if you just asked? Why did you come here, and not just come but tell everyone we're married and you've borne me a son? What did you plan to do next if I simply refused? You have no proof, because none of it's true."

Fanny's bravado wavered. She bowed her head and stroked her son's hair. "I'm desperate. It was a risk, but one I had to take, for my son's sake. I was wrong to say we were married, but I feared once you wed your heiress you would never agree to see me."

Anthony sighed again. "How old is the boy?"

"Two years," she said, her voice trembling. "Two years old, and no father. Only a penniless mother."

Anthony looked at the quiet little boy with a heavy heart. The child stared steadily back with no expression.

"He has a mother who loves him," he said. "Don't undervalue that."

Fanny bit her lip, then gave a little sob and held her son close for a moment. "But what good am I to him if I can't provide for him? If I can't protect him?" She dabbed her eyes with a threadbare handkerchief. "I never thought I would have a child, and then—he's everything to me now. But I'm not young, and I have no family; if something were to happen to me, what would become of my darling boy? Should I let him go to the workhouse or be cast on the parish?" A bitter laugh escaped her. "Oh, what a fool I am. It was a ridiculous notion from the start, but I—I didn't think clearly. I hoped—I hoped you would take pity on me, but I was wrong. He made me think this was the only way, and in my desperation I believed it. I am sorry, Anthony."

Anthony raised his head. "Who made you think that?"

Fanny flushed again. "I wasn't to mention him. He claimed he suggested the plan out of a sense of decency, but I see now he lied to me." She sighed. "Why should I keep his secrets, when he deceived me? It was your friend Mr. Childress."

Anthony didn't move for several minutes. He felt no surprise at the name Fanny said, only an odd sense of vindication. He hadn't been wrong to distrust Ned, then; but why? What had Ned to gain by attaching yet another scandal to Anthony's name? Surely he didn't think this contretemps with Fanny would cause Celia to fall into his arms. Was it just revenge for his disappointment?

"Here." Fanny dug in her reticule and pulled out a letter. "This is what he wrote me a week ago, saying you were about to make an advantageous marriage and resume your title. He suggested that if I were to act before the wedding, it could prove profitable. It—

it was a mad plan, and if I had been myself, I should never . . ." Her voice faded as Anthony took the letter, silently opening it and reading the damning message in Ned's clear, crisp hand.

At his prolonged silence, Fanny grew more defeated. Her shoulders slumped, and a shadow seemed to pass over her face. For a moment she looked even older than her forty-three years. "I am sorry," she said again. "So sorry. I shan't bother you again."

"Fanny," said Anthony as she reached the door, holding her son's hand. She paused and turned back. "I will help you."

Cautious hope sprang into her eyes.

"I will help you," he repeated, "but only on the condition that you confess to Exeter and the rest of his family that you lied to them about our relationship and that you never again claim any man as the father of your son except your late husband." He looked at the child again. "A boy should know who his father is."

Without a word she nodded.

"But Fanny, this is the last time." He shook his head slowly. "I would have helped you if you had only asked me."

Her chin trembled. "I know," she whispered. "I should have known."

"Where are you staying?"

"At the inn in Maidstone."

Anthony folded the letter with care. "I shall send a bank draft today."

She closed her eyes and sighed, then gave a little nod. "Thank you. I shall make my explanations and apologies to His Grace before I go."

"Goodbye, Fanny."

"Goodbye," she whispered, and then she was gone, taking her son with her.

Chapter Twenty-Seven

For a moment Anthony just sat in the drawing room, a ray of sunlight warming his legs but not driving away the chill he felt. Fanny had almost destroyed him—for money. Ned had incited her to do it—for spite. Perhaps he ought to break it off with Celia himself, Anthony thought darkly, on account of his extremely poor judgment of character, if these were the people he called friends.

Celia. Slowly he rose and turned to the door. He crossed the room and opened it, then started toward the library, his steps faster and faster until he was almost running. His heart thumped painfully against his ribs as he threw open the door. Was she still here? Was she—?

Celia looked up as he burst into the room. She was composed, unnaturally so for a woman whose betrothed husband had just been confronted by his supposed wife and son. Anthony's heart stopped pounding; it seemed to stop altogether.

"Celia," he said, then stopped. He didn't know what to say. He would be lost without her.

"Has she gone?" asked Celia. She was the picture of

calm, seated on a small sofa near the French windows that led into the garden. Her hands lay folded in her lap. There was no sign of the emotional storm he had expected. No trace of tears marred her cheeks, no flush of anger colored her complexion. Suddenly Anthony wished it did. He wished she had met him with all the fury of a woman betrayed, thrown things at his head and called him names. It would mean she cared.

"Celia, what you must think of me," he began desperately, coming toward her. "I swear to you she's not my wife. The child is not mine. . . ."

She shook her head. "No," she said. "You don't need to protest. I never doubted you, Anthony."

Anthony stood with his mouth open, staring at her. She never doubted him, not even when presented with another woman who called herself his wife and claimed to have his son?

"I knew you would never lie to me," she went on. "I knew you would never desert a child of yours. I knew—"

He hauled her into his arms and kissed her then, not caring what else she knew. He knew she loved him, and even stranger, she believed in him. When he lifted his head, she gazed up at him.

"Did you really think I could believe something like that of you?" she whispered, laying her hand on his cheek.

Anthony covered her hand with his own. "Most women would have."

"Ah, but I am not most other women." Her mouth quirked wryly.

"Indeed not." He gazed into the clear blue depths of her eyes. He would be worse than lost without her. "You are the only woman for me."

She touched his lower lip with the tip of her finger. "I knew that."

He took her wrist and held her hand in place, pressing his lips to her fingertips, then to her knuckles, then to her palm. "She's gone to admit she lied to your brother. She—Celia, she was once a friend of mine." He hesitated, clearing his throat. "She was once my lover. Years ago," he quickly added. "She invested funds in my tin mines and we had an affair. It was long ago, and she married someone else—the father of her child. She came here because her husband died and left her penniless, and she wanted to support her child. She said she was my wife because she hoped I would give her money to disappear, and not disrupt our wedding."

She studied him a moment with sympathetic eyes. "You gave it to her, didn't you?"

Anthony took his time answering. "Yes. But only because she confessed all to me, and promised to tell your family the same."

Celia smiled up at him. "How anyone thinks you are cold and calculating, I shall never guess. You're as soft-hearted as I, Anthony Hamilton."

He frowned in alarm. "Indeed not."

"Then why did you give her the money?"

"Are you saying I should not do so?"

"No," she said softly. "I would never condemn you for compassion."

Anthony closed his eyes and rested his forehead against hers. Celia slid her arms around him and just held him. The tension that had gripped him for what seemed like hours melted away, and he felt at peace. But after a moment he gently removed her arms and stepped away. There was more he had to say, more he needed to say before he could accept her love with a clean conscience.

"Celia," he said, "I have not been honest with you." Her expression slowly went blank. "There are things I ought to have told you—things you deserved to know before deciding to marry me. And like a fool, I thought I wouldn't have to tell you, wouldn't have to—" He broke off and ran his hands over his face. "I thought I wouldn't have to confess my failings."

"Everyone has failings," she said.

Anthony gave a harsh, despairing laugh. "Undoubtedly. But wait until you hear what I must tell you, before you judge." She opened her mouth, clearly about to protest, but then simply nodded. Anthony took a deep breath. Not even when the duke of Exeter had questioned him the other day had he revealed all he was about to reveal.

Celia had to know, though. She had to know before she tied herself to him for life, when she still had time to walk away. He had been fooling himself if he thought he could simply forget about his past, or that by not speaking of it, he could pretend it had never happened at all and that it wouldn't come back to haunt him. Celia was trusting and warmhearted enough that she wouldn't ask, but that didn't pardon his silence. Haltingly, barely able to look at her, he began to speak.

"I told you my father was angry when I was dismissed from school. No doubt he was, but more likely he was relieved. My mother had just died. She had been the only reason I ever tried to please him. He made her life miserable when I disgraced him; he blamed her for my faults. When she died he told me not to come back to Lynley Court, and I was only too glad not to.

"I was only fifteen and had no way to live. Celia, I—

I—" He sighed. "I cheated," he said softly. "I took exams for other people, for money, until I had finished school. I gambled. I had always been good at cards, and became much better. In London one can wager on anything, and I did. But it was still small money, enough to live but not enough to be settled. I couldn't give it up for long. I wanted more. I wanted wealth. I wanted to show Lynley I didn't need him or his estate or his money.

"I decided I must make investments, and took to playing on the 'Change. By sitting at tables with men in finance I learned things, and got ideas. I read the lists and found patterns in numbers that meant something to me. I liked making money," he confessed. It was a rather low-class thing to admit to, which was why Anthony never discussed it with anyone. "But to invest money, one must have it, and to get it . . ." He didn't want to tell her this part especially. He was too afraid of her reaction. "I got the money from women," he finally said, very quietly.

Her eyes were perfectly round. One hand crept to her stomach. "How?"

"As loans," he said, knowing it still sounded suspicious. "I would propose a bargain, one where they gave me money to invest and I repaid it with interest. I made money for them when their husbands would give them none. I told myself I was giving them some independence, some control of their lives."

"But that's not so bad," Celia exclaimed, as if he had just shown her the noble motive in his ignoble actions.

Anthony felt sick. "Perhaps not," he managed to say, "but I had affairs with some of them." He paused. "With several of them. Including Fanny."

"All of them?"

"No," he said even before she completed her question. "Not all of them."

"Oh." She quieted again, gazing at him with sad eyes.

He swallowed. "Some no doubt would say I seduced them to get their money. I never thought of it as such, but I was young—it was almost a game to me. I saw only the pleasure and the money, and the thrill of success. I made mistakes. I became entangled with women who could not be discreet, and as a result I became known as a seducer and a rake."

"Oh, Anthony," she whispered. "If I had known what you endured—"

"Don't." She flinched from his harsh tone. "What I *chose*. I chose to do it all, every wager, every seduction, every lie. A better man would have found a better way—"

"But you chose the more difficult way." She stepped toward him, her face filled with compassion. "Another man would have borrowed and borrowed, or lived off relatives and friends, or even stolen it. You chose to make yourself an island, didn't you? Where no one else would be hurt by your actions. And that way you were free to do what you must to survive."

"But I've hurt *you*."

She shook her head. "It hurts me to think that you have felt yourself less than worthy. That your father made you to feel like an impostor and a thief. But you . . . how can I judge you? I have never been poor with no way to live. I have never found myself alone in the world. I hope I would have been strong enough to endure the slurs and slights you suffered, but I never had to."

"How very charming," said a voice behind him. "No wonder you want to marry this one. She's making your excuses for you, Ham."

Anthony turned at the voice. Ned stepped into the

library through one of the open French windows. He was dusty and a bit disheveled, and there was a curious brightness in his eyes. Something was off.

"I thought you were required in town, Ned."

"Ah, yes. So I was. So I am. I just have a few things here that needed doing first, however."

Anthony put the pieces together then. Ned, who had wanted to marry a wealthy bride—namely, Celia. Ned, who had barely spoken to him since Celia's engagement to him was announced. Ned, who couldn't resist little jibes and barbs, who had been out riding this morning early, and who knew all about Fanny and Anthony's relationship with her. Ned, who brought a pistol from behind his back even as he smiled at them.

"You shot at me earlier," Anthony said, shifting his weight slightly to one side. Celia gasped, her eyes flying to Ned and growing wide at the sight of the gun. "And now you've come to try again?"

Ned sighed. "Well, I don't *want* to. But a fellow's got to live, doesn't he?"

"You *shot* at him? How does shooting Anthony help you?" cried Celia. "You're his friend!"

"That's why I'd prefer not to shoot him," said Ned patiently, as if she and Anthony were both being obtuse. "He's a capital chap, and I have really nothing against him except his infernal luck at cards. But the fact remains that I'm in desperate straits, and he's snatched away the wealthy widow I had my eye on." Celia's mouth dropped open in outrage. Ned laid one hand over his heart. "I swear to you, dear lady, that I would be a most devoted husband. If you could be persuaded to transfer your affections to me, there would be no need for any of this . . ." He waited, eyebrows raised in expectation. Celia clamped her lips together and shook her head, glaring at him. Ned sighed again. "I feared as much. There's nothing for it, then, but a little persuasion. Come along, Lady Bertram."

"I will not, you cowardly, shameful, lying—"

"Yes, yes, I take your meaning. But I really must insist."

"What will it gain you?" Anthony's eyes never wavered from the pistol. He moved another step to the side, subtly easing between Ned and Celia.

"I did think to marry her myself . . ." Celia hissed at him, and Ned laughed. "But I've no fancy to be killed in my sleep. Don't fret, Hamilton, just a spot of ransom. You'll get her back in good order. Most likely in time for the wedding, even."

"I might agree to that," said Anthony slowly, "but I don't trust you, Ned. So I must refuse on Lady Bertram's behalf, as her betrothed husband."

Ned sighed. "Please? I won't beg, but it would make things easier if you both cooperated."

"Why did you involve Fanny?" Anthony asked instead.

"Oh." Ned made a face and gave an embarrassed little laugh. "A rash decision. I had a bit much to drink after Exeter announced your engagement and . . . well, I dashed off the letter to Fanny without thinking. Rather forced my hand, too. Once she was en route, I had no choice. See, I really didn't want to shoot him," he turned to explain to Celia. "I *had* to. She was on her way; the die was cast. There was no room for retreat, and I had to go on with the plan."

"You might have killed him," Celia said through her teeth.

Ned appeared wounded. "I am not a killer, madame. I aimed for his arm."

"And hit the ground, my hat, my horse, and Lord

knows what else," said Anthony. "Being a bad shot is no defense against murder."

"He hit your horse?" Something shattered against the wall beside Ned, making both men jump. "And your hat?" Ned yelped, barely ducking out of the way in time as Celia hurled a small china figure at him. It wasn't quite sporting, but it was opportune. Anthony dove across the sofa, tackling Ned to the floor as Celia threw another figurine at him.

Ned cursed, trying to roll him over, but Anthony jabbed an elbow into Ned's stomach and held onto the hand that held the pistol. They rolled back and forth on the broken china, struggling to gain possession of the pistol, or at least aim it, until Ned gave a whoof of surprise, and his grip loosened. Anthony twisted sharply, but Ned managed to maintain a grip on the gun.

"You despicable, wretched liar!" Celia whacked at Ned's head again with her weapon, a leather-bound book. "You're a horrible person and a bad shot and a miserable poet—"

"Celia, get out of the way!" Anthony commanded, still wrestling with Ned for the gun. His supposed friend had looped an arm around his neck and was pressing on his throat.

"I want to help!" she cried.

"Ring the bell," Anthony croaked. Ned wrenched his head around, and Anthony felt his cramped fingers begin to slip from the pistol's stock. He sucked in as deep a breath as he could and slammed his shoulder into Ned's stomach, letting his weight fall on the other man. Ned grunted, and Anthony ripped the pistol out of his hand.

"Ring the bell," he repeated, staggering to his feet as Celia ran across the room for the bell rope. Ned stayed on the floor, curled on his side, his chest heaving. "Good God, Ned, why?" It was all he could think of to ask: Why, why, why?

Ned squinted up at him. "For the money, obviously."

"I would have helped you," said Anthony, still shocked to his core that a man who had been like a brother to him would try to kill him. "Warfield would have."

Ned gave a sharp, bitter laugh. "I don't need a few pounds. I don't need a loan. I have debts, Ham. Rather crushing debts. It's expensive to lead a gentleman's life with no title and no fortune waiting for a fellow. If only I'd had your luck at cards."

"It's not luck!" said Celia furiously.

Ned rolled his eyes and pushed himself up with a grimace. "As you like. The fact remains that I need money, and this lady is the key to the treasure chest."

"You would threaten her life over a few thousand pounds—"

"*Crushing* debts," Ned repeated. "I really can't settle for less than thirty thousand. I know you can't pay out that much immediately, but Exeter could. Come along, my dear. We really must go." And he pulled another pistol from the pocket of his coat.

Anthony raised his arm at once and pulled the trigger. The only sound, though, was a tinny click. Ned looked at the pistol pointed at him and grinned, a cruelly bitter expression. "I really didn't want to hurt anyone," he said as he got to his feet. "You'll notice that pistol was unloaded. This one, however"—he raised his second gun—"is. Now, my lady, come along, and please don't throw any more china at me."

"Celia, leave the room," said Anthony as he lowered his arm. She hesitated, then began backing toward the door. Ned swung the pistol around to point it at her. Celia froze, glancing at Anthony.

"This way, Lady Bertram," repeated Ned. His face had hardened, and he didn't look half so charming or handsome now. A trickle of blood ran down his cheek from a cut by his eye, and the light in his eyes was no longer amused but deadly, madly serious. Celia didn't know what to do. She had been so angry a few minutes ago, it hadn't occurred to her to be frightened, but now she was—and grew more so when Anthony stepped directly between her and Ned's cocked pistol.

"Go on, Celia," said Anthony in the same eerily calm tone. "You aren't going with him."

"I would prefer not to shoot you, Hamilton, but I will. Don't tempt me to tell you how I shall persuade the lady if I must use this shot on you."

"No," said Anthony. "Put down the pistol, Ned." Celia edged backward, thinking frantically. She did not want to leave Anthony alone with an armed madman, but if she stayed, she would only distract him. She reached the door and felt behind her for the knob, unable to look away from the two men, unable to blink. Every time Ned moved a step to one side, Anthony moved with him, staying squarely between him and Celia. She had to get help, if only she could get out of the blasted room. She ran both hands over the wood behind her, searching for the blasted doorknob as her stomach knotted in incipient panic.

"God damn it," said Ned impatiently. "I'm not going to regret this as much as I thought." And the pistol went off.

Celia froze in anguish as Anthony jerked. *No,* wailed her heart. *No, no, no . . .* But he didn't fall to the floor. He spun around, gazing incredulously somewhere to

Celia's left. She turned her head and saw that she had missed the door entirely; she had been feeling the wainscoting several feet away from it. Which was probably rather fortunate.

Lord Warfield stood in the doorway, a smoking pistol in his outstretched hand. His face was stark white, carved with lines of grief. Ned stared at him a moment, shock written large on his face, then dropped to the floor without a sound. The pistol clattered to the floor beside him.

Celia scrambled across the room, her heart almost bursting out of her chest. Was he hurt? Had Ned managed to fire and hit him? She'd only heard one shot, but if they had fired at the same moment . . . Anthony was just standing there, seemingly stunned. She threw herself at him, holding on tightly in case he was about to collapse. "Are you hurt? Did he shoot you?"

His arm came up around her. "No," he said, his voice dazed. "He didn't."

Celia choked, then gave a sob, and another. Anthony closed his eyes and held her close, absorbing every shudder and tear. If Ned had shot her, he would have died, too—in spirit if not in body. His only thought had been to get her safely out of the room, and then . . .then . . .

Anthony didn't want to think about Ned. He still trembled from the white-hot anger that had gripped him when he realized Ned meant to hold Celia—with a pistol to her heart—for ransom, but he knew later would come sorrow, for the betrayal by such a friend, and regret, that he never knew how desperate Ned had become before turning to attempted murder and fraud. Later . . . later he would feel the loss of a friend he had trusted and liked.

But he still had Celia. His arms tightened around her, and his eyes burned. Thank God he had her.

"Oh, good heavens—Celia!" Rosalind had heard the shot from the hall and come running. She rushed up behind Lord Warfield, who was just standing in the doorway for some odd reason, and pushed at him. "Celia!" she cried again, unable to see into the room.

"Don't fear," said Warfield in a heavy voice as he moved aside to let her pass. "She's in no danger now." He had a pistol in his hand and he wore riding clothes; she remembered that he had been on his way to meet David and ride out looking for Mr. Hamilton. Rosalind turned to search for her daughter, fearing the worst, only to realize Celia was fine. She clung to Mr. Hamilton, and he to her, as if neither would ever let go. Behind them Mr. Childress sat slumped on the floor, his shirt front red with blood and a pistol on the floor beside him.

"What happened?" Rosalind gasped. Warfield turned away, staggering toward the wall, and instinctively she reached out to steady him.

"Ned," was all he said. "Ned."

Rosalind looked at his ashen face and without a word took the pistol from his shaking hand and let him lean on her shoulder.

The room filled with people, alerted by the gunshot and by the servant who had come when Celia rang the bell and then gone in search of help. Marcus directed some footmen to carry away Ned, who was seriously injured but not dead, and to send for a surgeon at once. David handed Anthony the pistol Ned had dropped. Anthony let go of Celia long enough to see that it was loaded, and then he handed it back to David without a word. Celia tried to murmur an apology to Hannah for destroying the collection of china figurines that used to stand on the table near the fireplace, and Hannah only remarked on her excellent aim. Rosalind undertook to comfort Lord Warfield, and the servants began filtering in to clean the room.

As others stepped in to take control, Anthony took Celia by the hand and led her out of the house, almost running through the garden, across the lawn. There he stopped and turned to her. "Do you still want to marry me?"

She blinked, out of breath. "Why—"

"I would understand if you said no," he said, almost arguing. "I've brought nothing but scandal and danger upon you, and any sensible woman would no doubt be grateful to be released from our engagement."

"But I'm not," Celia said. "I want to marry you."

"Because I love you." He spoke almost over her words. "I have never loved another—never. It was affection, or lust, or friendship, but never love. Not like I feel for you. If he had shot you—"

She put her hand over his mouth. "He didn't."

Anthony bowed his head. "If you don't want me, say it now, I beg you. I don't know how I'll bear it, but . . ."

"You won't have to," she said. "I want to marry you. I love you."

"I love you," he repeated. His grip tightened on her hand. "I love you."

Celia smiled. If she didn't smile, she might cry. "I know," she told him softly. "I've known that for a while now."

That night he knocked on her door late, very late. Celia started to exclaim in surprise when she saw him standing there, but he pressed a finger to her lips, warning her to be quiet. He took her hand and together they stole out of the quiet house, down to the lake. Anthony helped her into one of the boats and handed her a thick blanket. He rowed them out a short way, until it seemed the two of them floated alone in a world of stars, above in the sky and reflected below in the water.

Then he sat on the bottom of the boat and pulled her into his arms, tucking the blanket around them. Celia leaned back against his chest, his arms around her, and gazed up at the night sky.

"You asked me once, here on the lake, why I wanted to marry you," he whispered. "I couldn't tell you. I still can't."

She turned her head to look at him in confusion.

"I can't tell you because there isn't a single reason," he went on. "There are as many reasons as there are stars above us. I could no more list them all than I could name those stars, but my reasons are just as real and just as fixed."

"I was wrong to ask you that," she murmured.

"No, you can always ask me anything you want. I have nothing to hide from you." He shifted, settling her more comfortably against him. "I have known you were the girl for me since you threw my boots in the lake, right over there." He indicated the rock they used to dive from when they were children.

Celia frowned. "I never threw your boots in the lake."

Anthony laughed, a low, warm rumble in his chest she could feel through her entire body. "It was the first time I had come to Ainsley Park. Your brother invited several of us from Oxford, and we wanted to go fishing. You clamored to come along. David said you were too small to bait the hook and could not come with us, but you followed and threw in a pair of boots after we had all waded into the lake. 'There,' you shouted in a fine fury. 'I am not too small to do that!' And you stormed off. But they were my boots, not your brother's."

Celia's eyes rounded. "But—but I was only a child then! And why did you never tell me they were your boots? I surely thought I had punished David quite thoroughly, for he was always ruining his boots and never had a spare pair."

"You were eight, and you stood up for yourself," Anthony said with a smile. "And I thought, that girl has spirit."

"But that does not mean you loved me," she said slowly. His smile faltered.

"You were the daughter of the duke of Exeter," he said simply. "I was the cuckoo in the Lynley nest. Love was not something I was permitted to feel for you."

"Permitted," she said in disbelief. "Permitted by whom?"

"By society. By your family. By myself." He sighed. "I had a great deal of affection for you—like a sister, I told myself. And it was. But then I saw you again, years later, during your Season. It was right after Euston had made you an utterly absurd marriage proposal and you said something that night, as we were laughing at him. You were so beautiful that night." His voice softened. "You said you were the only person in London who knew I wasn't half so bad as I pretended."

Celia's mind whirled. She remembered Lord Euston's ridiculous proposal, and she remembered Anthony had saved her from it; she even remembered wondering what it would be like if he had kissed her. But that was so long ago. She had been a naive, silly girl then, still harboring romantic fantasies without a single thought about what marriage—of what love—was really like. Anthony, even then, couldn't possibly have had an interest in *her* . . .

"I could never see you in a sisterly way again." Anthony looked a little abashed. "I even dared to ask Exeter permission to call on you."

She gasped, sitting bolt upright and making the boat rock. "No! You did? But I had no idea! He never said a word to me. Did he refuse? Did he—?"

"He had just given Bertram his consent to marry you."

Celia closed her mouth. For a moment she tried to think what life would have been like, if Anthony had courted her, if she had married him then instead of Bertie. Bertie might have married someone better suited to him; he might still be alive and well, perhaps with children to please his father. Anthony would not have been so alone and aloof for those years. And she . . .

"There is no way of knowing what might have been, if I had asked him a few weeks sooner," said Anthony gently, as if he could hear her thoughts. "We were both different then."

Yes, Celia realized, she certainly was. Four years ago she was a silly, foolish girl, filled with shallow fancies of love and adoration. Could she have even appreciated Anthony then? Certainly not as she did now. Having been lonely and unhappy herself, she understood him—and knew all the better what he had gone through to make him the man he was. Wordlessly, she rested her cheek on his hand where it cupped her shoulder. The backs of his knuckles were scraped and bruised from his struggle with Ned.

"I would not change a thing," he murmured against her hair. "I would have waited fifty years for this."

Celia smiled. Anthony was a greater romantic than

anyone knew—anyone except her. Hannah had been right; the people who said he was wicked and cold-hearted didn't know him at all. "I'm glad you did not."

He laughed again. "It certainly felt like it at times."

"Especially today."

His arms around her tightened. "Yes."

Celia turned to face him. She didn't want to talk about that again, not now. "You teased me once about making love in a boat."

Even in the moonlight she could see his eyes gleam in a reluctant smile. "If we should tip the boat, it would be an ignominious end to the evening."

"Well," she said softly as she reached up to kiss him, "we'd better be careful, then."

Chapter Twenty-Eight

It was a small wedding, nothing like her first one. It was in the Ainsley Park chapel instead of St. George's in London, and only her family and a few friends attended. She simply wore her best dress instead of an elaborate gown specially made, and her bouquet was a bunch of flowers picked by the bridegroom in a nearby field instead of hothouse lilies wrapped in lace. But Celia thought there was a beauty and a joy in this wedding that had been lacking in the first. The spectacle of that occasion had filled her vision and left little room for anything or anyone else. Today, all she could see and think of was Anthony, standing straight and true at the altar waiting for her.

This time she heard every word of the vows they exchanged. Her hand trembled as Anthony slid the gold band on her finger. When the vicar pronounced them man and wife and said the blessing, it was all she could do not to fling herself into Anthony's arms.

"Happy, darling?" Anthony asked after they had signed their names together in the register.

"Tolerably," she said, then burst out laughing as he blinked. "Must you even ask?"

He grinned in relief. "I've forgotten all sensible conversation today. Everyone will wonder why you married such a fool."

"Then I shall tell them all, quite happily," she declared as they walked out of the chapel into the sunlight. "I married him for love."

Rosalind dabbed at her eyes as she watched her daughter and her new son-in-law walk down the steps. They had eyes only for each other. He truly did love her, she realized, as much as Celia loved him. In place of the anxiety that thought would have wrought only a few days ago, she felt only relief. And peace. Anyone could see Celia was happier than she had been in years. If Mr. Hamilton—Anthony, she reminded herself to call him now—could make her daughter so happy, now and for years to come, Rosalind would never have an unkind word or thought for him again.

Lord Warfield came up beside her. "Good day."

She smiled and hastily tucked her handkerchief into her dress's sash. "Good day, Lord Warfield." She could feel his eyes on her, although she continued to watch Celia and Mr. Hamilton. They were making slow progress back to the carriage, stopping to speak to everyone.

"You're . . . er . . ." Lord Warfield cleared his throat. "You're happy, aren't you?"

She took a deep breath, blinking away the last of her tears. "Of course. Why would you think otherwise?"

"Well . . . you're watching the two of them, and you're crying . . . I know you're none too fond of Hamilton."

"He is now my son, and I shall be as loyal to him as

if he were my own child." She gave him a quelling look. David had explained everything about Mr. Childress's plot to her, how wrong they had all been about Mr. Hamilton—Anthony—and she didn't want to speak of it ever again, particularly not today. "As the mother of the bride, I feel entitled to shed a tear or two of joy."

"Joy." His face relaxed. "Aye, joy is always permitted."

Rosalind smiled. "I should hope so, particularly at a wedding."

Warfield grinned back. He had a nice grin, she thought suddenly, when he wasn't provoking her or arguing with her. "Might I have a word with you?"

"Of course," she said, surprised. They had talked quite a bit the last few days, ever since he had patted her hand so comfortingly that horrible day a week ago. She realized he was more of a father to Anthony than old Lynley ever had been, and Rosalind wasn't above surreptitiously discovering more about her new son-in-law. And to her surprise, she found she was becoming rather fond of the earl as they talked. "What about?"

"Not here." He glanced out the door, almost nervously, to where the other guests still lingered in the sunshine, laughing and chatting with the bride and bridegroom. "Over here?"

Mystified, Rosalind went where he indicated, into the vestry near the register where Celia had just recently signed her name, beneath those of her brothers and Rosalind herself. Almost thirty years ago, she realized with a small shock, turning the page to look. For a moment she stared at William's signature beside her own youthful one, the ink now faded. What a long time ago that had been.

Warfield had followed her. "Your husband?" he asked gruffly. Rosalind nodded, remembering how nervous and uncertain she had felt that day, marrying a duke twice her age with two sons barely eight years younger than she was. He had seemed so imposing and elegant, so tall and dark and serious. She had loved Exeter, but with a sense of awe; she had been intimidated by him, especially at first. There had been none of the easy connection between them that Rosalind had just seen between Celia and Anthony.

"Do you miss him?" asked the earl. Rosalind turned the page again, back to the present, and then she turned away from the register.

"Yes. At times. He was a good husband."

"Good, good." Warfield seemed ill at ease. He kept glancing at the register uneasily. "But you've been a widow a long time."

Rosalind bowed her head. "Almost fifteen years."

"And have you never . . . That is, what I wanted to ask . . ." He wet his lips. "Have you never thought of remarrying? Or considered . . . having affection for another man?" She stared at him. Warfield took a deep breath, then, to her astonishment, took her hand in his. "Your Grace, I have the greatest admiration for you," he said. "And the deepest respect."

"You hardly respected my opinion a fortnight ago," she said in surprise. "You said I was judgmental and irrational."

He dismissed it with an impatient flick of one hand. "That was when you thought Hamilton the scourge of the earth."

"With reason."

"Well, perhaps, but—"

"I wonder how you would react if I had been right and you had been wrong."

"But I *was* right, wasn't I?" he pointed out.

Rosalind pressed her lips together. "You cannot always be right."

He paused. "No, no, of course not. I hope you shall be gracious when I am wrong."

"Is this what you wanted to speak of?"

"I would like to call on you," he said in a rush. "After Hamilton and his bride have gone. When we have nothing else to argue about."

"Perhaps we shall always have something to argue about," she said tartly.

"I should hope so, it adds spice to a marriage," he replied, unperturbed.

"Marriage!" She laughed in surprise. "Who mentioned marriage?"

"I did. Not that I'm asking for an answer now, mind. You might not turn out to suit me after all—" Rosalind gaped at him, and he grinned hopefully. "But I think you might. And I should like to know if I might be to your liking as well."

"Lord Warfield." She tried to gather her wits. He was unbelievably outrageous, but she found it a little exhilarating at the same time, and oddly charming. "I hardly think—"

"Are you saying no?" He took a step toward her. Rosalind put one hand on her bosom. She had to look up at him. "Are you?" he repeated. Mutely she shook her head. She wasn't saying anything at the moment. "Thank heaven," he declared, before taking hold of her shoulders and pulling her forward to kiss her.

Off balance, she had to grab onto him to keep her balance. His arms flexed under her grip, and he gathered her closer, right into his arms. He lifted his head and looked down at her. "All right?"

"L—Lord Warfield," she stammered.

"Patrick," he said. "Call me Patrick. Do you want me to turn you loose?"

Rosalind looked at his wide, firm mouth. Her hands were still clutching his broad shoulders. She must be mad. "No."

"All right, then." And he kissed her again.

Chapter Twenty-Nine

The earl of Lynley arrived one morning several days later, unannounced except by a terse message sent on ahead from the local inn: "I shall call on you directly" was all it said.

Anthony read it, then put it aside to continue his breakfast. He didn't care if Lynley had come all the way from Sussex, or why. Lynley had never cared a fig for him, and Anthony felt the same about him.

Celia came in, filling the room with cheer and light. "Good morning, darling. You rose early today."

He got to his feet and bowed his head. "I didn't want to disturb you."

She wrinkled her nose at him. "Perhaps because you kept me from my rest all night. Yes, I see your consideration."

Anthony laughed. "No, it was not about last night. I let you sleep because I plan to keep you from your rest again tonight."

Pink flooded her cheeks. "Hmm," she said with a mischievous glance at his plate. "You'd best have some more to eat, then. To keep your strength up."

Anthony smiled at her, his feral rake's smile. Her

eyes widened, and she darted a quick glance at the door. "Not to worry, madame," he reassured her, prowling around the table toward her. "I have plenty of strength for that endeavor. Shall I demonstrate?"

She licked her lips and tried to look stern, but he could see the pleased flush. He, too, glanced at the door. Good God, marriage suited him just fine. If he turned the key, he could find out just how far that flush extended, right now. . . .

"What is that?" Celia asked, shaking him out of his thoughts. Anthony followed her gaze to the crested letter on the table beside his plate.

"Lynley wishes to call." Celia's gaze flew to his. Anthony gave a small shrug. "I suppose it had to happen sooner or later."

His wife tilted her head. "Do you not wish to see him?"

"I? I don't care, one way or the other. No doubt he wants to inspect you, to see if you measure up."

She came across the room to him and took his hand. For a moment she just held it between her own two, her hands small around his. "If you don't wish to see him, tell him not to come. Marcus will understand."

He considered it. He hadn't seen Lynley in years, not since the man had walked away from his mother's grave without a word or a backward glance at Anthony. He no longer hated the earl, but he didn't feel any interest in him, either.

But in denying Lynley, he would also be denying Celia. She was the daughter of a duke; she deserved to be a countess, even if Anthony didn't deserve to be an earl. Celia had taken him even given his past, and he owed it to her to be as respectable as he could be, including tolerating Lynley's visit. He curled his fingers through hers. "I should see him. And you might want to meet him. He is your father-in-law."

"I don't seem to have much luck with fathers-in-law," she remarked. "But if he hurts my feelings, you shall have to console me."

Anthony smiled. "I should like nothing better. But perhaps . . ." He hesitated. "I've been thinking," he said carefully. "Perhaps I should allow people to call me Langford again. I never cared when it was only my name in question, but now—"

"I think Celia Hamilton sounds very well," she said, as lightly as if he hadn't spoken. "I've already ordered calling cards."

He stared at her. "You don't need to."

"All that you are, I am, too," she said.

He turned their linked hands over, raising her knuckles to his lips. "No, my dear, I think you are much better."

Lynley arrived later that morning. Celia glanced at Anthony and, at his shrug, told the butler to show in the earl. Her husband put aside the book of poetry he had been reading to her, and Celia put her slippers back on. It had been such a cozy morning up to that moment, as they hid away in the sun-filled small drawing room. "We could summon Mama to face him down," she suggested, but Anthony shrugged again.

"No, better to get it over and done with."

"The earl of Lynley," announced the butler a few minutes later. Celia got to her feet, curious in spite of herself. Anthony stayed in his seat. She composed her face, to hide her interest in the earl, and placed her hand on Anthony's shoulder. Anthony didn't say anything, but he turned his head and pressed his lips to her knuckles. Then he rose to stand beside her.

Lynley was not at all what Celia had expected. He

was old—older than she had thought. A few inches shorter than his son, he was thin and stooped, with a long, slightly crooked nose and wiry gray hair. He leaned on a cane and wore clothing as austere as any minister. For a moment the room was quiet as he simply peered at her over his spectacles.

"Lady Langford," he said at last. He extended one foot and gave her a formal, if painfully slow, bow.

"Welcome to Ainsley Park, sir," she replied, curtsying.

"Hmmph." He continued to study her. "How old are you?"

Celia narrowed her eyes at him. "Not yet three-and-twenty."

Lynley harrumphed again. "Not too old, then. Good."

"Shall you inspect her teeth next?" drawled Anthony.

Finally the earl turned his gaze on him. "As rude as ever, I see."

Anthony's mouth twisted in a faint smile, but he only inclined his head.

"Won't you be seated?" Celia couldn't help but agree with Anthony, but this was her brother's house. Best they should discover Lord Lynley's purpose so he could be on his way that much sooner. With short, jerky steps the earl moved to a chair and seated himself. Celia took a seat near her husband, trying not to think that the earl reminded her of a large spider.

"To what do we owe this visit?" asked Anthony in a bland voice.

Lynley's left eye twitched. "I received word of your marriage too late in time to attend the wedding."

Anthony nodded once. "It was a very small ceremony."

The earl didn't look entirely pleased. "Yes, I know,"

he said sourly. "As the future earl, you ought to have married in the Lynley chapel."

"I was under the impression I wasn't to set foot on the property again," Anthony said. "It would be difficult to conduct a wedding with the bridegroom some miles distant from the chapel."

Lynley grunted. "I suppose the Exeter chapel will have to do."

"Thank heavens," murmured Anthony wryly, "since it's already done."

By now Celia was almost sorry she'd let her mother write to Lord Lynley about their marriage. What a sour old man, she thought. No wonder Anthony didn't want anything to do with him.

The earl turned to her then. "You may leave us."

Celia couldn't hide her surprise. Her eyes widened, and she instinctively looked to Anthony. His face was set, but he nodded, rising to his feet. Celia stood and bobbed a very slight curtsy to the earl, then turned to Anthony. "I will stay if you want me," she whispered.

"Make your escape and be glad," he murmured back. "I'll find you when he's gone."

After she left, Anthony remained on his feet. He hated sitting and staring eye-to-eye with the earl, as he had been forced to do for years as a boy when he was being punished. Lynley would make him sit on a stool in the corner of the study, and if Anthony so much as sneezed or twitched, he risked a blistered palm from Lynley's riding crop. Anthony admitted he had often misbehaved as a boy, but he refused to relive the experience every time he had to see Lynley.

As the earl groped for his cane, Anthony strolled to the windows. After a moment Lynley came up beside him.

"I see you have finally made something of yourself," said the earl, his gaze fixed on something outside.

"I am as I have always been." Anthony, too, gazed out the window.

The earl grunted. "Hmph. Perhaps you're my son after all."

Anthony turned a cool gaze on him. "Good God, I hope not."

Lynley's eyebrows shot up. Then he gave a bark of laughter. "That's proof of it, if nothing else."

Anthony had no trouble looking bored. "Have you seen what you came to see?"

Lynley nodded slowly. "A pretty girl. Good family."

"Better than yours," said Anthony.

"Better than I thought you would land," Lynley returned in the same flat tone. "I expect she brought you some funds. No need to crawl back and beg forgiveness, eh?"

"Forgiveness? What, for being born?"

He grunted again. "I was never convinced you weren't mine. I was never convinced you were, either, but that's neither here nor there now. I have no one else to inherit. It might as well be you."

It was on the tip of Anthony's tongue to say he didn't need the estate or the bloody title, that he had made his own fortune and place in life. But it occurred to him that this was an enormous concession from Lynley, if the man really believed Anthony was not his son. "Why did you think my mother would have lied to you?" he asked instead.

Lynley didn't respond for a moment. "Your mother was a child when I married her. I suppose it was drummed into her head that she must not disappoint me or anger me. She barely spoke for the first few years of our marriage; I hardly knew what her voice sounded like."

Bits of memories floated back to Anthony. His mother, her face fearful, taking his hand and hurrying him down the stairs and out of the house. Her frantic pleas for him to stop crying when he had fallen and scraped his knee. She had been terrified of Lynley. Anthony had recognized that even as a small boy.

"But eventually she came to me and said she was with child." Lynley snorted. "Ten years it took." He turned a piercing gaze on Anthony. "You could be mine. You could be the butler's, or the stableboy's, or a passing peddler's. No one can prove a thing."

"If she was so frightened of you," Anthony asked in a cool tone, "why would she risk deceiving you that way?"

Lynley's eyes narrowed. He said nothing, just tapped his fingers on his cane.

"I think you know she didn't," Anthony went on. "I think you never would have allowed her to stay, had you truly thought she carried another man's child. No matter how little you cared for her, you knew I was your only chance for an heir, and that's why you've never repudiated either of us."

A vein in Lynley's forehead pulsed. "You might have shown some deference, even a little gratitude. A proper son does not humiliate his father at every turn."

"A proper father takes a kindly interest in his son."

The earl pursed his lips. "I did my duty. The best schools—and you were thrown out of all of them."

Anthony's lips curled in a mocking smile. "Ah, yes, for beating the mathematics tutor at cards. How dare I."

"And fighting." Lynley's nose flared at the memory. "Like a common street brat. Disgraceful."

"They insulted my mother," said Anthony. "I know you didn't care, but I did."

"Well. Hmph. That's all in the past now." Lynley flicked his fingers as if to brush aside the distasteful history. "I expect you'll take your proper title again, now you've got a wife."

Anthony shrugged. "I've gotten along well enough without it."

"See here," Lynley warned him. "You'll not be an embarrassment to me still."

For a moment Anthony stared at him. An embarrassment? He embarrassed Lynley? He had his own fortune, and the hard-won knowledge to keep it and increase it. He had friends, not numerous but loyal, who would stand by him. He had a beautiful wife who loved him and believed in him. And he didn't owe a single bit of it to anyone, especially not to Lynley. "Good day to you, sir."

"Take the title, and you may pay a visit to Lynley Court," said the earl as if Anthony hadn't spoken. "I should like to see how the girl comports herself as mistress of a household."

"The girl is called Mrs. Hamilton," said Anthony. "And I have great faith she shall comport herself splendidly as mistress of a household, just as she does in all things. But she shall be mistress of my household, in London. I do not intend to give her up or share her, certainly not with you and certainly not at Lynley Court." He bowed. "I think we have quite exhausted this conversation. Good day, sir."

Lynley stared at him in amazement. "What?" he cried. "You're tossing me out?"

"No," said Anthony. "It is not my house." He walked to the door. "I shall notify His Grace you are here. You must excuse me." He opened the door and left Lynley staring, open-mouthed, after him.

Anthony found Celia in the garden, supervising the children. She turned to him with a beaming smile, and his heart turned over in his chest. She would be a splendid countess—*his* countess. Eventually, he supposed, he would give in and take the title again; he would visit Lynley Court again. He'd even speak to the earl again, someday. It would be an insult to his mother if he didn't accept his inheritance, after what she had suffered for him to get it. But it would be on his terms, in his own time, and not because Lynley deigned to bestow any of it on him.

"What are you working on?" he asked, coming down the steps to where the children worked.

"Paper boats." Celia tousled her nephew's hair. "Thomas would like to be an admiral, so we must construct his fleet."

"And Edward will be a captain," said the boy without looking up from folding his paper. Edward waved a half-folded boat in the air, then put it in his mouth. Celia exchanged a look with Molly, who grinned and went back to work on her own boat.

"Ah. I shall see that Aunt Celia is returned to you in time to christen the fleet, but I must steal her away." He took her hand and tugged, drawing her away as the nursemaid stepped up to take her place.

"Has he gone?" Celia asked as they strolled the garden paths, arm in arm.

Anthony lifted his shoulder. "I don't know. He was still in the drawing room when I left."

"You left him?" He nodded. Celia made a small noise of surprise. "I thought you might mend fences with him."

"I think it best if a very tall fence divides the earl

and me." Celia laughed. "I have everything I want," he said quietly, squeezing her hand. "I don't need anything Lynley can give me."

"Perhaps I shall set myself to charming the earl for you," she said. "Not because you need it, just to see if I can. If you can set yourself to charming Mama . . ."

Anthony chuckled. "I assure you, my task is by far the more pleasant."

"Then that will make my triumph all the sweeter," she told him with a saucy grin.

He stopped, turning to face her. "Shall we make a wager on who will succeed first?"

Color rose in Celia's cheeks. "There are no cards you can count."

"I still like to win," he informed her with a leering smile.

"Do you?" she murmured, her eyes lighting up.

"My darling, you know I do. And you are by far the greatest prize I have ever won."

"I am not a prize to be won," she declared indignantly. "I gave myself to you quite freely."

Anthony laughed, pulling her into his arms. "And that is what makes you so valuable."

She frowned at him. "I don't want to be taken for granted. Perhaps I should make you pursue me a bit more."

He smiled, holding her closer until her breathing hitched and she put her arms around his neck and lifted her face for his kiss. "And I would," he whispered against her lips. "To the ends of the earth and back, my love."

About the Author

Caroline Linden was born a reader, not a writer. She earned a math degree from Harvard University and wrote computer software before turning to writing fiction. Twelve years, eighteen books, and three Red Sox world championships later, she has never regretted her decision. Her books have won the Daphne du Maurier Award, the NJRW Golden Leaf Award, and RWA's RITA Award, and been translated into over a dozen languages. Visit her online at www.carolinelinden.com.